T

By

Helen Ellwood

and

John Raybould

To Maggie

H Ellwood

J Raybould

1

Special thanks

to

Henry and David

for their support,

and to

Elliott and Malichai

for the design of Grizelda's

birthday cake.

TARANOR

ELVES

Arbour Glenn

Goldendale

Ogman's cave

TARANOR City

Crystal pool

Chapter 1

Bryony and Sheean held on tight as Fable, the Faerie horse, leapt through the magic portal: away from the Human realm, away from the danger of Cucapha castle, away from all the friends they had known for the last eight years.

Bryony spread her wings and held Sheean's waist for balance. She could feel fear in his mind. She turned round, looking back at Albert. He was stuck on the Human side of the portal, calling her name. She blew him a kiss then turned to face Taranor: the Faerie realm, her own kingdom, her home.

* * *

Without thinking of the consequences, Albert jumped through after her. In an instant, the golden hills and pink sky he'd seen through the portal turned to a swirling grey mist. A strong wind buffeted him, knocking him and turning him over and over. He felt himself falling.

"Bryony," he shouted, "where are you? Help me!"

* * *

Bryony's heart leapt with excitement as she saw the Sentinel Trees up ahead: the ancient guardians of the Faerie realm of Taranor. She gave out a triumphant yell of victory. Sheean's ragged wings flapped against her face. As she brushed away their gossamer softness, she saw that he was still gripping Fable's mane tightly, his knuckles white with tension.

"Relax, Sheean," she called out, "we're through, you won't fall."

She leaned a little to one side and looked ahead to check on Dog. The poor animal dangled by his scruff from her horse's mouth; a mixture of amazement and excitement on his hairy face.

Fable landed and continued in a rhythmic gallop towards the trees.

"If it's all the same to you," gasped Dog, "I'd like to get down now."

Bryony smiled. All the time in the Human realm she had heard and understood the animals only through mind speech. Now, here in Taranor, she could hear Dog's true voice. She was looking forward to being able to talk aloud to all the insects and birds, and for her and Fable to be able to chat openly.

* * *

Albert felt himself falling more slowly. The mist around him changed from grey to pink, gradually clearing. He landed hard in shallow water. He licked his lips. Salty water. The sea. A wave knocked against his back, throwing him forward. He tried to get up, but was still dizzy from the effects of the portal. Another wave crashed into him.

He stood, letting the surf caress his legs as he scanned the cliffs ahead of him. A golden beach stretched away in both directions as far as he could see. Tears sprang to his eyes as he saw that he was totally alone. There was no sign of Bryony.

* * *

Within a few heartbeats, Bryony and her friends arrived at the ancient oaks. The Sentinel Trees lifted their leaves in greeting. Fable came to a halt and lowered Dog to the floor while Sheean and Bryony got down from his back.

"Sorry about that, Dog," said Fable. "Are you alright?"

Dog lay down on the floor. "No. Got bellyache."

"Oh, Fable," said Bryony, "it's so wonderful to hear your real voice again. And yours, Dog. I'd almost got used to hearing only mind speech from animals." She patted Dog on the head. "I'm sure we'll find a way to get the Portal Stone out of you, Dog."

"Only one way," said Dog, giving a brave smile. "Is in my tummy. Have to wait."

Sheean folded his arms and held his wings tightly against his body. He was scowling.

"What's the matter?" asked Bryony. "Aren't you happy to be home? I'm so happy I could burst. I could explode into a thousand stars!" She whirled into the air, spinning in delight, giving off turquoise sparks into the pink evening light. "Wheeeeee!"

Fable looked up at her patiently. "Sheean is traumatised," he said. "It may take him a long time to recover from his ordeal in the Human realm. You cannot expect him to be as happy as you are. We must be compassionate."

Bryony landed and touched Sheean's hand.

"I'm sorry, Sheean. I'm just so happy. I never thought I'd be able to rescue you. There were so many days and nights when I despaired and now..." She turned in a circle, her feet hardly touching the ground, taking in the glorious golden hills, the trees and the fresh clean air. "There are no more witches now, no more drugs, no more captivity. Believe me, Sheean, we're going to live happily ever after."

Sheean turned away from her, his voice low and uncertain. "Really? You believe that? How do I know this is not just another dream? Soon those trees are going to come towards me, evil eyes are going to peer at me from the darkness and then I'm going to wake up in my room at the castle."

Fable took a step towards him, tossing his head to clear his long white mane from his eyes. "My dear Prince, this is real. This is Taranor, your homeland, from which you were kidnapped eight mortal years ago."

Sheean shook his head. "You wouldn't believe what I've had dreams about. I've been inside a wolf's mouth and talked to eagles who said they were Wizards. This dream is just more fanciful, that's all."

Fable nuzzled him. "This is real, Sheean. You will know that in time."

"Green skies, pink skies; I don't know what's real anymore."

"But look around you," said Bryony. "Don't you remember the Sentinel Trees and the crystal pool? Don't you remember your parents? Fable, why don't we take him to the crystal pool? That might help him remember."

Fable shook his head. "We have to go and see Queen Rhyannon. She has waited anxiously for our return. She will be keen to know that the Light Prophecy will be fulfilled and that peace can now reign in the Seven Realms."

* * *

Albert walked to the beach. The sun was very low in the sky, hidden behind the cliffs. He remembered it being midnight at the castle, just before he jumped. Now though, he had no idea whether the sun was rising or setting.

"Keep calm," he said aloud, hoping the sound of his voice might anchor him in reality. "Bryony and Dog can't be far away."

He stared at the sea. It was stunning. The sky's reflection in the water was like liquid gold. He took a deep breath and shouted with all his might, "BRYONYYYY!"

Only the high-pitched cries of gulls on the wind answered him. The sun sank lower. "Keep calm. It's sunset. I'll have to stay on the beach until morning. I can't risk the cliffs in the dark."

He looked up and down the beach. "Get your bearings, Albert. Make Dad proud." He pointed to the sun, "West." He turned himself round a quarter of a circle, "North," he said. He turned again to face the sea, "East." Another turn, "South." The final quarter turn brought him back to face the cliffs.

He noticed a large rock nearby and settled himself behind it, hoping that it would provide some shelter. As he lay there, his back propped against the rock, feeling the warm night air begin to dry his clothes, he remembered his beach holiday with Bryony. They had slept on a beach very like this. Those happy days seemed so far behind him now. Then he thought of his parents. A lump of fear came to his throat as he imagined how frightened they would be at discovering him missing.

* * *

Dog ran up and down among the oak trees, paused at a particularly large one and cocked his leg. Bryony gasped. Fable ran towards him and nudged him away from the tree. Dog shook himself, looking up at Fable with annoyance.

"Why you do that? Piss on me leg, not up tree!"

"These are sacred trees. Please urinate somewhere else in future."

Dog began to lick himself clean.

"Somehow," Fable continued, "I must get the Sentinel Trees to accept you."

He turned towards the trees and bowed low. "Oh Great Trees of Guarding, please accept this mortal hound. He has helped to rescue the Prince and Princess of Taranor from the Human realm. He has played a part in the saving of the Faerie Kingdom."

The trees nearest Dog bent their trunks down with a slow, creaking sigh. Two branches reached out, their twigs as strong and supple as the fingers of a giant.

They caressed Dog's head with light green oak leaves, exploring his mind and soul. Dog cowered and whimpered, tucking his tail between his legs in fright.

"Sorry I piss on you," he said quietly.

The sky darkened to lilac and the birds lessened their song.

After a few moments the sky became light pink once more and the birds began singing with renewed energy. The leaves pulled back with a soft chiming sound of acceptance. Fable bowed his head.

"Does that mean Dog can stay here?" asked Bryony.

"Yes, my sweet one," said Fable. "He has been given the freedom of the city and an audience with Queen Rhyannon." Fable gave Dog a hard stare. "You'd better be on your best behaviour, Dog, and do not, under any circumstance, sniff the Queen's bottom."

Dog grinned. "Not sniff Queen's bottom. Me be good."

The trees began to sound their chimes once more, telling the whole kingdom of a royal celebration to come. A shout rose up from the city walls.

"They have arrived! The Prince and Princess; they have arrived!"

* * *

No matter how many times Albert scanned the horizon, Dog, Sheean, Bryony and her awesome white horse failed to appear. It was just him and the sea. For a long time he sat watching the sky darken to pale lilac. The moon rose and a few stars emerged. The sound of gulls quietened. His shoulders slumped in defeat. He closed his eyes, hoping to sleep.

* * *

Once through the trees, Bryony caught her first proper glimpse of the Faerie castle beyond the city walls. Warriors with spears held upright stood at sentry posts, their long, golden hair fluttering under helmets of bronze. Banners flapped in the breeze.

The castle spires seemed lit from within by a pale turquoise light, creating a soft glow around the city.

Ten Royal Guards appeared before them. The most Senior bowed low, sweeping his helmet to the floor and replacing it as he stood up, tall and proud. His grey-green eyes seemed to notice everything: Sheean's ragged wings, Bryony's tears of joy, the mud on Fable's hooves and the mortal dog.

He addressed them quietly. "Prince Sheean, Princess Bryony, it is an honour to welcome you home. Would you rather fly through the streets as the people wish, or portal straight to the Meeting Hall within the castle?"

Although he looked at Sheean for an answer, Bryony spoke up first.

"I think Dog's had enough of using the Portal Stone. He ate it. It's stuck in his tummy."

The guard controlled a fleeting expression of distaste and held out a glittering gem in his gloved hand. "We are privileged to have been given the responsibility of holding the Gem of Glittering Magnificence."

Dog jumped up and down at the guards, trying to greet them, but they remained like statues, scanning the trees and fields beyond for threats. Bryony peered at the tiny crystal in the guard's palm.

"We can transport you anywhere within the city, Your Royal Highness," said the guard.

Bryony looked at Sheean, but he merely shrugged, apparently uninterested in what was happening around him. At that moment she felt a pang in her heart as the damage that had been done to his mind and soul became apparent. She saw his ragged wings and realised that he would be unable to fly far.

"How far is it from here?" she asked.

"We have to fly through the residential streets, where people are already beginning to gather, then there is the Market Square, the Blossoming Grove and the Public Scented Gardens. And then we would travel over the Moat of Crystal Water and into the Castle where we would fly into the Meeting Hall itself."

Bryony was so excited at the names of these places. They were familiar and yet so strange, places she hadn't seen since she was a little girl. "We should use the gem and save Sheean's wings. I expect they're rather sore."

Sheean shot her a look of gratitude. Bryony smiled, glad that she had made a correct judgement and strangely proud that she had the modesty to save the processions and the public appearances for later.

* * *

Albert woke with a start. The sky was darkening, and the stars shone out with a brilliance that stunned him. There were so many stars. Their light left him breathless. The rock felt hard against his back. As he repositioned himself, he looked out over the sea and gasped. Just above the horizon a second, smaller moon was rising. Two moons in the sky! And both almost full.

* * *

Bryony looked around in awe at the Meeting Hall of the Great Castle. The high vaulted ceiling soared overhead, its arches painted with stories from olden times, its points decorated with oak leaves and acorns. Magical three-dimensional images of previous Faerie queens and kings hovered in niches on the walls, fluttering forever in varying hues of turquoise and blue.

She looked around at the empty niches on the walls behind her. A smile played around her mouth as she realised that, one day, her image too would be hovering up there. She would be admired by young Faeries visiting the castle and discussed in great ballads for all time.

She landed. To her left was a floor-to-ceiling window, fluted with arches. Through it she saw Silvin, the first moon, already high in the darkening sky. Orba, the second moon, followed. She could hear the murmuring of Faerie kin in the courtyard outside. People were gathering to welcome her.

Fionna and Alondil rose to meet them. At first their eyes were for Sheean only. Fable and Bryony waited patiently while they greeted their long lost son. Bryony's wings glowed pale green with happiness. Dog hid under a nearby chair, trembling.

"Oh my boy," sobbed Fionna as she held him tight. Alondil stepped forward and laid a gentle hand on his wife's shoulder. "Welcome back, Sheean. Happy Birthday."

Bryony watched Sheean being held by his parents. For a moment, the happiness that had filled her heart since arriving home deserted her. There were no parents here for her. She looked up again into the heights of the ceiling. Pastoral scenes flowed over the stone: scenes of wooded glades and magic gardens, famous heroes in flight and fair babes playing in pools of clear water. She felt her mother's presence then, a light hand on her head, a prickling sensation down her spine. She smiled. She imagined her father clapping his hands and settling down to create a poem for the occasion.

Trumpets blasting from the balconies shook her out of her daydream, heralding the arrival of Queen Rhyannon. In a blaze of golden-winged glamour, she flew through from one of the side rooms, followed by nine attendants. Light from the wall torches caught glints in the jewels of the queen's crown. Her tiny feet touched the stone floor and the fanfare ended. Everyone stepped back to create space. Bryony stepped back with them, but was shoved forward by Fable's nose.

"Go on, little one, this is your moment."

Sheean and Bryony stood alone in the middle of the Meeting Hall while Dog retreated further under his chair, tucking his tail between his legs.

In a loud voice Queen Rhyannon declared, "Bryony Winkleweed. Sheean Meranon. I Queen Rhyannon Elrowan Oakenflower welcome you. The future king and queen are home! The Light Prophecy can now be fulfilled!"

The sound of trumpets and cheers came to them from outside. The queen took their hands and looked from one to the other. Sheean looked flustered and confused.

"You have endured," she continued in a quieter voice, just for their ears, "you have shown courage fit for your royal status. I welcome you both into my heart and hearth. May your flowers all bear fruit and the acorns of your dreams come into full leaf."

There was an awkward pause. An attendant, hovering beside the queen, coughed politely. Fable nudged Sheean.

"Er, thank you."

Bryony took the hint. "It was a hard task, but Sheean showed a brave heart. I did what I could, but honestly..." She hesitated as she realised the truth of what she was saying. "I simply kept an eye on him. We owe our lives to Fable. And to Dog."

"Step forward, noble Horse. When you were born as a foal into the house of Oak, I knew you would play a special part in the saving of our kingdom. I want to thank you for guiding these two as children, and supporting Bryony as she lived among mortals. Your wisdom, patience and bravery will be rewarded."

Fable tossed his head, sending sparkles of diamond light into the room. He bowed low, touching his white nose to an outstretched front leg. Then he rose and nuzzled Bryony, a huge smile showing deep in his soft brown eyes.

Queen Rhyannon bent down and patted her knees. "Come here, little dog. What is your name?"

Dog wriggled out from under the chair and approached the queen. "Dog. Name is Dog, Your Majesty."

She stroked his ears and smiled. "Dog, you are welcome in our land. Without your help these great beings would not have been able to get home and the Light Prophecy would never have a chance of being fulfilled. I owe a debt of gratitude." She frowned and passed her hand over Dog's back. Then she smiled. "I hope the Portal Stone in your belly passes without discomfort."

A tall, imposing Faerie hovering near the queen, frowned.

"By your leave, Your Majesty," he said. His wings were indigo, showing his high rank and level of authority. Queen Rhyannon turned, still smiling, one hand stroking Dog's ears. Dog relaxed and grinned sloppily at Bryony.

"Yes, Agaric?" said the queen.

"By your leave, Your Majesty, it is not customary for mortal hounds to frequent the royal environs."

Bryony remembered him from her early childhood. Sheean often used to tease her, when she was naughty, that he'd tell on her and get her into trouble. It was only ever a joke, but the imposing figure of Agaric, Chief of Security, had always filled her with fear.

The queen laughed lightly. "This dog is special. He is welcome." She leaned close, burying her face in Dog's ruff and whispered, "Please behave yourself. Don't get me into trouble."

Dog wagged his tail as hard as he could, his tongue hanging out with delight. "Will be good. Love you!"

The queen ruffled his fur and rose to address Sheean. She spoke again in a loud voice that seemed to echo throughout the castle and the lands beyond. "Sheean Meranon, you are destined to be King. It was seen at your birth and by the signs thereafter." Then to Bryony. "Bryony Winkleweed, you are destined to be Queen. It was seen at your birth and by the signs thereafter. Tomorrow night the two moons are in alignment. You will both be crowned and married, as to our customs. May you live long and in peace."

The queen's voice became less formal. "Now, let us meet your subjects and then you may rest. Later there will be a banquet. Follow me."

She turned quickly, showering the room with gold sparks. They flew up the staircase towards one of the large windows and out onto a balcony. As soon as the crowd saw their future king and queen, safe at last, the cheers erupted, trumpets blew and fireworks lit up the sky.

Bryony's heart soared as she looked out over the courtyard, filled with her multihued people. She looked out over the city to the Sentinel Trees and up into the sky. The fireworks danced as Silvin and Orba rose higher.

* * *

In the Human realm, a gloomy dusk settled like a moth-eaten blanket over the city of Cucapha. Inside the castle, candles had been placed all around Queen Grizelda's planning chamber to banish the encroaching darkness. She clapped her fat hands together. A tall Goblin entered. He was slender, athletic and pale. Almost Human. Almost attractive to her eyes.

"What news of the prison camps?" she asked, indicating to him to come closer. "Don't be shy, I don't bite."

The Goblin took a few hesitant steps towards her. "The tents are erected and we have press-ganged a decent sized workforce. We can take as many Goblins as are willing, or even unwilling, to help contain the threat, Your Majesty."

"Right. Round up everyone with green eyes and keep them. Make them work. Make them produce beautiful things for me. Sheean had green eyes. He might return, or maybe his mother will come for revenge. By keeping everyone with green eyes in a prison camp, no Fay can attack me. We will keep them there forever if necessary."

"As you wish, Your Majesty."

"I like your uniform," said Grizelda. She licked her lips while her eyes trailed up and down the creature's body. "It fits you well. I want my name on it. I want my name on the uniforms of all my new soldiers."

The Goblin's eyes glittered a dull red in the candle light. "May I suggest an armband be worn by officers like myself. The simpler Goblins do not have the discipline to wear uniform."

Grizelda slapped her massive thighs in glee. "Yes, you are cleverer than the little green ones aren't you. Mmm. An armband with my initial on it. That's G for Grizelda. Make it red like your eyes and black like my heart. Show them I mean business."

The Goblin bowed and retreated from the room. Grizelda swivelled in her seat to look out of the window. From her room she commanded a view of the entire city. She smiled. "My reign will be long and beautiful, and no jumped-up Faerie will threaten my crown ever again."

* * *

Bryony flew through the state rooms at Taranor Castle, enjoying the soft, white curtains that billowed in the gentle evening breeze. Fragrant scents from the gardens flowed through the air. High ceilings constructed of the finest crystal filtered Faerie moonslight in lilac and pink hues over petal-strewn floors.

"Now that you have bathed, Your Royal Highness," said her maid, Lorella, "I'll do your hair, ready for the banquet."

Bryony's heart soared with excitement when she saw her bedroom. In the centre of the room was a deep, rose petal bed with a cover embroidered in the finest threads, and pillows made from summer clouds. Honeysuckle and jasmine grew intertwined to form a roof. An arched window opened out onto the prettiest garden she had ever seen.

As a child she had slept in her mother's arms in their oak tree, or curled up in a leaf. Now she was a Princess, she had the best bed in the realm.

Bryony sat down at a dressing table in front of a mirror, smiling at her reflection. Lorella began to brush her hair with a brush so soft that Bryony could hardly feel it. She remembered having her hair brushed by Mrs Hogarth, the Baker, in the Human realm, and how it had hurt sometimes. Mrs Hogarth hadn't meant to cause her pain, but her hair was often tangled and Mrs Hogarth was not renowned for her patience. Bryony relaxed as Lorella drew the brush tenderly, again and again, through her long brown hair.

She thought of the Baker's house and the hard little bed she had been given there. She remembered trying to see Sheean and communicate with him through the water bowl in her room. She remembered Albert, the blacksmith's son and her dear friend Edna.

"Everyone is so happy that you've returned," said Lorella. "It's going to be such a feast tonight. I've heard they're arranging the Coronation for tomorrow."

Bryony dragged herself back from her memories. "Yes, that's what Queen Rhyannon said earlier."

"Is everything to your satisfaction, Your Royal Highness?"

"Yes, thank you."

Bryony met Lorella's eyes through the mirror. Her maid was looking at her with concern.

"You look thoughtful. Was it so very bad in the Human realm?"

"No, there were some nice people. I was just thinking about some of them."

Lorella paused in her work. "The Humans?"

"Yes. There was a lovely old lady called Edna who had magic. And there was a young man called Albert."

Lorella put the brush down. "Poor things," she said, as she began plaiting Bryony's hair into an elaborate formation on the top of her head. "I feel sorry for Humans. They live for such a short time. My friend Silverbella says some of them have thoughts and feelings, just like us. Is this true?"

"Yes, they are very like us in many ways."

"I know many of our kin don't even give them a thought, but I feel sorry for them."

"They have terrible eyesight," said Bryony, "and they smell awful. Although I did get used to that after a while. They eat..."

Bryony paused as she remembered the dead animals the Humans ate almost every day. She felt sickened. She took a deep breath and tried to put the picture out of her head.

"What decoration would you like in your hair, Your Royal Highness?"

"I'm not sure."

"Dragonflies are very fashionable, or you could have butterflies and glow-worms."

"Do whatever you think is right," sighed Bryony.

Lorella sang a short melody. Within a few heartbeats, five butterflies and three glow-worms flew into the room, settling on Bryony's hair. Bryony smiled. Her nausea was fading, but she still felt uneasy. She kept thinking about Edna and Albert, left behind in the Human realm. At least her friend Alex the Dwarf had come through with them, albeit not in his Dwarven form.

She was aware that she had almost failed in her quest. If it hadn't been for Fable, Sheean would have been killed as they jumped from the castle tower.

The butterflies moved around her hair, unsettled by her anxiety.

"What do they eat, Your Royal Highness?" asked Lorella.

"Mmmm?"

"The Humans, what do they eat?"

Bryony looked down at her hands on her lap. "I'd rather not talk about it."

"As you wish, Your Royal Highness. When I finish your hair, I'll send for the tailors."

"Why?"

"So that you are properly attired for the banquet, Your Royal Highness."

"What's wrong with my appearance?"

Lorella curtsied and bowed her head. "Nothing. It's just this is a formal banquet which requires the wearing of pearls and silver. Plus it has overtones of heroic victory which as I'm sure you're aware, requires gold and a hint of royal blue. So the tailors are trying to come to an agreement."

A tinkle of bells announced the arrival of a tall, elegant Faerie. She wore a slim-fitting blue robe that showed her shoulders and upper arms. On her hands she wore silver gloves.

She curtsied low. "By your grace, Your Royal Highness, the Royal Tailors have come to a decision. You are to create a golden full length gown with royal-blue sleeves adorned with pearls. A silver bouquet is to accompany the outfit."

Bryony concentrated for a second and in a small flash of light a golden gown appeared on her slender frame. Bryony looked in the mirror. "By the gods, I look good."

"You do indeed," said Lorella.

Bryony turned to her maid. "Oh I'm sorry, I didn't mean to sound arrogant. You look lovely too."

"Your beauty," said Lorella, her wings turning pale in modesty, "outshines all but the Queen's."

"Might I suggest, Your Royal Highness," said the tailor, "the sleeves need to be a little less full. If they are fitted, you will not trail your sleeves as you eat."

Bryony changed the sleeves, and watched as the butterflies settled around her tiara. She tipped her head on one side. The butterflies adjusted to the tilt of her head.

"With your permission," said Lorella, "I will go and find out what time the banquet begins."

Bryony dismissed the maid and the tailor with a nod of her head, hoping it looked suitably regal and distant, without being rude.

Alone for the first time since her arrival, Bryony looked at herself in the mirror. The tiara fitted perfectly. Its gems glittered in the moonlight. The butterflies, now a delicate shade of silver, shifted in her hair, still a little unsettled.

"Hello, little wings. Thank you for helping me dress my hair tonight," said Bryony, smiling at their reflection in the mirror.

Tiny squeals played around the room as the butterflies wriggled, clearly delighted to be addressed by the Princess of Taranor.

"It is an honour," said one, in a voice almost inaudible, even to Bryony.

* * *

Sheean stood in his bathroom, surrounded by attendants. One kept bothering him, asking him questions and insisting he have a bath.

"Who are you?" asked Sheean.

"I'm just your butler, Your Royal Highness. You would have no need to know my name."

"Mmm... even so, I would like to know it."

"It's very kind of you, Your Royal Highness. My name is Jerremoy-Droford-Rosethorn. My friends call me Jerreh."

"OK, Jerry, I'm not bathing in front of all these people, so please tell them to go away."

Jerremoy swallowed nervously. "That's very irregular, Your Royal Highness, but if it is your wish. Wouldn't you like your back washer to stay?"

"No, I can wash my own back."

Jerremoy clapped his hands and shooed the bathing assistants out of the room.

"I will burn the human clothes, Your Royal Highness," said Jerremoy as Sheean got into the bath. He picked up the Human shorts. "I will burn these."

Sheean lay back in the fragrant water. The bath was big enough to stretch out. The petal-strewn water felt wonderful.

"Burn them?"

"Yes, we cannot allow the smell to linger here."

"OK. Can you find me some more clothes?"

Jerremoy looked shocked. "We don't have any clothes, Your Royal Highness. Are you unable to use your Faerie glamour?"

"S'pose I could. It's just easier to wear clothes, and then I don't have to think about what I'm wearing."

"I see. Might I offer the humble opinion that you will soon become familiar with your magic, Your Royal Highness?"

"S'pose. Can you stop calling me Your Royal Highness?"

"No! Your Royal Highness."

* * *

From the doorway to Bryony's room there came a peal of tiny bells. At first she couldn't remember what it meant, and then it came to her. "Enter," she shouted. The silver curtain over her doorway billowed open as Fionna flew into the room. Bryony ran into her arms.

"Oh my dearest Bryony," said Fionna, "your parents would be so proud to see you now."

Bryony felt tears come to her eyes. Fionna stepped back. "Look at you. That tiara fits perfectly."

"Thank you."

Fionna's deep green eyes became serious. "You said you were fine during the audience with the queen, but I want to know. I've just been to see my son and... well I'm worried."

Fionna flitted around the room, finally settling on the window seat overlooking the garden. Night scented flowers filled the room with fragrance.

"Is Sheean alright?" asked Bryony.

"No. I'm worried about him. I knew he would be altered by his experience in the Human realm, but I didn't expect such a dramatic change."

For a moment Bryony wondered if Fionna was going to cry.

"He seems so sullen," continued Fionna, "so unlike how he was as a little boy. He seemed almost unhappy to be home. You seem much as you were. Bright, enthusiastic, happy."

Bryony sat next to her, arranging her royal robes over her feet. She fingered the bright blue tassels of her belt. "He had a hard time. He was drugged and held in a castle. It took years before I could speak to him in his dreams. Magic blocked us at every step."

The words spilled from her mouth; at last she could tell her story. She told Fionna all about seeing Sheean in his nightmares and about travelling through the Goblin realm. She told her how he had tried to save her when a beast took her into its lair and how courageously he had endured his captivity. "A lot of the time, he didn't know who he really was. He didn't know he was Fay."

Fionna turned to her. "For me, this has been the longest petal and a half of my life. I can't imagine what it must have been like for you. How have you coped with being so long in the Human realm? Has it scarred you?"

"No - I'm fine, honestly. I had Fable with me and I never forgot Taranor or why I was living with mortals. I even made friends. One of them, Edna, was like a mother to me. She looked after me and taught me things. So did Sandy, Albert's mother."

"Who is Albert?"

Bryony found herself blushing. To hide her face she turned and arranged some flowers on a small table. "Oh no-one. Just a young man." As her blush faded she turned to Fionna and laughed. "He was in love with me. He never knew I was Fay. I kept him away from me."

"Well done. It sounds like you've dealt with this very well. You are clearly suited to rule. I'm just not sure about Sheean."

"He'll be fine. He's strong and brave."

Fionna smiled and rose into the air to leave the room. "He's still my boy, even though he's grown up now. Well, I'd better be going. See you at the banquet."

* * *

Sheean had to admit he did feel much better after his bath. The oils and scented lotions had a marked effect on his mood and the healing waters had repaired his wings. He heard noises in his bedroom and hoped Jerry had returned with something practical to wear.

Sauntering out of the bathroom, he found his bedroom full of people again.

"Jerry!" he shouted. "I thought you'd sent them away."

"These are different people, Your Royal Highness. These are the tailors."

"Tailors? But you said we dress by magic here."

"They will help you design a magical glamour that befits a king. After all you are to be married and crowned tomorrow evening."

"So soon?"

Jerremoy bowed his head. "The two moons will come into alignment tomorrow night. It is the right time."

Sheean shrugged. He thought for a moment and brought an image of his usual clothes, ones he had worn every day in the Human realm. They had been comfortable and hard wearing, especially during sword training. The image in his mind transformed into a magical glamour that clothed his light-filled being.

"No!" shouted one of the tailors. "Jerreh, please inform His Royal Highness that he cannot wear animal-skin trousers!" The other tailors shuddered at the sight.

Sheean closed his eyes and concentrated.

"Or shorts, Your Royal Highness. You need to imagine petals, delicately sewn together with gold thread, long and flowing, with the hem just touching the ground."

"I can't imagine wearing anything like that. Maybe if you show me."

"Oh we can't wear anything meant for a king," said Jerremoy, "it would be unthinkable."

"What if I order you?"

"Oh, well, yes. If the future king orders it. I suppose that would be alright."

One of the tailors, approximately Sheean's height and build, was chosen to show Sheean different combinations of royal clothing while the others crowded around him, making suggestions about shape and colour.

Eventually, after many arguments, Sheean was dressed in something light and graceful, something acceptable to all. Underneath the finery, in a small act of defiance, he added a pair of leather shorts.

Once the tailors had gone, Sheean wandered around his room, finally stopping by the window. He looked at the garden. It had been a long time since he'd seen anything so beautiful. The moonslight shone so brightly; it made everything look as if made out of silver. He saw Bryony walking near a pool. She looked wonderful, just like a Faerie Queen.

Jerremoy interrupted his thoughts. "Would you like a snack? I have taken the liberty of ordering a few fine dishes to satisfy you until the banquet."

"Oh, I am a bit hungry. What have we got?"

Sheean looked at a series of tiny crystal dishes set on a round table in the middle of the room. Each held an array of different flower petals, leaves and nuts. An attendant entered the room and stood close to Sheean. Sheean hesitated.

"Is there something wrong, Your Royal Highness?" Jerremoy asked.

"It looks very pretty, but don't you have any real food?"

"I'm sorry, Your Royal Highness. Have I missed something?"

"Perhaps a bit of cheese, potatoes, maybe some pastry and a glass of ale?"

"I have no idea what you are talking about, Your Royal Highness."

Sheean reached out and picked up a yellow petal. The attendant, who had been hovering near Sheean's side, snatched the petal and put it in his mouth. He swallowed.

"It's safe to eat, Your Royal Highness," said the attendant.

"Who are you?"

"Your food taster."

"Oh, sorry, I didn't know I had a food taster."

"Your Royal Highness, I have to try each dish before you do, just in case. Would you like to continue eating?"

"No. I'm not hungry anymore," sighed Sheean.

"Of course, Your Royal Highness."

* * *

Fable grazed the sweet grasses of the Wildflower Meadows, while Dog cavorted around, chasing moon shadows. Finally, exhausted by his games, Dog ran to Fable and nuzzled his nose.

"Do you understand the rules now, Dog?" asked Fable.

"Yes."

"The rules are: no running into the meeting hall, no barking inside the castle unless it's to ward off danger. If there is danger you can bark as much as you like. Your job is to guard the new king and queen."

Fable was convinced Dog wasn't listening. He seemed mesmerised by the two moons in the evening sky. Dog looked back at Fable with bright eyes. His tail wagged back and forth.

"Me get it," said Dog.

"I'm going to test you now," said Fable.

"OK."

"Where are you permitted to dig?"

"In Sheean's garden."

"Good. Where can you go to the toilet?"

"Back of Sheean's garden." Dog scratched himself, then tipped his head on one side. "Why not Bryony's? Me like Bryony too."

"Because Sheean won't mind. Now what happens after you go to the toilet?"

"Sheean does magic, make it go away."

"Well done. I believe you're ready to join the Royal Family. Tonight we're having a banquet and tomorrow we will go through the crowning ceremony."

"Good times for Dog!"

Fable smiled as Dog began scampering after a cloud of midges, snapping at them as they broke formation.

"Remember, Dog," called Fable. "Respect all life here."

* * *

Bryony walked out into the garden. As much as she loved the beautiful garden Edna had created behind her cottage on Maltbrook Lane, no Human could grow a garden as opulent as that made by Faerie hands. She looked up. The early stars were out and the second moon had risen higher, casting a fine sheen of silver over the flowers and trees.

She sighed and walked towards the pond, with its golden clockflowers and sparkling fountain. The clockflowers were a little like the drawings of lotus flowers she had seen in the Human realm. Each flower had twelve petals and an iridescent gem in the centre. She reached forward. The petals were soft to the touch, yet unyielding, like warm gold. Five petals of every flower lay open, catching the moonlight. The other seven curled upwards, just touching the central jewel.

Lorella flew into the garden, brimming with excitement. "By all that's beautiful, Your Royal Highness," she gushed, "you will make a wonderful queen."

Bryony smiled. She wished her entire being could smile, not just her mouth, but everything felt rather hollow. She had been looking forward to this time for so long. How often had she lain there in her little bed at Mrs Hogarth's house, her arms tired from preparing pastry, thinking of the day when she would finally return home? She used to imagine the fanfares, the fireworks, the music and the dancing. Thoughts of her coronation had kept her going through many a long night. Why couldn't she enjoy it now that the time had come? She kept thinking of the Human friends she'd left behind. She missed them. Tears came to her eyes.

"The banquet will be at seven petals, Your Royal Highness," said Lorella.

Bryony looked at the clockflowers. "Do you know anything about the time difference between realms, Lorella?"

The maid curtsied and lowered her head modestly. "A little."

"I was away in the mortal realm for eight years. How long have I been gone from here?"

Lorella's response was immediate, as if all her kin had been measuring the time closely. "One and a half petals, Your Royal Highness."

Bryony brushed the clockflower petal with her finger once more and flicked it with her fingernail. A tiny bell echoed around the garden. Lorella giggled. Despite her growing anxiety, Bryony laughed too.

"You would be in dreadful trouble if you did that, wouldn't you?" said Bryony.

Lorella, still laughing, curtsied once more. "I would, Your Royal Highness."

Bryony flew over to a rose-covered arbour. She hovered there in midair, trying to relax and enjoy the scent of the flowers, but the Human realm continued to nag at her mind. "So one petal here is how long in the Human realm?" she asked.

Lorella paused to think for a moment. "Six mortal years is roughly equivalent to one of our petals."

At that moment, in each of the clockflowers, a petal relaxed downwards and joined the other open ones. Simultaneously, six tiny bells sounded. The gentle chiming echoed around the entire city, as the time of six petals was announced all over the kingdom by clockflowers in gardens everywhere.

Bryony smiled. Happy memories of her early childhood flooded her mind; memories of her mother holding her in her arms and singing Faerie lullabies at the sound of the sixth petal. It was the time all young children went to bed. It was the time when half the central gem of all the clockflowers shone outwards into the gardens of Taranor, the other half being hidden by the closed petals.

She had often seen the gems fully revealed at midday, but the most exciting event in the life of a Faerie child was to see the light of the clockflowers at midnight on the night of their birthday.

"If there is nothing else, Your Royal Highness," said Lorella, "I will call for you at seven."

Bryony dismissed her with a nod.

She stepped closer to the pool of water in the centre of the garden. Lily pads as large as dinner plates covered the surface of the water. Dragonflies flitted among the waterlilies. Glow-worms began to shine and fly around the garden, creating motes of light that darted in and out of the flowers and gathered in clumps in dark corners, bringing a shifting, uneven light to ivy clad walls. Bryony thought of Edna. She looked into the water, wondering where her old friend was now.

* * *

Queen Rhyannon settled herself at the Meeting Room table. "I have a lot to do before the banquet, Agaric. This had better be important."

"I trust I can speak for all," said the Security Chief, glancing round the table at the other Council members. "Please interject if I say anything with which you disagree. Your Majesty, I have called this meeting with the utmost urgency. My agents have reported disturbing information regarding the Chosen Ones. As we are all aware, Bryony Winkleweed is an orphan with uncertain parentage. She is untried and untested. She is talking of having... friends in the Human realm."

The queen opened her mouth to speak, but Agaric pushed on. "And as for Sheean Meranon, well, he is completely unsuited to be king. He will lead Taranor into chaos. He is tainted by Human contact. Bryony was at least at liberty in the Human realm and never forgot, or revealed, her identity. However Sheean seems to have become almost Human. He spent a lot of time with..." Agaric gave a theatrical shudder, "... a Human woman."

Queen Rhyannon looked at the tapestries on the walls showing scenes of the halcyon days of the Faerie kingdom, when all races lived in harmony. She sighed.

"I believe Sheean is the rightful king," she said. "He has shown tremendous strength and endurance during his captivity. And as for Bryony being untested, what greater test can there be than to remain in the mortal kingdom, ageing as they age, risking sickness and death to save your betrothed? I believe with all my heart and soul that Bryony Winkleweed should take my place as Faerie Queen of Taranor. I would remind the Council of the

34

Prophecy. It was foreseen that Bryony and Sheean would experience and overcome hardship. They are the Chosen Ones."

"With respect, Your Majesty," said Agaric. "The Prophecy could have been fulfilled by any pair of children."

Queen Rhyannon silenced him with a long, withering look. "I also believe that with the right rehabilitation, Sheean will make an excellent recovery from his trials."

"Your Majesty, there are rumours of other contenders for the throne."

"Who are these others?"

Agaric shifted in his seat. "There is only one at this exact time, Your Majesty. Prince Liedinroad of Goldendale. He will keep order in Taranor. He will keep Bryony in order as well. I believe he is a better choice."

The Queen's golden light flashed bronze. "Keep order! That's all you think about! There is more to ruling a kingdom than keeping everything controlled and unchanging." She gave a small laugh to show that she had not lost her mind. "But don't worry; I'm not going to be inviting Goblins to tea!" Her face became serious once more. "I wish to bring the Faerie Kingdom to its true power. Our race has been dwindling for thousands of years. We need a couple on the throne who will give our race courage in these difficult times. They will show the way in a new era of co-operation and love. If you have nothing else to say, then I consider this meeting closed."

Agaric's lips formed a thin, tight line. The queen rose into the air and flew directly over him.

"And, Agaric, I'll ask you NEVER to interrupt me again. You saw that I was about to speak and continued with your own point of view. This is unacceptable. If it happens one more time I will remove you from office."

* * *

In the scented waters of the Great Bath, Grizelda was able to move freely. She lifted her arms, letting the flabs of fat fall down.

"My armpits, wench, don't forget my armpits!"

The servant girl flinched at the sight. "Do you want me to shave you, Your Majesty?"

"NO!"

Grizelda's face turned puce in her fury. "The hair is to collect sweat you fool. The last time I was shaved, I itched so badly afterwards that I banished the person responsible to the Demon realm. Forever!"

"As you wish, Your Majesty."

The girl moved the folds of flesh aside and rubbed at the dense black hairs of Grizelda's armpit with a cloth.

"What flavour is my birthday cake?" asked Grizelda.

"I don't know, Your Majesty."

"DON'T KNOW! Then go and find out. I want to imagine it before I eat it."

The girl left, making her way to the kitchens, while Grizelda sat in the steaming water flexing her giant thighs. "I hope it's spiceberry. Cook does a great spiceberry cake. I want apple pie in the middle and meringue on top with orange. And custard."

As she reached for the sugar-pop drink at her side, she slipped. Soapsuds sprayed into her face and waves of water sloshed over the side of the bath.

"WENCH!"

The girl came running back, breathless.

"Get me back upright, you fool! Or I will send you to the howlings!"

Trembling, the girl grabbed Grizelda's vast arms and tried to lift, but the queen's hips were stuck.

"I'm so sorry, Your Majesty, I have to get help."

Grizelda's face was purple with rage by the time three soldiers arrived to get her free. Each wore a blindfold to preserve her dignity. They did their best to manipulate her bulk without injury, but none of them truly knew where they were putting their hands.

Once she was free, she sat on a towel on a chair and patted her face dry. The exertion had made her sweat again.

"Well, what flavour?"

"It's chocolate, Your Majesty," said the girl, bowing her head.

"SPICEBERRY! I want SPICEBERRY!"

Grizelda turned to a soldier standing nearby. "When you are outside this room, take off your blindfold and go to Cook. Tell her I want spiceberry, with apple pie, meringue, orange and custard. In that order. The rest of you can go. Not you girl."

Once alone with the servant girl, Grizelda turned on her.

"YOU!" she screamed, pointing a wrinkled, pulpy finger. "You left me alone in the bath! I could have drowned!"

The girl lowered her eyes. "But, Your Majesty, you asked me to go and find..."

"NO-ONE says '*but*' to ME!"

There was a flash of light and the girl was gone. A faint whiff of sulphur filled the air. Grizelda looked around for her clothes.

"Servants! Here! Now!"

Later that evening, trumpets sounded all around Cucapha castle as Grizelda's sedan chair entered the banqueting hall, carried high on the shoulders of six Goblins.

"All hail, Queen Grizelda!" shouted the crowd as she was lowered onto a platform at the head of the table. The seat had been specially built to take her bulk. On her right, sat a pale Goblin officer and on her left was Edna, the Wise Woman. Queen Grizelda settled herself onto sequined cushions and signalled for silence.

"It has been six years since the death of King Yuppick and the escape of the Fay Prince. As promised, since then I have been a fair queen and a wise one. As before, everyone who does my bidding will be happy. Let the party commence."

The people applauded as servants arrived carrying trays of food. There were quails' eggs in jelly, melons sculpted in the shape of swans, piles of hot buttered toast and dishes of sea creatures in batter. Grizelda waved the trays away. "No. I don't want that! I want my cake!"

A flurry of disappointment rippled down the room as the fresh food was taken away. A hush fell on the banqueting hall as servants on each side extinguished the wall torches. All eyes turned to the door.

To the sound of another fanfare, four servants carried a teetering tower of sweetness into the hall. The cake was the width of a cartwheel and as high, its top surface covered with candles. The servants staggered up the hallway between the tables and laid the cake in front of Queen Grizelda. They curtsied and retreated backwards, bowing and grovelling until they were out of sight.

There were so many candles on the cake that the wax began to catch and the cake began to blaze. Grizelda clapped her pudgy hands together, cackling in delight. She sniffed the bottom of the cake and smiled in satisfaction. "Spiceberry," she muttered. She stuck her fat finger into the middle layer of cake, pulled it out and sucked. The room fell silent. "Apple pie, yummy." With the same finger she swiped some of the soft coating from the top and put it in her mouth. "Custard and meringue." She looked around the banqueting hall.

"The Cook has done well. The Cook will live!"

The diners erupted in cheers, hats were thrown and it took quite a while for the applause to die down. By this time flames were spluttering on the top of the cake, the heat melting the meringue.

Grizelda took a huge breath. Ladies lifted their fans to shield their faces and the men averted their eyes. She blew. Spittle covered the cake and a few candles went out.

Grizelda's face was covered in icing and custard. She clicked her fingers and smoke issued from a few more candles. Her face grew dark. Many candles on the far side of the cake continued to burn.

Edna muttered a discreet word and all the candles went out. The diners cheered and clapped, wishing Grizelda a happy birthday. She did not smile. "I'm going to light them again. I want to make another wish. I am Queen and I can have as many wishes as I want!"

Grizelda glared at the cake. She clicked her fingers. Nothing happened. Some people near the door scraped back their chairs, ready to escape. Edna glanced in compassion at the queen's unhappy face. Under the table, she clicked her fingers and all the candles blazed into life once more, the flames hovering just above the cake.

Queen Grizelda shook with rage, her cheeks quivering, dropping crumbs of meringue onto the table. She turned on Edna.

"I hired you to protect me, not show me up in front of everyone! For your insolence you will be BANISHED!"

There was a puff of smoke. Edna's chair was empty.

Chapter 2

Edna fell for a while through sulphurous fumes, then landed on the side of a vast sand dune. She lost her balance and began to slide downwards, out of control, scraping her ankles against submerged rocks.

"Halt!" she cried. Her descent slowed a little. "HALT," she yelled, using every ounce of her power.

An outcrop of boulders sprang up from the sand like a hand rising from the desert to stop her. She slammed into the obstacle, banging her forehead. She lay still for a moment, catching her breath, while the hot wind blew sand over her skirts. The air smelt foul; a mixture of rotten eggs and burning pitch. Her head throbbed. She reached up to touch her forehead. Her fingers felt warm, sticky blood and the tenderness of a bruise.

* * *

Bryony moved some lily-pads out of the way to create a clear patch of water. She thought again of Edna. "Oh Edna, I'm so sorry I had to leave you behind. Edna, can you show me where you are?"

A vision formed. Bryony caught her breath as she saw her friend slumped against a boulder in a desert. Blood trickled down her wrinkled cheek and her skirts lay tangled round her legs.

Bryony whimpered and turned from the water's image.

* * *

Edna shut her eyes and visualized a simple healing spell. Within seconds her pain diminished and she felt

41

strong enough to stand. She had come to rest almost at the foot of the dune. Before her stretched a wide, barren valley. Ahead was a forest, and beyond that a river so wide that its further shore lay shrouded in mist. Far to the right lay a range of mountains.

She gave a short laugh as she recognised where she was. "The Demon realm! Thank you Grizelda. I was going to come here next month anyway. I'd have preferred to have my spell books, but I'll manage." She shrugged her shoulders, lifted her skirts and began to walk. "At least I've landed near the River Styx."

Away from the dunes, the sand gave way to grey, volcanic grit. Stunted trees and bushes provided little shade from the heat. From the forest came screams of anguish and cries of despair. Edna shook her head sadly and continued to walk towards the river.

She heard a tiny voice calling out. "Meeeuw." It sounded just like a kitten. Edna dragged her shawl around her shoulders and walked faster towards the river, keen to leave the Dunes of Despair behind her. "I'm not going to respond to every little sound I hear in this land of lost souls," she said aloud. "Let me pass unhindered."

"Meeeuw." The sound came from somewhere up ahead.

"I'm going to hear howls and wails of despair. I'm going to hear the rattling of chains and screams of agony, and I know full well most of them will not be genuine. Nearly all of them will be traps."

"Meeeuw."

"I'm going to ignore the charming voices: the voices that sound so persuasive and intelligent; the voices that sound like they belong to innocent beings, trapped here through no wrongdoing of their own. I've been here before, little creature, and I know that those are the most dangerous."

"Meeeuw."

"Your little cry sounds so sweet and pathetic, but if I actually look for you, I'll find that you're a great big creature, intent on eating me for supper. Not just my body but my soul as well, and there is no way I'm staying here for eternity with you. I have an important job to do. Now if you don't mind..."

A scratching sound came from nearby, as if made by tiny claws against wood.

"Meeeuw."

Her heart melted. She scanned for magic and could sense nothing evil.

"Alright, little creature, call me and I'll find you. But I promise you, if you treble in size and devour me, I will give you such indigestion you'll regret you ever met me."

"Meeeuw."

She followed the sound until she came to a small wooden box. The creature inside scratched against the lid.

Edna knelt down on the burning volcanic grit and picked up the box.

"Here goes. I'm opening a box in a dangerous place, something my husband told me never to do, but be warned little Demon, I'm ready for you. I'm not the simple old lady you think I am."

Calling strong defensive magic to mind, Edna began to open the lid. She paused. A tiny, fluffy paw reached out, searching. She opened the lid further to reveal a ginger and white kitten. It had white paws and a little white splotch on its nose. Its eyes were blue. It reached out towards her, touching her with a paw as soft as velvet.

Edna waited. "Well, go on then, reveal who you are. Turn into a monster."

The kitten climbed out of the box onto her skirts, wobbling in its weakness.

"Oh my goodness, you really are a kitten! You can't be more than eight weeks old! What's your name?"

The kitten looked up at her. "Timoffy."

Edna smiled at the kitten's cute voice. "What are you doing here?"

"Queen Gwizelda got bored wiv me."

"That woman is evil. She will know my wrath!"

Edna reached among her skirts for the tiny crystal she always carried. It was not capable of big magic, but she hoped to be able to contact Azabyandee for long enough to save this helpless creature. The kitten climbed up onto Edna's shoulder, perching there like a ginger parrot. Edna closed the wooden box and placed the crystal on its lid. She drew symbols in the air. Soon the sparkling gem turned opaque.

"Azabyandee, I need to speak with you."

In every facet of the crystal there appeared a cat with cream fur, each with a dark, pointed face and bright blue eyes.

"Wife, why are you calling?" The voice that came from the crystal was tinny and indistinct. "What can be so urgent that you use the crystal?"

"I have accidentally enraged Grizelda. At least I am alive and not frazzled into dust. I'm in the Demon realm."

A gentle hiss escaped Azabyandee. "It could be to our advantage that you are in the howlings. Maybe

44

you can try again to discover the whereabouts of the Wyvernhope Torc?"

"I'll do my best. I'll make my way to the ferrywoman. She might be able to help."

"Good luck, my dear."

"Darling. I've just come across an innocent soul, another victim of Grizelda, who needs our help. I'd like to send her through the crystal to you."

Azabyandee's eyes narrowed. "Surely you have the wisdom to know that you cannot send back every hapless soul you come across."

Edna smiled. "Of course, my love." She took the kitten from her shoulder and held it up so that Azabyandee could see. "I thought that since you are in cat form at the moment you would sympathise. His name is Timothy."

The kitten wriggled in her hand. "No. Me is girl."

Edna smiled at the kitten. "Sorry, my dear." She looked at the crystal again. "Grizelda banished her to live in perpetual thirst and hunger inside a wooden box among the Dunes of Despair. I wish to send her back to you to live in comfort."

"You do realise that only one soul can be sent to me this way."

"I do."

A blue mist drifted from the eyes of Azabyandee and into the air around Edna and Timothy. In seconds the kitten was gone and the blue mist retreated back into the crystal.

"She's here," said Azabyandee. "She's eating the mouse I caught this morning. I will give her safety. Good luck my love. Only contact me in an emergency. The crystal will not last much longer."

Edna blew her husband a kiss and closed the connection.

45

She paused near the edge of the forest, sucking on a moist stem of aloe-vera. The trees were twisted, contorted as if in pain. Among their roots, mushrooms and patches of grass struggled to grab moisture from the parched, volcanic dust.

She picked one of the mushrooms. "Reveal... good or ill." Magic sparkled round it, but Edna couldn't tell whether it was safe to eat or not. It had a smooth brown top and creamy gills. It looked delicious. Not fooled for a moment, Edna tucked it into her waistband.

As she did so, a deep, mind-numbing fatigue came over her. Her head began to hurt again. She sat down. She was hungry. She had not eaten for hours. She took out the mushrooom and looked at it, nibbling its edge. She waited before eating any more to see the effect. She felt better for resting on the ground. She thought about getting up and continuing to the river but decided against it.

She looked up. The sky was pale yellow from horizon to horizon. Every now and again vague cries of distress came to her; howls deep in the forest rose and fell. Her heart went out to the suffering beings.

After a while she heard footsteps and turned to see two young men walking towards her. They approached and bowed politely. "We are lost," said one. "Can you guide us out of here?"

The other man bent down to pick up two mushrooms. He shoved one into his mouth, and gave the other to his friend.

"Be careful with the mushrooms," said Edna. "I don't know yet whether they are safe."

The man who had spoken ate his mushroom, speaking with his mouth full. "We are so hungry and thirsty. Where are we?"

Before Edna could answer, both men became stiff in their movements, their faces froze, their mouths contorted in pain. A terrible howl came from both of them as their bodies elongated and contorted. Edna tried to rise, hoping to end their suffering, but she couldn't get up.

The men's arms grew longer and their fingers became thin and brittle. Their feet turned into roots, plunging deep into the ground. Edna tried once more to rise. She looked up, and where the two men had been standing were two twisted trees. From deep within a large knot on each trunk came shrieks of despair.

Edna stood up with great difficulty. Her muscles felt stiff and wooden. "Oh dear," she said, "I've made a terrible mistake."

Although the heat of the land and the quality of light didn't change, Edna knew many hours had gone by, possibly days. All sorts of creatures had come to the edge of the forest where the mushrooms grew. Each turned into a twisted tree, despite her warnings. She stood in a clearing having used magic to keep them away from her. She alone had leaves; all the others looked blasted and dead, even though she knew they were alive.

Her leaves allowed her to stay refreshed and alert, gathering what energy she could from the light. Her roots dug deep into the ground, finding moisture.

One of her roots hit something hard. She explored it and found it was a semicircle of metal. She gasped as she wondered whether it might be the

Wyvernhope Torc. As she reached her root around the metal object and held it, the ground began to move. Snakes began to writhe at the base of her trunk.

"Leave it alone!" hissed the snakes. Convinced it was indeed the treasure she was seeking, Edna hung on tight.

* * *

The glow-worms in Bryony's hair became dislodged as she flew round and round her room. "I must find a Portal Stone. I'm the Princess of Taranor! They must have a spare stone for me!" She flung open drawers and looked in all the glittering boxes on her dressing table.

She paused, catching her reflection in a full-length mirror. Her tiara had slipped across one delicately pointed ear and most of the butterflies had fallen down her long brown hair. She pushed the tiara back on her head and fanned out her wings. The upper set were a beautiful turquoise. The lower set had flashes of royal blue. The image of Edna returned to her mind, forcing her to continue her search. Then she remembered Dog.

She flew through the Royal Gardens to the Wildflower Meadows where she found Fable and Dog sitting together in the moonlight. Fable smiled, and Dog ran up to her wagging his tail round and round. She patted Dog on the head and stroked Fable's velvet-soft nose.

"Dog, have you still got the Portal Stone in your stomach?"

"Yes. Not hurting now."

"Do you feel the need to... to go to the toilet yet?"

Dog scratched his ear. "No."

Bryony sighed.

"Why do you need a Portal Stone, sweet one?" asked Fable.

"Um... just need to... um..."

"You're not going back to the Human realm are you?"

Bryony looked into the wise brown eyes of her horse: the horse that had cared for her since infancy, that had travelled with her during her years in the Human realm, that had risked his life to save hers. She couldn't lie.

"I'm going to rescue Edna. I used the water in my pond to check on her. She's in trouble."

Fable snorted and tossed his head. "Oh no you're not."

Bryony looked down at her feet. Fable took one step towards her and nuzzled his face against her shoulder.

"Edna is a fine woman," he said. "She is more powerful than you can possibly imagine. Even though you saw her in jeopardy just now, she will prevail. The troubles of the mortal realm are no longer our concern."

Dog licked Bryony's hand. She looked once more into her horse's eyes and saw the truth of what he was saying. She smiled and turned to go back. "OK Fable. I'd better carry on getting ready for the banquet."

Fable chuckled. "Try not to lose the glow-worms and butterflies. They've slipped quite a long way down your hair."

Bryony smiled and helped the insects back onto her tiara. "Thank you Fable. I'll see you later."

As she walked back through her scented garden, she couldn't resist one more look in the pool. She thought of Edna: of her round, apple cheeks, of her potions and her nine cream cats. She remembered how much she had enjoyed Dragonfest the previous winter. She remembered the pine tree with its little decorations and the presents underneath. She remembered Edna's smiling face.

The pool showed a forest of trees. Howls of despair filled the air. She looked closer and saw that one of the trees stood alone in a clearing. It had a twisted knot in the centre of its trunk. The knot looked just like a face. Edna's face!

"Edna!" shouted Bryony. "I'm coming!"

She took one of the butterflies from her tiara and held it gently on her finger.

"Please go to the rose arch at the entrance to the Wildflower Meadows, little Butterfly. Count to ten, and if I'm not back by then, tell Fable where I've gone. I have to rescue my Human friend, Edna. She would do the same for me." Her voice cracked. She took a deep breath to try to push away her fear. "There's no time for tears. I must hurry."

The butterfly flew away towards Fable while Bryony rushed towards Sheean's room. "He'll have a stone, I'm sure he will."

* * *

Finally alone, Sheean threw himself onto the thick, rose-petal bed. He felt utterly miserable. He knew he couldn't spend the rest of his life like this, never able to do anything for himself. He wondered whether when he got to be King he could pass a few laws to make everybody leave him alone.

He shut the curtains round his bed, trying to shut out the brilliance of the moons, hoping for peace.

Instead he heard bells tinkling as Bryony hurtled into his bedroom.

"Sheean, wake up," she said, yanking his curtains open.

Sheean sat on the edge of the bed, rubbing his eyes. "How come you look alright in that dress and I look so stupid? Men don't wear dresses."

"You're not wearing a dress, it's a royal robe. Listen, I haven't got much time."

"Are you OK? Is something wrong?"

"Yes, but it's nothing for you to worry about. I'm going out for a while. Can I borrow your Portal Stone?"

"My what? Where are you going?"

"To rescue Edna. If anyone asks," she said, "I'll be back by the banquet."

Sheean felt too weary to argue. He lay back down and closed his eyes again. He could hear Bryony moving round his room, opening and closing drawers.

"OK, I'll wait here for you shall I?" said Sheean, sarcastically.

"Whatever."

He heard Bryony rush out of the room. He opened his eyes and saw the white curtains that surrounded his bed wafting with the speed of her departure.

* * *

Butterfly reached the rose arch at the entrance to the Wildflower Meadows. She saw Fable, his white coat shining in the light of the moons, nuzzling up to the mortal hound. The two animals seemed to be friends. Fable kept licking the dog to try and clean it. Butterfly laughed at the thought of how long it would

51

take to clean such a dirty creature. How could Queen Rhyannon have allowed such a thing to enter Taranor?

Butterfly trembled with the responsibility of her task. She knew that Bryony should not have gone. No-one ever left the city without telling one of the administrators. Certainly the Royal Attendants should be informed. The roses tumbling over the arch were intertwined with sweet jasmine. She was tempted to pause and drink, but Bryony had said to count to ten and then tell Fable.

Why? Why not tell Fable sooner? Butterfly had never had a conundrum to deal with before. She spiralled her tongue tighter in her mouth, struggling to come to a decision. She took a deep, fluttery breath and began to count to ten.

* * *

Bryony dismissed the remaining tiny creatures in her hair and sat on the edge of her pond. She looked up at the stars and moons.

"Goodbye Orba," she whispered, "goodbye Silvrin, I'll be back in a flash."

She turned to the water and thought of the town of Gavelkind in the Human realm, the town where both Albert and Edna lived. Almost a whole petal had gone past since she was last there; so much could have happened in six mortal years.

The water grew cloudy and dark. Soon the main street of Gavelkind appeared in the water. It was night. An owl hooted in the woods. Bryony could sense changes: the presence of iron was stronger at the blacksmith's cottage than it had been, and the track through the town seemed wider and smoother.

To her shock she saw two Goblins sitting side by side in a sentry box, spitting onto the street.

Goblins? What, by the gods, had happened? Holding Sheean's Portal Stone, she shrank down to the size of a wasp so that the portal would be small and less noticeable. She didn't have Fable to protect her this time. She would have to be very careful.

She heard a faint pop as the portal shut behind her, cutting her off from the Faerie world. She flew straight into a deep bush and hid her Faerie light.

"Wazzat?" said one of the Goblins.

"Wot?"

"Somefink over there." It pointed towards Bryony.

"Nar."

"Wuz."

"Wuzzant!"

Bryony changed her appearance, taking on the glamour of a leaf. She heard footsteps. A young woman, wearing a shawl held tightly round her thin shoulders, passed by.

"YOU!" shouted one of the Goblins. "STOP!"

The woman paused.

"Why you out? Is curfew!"

"I'm sorry, my friend was ill. I was delayed in getting home."

"Say Sir!"

With a deep sigh the woman added a tiny, "Sir."

The Goblins looked her up and down. "We let you go this time. We see you after curfew again, we eat ya!"

The woman walked past the Goblins and let herself into the blacksmith's cottage. Bryony hid behind the leaves, trembling. The Goblins leaned back in their chairs and laughed, continuing to spit, each competing to see who could get their green phlegm to go the furthest.

A short while later they fell asleep, allowing Bryony to fly unnoticed into the blacksmith's courtyard. She looked in through the kitchen window and saw Albert's mother Sandy talking to the young woman, who seemed to be crying. Assuming Human form and dressing herself in loose trousers and an embroidered smock, Bryony knocked. Immediately, the light in the kitchen went out. A voice hissed through the back door.

"Who is it?"

"It's Bryony."

Sandy opened the back door. For a second the two women stared at each other. Then Sandy shook her head and grabbed Bryony's arm, pulling her into the room. The young woman lit the lantern once more and stood with her back to the range, delicately dabbing at her eyes with a handkerchief.

"Bryony! I never thought I'd see you again! Are you alright? Where have you been?" The questions poured out of Sandy as if they would never stop. "Where's Albert, is he with you?"

Bryony wanted to hug her, but the tension in the room made her cautious. The two women looked thin and their faces were pale and drawn. Their clothes were ragged.

"Her eyes... she has green eyes," whispered the young woman.

The shock on Sandy's face faded, to be replaced by anger. "How have you escaped?"

"Escaped from where?" asked Bryony. "Where's Albert?"

Sandy's wrath grew. She placed her hands on her hips and glared at Bryony. "Albert ran off with you, so you tell me!"

Bryony wanted to run from this horrible world, with its spitting Goblins and its shouting, its awful smells and its anger. She backed away to the door. "I don't know. I thought he would be with you. What's happened? Everything seems like a nightmare."

Sandy's voice, when it came, was softer. "You mean to tell me you have no idea where Albert is? I assumed you both ran off to avoid the prison camps."

Bryony shook. By now her back was against the door and she was ready to fly. Sandy sank into a chair with a small cry of despair. The young woman went to comfort her, still glaring at Bryony. Sandy looked up.

"When did you last see him?" she asked.

"I haven't seen him since yesterday. I mean since we delivered the cheesecakes to King Yuppick at the castle."

"But that was six years ago! Before the occupation."

Bryony's mouth opened to speak, but no sound came.

"Bryony," continued Sandy, "what are you up to? You're in terrible danger being here. I need to make you understand. Finella, please serve us all some soup."

"Are you Albert's sister?" asked Bryony as she joined Sandy at the table.

"Yes," replied Finella. She lifted a saucepan from the range and began ladelling soup into wooden bowls. "Mother, the soldiers will be looking for her. We shouldn't have her here in the house. It's dangerous."

"Just for one night, my dear. Just for one night."

Finella placed a bowl of thin soup in front of Bryony, before sitting down next to Sandy.

"Bryony," said Sandy, "tell us what you've been up to all this time."

Bryony played with her soup.

"Don't worry," said Sandy, "there's no meat in it. We can't afford it any more. I suppose it could be worse. If it wasn't for Roger working up at the castle, we'd be in trouble. We're doing quite well really, we've got..." She stopped speaking, her voice caught in her throat.

Bryony looked up at her friendly face. Fine lines of stress showed around her eyes.

"Who's Roger?"

"Albert's uncle, my brother-in-law."

"What about your husband? Where is he?"

Bryony knew, as soon as she'd spoken, that she'd made a mistake. Sandy's face crumpled. Finella shot Bryony a thunderous look.

"He was killed by the Goblins," said Sandy, "three years ago."

She looked down at her bowl. Bryony cleared her throat.

"I'm really sorry."

There was a short silence. Sandy drew in a shaky breath and began eating her soup.

"Have you been in hiding?" asked Finella. "How have you avoided the camps?"

"I've been far away. I don't know anything about the camps."

"But surely, word of Grizelda's campaign must have reached the South. Have you been at Shalimar?"

Bryony made an effort not to blush as she lied. "Yes."

"How is Ruth?" asked Sandy. "Merik's wife. You know Merik."

"Ah yes."

"She's at Shalimar with her sister. She's got green eyes too, so Merik thought she'd be safe there. Did you see her?"

"No."

They ate in silence, their spoons scraping the bowls until every scrap of the soup was gone.

"Bryony, you can stay the night, what's left of it, but at first light you must leave. It's not safe here. I can't harbour a green-eyed person, no matter how well I know them."

"Please Sandy. Please explain what this is all about."

"You know full well that Queen Grizelda would have me killed if she knew you were here."

Bryony stood up in shock. Her chair clattered to the floor. "Grizelda is Queen?!" The urge to revert to her natural Faerie form grew overwhelming. "I really don't know anything. It's true. I've been far away, but not in Shalimar. I've been in the mountains. I came to see Edna."

"Why didn't you say so before?" said Sandy as she bustled about, getting some blankets from the corner of the room. "Look, rest here for the night and I can explain in the morning. You're best off going back to the mountains, my dearest. Edna has been banished. You can't help her."

"Why? What did she do?"

Bryony picked up her chair and sat down again.

"She upset Grizelda."

"Do you mean that Grizelda is the queen at Cucapha Castle? How can that be?"

"Enough questions. Make your bed here, by the range. Or you could share with Finella."

"No, please don't go to lots of trouble. I need to go to Edna's cottage. I need to see Azabyandee."

"Who?"

"Her cats. Who's looking after her cats?"

Finella made a small tutting noise with her teeth and glanced across at her mother. "I think she's lost her mind."

"Are you quite well, Bryony?" said Sandy. "You're talking as if you have a fever."

Bryony got up and moved to the door. "Please Sandy, let me go."

"You can't go out now, the Goblins will catch you."

Thinking quickly, Bryony changed her strategy. "Actually, to tell you the truth..."

"Here it comes," said Finella.

"I was staying in the mountains. As I made my way here I bumped my head and feel very confused. I can't remember anything. I'd like to stay here, by the range, and I promise I'll be gone by first light. I don't want to get you into any trouble. You have always been so kind to me."

"Stay the night, and I will try and get a doctor for you in the morning. I want someone to take care of your head."

As soon as Sandy and Finella had gone to bed, Bryony ruffled up the blankets as if she had slept on them and tiptoed to the back door. Opening it as quietly as she could, she slipped into the courtyard and made her way towards the field at the back.

She felt a pang of nostalgia as she passed the stables. The warm smell of the horses reminded her of all the happy times she'd had here with Albert and Fable. She felt like she had returned to a different world; everything was so strange.

Just as she was about to revert to Faerie form, she heard a familiar voice in her mind.

"Bryony? Is that you?"

Bryony went back to the stables and looked inside. She saw her old friend Bracken lying in the straw. The kind old horse got up and nuzzled her with his nose.

"Hello, Bracken, how are you?" she whispered.

"I'm fine, Bryony," said Bracken, straight into her mind. *"It's good to see you again. But you must fly! Away! Don't return until this madness is gone."*

Bryony shifted to Faerie form and muted her light until she matched the grey and brown of the night air. Looking down at her body, all she could see was a changing pattern of light. "That'll have to do. Oh my sweet Bracken. Take care of yourself. I'm going to rescue Edna and sort out all this mess. I can't wait to tell Fable that I've seen you again."

"Please send him my love."

"I will."

Bryony kissed Bracken on the nose and flew as fast as she could towards the edge of town, keeping to the trees and outbuildings as much as possible.

Within a few minutes, she saw Edna's cottage on Maltbrook Lane. It looked the same as before, pretty, even in the night-time, with roses over the front door and wild flowers in the garden. She flew to the back door and looked in the window. The cottage was dark. She jumped as a dark faced, cream cat popped into view, followed by another, and another. Bryony laughed. "Let me in, Azabyandee." All three cats looked to the door and then at Bryony. She tried the handle and found the door was unlocked.

Bryony entered Edna's cottage and paused to allow her Faerie sight to adjust to the darkness. Dust lay on every surface and the air smelled musty. The fireplace was dark, cold and dead. The three cats rubbed against her leg in greeting.

"Are you alright, Azabyandee? The last time I saw you, you were battling King Yuppick, hissing at him to destroy his mind. Did you kill him? The noise you made almost finished me."

A well spoken, nasal voice issued from the minds of all three cats in unison. *"No. You passed out, and he escaped. He died jumping after you and Sheean from the balcony of the tower. I am fine but I am rather distressed."*

Bryony looked around the room at all the familiar ornaments, cushions and tapestries.

"Edna is in trouble isn't she?" she said. "I've come to rescue her. I saw her in the water. I simply couldn't stay at home and leave her suffering. Where is she?"

Six more cream cats streamed into the room. They curled round her legs, rubbing their faces against her. Once all nine cats were in the room they settled down on the hearth rug and gazed at her with their china blue eyes, each with a tail curled neatly round its front paws.

A crashing sound came from the kitchen. It sounded like crockery falling onto the stone floor. Bryony felt her hair rise with static as a ginger kitten charged into the room, chasing a ball of fluff.

"Oh, how adorable!" said Bryony. "What's your name?"

The kitten skidded round the chairs and bounced up to her, grabbing at her hands with tiny paws.

"Me is Timoffy."

"You're so sweet. How did you get here?"

"Froo da cwystal."

The kitten chewed on Bryony's fingers making her laugh.

"Alas," said all nine cats at once, as if with one voice, *"Edna has been banished to the Demon realm, due to an argument with Grizelda. She sent this juvenile through to me. She would save all the lost souls in there if she could."*

"What happened?"

"I will tell you later. It is imperative that you go to her with all haste. I expected Edna to return almost immediately following her banishment. Her magic is strong enough to deal with the realm of shifting shapes and howling, but she has not come home. Something has kept her there. I cannot see her, or communicate. Something blocks me."

Bryony shivered at the thought of her kind old friend in trouble in such an awful place. "How long has she been there?"

"Eight weeks, and although I fear for her safety, I hope that she is in fact alright and searching for the Wyvernhope Torc."

"The what?" Bryony sat down on the rug in front of the cats to listen, allowing Timothy to chew her hair.

"During the Wizard Wars, a torc, that's a type of necklace worn by the Great Mage, was taken into the Demon world. It has remained hidden for a long time. Many have gone to search for it, keen to gain its powers, but all have failed. It is my hope that my wife is not trapped there, but is simply delayed while searching for this artefact."

"Why would she want it?"

"My child, you still have no idea who I am, do you?"

"Not really."

"For now it is enough for you to know that with the torc I can be restored to Wizard form and my former Wizard power. Then, with Edna by my side, we will be able to overthrow the tyranny that strangles this land."

"Please can you tell me what's happening with the Goblins? Everything seems to have become so terrible."

"Time is of the essence, we must make haste. However I will tell you a little. Six years have passed in this realm since you and Sheean escaped the castle and flew through the portal, back to the Faerie Kingdom. Although King Yuppick died that day, the Human realm is still filled with evil. The witch Grizelda took his place, setting herself up as Queen. No one dares to defy her.

"During the first year of her reign, many people who resisted her rule were put to death or banished to the Demon realm. She soon began to fear Sheean's return. To prevent being taken by surprise, she organised teams of soldiers to arrest anyone with green eyes. Prison camps were built in the Tirach desert. However, Humans were reluctant to follow her orders, so she opened a permanent portal into the Goblin realm and drafted in an army of willing fighters. She uses these to keep order."

"How awful. Doesn't she realise the Fay can change their eye colour at will?"

"Clearly not - which is useful for us. Princess Bryony, I ask you to venture where I cannot go, and to find my wife. If I had the power I would go myself, but sadly I do not. Please help her to find the Wyvernhope Torc. It is made from the finest gold and silver and fits anyone who wears it, giving them tremendous power."

"Of course. No problem. I'll bring Edna back with her magic necklace and be back in time to go to the banquet in the Faerie realm. I'm being crowned Faerie Queen tomorrow night."

The cats purred momentarily. *"I am pleased for you. I just hope this is as easy as you think it will be. Now, please close the shutters. We do not want any light escaping the house and drawing the attention of the Goblin Watchers."*

Bryony flew to the window and pulled the shutters closed. "Who is looking after you, Azabyandee?"

"I can get in and out through the kitchen window which is always open, and I can hunt. I am not in jeopardy. Please make haste. Stand on the rug."

Bryony did as she was told. "I have a Portal Stone, will that help?"

"Yes," said Azabyandee, as he moved into a circle round her. *"Use your mind and the stone, but you will need my energy too. It is hard to travel to the realm of horrors alone."*

* * *

Grumbuk leaned on the bar of the Snot and Bucket, his head lolling closer and closer to his pint of green ale.

"You ever been Human realm?" he asked.

The barmaid laughed, showing a mouthful of rotten teeth and a small black tongue. Her breath was disgusting. "Why bother going there? Goblin realm good place."

"True. Specially now Ogman dead. Was me what killed him."

"You joking yes?" said the barmaid.

"Nope. Me hero. Me kill bad king. Save all worlds."

"You always same. You mad artist."

Grumbuk tried to straighten up. "It true!"

63

The barmaid wandered off, still laughing, to wipe the tables with a filthy cloth. She paused by some Goblins in the corner. "He think he hero," she muttered. They all laughed. Grumbuk drained his glass and left the inn, trying not to stagger into the door frame on his way out.

Once in the street he breathed in deep. The flowing sewers smelled good, reviving him and reminding him of his hunger. A food seller cried his wares nearby. "Bugrat pie! Best in town!" The smell coming from the trolley on wheels was ripe; a sickly sweet stench that made Grumbuk's stomach rumble. As he made his way over to the stall he noticed a soldier in leather armour, wearing an armband bearing a red G on a black background. The tough ones all had these now.

When these armbands had first appeared in the Goblin realm, Grumbuk used to joke with friends that the G was short for Grumbuk; that the worlds were being united under his name. It was harsh enough that no one believed he was responsible for the death of the evil King Ogman, but to have the whole of the Goblin realm under the thumb of a poxy Human queen, well that was bogshit.

He walked over to the stall. "How rotted?" he asked.

The food seller was covered in the finest set of warts Grumbuk had ever seen. They covered his face, hands and even his eyelids, giving him the appearance of a lichen covered tree. "Very. Fall apart in mouth." The food seller scratched his head and a shower of flakes of skin fell onto the pies. Grumbuk licked his lips.

Before he could buy a pie, the soldier approached and touched him on the arm with a shock stick.

"You fit Goblin," the soldier grunted, "what you do here?"

"Me buy pie, stupid."

Pain shot through Grumbuk like lightning. His arm burned, his hand clenched shut against his will. Black and orange lights flashed behind his eyes.

"You stupid!" shouted the soldier, grabbing him by the arm and leading him away. "You come with me! Any trouble I hit you with shock stick again. Turn pain level up!"

Grumbuk rubbed his sore arm. "Where we go?"

"You in army now."

Grumbuk tried to make his voice sound thin and weak. "No - me artist. Me really weedy."

"You strong enough."

Grumbuk sat on the back of a cart pulled by a team of bugrats. He was tightly packed in with fellow conscripts. He was really hungry now, as they had not been allowed to stop for food at the border control.

Once through the portal into the Human realm he noticed the air smelled empty and the sky was a weird blue colour. As the cart rolled at a steady pace along a paved road, a small hand touched his.

"Am frighted," said a tiny Goblin child.

Grumbuk squeezed the hand gently.

"Me too."

* * *

Butterfly gripped the rose with her tiny feet and concentrated. Four... five...

* * *

Bryony stood in the cottage, clutching her Portal Stone and thinking of Edna. Beams of blue energy came from the cats, mixing with her own Fay light. A small portal appeared in the air in front of her.

BANG! BANG!

"Open door!" shouted a voice from outside the cottage. "No magic allowed!"

"The Watchers!" hissed Azabyandee. *"We must hurry!"*

The kitten bolted under the chair. Bryony concentrated once more and the blue light from the cats' eyes grew in intensity. Bryony watched as the portal widened, opening into the Demon realm.

"Bash in door!" shouted the voice outside.

The blue light grew brighter. Through the portal, now as wide as a cartwheel, Bryony saw forest of twisted trees. Behind her, the sound of splintering wood and hissing cats came to her ears. Bryony turned to look at Azabyandee. The blue light coming from his eyes faltered, and the portal snapped shut.

"Save yourself!" yelled Azabyandee, as he ran into the kitchen. Bryony followed. Two enormous Goblins stood by the sink, each wearing red and black armbands. The front door lay smashed into pieces around their feet.

"Run!" shouted Azabyandee. She saw the last two cats jumping through the kitchen window.

"We got Fayri! Grizelda give us prizes!" shouted one of the Goblins, punching his colleague in the arm. "Get her!"

Before the other Goblin could act, Bryony drew a deep breath and shouted, "FREEZE!"

The two Goblins stood as still as statues. Bryony assumed Human form and, careful not to touch them, she crept past. Out on Maltbrook Lane she saw a few cream coloured shapes, visible even in the darkness, hiding in the hedge further down the lane.

Azabyandee's voice came into her mind. *"Eyes!"*

"What?"

Another Goblin lounged nearby, picking his nose. He approached.

"You! Is curfew! Why you out?"

Bryony turned to run, but strong hands caught her hair and pulled her back. The Goblin peered closely into her face. She could see every hair in the creature's nostrils and every blackened tooth in his mouth. His foetid breath made her feel faint.

"Green eyes," it chuckled. "Oh goody, me be rich now! Got place for Humans like you."

With a hiss, Azabyandee attacked. He clawed at the Goblin's legs, leapt onto his shoulders and raked the Goblin's face with claws as sharp as shards of glass. The Goblin screamed, letting go of Bryony's hair. It flailed in the air, trying to grab Azabyandee. Bryony heard a noise behind her and turned to see the two Watchers, woken by the screams of their comrade, rushing towards her, their arms outstretched, their eyes red with hatred and greed.

"FREEZE!"

She stepped back to the edge of the road and looked at her handiwork. The two running Goblins were frozen midstride. They looked almost comical. The one fighting Azabyandee looked like a grotesque carving, entangled with cream cats. A trail of blood stopped halfway down his contorted face. She counted. Only eight cats had been frozen in the midst of battle. The ninth approached her from the side of the road.

"Well done," he said, pausing to wash briefly. *"I could have killed them all easily, but your spell was swift. Now we need to get rid of the evidence as quickly as possible."*

"Do I have to kill the Goblins?"

"It would be wise."

As Bryony woke each cat with a gentle touch, she noticed a dagger in the belt of one of the Goblins. Inch by inch, she eased the weapon from its sheath, and then, one by one, she slit the throats of the Goblins. The stench of their sticky blood made her want to vomit. She looked up at Azabyandee. He was standing in a neat line on the side of the road.

"This is horrible," she said. "I know these beings are really nasty, but it's a shame they have to die. They were only doing their job."

"Bryony, your compassion is noble, but don't allow yourself to get too soft," purred Azabyandee.

Bryony threw the dagger away and began to drag the bodies into the ditch. They were surprisingly heavy, and the touch of their protective clothing disgusted her. She found herself shedding tears for the animals that had died to make their armour. The third Goblin proved the most difficult; she was getting tired.

"You must hurry, Bryony," said Azabyandee. *"The sun is coming up soon and more Goblins will be on this road. We must get you to the Demon realm. It is not safe for me to remain here. Meet me under Dringle Bridge in one hour. Our actions will be hidden there, and the reflections of the water will hide the magic light."*

Bryony dropped the Goblin and stood, placing her hands on the small of her back, easing out her muscles. "I'll see you there. Don't worry, I won't let you down."

Azabyandee ran off down the road towards the village of Dringle. With a deep sigh, Bryony took hold of the last Goblin and pulled. Suddenly, a sharp, burning pain shot through her. She dropped her burden. Losing her Human shape she cried out, sinking to the floor. Never before had she felt such pain. It had a searing and a drawing quality, sucking the air from her lungs, making her guts cramp in terror.

She looked at the Goblin and saw that she had accidentally touched a metal band wrapped around its wrist. It was iron. Her fingers throbbed, pulsing with each beat of her heart. Her breath caught in gasps. With the last ounce of her strength, she dragged the Goblin to the ditch.

Exhausted, she sat by the side of the road, curled up in pain. Far away, coming from the town of Gavelkind, she heard the sound of Goblin voices. She forced herself to stand. She wanted to fly, but her wings completely failed her. Afraid of being found by the guards, she attempted to resume Human form. This normally happened in an instant, but now the change was slow, as if her magic was dampened. Eventually her wings, pointed ears and teeth were transformed. She got up and began to walk to Dringle Bridge.

The thought of the cool water drew her, giving her legs a little strength, but soon she was spent. She sat underneath the shade of an oak tree, a little way back from the road. The fingers of her right hand were red, and the skin was peeling away in blisters. Her legs felt like jelly. Never before had she felt so overcome, so weak mentally and physically.

The dawn light began to appear. Birds sang sweetly in the trees as if nothing was wrong. Snails moved slowly across warm stones, looking for food, and flowers turned their faces to the sun. If it wasn't for the three dead Goblins on the lane and the dreadful pain in her hand, it could have been a day like any other in the Human realm. On days like this, she had enjoyed delivering bread to the castle with her Edna. She remembered Bracken, pulling the cart, the sun on his warm, brown back, and his ears pointed forwards in interest.

The pain made her feel faint. It felt as though creatures were climbing under her skin, burrowing deeper all the way to the bones of her arm. A deep sadness welled up.

"Who am I to think I could come here and sort it all out? Ridiculous! What would Fable say? He'll be so cross with me when he knows where I am."

Her eyes filled with tears. Angry with herself for being weak, she wiped them away. As soon as the moisture touched the burn, the pain ebbed away. She looked at her fingers. The skin was healing. Flooded with relief, Bryony blinked her eyes over the wound, feeling each drop of salty water ease the pain further, taking the burn away and healing her skin. She was so caught up with this that she failed to notice two Goblins creeping along the road.

A shadow fell across her. She looked up. They were small in stature and dressed in ordinary grey-green ragged clothes, glaring down at her with wicked grins on their faces.

"Hey Gorid, she got green eyes," said one.

Bryony blinked, making a massive effort to change her eye colour to brown.

"No stupid, they brown," said Gorid.

"Who you calling stupid?"

"You!"

They began punching each other and kicking, squealing as they inflicted damage. Bryony stood up, careful not to draw attention to herself. She inched away.

"Tribit, you clotpole, she running away!" shouted Gorid.

Bryony turned to run, but they were on her in an instant. A sharp blow to the back of her knees took her to the floor. With surprising speed they tied her wrists and ankles with rope. Bryony felt faint.

Tribit stared at her. "Like I said. She got green eyes."

Gorid peered closely. Bryony tried again to change her eye colour, but her magic felt so weak.

"They got bit brown in," he said.

"Mostly green," said Tribit. "We take to camp."

She was thrown over Tribit's shoulder like a sack of potatoes, and they began to march down the road, laughing.

"Human with green eyes," said Tribit. "We get loads of money."

"Brown and green. I saw first."

"Did not. Tribit carry, so is Tribit's prize."

"We share."

"We share carry then?"

"No."

"Why?"

"Cos I bin school," said Gorid.

Tribit's bony shoulder dug into Bryony's belly, bouncing her up and down with every step. His stubby arms held her with an amazing strength. Her legs flopped over his front, and her head hung down the back. The stench that came from his clothing was disgusting.

"Freeze," she said faintly.

They didn't even falter in their stride.

"FREEZE!"

The Goblins laughed.

"Why you pretend to be Fayri?" asked Tribit. "Just 'cos you got green eyes, don't make you magic."

She tried to revert to Faerie form, to use her full power, but apart from a mild itching in her back, nothing changed. Although the skin on her fingers looked healed, she felt as weak as a kitten, and a deep ache travelled from her hand up her right shoulder and into her back. She went limp and closed her eyes.

Chapter 3

Queen Grizelda sat on a massive sequinned cushion in the courtyard of Cucapha castle, looking at the outside of her North West tower. A pair of metal tracks had been fastened to the stonework and on the floor was a metal cage, big enough to hold the queen's frame. A man stood nearby, fidgeting with nerves.

"What's your name again?" asked Grizelda.

"Gladwyn, Your Majesty. Roger Gladwyn."

"If this works, Roger Gladwyn, I'll give you a Royal Warrant. If it doesn't, I'll have the dragon barbeque you."

"Thank you, Your Majesty. I'm certain you will be pleased with my invention."

"What's it called?"

"A personal ascending platform, Your Majesty."

"Is it ready for testing?"

"Yes, Your Majesty. I'm just going to send this sack of potatoes up and down in the cage."

Roger loaded the cage with the potatoes and closed the door. He pulled at the lever attached to the wall. The cage rose, carrying its load to the top of the tower.

"It's looking good, Your Majesty," said Roger as he pushed the lever upwards to make the lift come back down.

The lift descended. At first everything seemed to be working well. It moved slowly down the tracks for a few feet, but then, without any warning, it gave a shudder and dropped to the ground like a stone. The floor of the cage was white with smashed potatoes.

"Teething troubles, Your Majesty," said Roger. "It just needs a small adjustment and it will be fine."

Grizelda scowled. "I think you should ride in it next time."

Roger looked at the mess in the bottom of the cage and began to sweat.

"Of course, Your Majesty. I have every confidence in it."

* * *

As the sun reached its highest point in the day, Tribit and Gorid arrived at the outskirts of the village of Dringle. Tribit gave out a theatrical groan and dropped Bryony on the main road.

"Me tired of carrying," he moaned.

Gorid glared. "You carry again when get to camp. Look like we is hard bounty hunters."

"We is."

"Just do what I say or I knock teeth out."

Bryony got to her feet. She was shocked at how the village had changed. Dringle, once a pretty rural village, was now swarming with Goblins. The main track had been widened into a proper paved road and on either side of the street Goblins were selling rancid meat. The air was thick with flies and the smell of Goblin sweat.

Tribit grabbed Bryony by the hair and led her through the village. Humans peeped out of their cottage windows, hurriedly pulling the curtains so as not to be seen. On the other side of the village loomed the mountains. Beyond them lay the Tirach desert.

"Why is Queen Grizelda collecting everybody with green eyes?" asked Bryony.

Gorid grunted, keeping his face stern. "You prisoner. You no ask questions no more."

By late afternoon, Gorid, Tribit and Bryony were picking their way, in single file, down a ravine on the far side of the mountains. Bryony felt faint with fatigue.

As she trudged along between the two Goblins, she thought about her first arrival in the Human realm. She had been with Fable then, safe in her innocence, utterly unaware of the enormity of her quest. They had arrived on this very track, higher up, on the pass.

A stone struck the back of her leg. She heard Tribit laughing.

"Oops," he chuckled.

The urge to turn around and rip his throat with her teeth was desperate, but she held her temper and marched on. Another stone hit her leg near the ankle, stinging the bone. A wave of fear swept over her, dousing the flames of her anger. She hadn't slept for two whole days. She thought of her kin preparing her banquet. She thought of her garden and the pond.

Her hand strayed to her Portal Stone in its pouch at her waist. For a heartbeat she was tempted to use it - to go back and start again. Then she thought of Edna, bleeding in the desert. Maybe Azabyandee was wrong, maybe Edna had been banished to the Tirach desert.

The ravine was steep, and where the shadows fell, the air was cold. Another stone stung her leg.

After a while the ravine widened out into an expanse of sand criss-crossed with Goblin tracks. Further ahead, Bryony saw a barrier across the road and a cluster of tents flapping in the breeze. The prison camp.

Tribit puffed himself up with pride and threw Bryony over his shoulder. The Goblins at the barrier clapped their hands.

As Tribit marched forward, Bryony could feel strong, defensive magic running across the road like a farm fence. It was similar in style to the one that had held Sheean prisoner in the castle during his childhood. She hung upside down over Tribit's shoulder, glaring at the world.

"She been tested?" asked a sentry. He was chewing on a piece of meat and crunching bones.

"No," said Gorid.

"Interrogation tent that way."

The sentry gestured with the piece of meat towards a marquee just to the right of the barrier.

"How much we get?" asked Tribit.

The sentry looked at Bryony critically. "If she Fayri, get lots. If not, get some."

The air was hot inside the tent. Bryony was made to stand. All round the walls, lounged an array of Goblins, male and female, all with expectant looks on their faces. It was as if they were there for some kind of performance or sport.

A Goblin in dark uniform, with a red and black armband, sat at a desk in the centre of the tent. He gestured for her to come forward. Her knees were shaking, her tongue was sticking to the top of her mouth and she could hardly swallow. She noticed that Gorid and Tribit were drinking ale and laughing, clapping each other on the back. They were taking sly, greedy looks at her from the corners of their eyes.

The Goblin at the desk leered at her. "Name?"

Despite her fatigue and the evil magic that flowed through her blood from the ironburn, Bryony's mind was sharp. "Sandy. Sandy Gladwyn."

"Race?"

"Human."

"Age?"

"Eighteen."

The Goblin took a box from a drawer in the desk and placed it on the table. She felt evil emanating from under the lid. Her heart began to thump faster. She noticed the Goblins around the edge of the tent leaning forward, greedy anticipation showing on their nasty little faces. The Goblin opened the box to reveal a metal plate. She recognized it instantly. It was iron.

"What's that for?" she asked, feigning ignorance.

"That last question you ask. You gave up right to speak when you walked in here."

Bryony leaned forward and brought her nose one inch from his. "I was carried."

She heard Gorid and Tribit snort with laughter.

Pain exploded behind Bryony's eyes, lights danced in her vision and her ears rang. She clutched at the desk for support, refusing to give the audience the satisfaction of watching her collapse to her knees. She turned. Behind her a Goblin held a raised stick. The tip of it was glowing.

The Goblin at the desk spoke calmly. "Touch plate."

Bryony looked back at the plate and shook her head, stalling to give herself time to think. She could sense the Goblin behind her raising the stick again.

She moved her hand toward the plate, thinking fast. Her magic felt weak. She concentrated and created a layer of fine fur on her palm, laid her hand on the metal and met the eye of the Goblin.

"Turn hand over."

Bryony removed her hand from the plate, got rid of the fur and turned her palm over. It was undamaged.

"You Human," pronounced the Goblin at the desk.

Groans of disappointment followed her as she was led out of the tent.

* * *

Butterfly opened and closed her wings. Fable was a long way from the arch, at least fifty wing flaps. How long would it take to get to him? At least she was able to fly by the light of the moons. She remembered the tales she'd been told when she was just a fat little caterpillar, tales of the mortal realm where butterflies only lived for a few days, and where they needed the sun's warmth to fly.

She sighed as she realised she'd lost count. She started again. One... two...

* * *

The stench in the dining tent hit Bryony like a blow. There must have been at least a hundred Humans packed together, eating. Many children simply sat on the sand, using their fingers to shovel rice into their mouths as fast as they could. The adults sat at tables. No one spoke. The only sounds were the barked orders of the wardens and the cook's shouts of "Next!"

"Better get a move on love," said a woman eating at a table nearby. "You're nearly too late for feeding time."

Bryony smiled, thanked her and made her way to the cook.

"Next!"

Bryony went up to the pan. It was nearly empty. At the bottom was a wodge of dried up rice.

"Bowl!"

She lifted her bowl forwards. Her stomach growled, having had nothing since... she couldn't remember when. The ladle smacked against Bryony's bowl, almost knocking it from her hands.

The Goblin cook leaned forward, her wrinkled green face attempting a smile. "You new. You get extra. Pan nearly empty."

Bryony managed to stammer a tiny, "Thank you". The cook looked down at a child queuing behind Bryony.

"Too bad! None left."

Bryony held her bowl, unable to take her eyes from the child's face. Instead of crying, he simply nodded and began to walk away, his bowl held loosely in his hands. His arms were stick thin.

Bryony found herself shaking with shock and fatigue. She couldn't bear the thought of the child going hungry, so she followed him and touched his shoulder. He turned towards her.

"We can share," she said.

The boy clutched at her hand, still silent.

"Come on, let's find a safe place to eat," said Bryony.

"There isn't a safe place," said the boy. His voice was small; it held no hope.

They held hands and found a corner to sit down. As they took alternate bites of the rice, tears began to flow down the boy's face.

"What's your name?" asked Bryony.

"Malichai."

"My name is um, Sandy. It's not very nice here is it?"

The boy shook his head, chewing thoughtfully. His eyes were huge, his pale skin almost translucent. She ran her hand through his unkempt hair.

"How long have you been here?"

"Don't know."

"How old are you?"

"Nearly twelve."

"Are your parents here?"

At this, the boy broke down into sobs, curling himself into a ball.

"I'm so sorry. Please don't cry. We can be friends."

The boy's tears slowed. Bryony pressed on. "We have the same colour eyes, maybe we're related."

Malichai looked up. His eyes were startling. Bryony began to wonder if he had Fay blood in his veins.

"I'm an orphan," she said, wiping his tears away with her fingers. "Maybe later, I'll tell you my story. Or... well... I'll tell you a story anyway, maybe not mine. Would you like that?"

Malichai smiled and sniffed back his tears. "Can my brother come too?"

"Yes of course. Where is he?"

Malichai looked around and pointed. To one side of the tent she saw a young lad, he looked about fourteen years old, mimicking one of the wardens. He stood behind the Goblin and pulled faces. The prisoners nearby struggled to control their laughter.

"He's always getting into trouble."

"What's his name?"

"Elliott."

"Well, Malichai, I think this is a terrible place. I think Grizelda is awful. I'm going to change things around here."

Malichai looked up at her in wonder.

The sound of a gong brought everyone to their feet.

"What's happening now, Malichai?" asked Bryony.

"It's time for bed. It gets dark quickly here. And cold. Come on, stay in our tent, you'll be alright."

Malichai jumped to his feet, as quick as a frog, and reached out his hand. They walked together towards the exit, shuffling behind the people queuing to get out.

"Elliott!" hissed Malichai. "Come on!"

Elliott gave an impish grin, tossed back his long fringe and wriggled through the throng to join his brother.

"This is Bryony. She's in our tent."

Elliott looked at her. He was almost her height and his green eyes reminded her of Sheean. He tipped his head on one side like a bird. "Hello."

At the exit a female Goblin grabbed at Bryony. "You. With me."

Malichai clung to Bryony's hand, a small wail starting from his lips. Elliott took him gently by the shoulders. "It'll be all right. We'll see her tomorrow."

Malichai's little hand slipped from hers as she was pulled away. She heard the boys arguing. Malichai seemed to be very worried about something.

As she followed her guard, Bryony had time to take in her surroundings. It was getting colder. The mountains loomed up on her left, already dark. She was being led down a track, hardened by countless feet, through a series of tents. Occasionally she caught glimpses of people settling down for the night, sorting out their belongings and comforting their young.

The guard stopped at one of the tents and pointed. "You. There. Female tent. Bed on right."

"Thank you."

Bryony smiled to herself as she thought how proud Fable would be. She was remaining polite when all she wanted to do was bite.

She lay down and pulled the thin, dirty blanket over her shoulders. She was right near the edge of the sleeping tent, where a draft of desert air chilled her bones. She rolled over and lifted the side of the tent to peep out at the late evening sky. The first few stars were bright. Guards sat around on the track between the tents, shocksticks held idly across their knees. She could tell from their snores that they were asleep.

Bryony had been awake for hours. Every time a child whimpered, or a mother cried softly, she woke, her heart breaking. Her arm and shoulder ached and her mind felt dull.

Getting up as quietly as she could, Bryony made her way to the area in the corner marked out as a toilet. She pulled back the curtain. There was a hole in the floor and a plank of wood on each side. Near the door was a bucket of water for washing. At least here she had some privacy.

She used the toilet and washed her hands. Looking into the water in the bucket, she thought of Fable. She saw him prancing around in a meadow in Taranor, tossing his mane. Dog was with him, barking happily, trying to catch moonbeams in his mouth. She called out, but they couldn't hear her. She gazed at the lilac sky of Taranor where the two moons floated, bright and shining. She thought of Sheean.

She saw him asleep in his fine bed.

"Sheean."

Her voice was just a whisper. He didn't look up. She thought of her two new friends, Malichai and Elliott. She saw Elliott sitting up, with a blanket wrapped around him, barely able to keep awake. He held a tiny twig in his hands. It had been carved in the shape of a sword. He held it like a soldier, ready to attack anyone who came near, while Malichai slept peacefully.

She pulled her visual field back a little to see where they were, finding them near the middle, in the next tent. Pulling out further, Bryony got a view of the entire camp from above. She saw the barrier and the tent where they had tried to test her. Near this was a roped off area of trampled sand. On the desert side was a series of tables, loaded with fine cloth and beads. Behind them was a small hut. It was the only brick building in the camp.

She was pleased to see how pathetic the perimeter fence was. Metal stakes had been thrust into the sand with ropes slung between them. Bryony's heart sank when she saw that it was guarded every few paces by Goblins. Each stood, wide-awake, holding weapons at the ready. Torches blazed all around the perimeter, flooding the fence and the edges of the tents with light.

She felt in the pouch at her waist. The Portal Stone, stolen from Sheean's room, was warm, almost as if it was calling to be used. She took it out.

Imagining the land on the hill above the camp, Bryony tried to open a portal. The stone glowed, but no portal opened.

"Oh dear," she breathed. "There's strong magic here. What should I do Fable?"

Brushing the tears from her eyes, she put the Stone away, went back to her bed and picked up her blanket. After a quick glance round the tent to make sure no-one was watching, she slipped away, as silently as thistledown.

Bryony's breath steamed in the cold night air. Hugging her blanket around her shoulders she slipped past the sleeping guards and made her way to the boys' tent.

There were so many sleeping bodies packed tightly together for warmth that it was hard for Bryony to walk through them without disturbing anyone. Going as small as a butterfly would have helped, but she couldn't risk her Faerie light showing, not even for an instant. Besides, she wasn't sure she had enough power.

She found her new friends in the middle, just as she'd seen in her vision. Elliott turned his head, his eyebrows shooting up in surprise, as she approached. Bryony wriggled down next to him.

"Where have you been?" asked Elliott.

"They made me sleep in the ladies' tent. But I slipped away."

She glanced at his twig. "Why have you got a sword?" she asked.

Elliott looked down. He leaned closer to Bryony, tossing his fringe out of the way to see her with both eyes.

"There's rats here. Malichai is afraid they'll run over his blanket. He's afraid they'll eat him."

"Rats? But they won't hurt him."

"Won't they? Everyone knows they bite."

Bryony reached for the twig, taking it from his fingers gently.

"You rest. I'll keep watch for the rats."

Elliott's face flooded with relief. Within seconds he was cuddled next to his brother, relaxed in sleep.

Bryony took off her blanket and laid it over the boys' bony shoulders. She imagined herself becoming warm. A glow of comfort spread from her belly, moving all the way down to her toes and up to the top of her head. The only part of her that remained cold was her arm, where the iron had touched.

A scuttling sound nearby attracted her attention. She looked down to see a rat poking its nose out from under an old man's blanket.

"Hello Rat," said Bryony, using mind speech.

The rat jumped in surprise. *"Oh, you frightened me,"* it squeaked.

"Sorry."

The rat made as if to move away.

"Before you go, Mr. Rat," said Bryony, *"may I ask you a favour?"*

The rat turned its black, beady eyes to her. *"Certainly."*

"Could you ask all your friends and relations not to crawl near these boys, please?"

The rat looked at Elliott and Malichai. *"Why?"*

"Because it frightens them. They think you're going to bite."

The rat laughed. It was a tiny, gentle sound in Bryony's mind. Quite mouse-like, but a little more woolly.

"We don't bite unless we're scared. We crawl ever so quietly. We're only looking for food."

"Yes, but please could you keep clear of these boys?"

The rat sniffed around in the air. *"Got any cheese?"*

85

"I'll try to steal you some bread if I can."
"Deal."

The next morning, after a breakfast of watery porridge, Bryony was taken outside to the tables where many of the prisoners were already at work. Bryony looked in confusion at the array of needles, pins and cloth on the table. Men, women and children worked away, sewing pieces of fabric together. Some embroidered, while others sewed sequins on garments that sparkled in the desert sun.

"You!" shouted a Goblin guard, pointing a bony finger at Bryony. "Sew!"

"I don't know how."

"Learn fast," said the Goblin, "or I make you dig in desert for pretties."

Bryony had no idea what the Goblin meant, but it didn't sound good. She'd noticed a lot of the younger men heading off to the desert in the early morning, carrying shovels.

For a moment, Bryony watched the other people sew. Then, before any of the warders could hit her with their sticks, she picked up a needle. She breathed a sigh of relief as she found the metal didn't bite.

A woman smiled at her. "You look so familiar," she said. "Are you from Cucapha?"

"No, I'm not from round here," said Bryony.

"We met briefly last night. My name is Ruth. This is Luci and this is her uncle, David. They're from Dringle."

Luci nodded and continued sewing. David smiled, his eyes crinkling kindly at the corners. Bryony was just about to tell her new friends that she was a stable hand called Sandy Gladwyn, when Ruth squeaked and pointed a finger at her.

"I know you. You're Bryony. You used to deliver the bread and cakes to the castle. How are you? I'm Merik's wife."

Bryony wanted to disappear, to fly away somewhere else. She hadn't thought things through at all, but her instincts told her it would be better if she remained a stranger here. She felt she had a better chance of escape if nobody knew her. Anonymity was impossible now.

"It's nice to see a familiar face," said Bryony, trying not to blush. "Can you show me what to do?"

Luci showed her how to sew sequins onto a vast cushion. They worked quietly together for a while. Goblins turned up with jugs of water. The sun burned down relentlessly.

"Who are these things for?" asked Bryony.

"Queen Grizzie," said David. "I keep wanting to leave pins in, so they stick in her vast behind."

The group roared with laughter.

"No larfin!" shouted a Goblin.

"Oh shut it," chuckled David.

Despite his rebellious words, the group calmed down and got on with their work.

That night, Bryony sat next to the boys in the family tent. The rats kept their promise and stayed away. Bryony's thoughts whirled round and round. She'd tried scrying again earlier, but Sheean was still asleep. Only minutes had passed for him. He couldn't hear her, nor could Fable. Something was blocking her magic. She was trapped. Her wonderful royal future shattered.

All the lives of these kind people had been turned inside out by the paranoia of one foul, loathsome Human. A mere mortal. Bryony wished she'd squashed the bloated bug of a witch when she had the chance.

She placed a blanket over the boys' shoulders and looked at all the sleeping children. She couldn't imagine herself escaping and leaving all of these little people behind.

Malichai woke up and crawled into Bryony's lap. "I want my mummy."

"So do I my lovely, so do I"

Malichai wriggled into a sitting position. "Is your mummy missing too?"

"No, my mummy died a long time ago."

Sympathy flooded Malichai's huge eyes. "Oh that's sad. Do you miss her?"

"Every single day. I miss my father too."

She stroked his hair and he settled back down, curling up in her lap like a squirrel in a tree.

"When did you last see your parents?" she asked.

The reply was muffled. "It was a year ago. The soldiers came. I haven't seen mum or dad since."

"Would you like to hear a story?"

Malichai nodded. Bryony tipped back her head and thought for a moment. "Once upon a time, there was a Faerie Princess..."

"I hear you're a storyteller," said Ruth, the next morning.

"Well not really, I just thought it might help some of the little ones get to sleep."

"They're all talking about it. They're all looking forward to the next installment tonight. They loved the bit about the talking dog. And the beautiful white horse. I hope you tell some more soon, because I'd love to listen. It would take me away from this horrible world for a while."

Bryony smiled. "I'll see what I can do."

Just then shouting broke out near the interrogation tent. Bryony listened as closely as she could without changing the shape of her ears. She heard screams and Goblin curses. As the noise got closer to the sewing area, everyone saw a woman struggling in the hands of three Goblins.

"Give 'em hell girl," muttered David.

"Get your hands off me!" shouted the woman.

The guards threw her to the ground like a sack of coal. She got up, tossed back her long black hair and glared at the Goblins. Her green eyes flashed. "Touch me again and I'll have you!"

The three Goblins approached her, shocksticks raised.

A shrill scream cut through the air.

"Mummy!!!"

Malichai came running across the sand, quickly followed by Elliott. The boys threw themselves between their mother and the sticks, glaring in defiance at her tormentors. Elliott lowered his head like a goat about to butt.

"Don't you touch her," he growled.

The Goblins continued to advance. Bryony stood up, her hands balled into fists at her side. "Leave them alone!"

David stood too. He said nothing, but he looked ready to fight.

Behind her, Bryony heard running feet. She whipped round in time to see a whole troop of Goblins. Each one was clothed from head to foot in leather armour. Each one wore a red and black armband and wrist protectors of metal. Bryony shrank back.

"All Humans will sit and be quiet."

The Goblin who had spoken walked forward. He was tall and pale. His eyes were red. Everyone sat down at the table. The Goblin drew his arm back as if to strike at the newcomer with the metal band on his wrist. Bryony flinched. He noticed and turned.

"Did I frighten you little girl?" His red eyes glared at her with more intelligence than she'd ever seen in a Goblin. "You will all learn, or you will die. Your choice."

With a barked command he continued onwards to the gate. The new woman smiled at Bryony. "Hello," she said, "I'm Kerry. Thank you for standing up for me."

Ruth took charge of the sewing table, giving everyone a job to do, while Kerry hugged her children tight, her tears wetting their hair.

* * *

A slight breeze shook Butterfly as she sat on the rose. The stinking dog ran past her, out of the meadow towards the Royal Chambers. She opened her wings again. For the third time in a row, she'd lost count. It was just too hard to count to ten. She took a quick drink and tried again. One... two...

* * *

Sheean lay on his bed with his eyes closed.
"Alex, are you awake," he said to his sword.
"I'm always awake."
"I wonder what Bryony's up to? Maybe I should check to see if she's OK." Sheean closed his eyes again. "Then again, maybe not."

Alex chuckled. "She's only been gone a very short time."

Anxiety about his childhood friend preyed on Sheean's mind. "A very short time here is a really long time there. She's been gone a few minutes, and she's not come back yet," said Sheean as he climbed out of bed. He grabbed Alex and flew out of the window into his private garden.

"True," said Alex. "Oh dear. I should have thought of that. Are we going to rescue her?"

* * *

Butterfly gave up. She opened her wings and pushed off with her little feet. She felt a quiet thrill at being chosen. She was no longer a simple hair ornament. She was a Messenger.

Butterfly flew as fast as she could towards Fable. She saw Fable looking across at her.

"Little Butterfly..." he said.

"Yes Fable," she panted, continuing to fly as fast as she could.

"Why are you flying so fast? It's dangerous. Stop!"

Butterfly felt a wave of relief as she landed on his nose. Fable was still senior to Bryony right now, and if Fable said she could stop, she could. She clung onto his long white whiskers with all her tiny feet.

Fable carried her to one of the flowering bushes, where she jumped off and took a long, deep nectar drink.

"What's the matter?" asked Fable. "You look all of a flutter."

Butterfly spoke between slurps of nectar, coiling and uncoiling her tongue. "Bryony said... I should... count... to ten."

"Why?"

Finally sated, Butterfly folded her wings and concentrated on her message, her big moment.

"She told me to count to ten and then come and tell you. But I couldn't count very well. I tried my best."

"Tell me what?"

Butterfly could see that Fable was trying to be patient, but he was pacing up and down, his delicate silver hooves making patterns in the grass.

"To tell you that she has gone."

"Where has she gone?"

"To rescue her friend Edna."

Fable tossed his head wildly and snorted. Butterfly almost lost her balance on the flower.

"How long has she been gone?"

"Not long. I counted almost to ten. Almost, but I got lost at around five. A few times."

"Oh dear!" said Fable. "I must run and get help!"

"Have I done the wrong thing?" asked Butterfly.

She didn't get an answer. Fable was away in a flash of light and a blur of diamonds. Butterfly drank from the flower again, but anxiety over what she'd done took all the pleasure of the nectar away. She folded her wings and rested, thinking of how she could make amends for her mistake.

* * *

Fable flew down a long corridor towards the Queen's rooms, almost knocking Jerremoy over in his haste.

"What's the matter Fable?" he asked.

Fable skidded to a halt.

"Bryony is missing!"

"What?"

"She has returned to the Human realm to rescue a friend."

"Oh this is too much," wailed Jerremoy. "It's almost time for the crown fitting. What is she doing?!"

Jerremoy turned and flew as fast as his wings could take him.

"We have to tell the queen. She's in the meeting room. Follow me."

* * *

Sheean looked into his pond and thought of Bryony. The water turned cloudy. Then he saw her lying in the dark. She was crying.

"Bryony!"

An intense burning crept up Sheean's right arm and into his back. He felt his Fay light dimming. The vision evaporated. Bryony was gone. Sheean jumped to his feet.

"Where is she? How do I get to her?"

"She is in the Human realm," said Alex. "That's where she said she was going. She could be in prison at Cucapha. You need a Portal Stone to open a window between the realms. Dog has one in his belly."

"Dog!" called Sheean. "Dog, I need you."

Dog came running into Sheean's garden, panting and grinning, jumping up in delight. He ran off a little way, and returned dragging a sapling from the back of the garden. He dropped it at Sheean's feet. "You throw yes?"

Dog's eyes widened in surprise as Sheean picked him up and held him tightly. Sheean thought of Bryony, but nothing happened.

"What doing?" Dog asked.

"Where's the Portal Stone, Dog?"

"Under bush."

"What's it doing there?" Sheean asked.

"Time for stone to come out. Had go somewhere."

Sheean put Dog down. "Show me."

"There," Dog said, indicating a small mound under a bush near the pond.

Sheean prodded the area with Alex.

"What are you doing, lad?" said his sword.

Shean found what he was looking for and stabbed the turd with Alex's point. Concentrating on Cucapha castle, Sheean visualised the gatehouse.

"Dog. Stay," he ordered. A circular window appeared to one side of Sheean's pond, its edges crackling and steaming in the moonlight. As Sheean jumped through into the Human realm, the Portal Stone fell from the tip of Alex's blade. The stone, his only means of getting back, landed near the pond, beyond his reach.

It was dark. Sheean saw something in his peripheral vision. He whipped round to face his enemy. It was a Goblin. With the strong momentum of his turn, Alex's blade took the Goblin's head clean off at the shoulders.

Sheean kicked the body away from him and crouched in the darkness. He could see the gatehouse in front of him, and the ugly, grey castle looming up into the night sky. The gates to the castle were closed. He stayed crouched down in some bushes until he was sure there was no further attack.

"I didn't appreciate that at all," whispered Alex.

"Didn't appreciate what?"

"Having Dog's excrement on me."

"I'm really sorry, I couldn't think of what else to do."

"I don't mind Goblin blood, but I do mind dog excrement. Now kindly clean me."

Sheean looked around, found some leaves, and began cleaning his blade.

"If you do that again," whispered Alex, "I will refuse to come out of the scabbard. I will refuse to fight. I don't care how bad the enemy is, or what's at stake, I demand more respect!"

"I said I was sorry."

There was a light on in the window of the gatehouse. Sheean saw his old friend and sword trainer, Merik, sitting at a table. The soldier was leaning back on his chair at an alarming angle. Seeing Merik again made him aware of how silly his own Faerie clothes looked. Sheean glanced down at his royal robes and ridiculous shoes. There was no way he was going to let Merik see him dressed like that. He reverted to the plain turquoise light of his family and flew over the gatehouse wall.

* * *

Bryony walked with her fellow prisoners to the sleeping tents. She wasn't sure how long she'd been at the camp, but it seemed a long time. Day had followed day, each the same: sewing all day with breaks for exercise, rice and greens every night, threats every minute. She still had no idea of how to get out. She felt sick at the thought of what might have happened to Edna by now.

As Bryony got to her blanket, she found a huddle of children gathered. Parents shot her looks of deep gratitude as they settled to sleep. Ignoring her own fatigue, Bryony sat down in the middle of the children.

A little boy of around five years old clutched his bald teddy bear.

"Please tell us about the white horse again," he whispered.

Bryony smiled at him. "What's your name?"

"Little Eric."

"All right Little Eric. I'll tell you about how Fable saved me when my... I mean when Princess Lorella's parents died."

Some of the children look sad.

"Well maybe that's too sad for tonight. How about the one where Fable learns to fly?"

The children smiled and settled down.

"Well, the thing you need to know is that Faerie horses can't fly at first. They can walk on water and run as fast as the wind, just above the ground, but they have to be a bit more grown up before they can fly. And they don't have wings. When they fly, they just gallop into the air. It's very exciting. You can feel the clouds brushing past your knees and you feel really safe because the horse is big and broad and warm. You can't fall off a Faerie horse. Well, most Faeries can't."

She was about to launch into a tale of wolves and castles when the tent flap opened. Two Goblins approached.

"No stories," they shouted.

Kerry, who had been cuddling her two children, stood up, towering over the two Goblins.

"Why?"

"'Cos."

"But it helps them sleep," said Bryony, getting up to stand next to Kerry. Many of the children scuttled back to their parents to be shielded by protective arms and blankets.

The Goblins grabbed at Bryony. "You is trouble."

Bryony could take no more. She grabbed the one nearest to her and sank her teeth into its face, while Kerry kicked out at the other. She heard Malichai screaming in terror. Lights flashed behind her eyes as pain flooded her whole being.

Bryony woke to find herself in a stone cell. There were red marks on her arms and legs. She winced at a pain in her back. Kerry lay nearby, groaning.

"Are you alright?" asked Bryony, instantly rolling her eyes at the stupidity of her question.

Kerry turned her head. Her eyes remained closed. "I've said before I'll get your dinner, but you boys are old enough to get your own breakfast."

Bryony shook Kerry gently. "Wake up."

Kerry's eyes opened. She whimpered.

"Where does it hurt?" asked Bryony.

"Are you really going to eat all that?" said Kerry, closing her eyes again. Her hair was matted with dried blood.

"Kerry. Open your eyes. Talk to me."

Bryony stroked her friend's face. Kerry opened her eyes for a moment and grabbed at Bryony's hand.

"I have to get back. The children are inside the book. I have to..."

She turned to one side, threw up on the stone floor, and lay down again. Bryony moved over to her, ignoring her own pain.

"Let me have a look."

Bryony parted Kerry's long dark hair to reveal a deep cut. It had stopped bleeding, but the swelling was clear. Bryony remembered the healing she'd used on Albert's mother. Drawing the same magic into her mind, Bryony sent power through her fingers. Her Human glamour flickered off for a second, revealing her turquoise light.

Bryony stopped instantly, taking her hands away and hiding herself in her Human shape once more. Kerry looked round at her.

"What are you doing?"

"Nothing."

"I'm sure I saw lights just then. A beautiful blue."

"That can happen when you've had a bang on your head. Edna told me. It's called concussion. You need to rest."

"Who's Edna?"

Bryony's lips trembled. The sadness came from nowhere, like a wave threatening to overwhelm her. Kerry turned to her and took her hand.

"Is she your mother?"

98

Bryony couldn't contain her grief any longer. She bent towards Kerry and collapsed into her arms.

She had no idea how long she lay there, comforted and sobbing, while Kerry patted her back gently. After a while she sat up, sniffing. Kerry produced a handkerchief from her skirts.

"Use this."

Bryony blew her nose like a child. Her breath was ragged, besieged with gulps of air that wracked her body.

"Tell me," said Kerry. "It'll make you feel better."

"I should be looking after you."

"Oh don't worry about me. My headache is completely gone now. I feel fine. Tell me about Edna."

"She's not my mother, my mother died when I was very young, but she's been like a mother to me for years. She is a lovely, kind old lady who lives in Gavelkind. She works with herbs and healing."

"Why can't we just plan an escape together?" asked Kerry. "I know there's a lot of them, but each Goblin is quite small really."

Bryony stood up and began pacing. She had an irresistible urge to fly. She felt as if the walls were closing in on her soul. "I think about it every day, but I've heard that many people have died trying. We would have to be organised."

Kerry looked down at her hands. She rubbed the dried blood from her fingers and felt her head. "Those guards at the fence must be paid well."

"Or be afraid of something," added Bryony.

The rasping sound of a bolt being dragged across the door stopped their talk. A fat Goblin in a woolly hat walked into the room.

"Go on. Hop it. You done yer time."

As Kerry stood up she staggered a little. Bryony grasped her arm and led her through the door. The Goblin leaned close, his breath stinking of ale and rancid meat. "Don't come back. You come here three times, you is deaded."

Chapter 4

Merik put his feet on his desk and rocked his chair back on two legs. He closed his eyes. It had been a long day training the new Goblin recruits, most of whom didn't know a sword from a penknife. 'A really bad day,' he thought, as the legs of his chair gradually gave way, dumping him on his back on the floor. As he struggled to his feet, a bright turquoise light filled his room and a voice came from within the light.

"Sleeping on the job again?"

Merik grabbed a sword and shielded his eyes.

"Who?"

The voice sounded familiar.

"Don't you recognise me?" it said.

"I can't see a bloody thing for the light."

"Oh, sorry," he said as he lowered his Faerie light and replaced it with his usual human clothing: a leather tunic, shorts and sandals.

"Sean!" Merik bellowed as he ran towards his old friend, his sword clattering to the floor. "By the gods lad, I never thought I'd see you again."

Merik wrapped his arms around Sheean, making him wheeze in a crushing bear hug.

"Let me look at you," he said, putting his hands on Sheean's shoulders, pushing him back to arm's length. "You've not changed a bit. You look no older than you did when you left."

"How long have I been gone?"

"Must be the best part of six years," Merik answered, letting go of Sheean and counting the years on his fingers. "Yes, Grizelda's been Queen six years."

"Grizelda? That old crone? She's not royal!"

"I know. She took the throne as soon as King Yuppick died and no-one dares to challenge her. Now she's ruling Cucapha and the outlying towns with a tight grip. She's evil. Oh Sean, it's so good to see you!"

Merik moved to hug the lad again but Sheean backed away.

"My name is Sheean. You never got it right. It's not Sean, it's Sheean."

Sheean lengthened the sound of his name so that Merik could hear the difference. Merik drew up another chair and pulled his upright. "Sh... oh I don't know, Sheeeeeean," he laughed. "Tell me everything."

"Bryony helped to rescue me. We both went back to the Faerie Kingdom, but she's come back here to rescue Edna. I've seen her, she's in trouble. Could she be in the castle dungeons?" Sheean sat down next to Merik at the wooden table.

"Woah, slow down," said Merik. "Bryony is one of you lot?"

Sheean nodded.

"She won't be here," said Merik, "there's no room in the castle, the dungeon's always full. People keep rebelling, and when they do Grizelda has them locked away. She's had a big prison made out in the Tirach desert. Her army of Goblins rounded up everyone with green eyes and took them there. I suppose Bryony could be there."

"Army of Goblins?"

"The Goblins are everywhere. Didn't you see them when you walked through the streets?"

"I didn't walk."

Merik leaned back away from Sheean, careful not to tip his chair this time. "No, I guess you have your Faerie magic now. You know Sean, there hasn't been a day gone by that I didn't regret that day, fourteen years ago, when I helped kidnap you."

"Merik... friend. You were following orders."

Merik visibly relaxed. "Thanks, still... I..."

"What about the Goblins?"

"Grizelda recruited them from the Goblin realm. She's using the vicious little bleeders to keep us all in order."

"That's bad. Why arrest everyone with green eyes?"

"That's a strange one isn't it? You remember cook, don't you?"

Sheean nodded.

"Well, she says Grizelda's so frightened of you coming back with an army of Faerie folk, she ordered anyone with green eyes to be arrested. I think she's lost the plot." Merik stared at the table for a moment. "When I heard what was happening I sent my wife off to my sister's place down south, in Shalimar. She's got green eyes you see. It's OK down there at the moment, but they say Grizelda's power could spread, what with the Goblins and everything."

Sheean saw a washstand in the corner of the room. He stood and peered into the water bowl on its top and thought of Bryony. Briefly, he caught a glimpse of her, working at a table, sewing something. She was dirty and sweaty. She looked tired. The vision faded.

"So the prison is in the desert?" he said. "I'm going to need your help to rescue Bryony."

"Of course, although, we're going to need some help. We can't just walk in there and release her. We need an insider."

"Someone trustworthy?"

"I believe so. According to him, you two know each other."

Sheean coloured his eyes a deep brown and followed Merik through the winding streets of Cucapha's sprawling slums.

"Stick close to me, lad," said Merik. "It's after curfew and the Goblin soldiers can be mean."

"Have the people always lived like this?" Sheean asked.

"No. During your time here, while you were locked up, the old king made sure his people were generally well cared for."

On street corners, groups of Goblins checked anyone brave enough to be out on the streets. Brandishing shocksticks, the Goblins often approached Sheean and Merik, but always backed away when they recognised their superior.

"They seem to respect you," said Sheean.

"They think I'm one of Grizelda's men."

"And are you?"

"No... She thinks I am. I was with her outside your bedroom door the night you escaped. I guess she thinks I have as much to lose as she does if you come back, so she leaves me alone."

Eventually, they arrived at their destination, an old tumble down shed, standing a little way off a side road to Gavelkind. They made their way cautiously, in almost total darkness, through the gateway, trying not to break the gate as it flapped open on one hinge, and along the muddy path to the front of the shed.

"You know, I could have made light for us to see our way with," said Sheean.

"No, don't draw attention to us, you never know who's watching."

Merik knocked on the door. It creaked open a little. The voice of an old Goblin came from inside. "Who there?"

"It's OK, it's only me, Merik... and a friend of yours."

"Not got no friends."

"Well, that's nice, I thought you and I was friends. Can we come in?"

"If must, nearly bed time."

Merik and Sheean stepped into the shed and closed the door behind them.

"Bout time you come back, Fayri!" said a stout Goblin, sitting back down on a filthy bed. "You disappear. Leave Grumbuk in cave with dead king. Know how long take Grumbuk get home?"

Sheean smirked, pleased as pie to see his old friend. "Sorry Grumbuk, I didn't have any option."

"Is OK, me hero now. How you?"

"They want me to marry Bryony, and make me a king."

"And you not want?"

"No."

Merik looked at Sheean. "Do you know where Kanthy is?"

Sheean shook his head, frowning. "No."

"She ran away when she thought you was dead," said Merik, sitting next to Grumbuk on the bed. "I'd hoped she would have found you again. Her mother will kill her if she ever comes back here."

"There you are," Grumbuk handed Sheean and Merik a goblet each. "Enough talk about girls. Grumbuk have best Goblin ale. Girls no good. Ale best."

They sat in a row on Grumbuk's stinking bed, drinking and watching the light from the flames in the fireplace flicker around the room.

Sheean looked around and smiled. "This is better than any palace, any amount of riches. Just sitting with your best friends, not having to be anything other than yourself."

"Humans suffer here, very bad," said Grumbuk as he swilled more ale into their goblets. "Need kill Queen Grizzy."

Sheean's head was reeling, but he wanted another ale. "You want me to kill Grizelda?" He thought about the fat old witch and felt himself wanting to laugh.

"People need help, you hero, kill Ogman, easy kill her."

"You always say you're the hero," said Merik.

"Is joke. Fayri real hero."

"It was team work, Merik, just like you taught me," Sheean answered. "It needed both of us to fulfil the prossephy, I mean prophecy."

Merik laughed. "Had too much ale lad?"

There was scratching on the door.

"Go WAY?" Grumbuk shouted.

The scratching continued. Merik got up and opened the door a little to look out. As he did, nine cream cats with china blue eyes filed through the gap and sat with their backs to the fire. They turned as one and faced Sheean.

Sheean stared, amazed, as the cats arranged themselves in a long line, each with a tail tucked neatly around their legs. Merik sat back down on the bed.

"That's something you don't see every day," he said.

A voice, high and refined, came from the mouths of all nine cats, speaking in unison. "My name is Azabyandee and I have come to see you, Sheean of the Fay, on a most important matter."

"Talking cats!" said Merik, spluttering into his ale. Grumbuk rolled back on his bed, roaring with laughter, his little green legs kicking in the air. A fart erupted from him, making him laugh even harder.

Merik pulled a face and wafted his hand in the air to spread the stink. Sheean tried to suppress his laughter when he saw the nine cats looking offended. "How did you know where to find me?" he asked.

"I can see time future and time past. I am one of the last Wizards."

Grumbuk sat up bolt upright. "You Wizzud?"

The cats stared at the old Goblin with unblinking eyes.

"I am Wizard Azabyandee, rendered almost powerless many years ago by Grizelda and her minions in the Demon realm. By splitting me into nine equal parts, she thought to destroy me. My wife Edna saved me in the form of identical cats, and so I remain, with limited magic, until victory is won. Edna is now trapped in the Demon realm, banished by Grizelda. If Grizelda is not stopped, all that is good will be made foul. All that is foul will rule.

"Sheean, future King of the Fay, I implore you to rescue my wife. If you do, Grizelda can be defeated and the suffering in this realm can be stopped."

"What about Bryony?" asked Sheean.

"If she be in prison camp," said Grumbuk, "she be safe enough where is."

"How do you know?"

"Have people there. Can give extra rations."

Sheean felt overwhelmed with frustration. "How do I get to the Demon realm?"

Grumbuk opened his mouth, but before he could speak, the nine cats continued.

"I could assist you in opening a portal here, as I tried with Bryony, but I fear the same result could occur. The bright light involved might attract the attention of the Goblin guards and you, Sheean, would be taken to the prison camp, just as she was.

"If that occurs, the Human realm will fall and the Dark Prophecy will finally be fulfilled. To prevent this disaster, you must go far from here to the Goblin portal near the mountains. From there you can enter the Demon realm via Ogman's crater. There you will find my wife. Please make haste."

"Grumbuk know. Is at pass near Dringle."

Sheean sat in silence for a few seconds, unable to shake the image of Bryony's suffering from his mind. "Can't I get Bryony first?"

One of the cats leapt towards him, planting sharp claws into his hand. "Fool" it hissed.

"Ow!" yelped Sheean, trying to take his hand away. The cat held firm, glaring at him. Sheean saw the power behind those eyes, power filled with light and ferocious wisdom.

"Edna is my WIFE!" shouted Azabyandee. "Do you not understand? A wizard may only marry another wizard!" The cat let go of Sheean and joined the others. "If you rescue my wife, we will be powerful enough to defeat Grizelda. Then all will be free, including myself, and your queen to be. It's time you put that sword of yours to good use."

Sheean found himself trembling, suddenly sober. "Er... OK... Edna first, then Bryony." He looked at his Goblin friend. "Right Grumbuk. Let's get going."

"You're not getting rid of me that easily," said Merik.

"What about your job?" asked Sheean.

"If this all works out, I won't have a job soon anyway."

"Family?" asked Grumbuk.

"My wife is safe. Far away from here. My son..." He looked at Sheean, who shifted his eyes to look at the floor. "My son is dead."

Grumbuk nodded. An evil smell came from the folds of his night-shirt as he stood up. "Sorry he dead. We go now. Me in charge. Merik got brawn. Fayri got magic. I got brain."

"And what about me?" a muffled voice said from behind Sheean's back.

Sheean drew Alex from his scabbard and rested him across his knees. "You are important too Alex. Have you forgiven me for the dog turd?"

"Mmm."

"Your sword is more important than you can imagine," said Azabyandee. "Young prince, treat your sword with deep respect. Remember his sacrifice. Remember the Dwarf that was, who gave his life to become the King's Sword. Do not think of this weapon as an ordinary sword. That would be your undoing."

Grumbuk left his hut to arrange the extra rations for Bryony, while Merik returned to the castle to pack a bag and arrange for Kendro, his lieutenant, to take over his post in the gatehouse. They both gave Sheean strict instructions to stay in the hut and to not answer the door for anyone.

As there was nowhere to sit, Sheean lay on Grumbuk's bed, trying to sort out his feelings.

Azabyandee relaxed. The nine cats chose different places to lie down.

"You look troubled, Prince Sheean," he said.

Sheean sighed. "I don't know what to do for the best. Bryony's OK. We used to be good friends as children, but things change as you grow up. S'pose it could work. Maybe we would grow closer in time. But, what about Kanthy? Maybe she didn't betray me. Maybe she was just frightened of her mother and ran away to protect our child. I'm probably a father by now."

Azabyandee began to scratch his ear. "Who is Kanthy?"

"My girlfriend. Well, I thought she was, but I think she used me."

"You now have a greater mission than deciding between your future queens, young prince. I have to leave here. The fleas are too numerous. Good luck. Come back to Edna's cottage when you're done and report to me."

With a swish of nine cream tails, Azabyandede left the hut. Sheean hadn't had time to ask where Edna's cottage was.

Merik was the first back. "Right lad, all sorted. Are you ready?"

"Yes, I only have Alex to take with me. How far is the entrance to the Goblin world?"

"Not far I think, somewhere near the mountain pass to the desert," Merik answered.

"Merik."

"Yes lad."

"Have you always been a soldier?"

"Followed my father's example and joined up as soon as I was thirteen."

"So you did what your family expected of you?"

"I guess so, but it's what I wanted as well. I never dreamed of doing anything else. Mind you my uncle was another thing altogether. He didn't want to be a soldier and refused to join up. There was a big argument and my grandfather disowned him, told him to go and never come back."

Sheean was thoughtful for a minute. "Was he OK?" he finally asked.

"Yes, he found himself a girl with family money and went off somewhere to be an innkeeper. Had loads of kids and was doing well, last time I heard. He was called Merik as well."

"Merik."

"Yes lad."

"About what we're doing now... Do you think it's the right thing to do... I mean is it right to go and rescue Edna first and Bryony second?"

"Mmm, I'd say yes. Grumbuk says Bryony'll be OK in the camp until we get back. If we rescue her first, we could have problems with Grizelda before we can rescue Edna."

"S'pose. I didn't think of that."

Grumbuk came back a little later, in a bad mood. "Cost fortune keep girl Fayri in luxury."

Sheean smiled at Grumbuk. "Thanks Grumbuk, you're a real friend."

"No forget Fayri."

Sheean sat in the back of the cart with Merik, while Grumbuk drove. Sheean's hands were loosely tied with rope to make him look like a slave for the journey to the Goblin portal. Much to Sheean's delight, Merik agreed to be the slave on the other side of the portal.

"I was a slave for a while last time I was in the Goblin realm. You'll look just great in a loin cloth."

Merik said nothing, he just looked at Sheean through squinted eyes.

Grumbuk turned round in the cart. "Not walking this time, Fayri. Grumbuk pay lots for Fayri comfort."

Sheean put on his best royal voice and joked. "Thank you ,Sir Grumbuk, it is surely transport befitting a king."

"Don't make him anymore big headed than he already is," muttered Alex.

"Shud-up cousin. If not careful, have melted down."

"Grumbuk," said Merik, "are you part Dwarf?"

"Shud-up, if not careful, all walk behind cart."

The journey was slow and hot. They were stopped several times by Goblin soldiers demanding travel papers. Sheean watched in silence as the other two made excuses. The Goblins had obviously worked out a way of making money from their posting to the Human realm and would not allow the trio to proceed, threatening them with shocksticks unless Grumbuk paid the necessary bribes.

Only once did it get difficult, when one small group of Goblins wanted more money than Grumbuk was prepared to pay.

One of the Goblins left his comrades and walked up the track to have a look at the prisoner. Seeing Sheean alone, he prodded him with an unarmed shockstick and tried to drag him off the back of the cart.

Sheean threw off the loose ropes and reached for Alex. The Goblin fell back away from the cart, its head bouncing down the track towards the others, ending up in the centre of the group.

"Dangerous prisoner!" said Grumbuk. "Now me have to get back under control. Let us through, or else!"

The remaining Goblins backed off. The leader beckoned Grumbuk and Merik to continue on their way. For good show, Merik re-tied Sheean's ropes, making it look difficult.

Their progress between stops was slow. The old plough horse Grumbuk had purchased only had one plodding speed, and, no matter how much Grumbuk shouted Goblin insults at it, it refused to walk any faster.

"Have you tried being nice to the horse?" Sheean asked.

"It not understand."

"You'd be surprised how much animals understand."

"Mmm... say you."

It had taken most of the night to reach their destination. When they pulled up in front of the rope barrier, it was dawn. The sentry box was empty. There was a sign propped up outside which simply said, 'Gone.'

Sheean looked through the portal shimmering over the road in the form of an arch. Instead of the expected green cliffs of the Seven Sisters, he saw a rutted muddy track winding off into the distance. Rubbish was piled against makeshift food stalls. A hideous stench and a cloud of flies wafted into the Human realm.

"Where is everyone?" Sheean asked. "I expected the border to be crawling with Goblins."

"No need guards, no one go back Goblin realm," Grumbuk said as he jumped down. He removed the rope barrier, got back on the cart and drove them through the portal.

The temperature dropped markedly as the cart passed through the arch into the Goblin realm. The smell coming from the food stalls and piles of rotting garbage that lined the track made Sheean retch.

They paused and released Sheean's bonds. Merik put his hands forward and let Grumbuk place the ropes loosely round his wrists.

"Not too tight. I might need to fight, remember."

"Me know. Me not stupid."

Sheean shivered. He looked out over the cliff. Everything looked soiled. Even the Seven Sisters rocks, standing straight and untouched by the centuries, looked grey and grubby.

"It used to look so nice around here," he said.

"Not much different," said Grumbuk. "Look, nice murky green sea. Good food. No soldiers. Not so bad."

"I wouldn't know," Alex grumbled from within his scabbard on Sheean's back.

"You bin here before Alex, remember?" said Grumbuk.

"I didn't see much. I was nearly always in the dark, in here, never used."

"Alex... are you OK?" asked Sheean.

"A little more respect wouldn't go amiss."

Sheean swung the sword around and unsheathed it slightly, allowing the pure silver of the blade to shine in the green sunlight.

"Who disrespected you?"

"Well, as you ask. There was the dog poop."

"I said I was sorry about that."

"It takes time to get over something like that. Before I became the King's Sword, people respected me, even asked my advice. Now I'm lucky if anyone speaks to me at all. And you don't clean me properly. I've still got smears of Goblin blood on me."

Sheean sighed. "I guess I'm a disappointment to you. I s'pose a real king would ask your advice all the time."

"ALEX!" Grumbuk shouted. "How you say things like that? Me, you and Fayri, we sung about in legend. How important you want be? You kill beast in cliff. Great beast of legend."

"Yes, you're right. I'm sorry Sheean. Pay no attention to a grumpy old Dwarf, er... sword."

Merik paced up and down the track by the cart, peering into some stunted trees ahead. The horse snorted and backed up a little way.

"Was it really my fault you had to give your life to become my sword?" Sheean asked.

"No lad, it was an honour. Even if fate hadn't arranged for you to be there at the ceremony of transformation, I would have found my way into your possession eventually."

"What if I never become a king?"

"Have you lot finished?" Merik asked. "Only there's a very large winged lizard... dragon sort of thing near those trees, and because of all your talking, it's heading this way."

"Oh no!" exclaimed Sheean. "The beast!"

"The beast?" Alex shouted. "I thought I'd killed it! Lets get it. It's not getting away again. I'm... we're having the bleeding thing this time."

"Don't think you're going off to enjoy yourselves without me," Merik said, as he shook away the ropes and drew his sword. "Stay here Grumbuk, look after the horse. We're just nipping down the road to sort out this... lizard thing."

The beast crept towards them, swinging its huge head from side to side, sniffing and drooling. Pus oozed from an empty eye socket. The remaining eye glared at Sheean. A long low hiss escaped through its teeth.

"Grumbuk coming with. That not lizard, that monster of legend. Kill thousands everyday."

They tied the horse to a dead tree trunk and set off down the track. Grumbuk walked down the middle of the road, waving his arms about and shouting Goblin obscenities at the monster, while Sheean and Merik spread out on either side of the track.

Merik shouted across to Sheean. "Remember your training lad."

Sheean glanced at Merik. "You have to strike its heart. You can't kill it otherwise."

Merik nodded. They moved closer, muscles tense. Sheean could feel Alex growing warm. He loosened his grip and tried to steady his breathing.

"Watch the teeth. It's got venom in its spit too," he shouted. Merik nodded again, his eyes scanning the beast for a point of attack.

"See that scar on its neck?" shouted Sheean, settling into a fighting stance, "Bryony and Alex did that."

The beast turned its head further to glare at Sheean. It opened its wings with a creak of old leather. Slime dripped from its mouth. Muscles bunched as it settled onto its back legs, ready to spring.

Without warning, Grumbuk picked up a rock and threw it, hitting the beast squarely on the nose. The creature screamed and leapt at him, revealing a mouth filled with dagger-like teeth.

"Nooo," shouted Merik, as the beast's head came down, mouth wide open, lunging towards Grumbuk's head. Sheean and Merik looked on in horror as the scaled jaws snapped shut with a tooth-grinding crack. The old Goblin rolled between the beast's front legs, just missing its stamping feet.

Grumbuk released a long, thin knife from a sheath strapped to his leg, and as he rolled under the beast's breast-bone, he plunged it upwards into its heart. The beast lurched forward, then dropped to the ground, pinning Grumbuk's legs under its body.

Sheean and Merik put their swords away and looked down at Grumbuk's bloodied face.

"What's that awful smell?" asked Merik.

Sheean laughed, remembering how he and Bryony had smelled after their encounter with this same beast. "It's the blood. It stinks."

"You two just going watch hero struggle?"

Merik looked at Sheean and smirked. "I guess we should help our Beast Killer back onto his feet."

Sheean and Merik took an arm each and pulled. As they did, the beast seemed to take a last breath, releasing Grumbuk. They lost their balance and fell backwards into a pile of rubbish.

"Now who stink?" Grumbuk said with a big, toothy grin.

* * *

Bryony flipped the silk blouse inside out and examined the stitches. She marvelled at how her sewing had improved. The shoulder seam was almost invisible; the cuffs finished in delicate embroidery.

117

She shifted her inspection to the lower hem and smiled as she read the motto she'd placed there: "Queen Grizelda, your rule is over. Prepare to die!" Each letter was neatly done in pink thread, contrasting brightly with the green of the blouse.

Ruth put down her sewing and grabbed Bryony's arm.

"Watch out," she hissed, "here he comes again."

"Oh no," groaned Bryony. "Why does he keep picking on me?"

A tall, pale Goblin walked up to her, arrogance oozing from every green pore. He reached forward and grabbed her hair with one hand and brought his metal clad arm to her face. Bryony shut her eyes. She knew that one of these days this awful bully would follow through with his threat; she would find herself screaming as the iron burned her, disfiguring her forever, revealing her as Fay.

She felt the metal coming closer and heard a cruel laugh right by her ear. She tensed, ready to flash into Faerie form and rip out the throat of this tyrant with her needle sharp teeth.

Nothing happened. She opened her eyes to see David standing right by her, gripping the Goblin's arm in his fist. They were locked in a silent struggle of strength and will. As Bryony disentangled her hair from the Goblin's grip and moved out of reach, she felt a tug on the hem of her blouse. Ruth was pointing to the table, encouraging her to safety underneath.

Bryony glanced back briefly. The Goblin guards stood around with hands on weapons, waiting for instructions. David gritted his teeth; his arm began to tremble. Ruth tugged again. This time Bryony ducked down, following her under the table and along to the next. They peered out at the struggle.

A deep growl came from the Goblin's throat. David swore under his breath and shifted his footing. Using the tiny change in balance to his advantage, the Goblin pushed David back. Fear flashed in David's eyes as he fell to the ground.

At a signal, two Goblins jumped on him, punching and kicking David's curled up form. Another signal stopped the violence instantly. Bryony found herself trembling at these highly disciplined Goblins. These were not the simple mountain creatures she was used to. They even spoke like Humans.

"Drag him to the jail," said the leader. "He will be executed at Gobfest. Let his death be a lesson to you all!"

* * *

After the hot and dusty journey from the Seven Sisters, Grumbuk sighed with relief as their wagon rolled noisily into the yard of the Troll's Head inn.

"Thank the gods," Merik croaked. "I could drink the place dry."

"Not on own," Grumbuk chuckled.

After making certain their horse was settled in the stables with plenty of hay and water, they made their way around to the front door. Grumbuk strode forward, pulled the handle down and pushed the door inwards, crushing a Goblin busy being sick down the wall.

"I go first, they know Grumbuk. I hero. Follow Grumbuk." He beckoned to Sheean and Merik as he marched over the fallen door, making the Goblin trapped underneath belch with every step.

"Barmaid, you know Grumbuk. Need rooms, food and ale."

The barmaid looked at Grumbuk for a moment and then continued her conversation.

"Ten big crusty ones, under armpit," she said to an enormous Goblin, pulling up her sleeve. Her friend bent forward to get a better view.

"That nothing. Got twentyfive on backside. Look."

The fat Goblin stood and began to unbuckle his belt. Grumbuk banged his fist on the bar.

"You deaf?" Grumbuk demanded. "Is hero, Grumbuk."

"Know who is," spat the barmaid. "You not fix front door."

Merik turned to Sheean and whispered. "What is she on about?"

"When we were here last time," said Sheean, "Grumbuk broke the front door. I thought it had been repaired."

"When was that?"

"Just before I escaped from the castle."

"That's years ago."

"Goblins hold grudges forever," said Sheean as he looked around the room. "Nothing's changed. That broken bottle under the bar-stool was there six years ago."

"I already pay for door," Grumbuk reminded the barmaid.

"Didn't. It still hanging off."

Grumbuk sighed. "OK put on bill. Too tired argue."

The barmaid looked at Sheean and Merik. "No bring Humans inside."

"Not Human. Dangerous Fayris. Grumbuk friends, no mess with."

Sheean played along and smiled, showing his razor sharp teeth.

"OK," said the barmaid, "you sit. I bring food and ale. Share room though, AOWC convention later."

"AOWC convention?" asked Merik.

"Association of Wart Counters," the barmaid clarified. "Visit yearly, count warts, drink ale. Easy money."

They sat around a rickety table, while the barmaid brought jugs of Goblin ale and plates of food. Grumbuk dived in, taking fistfulls of food from each plate, while Sheean and Merik poked at the food with their fingers.

"Is anything safe to eat?" Merik asked.

"No," said Sheean, "not unless you have plenty of ale with it, to kill the germs."

"What's these small round things?"

"I had some of those last time I was here, they're... err... quite nice. They're not meat."

"What are they then?"

"The locals call them rabbit pellets."

"Oh, rabbit food?"

"More like what comes out after they've eaten."

Sheean and Merik settled for the ale, while they watched Grumbuk finish off all of the food.

"You not hungry?" Grumbuk asked as he wiped his greasy mouth on the back of his sleeve. Merik and Sheean shook their heads. Grumbuk gulped down a jug of ale and belched. "Plan tomorrow. We go up volcano, find way Demon realm. Easy... YES?"

"You said you knew the way," said Merik.

"Is there somewhere. How difficult can be?"

Next morning, Sheean and Grumbuk came downstairs to find Merik sitting at the bar, dipping toast into a lightly boiled egg and talking to the barmaid.

"How did you get Human food?" asked Sheean.

"You just have to be nice to people," said Merik. "Grimlooks," he gestured towards the barmaid, "told me that the portal to the Demon world is one-way. People are pushed into it from this side, but no-one ever comes back out."

Sheean gripped the scabbard of his sword a little tighter.

"We will," Grumbuk said confidently, as he dug into his pocket for some money. "How much?" he asked Grimlooks.

"All paid," she answered.

"Who pay?"

Grimlooks looked at Merik and batted her eyelashes at him. "He repair door and fix ale pumps, so no charge."

As they left the inn, Grimlooks shouted after them. "Careful Merik, is dangerous out there."

"I will," he shouted back.

"Made a conquest there," chuckled Sheean.

"There's a nice girl under that Goblin exterior. She drew me a map as well," Merik said, as he unfolded a dirty piece of paper and showed it to the other two. "She told me the main path up to the crater is guarded. But if we walk along the south edge of the volcano's base, we'll come across an old disused path that will take us right up to the summit without being spotted by the guards. The path was used in ancient rituals, apparently."

"Not hear about path," Grumbuk growled, a hint of jealousy in his voice.

Merik winked at Sheean. "Yes, they used to throw anyone who had Human friends into the bubbling lava from the ledge at the end of the path."

Sheean laughed aloud at the Goblin's shocked expression.

"You think funny?" mumbled Grumbuk. "Come, we not got all day. We go that way, we not take horse and cart. We walk."

The disused path was easy to find, but the path itself was very steep and Sheean felt tired by the time he got to the top. He looked down. In the depths of the crater, lava smoked and spewed.

"Where be portal?" Grumbuk asked.

"Grimlooks says it's at the bottom somewhere," replied Merik. "It's invisible until you get really close to it."

"I could fly down and have a look," said Sheean.

"Good idea, Fayri. We stay here, watch."

Sheean altered his glamour. His leather tunic and sandals faded away to be replaced by his adult wings. Dressed only in his favorite shorts, he stood looking down into the crater for somewhere to aim for.

Merik looked at Sheean with wonder and pride. "Nice set of wings lad," he commented. "Amazing colours! When I first saw you, your wings were only tiny. Now look at you!"

Sheean opened his wings to their full extent, showing the royal blue of the lower set. "Thanks, Merik. I'm going to start directly below us. There seems to be more steam there than any other part of the crater."

"Be careful son," Merik warned.

During Sheean's imprisonment in the castle, Merik had always been there when he needed someone to confide in. Alone in his room, Sheean had often dreamed of being Merik's son. Merik's words gave a warm glow to his heart.

"I will father," he said as he spread his wings and jumped off the rim of the volcano.

* * *

Grumbuk and Merik looked on in amazement, admiring the young man' s graceful form. They watched Sheean ride the hot thermals like an eagle, only flapping his wings occasionally to steady his descent into the depths of the crater.

As Sheean reached the cloud of steam, there was a sudden flash of red and he was gone.

"Shit!" Merik shouted. "Now what?"

"We go after," Grumbuk said.

"How? I can't see any way down from here."

"Like this," Grumbuk said, as he grabbed Merik's hand and dragged him off the edge.

"You'd better be right about this!" Merik shouted at Grumbuk, as they plummeted downwards.

"Soon see," Grumbuk shouted back.

* * *

Sheean watched as Merik and Grumbuk plunged through the hot, sulphurous air towards him. He stepped back a little to allow space for them to land.

"Don't worry," he shouted, "it's..."

Grumbuk bounced a little as he landed in a pile of rotting vegetation.

"... soft."

Sheean laughed at the expression on his friends' faces. "I was wondering how long it would take you to get here."

Merik and Grumbuk choked on the fumes that surrounded them. They looked confused, as if finding it hard to believe their eyes.

"Trees?" said Grumbuk, scratching his head in confusion. "Me thought would be lava and flames."

They were in a small clearing in a forest. The trees surrounding them were closely packed and twisted, as if wrung out like wet laundry. They were ancient and knotted, the bark in many looking like faces peering out into the gloom. A sickly green light filtered through the dense canopy of leafless twigs, making everything look jaundiced and sick. The forest stretched off into the darkness as far as they could see; the branches and roots reaching out, frozen in despair.

Sheean helped Grumbuk to his feet.

"Where is?" Grumbuk asked.

"The Demon realm, I guess," Sheean answered.

"Where go next?"

They looked around. Everywhere looked the same. There were no pathways, no breaks in the trees and no noise other than the sound of their own breathing.

"I haven't a clue," Merik answered.

Sheean looked around. "Maybe if we could find some water, I could use it to see which way to go."

Suddenly the trees close by started creaking and swaying, as though caught in a strong wind. "Waaaater! You said waaaater," breathed one, its voice soft and low. It stood tall and twisted at the edge of the clearing.

"He did say waaaater. I heard him," whispered another. This one was slimmer, its voice higher-pitched and brittle.

"Me heard him tooooo," creaked a stunted, broken tree to their right.

Startled, the trio stood back-to-back. Sheean drew Alex, whose blade glowed dimly in the sickly light. Sheean relaxed as he'd been trained, and held the sword loosely. "Who said that?"

A tree directly in front of him contorted, forming the semblance of a face. Its voice sounded like the rustling of dead leaves.

"We did. You said you have waaaaater."

Grumbuk stepped forward, dagger in hand, ready to do battle. "Fayri say, if could find some, not have."

The trees shrieked together, thrashing their limbs in the fume-laden air.

"That's not faaaair."

"You promised us waaaaater!"

Merik relaxed from his fighting stance. "The only water we have is a small amount of drinking water."

"Ah!... you have waaaater. Give it meeeee," said the stunted tree.

"There's only a bit, and we need that for drinking," said Merik.

"Pleeeease."

All around them trees reached forward with their dead branches, twigs groping in the air like skeletal hands.

"I said we need it for drinking. If we give it to you, we'll die of thirst."

"You can't die heeeere."

Sheean looked around. "Everything looks dead to me."

"Can neeeearly die," said the stunted tree. "I once like yooooo. Was hunting Faaayris. I fall down crater. Now I'm treeeee!"

"How come you tree?" Grumbuk asked.

"Ate mushroooom. Fell asleep. Woke up as treeeee! You, me same, Goblin friend. Pleeease give me waaaater!"

Grumbuk stepped back, shocked.

"What about the rest of the trees?" Sheean asked.

"Same as meeeee. Same as yoooo. You get hungry. You eat mushrooooom."

The tallest tree leaned forward, its bark creaking and cracking. Its voice seemed lesss like the wind, more like the Human it may have once been. "Tell me what brings you here? Most people here have been banished here. What have you done wrong?"

"Nothing," said Merik. "We've come here to rescue a friend. A Human woman called Edna."

The tree paused, holding its branches still for a second. "The magic user?"

All the trees waved their branches, dead twigs clattering against dead twigs. It was as if a terrible wind was blowing and yet the air was still.

"She's here, paaaaart of forest," said the thin tree.

"A tree?" Sheean asked.

"Eventually, everybody becomes paaaaart of the foressssst."

Grumbuk stomped up to the stunted tree. It stood a little taller than him. He held his dagger tightly. "How you know she here?"

"We talk through canopy. All of us. Is millions."

The thin tree joined in. "All near death, but unable to die."

"How we find her?" Grumbuk asked.

"I show yooooo," said the little tree.

"How you show? You tree, no move."

"One drop water. That all."

"And if we give you some of our water, you promise to take us to Edna?" Merik asked.

"Proooomise," said the tree, holding a root out towards Merik.

Merik unscrewed the top of his water flask. "How much do you need?"

The entire forest began to move, trunks bending and swaying, branches flapping. Roots deep in the ground writhed under foot, moving like snakes in a pit.

"Freeee meeeee!" they cried. "Freeee meee, give meee waaater!"

"Gimmeeee! On my rooot!" squealed the stunted tree. "Gimmeeee!"

Merik held the flask out. The tree dipped a root into the flask, drinking deeply. Sheean found himself trembling as the other trees drew nearer.

"Er, Merik the other trees are moving closer," he whispered. "I think we should go."

The root of the small tree shrank back with a sigh. Gradually, the dried, dead bark became green and soft. A knot in the trunk turned into an ugly little face. A few seconds later, a fully formed Goblin stood in front of them, shaking dead leaves and bits of twig from his clothes.

Merik looked into the flask. "You said just a drop!"

"Couldn't stop."

"It's empty!"

The surrounding trees became still. A groan of despair echoed throughout the canopy, disappearing away, repeated and repeated into the far distance.

Sheean felt the first flutter of despair. "How are we going to free Edna? That was the only water we had," he said.

"Blood might work," Grumbuk said, threatening the other Goblin with his dagger. He moved so close that their noses almost touched. "You said you was Fayri hunting," said Grumbuk. "Who your boss?"

"Let's find Edna first, then we can chat," said Sheean, stepping between them.

"Follow me," shouted the Goblin, as he scurried off into the densely packed trees.

Within a few minutes, they reached a place where the trees were so closely crowded together, it was impossible to make any headway without stepping on their roots. Almost every time anyone put a foot to the ground, it was accompanied by squeaks of pain from a nearby tree. Sometimes they really yelled. Sheean found himself apologising for almost every footfall.

At one point, the forest was so densely packed that their path was completely blocked and they had to hack their way through with swords. Alex didn't mind, but Sheean held back, unwilling to cause further pain. Alex grumbled as Merik led the way. The insipid light filtering through the twigs gave no indication of time. They seemed to have been going through the twisted forest forever.

Suddenly the Goblin stopped at a clearing and pointed.

"This place. I go now."

Merik grabbed the little Goblin. "Hang on a minute, where are you going?"

"Dunno. Away." The Goblin gave a little twist of its body and broke free, disappearing onwards through the trees.

The clearing was roughly circular. The ground ahead was covered in thick vines and in the centre of the clearing stood a single tree, its branches covered in dark green leaves. Mushrooms sprouted up here and there. They looked good enough to eat with their pale creamy brown colour, like little pixie hats on stalks.

"That's the first tree we've seen with leaves on," said Sheean.

"That has to be Edna," said Merik, as he stepped into the clearing.

"No!" Grumbuk shouted, grabbing Merik's belt and pulling him back. Merik lost his balance and sat heavily on the ground.

"What the...!"

Grumbuk pointed to the floor of the clearing, his little green finger trembling.

"Snakes!"

"Nonsense. Those are vines and roots," said Sheean, peering into the clearing.

"Not vines."

Sheean prodded one of the vines with Alex. It seemed to shimmer for a second, and then a head rose from the entanglement. Hissing and spitting, it unravelled itself until its head was level with Sheean's. "Who issssss?"

"We've come to rescue Edna," Sheean told it.

"No chancccce. Ssshe isss ssstaying here."

"I don't think so," Sheean said, as he sliced the snake in half.

The two halves dropped to the floor. A second later, a new head grew and there were two snakes, where previously there had been one. The whole clearing was now in motion, writhing and twisting around the tree in its centre.

"Now what?" Merik asked.

They sat in silence at the edge of the clearing, each deep in their own thoughts.

"If Bryony was here, she could have frozen the snakes," said Sheean. "I wonder... " He formed a small ball of fire in the palm of his hand and threw it at a snake. The fire hit its target but simply dissipated in a puff of smoke. Sheean shrugged. "I guess fire is not going to work then."

Feeling thirsty, Merik checked his water flask again and threw it in frustration into the middle of the snakes. As it spun through the air, a single drop of water fell onto a snake, turning it into black smouldering ash.

Everyone looked on, open-mouthed. Grumbuk jumped to his feet.

"Need water. Make rain Fayri!"

Sheean stood by his side, facing the tree. "I should be able to. Bryony did it once."

"Go on then."

"I don't know how to."

"Try."

Sheean closed his eyes. "I have to see it in my mind."

"Keep going Fayri," Grumbuk whispered in his ear. "Something happen."

Sheean opened his eyes for an instant to see the sky slowly turning black, plunging the clearing into near darkness. A distant rumbling of thunder rolled through the clouds, growing louder as it approached. A single flash of lightning lit up the forest and a drop of rain fell.

Sheean closed his eyes again and concentrated harder. The rain became a torrent. The snakes writhed and disintegrated into black smoke. It was impossible to see anything of the tree in the centre. All around them, as the rain fell, they were aware of the trees turning back into the beings they once were, taking flight into the depths of the forest.

* * *

Edna felt herself being pulled away from the treasure beneath her roots. Her tight and twisted tree shape was changing. A glorious, cooling rain fell. The ground was smoking as if a forest fire had swept through the area. Her leaves reached up, desperate for the water, while her roots hung onto the metal far below.

After a short while, the rain eased off and Edna found herself back in Human form, gazing at two familiar faces at the edge of her clearing. Sheean was there, grinning at her, and Merik the soldier. With them stood a Goblin.

She was aware of her grey hair hanging in rats' tails around her shoulders. Her blouse and skirts were muddy. Her shawl lay on the floor, covered in dust and leaves. She stamped her foot.

"What are you doing?!" she shouted. "I nearly had it, and now I'll never reach it!"

Their faces fell. She took a deep breath and relaxed. Even if she'd been able to get the treasure, what would she have done with it while living as a tree? A wave of gratitude flooded her being.

"I suppose you meant well," she said, breaking into a smile.

She walked forwards and embraced Sheean, careful not to damage his wings in her affection. She felt his young body go rigid with embarrassment. Holding him at arm's length, she tried to get the Fay youngster to meet her eyes. "Thank you," she said, "but I didn't really need rescuing at that moment."

The young prince simply looked at the floor, as if he'd been told off by his mother. She patted his arm. "Thank you. You did well."

She let him go and turned to Merik. "How did you know I was here? And how did you get here?"

"Your cats told us you were here," said Sheean. "Somehow they, I mean he, knew I was back in the Human realm and asked us to help you defeat Grizelda. What were you trying to reach?"

Edna hugged Merik in turn. "I'm so glad to see you. And Alex. Who's your little friend?" she said, looking at the Goblin.

Grumbuk strode forward and gave a big bow. "Grumbuk, hero of legend, at your service."

Edna smiled. "It is an honour to meet you Mr. Grumbuk, hero of legend." She looked at her rescuers kindly. "I was trying to reach an artefact, the Wyvernhope Torc. I could sense metal down near my roots. I grabbed it but couldn't bring it to the surface. Then when you lot turned up. I couldn't say anything, as I didn't want the snakes to know what I was doing. Now if you'll give me a minute, I'll just see if I can see it."

"What does it look like?" asked Sheean.

Edna lifted her skirts and bent down to look among the ash and leaves. She began digging with her hands. "It's a torc, a necklace made from gold and silver. I need it to turn my husband back into Wizard form." She paused and looked up. "We need his help to defeat Grizelda."

Grumbuk and Merik searched among the leaves using their blades. Sheean was about to do the same, but Alex refused to come from the scabbard.

"Come on Alex."

"I'm not a shovel! I've told you before."

"Sorry Alex. I didn't think."

"You never do!"

Edna stood up. "Alex, would you be so kind as to help to search for this magical item? Your Dwarven abilities to differentiate metals may point us in the right direction. I would be much obliged."

Sheean drew the sword from the scabbard with ease. "It would be my pleasure," said Alex. "Maybe I should be the Wizard's Sword rather than the King's Sword. What do you think, Sheean?"

Sheean growled.

"No more arguments," said Edna. "Sheean take Alex and point him at the ground about here." She indicated an area near where her roots had been. Merik and Grumbuk watched as the sword glowed deep silver, like moonlight reflected in a dark lake. "Here," said Alex. "I can sense metal here."

Edna looked down at Grumbuk. "You have strength, Mr. Grumbuk. Would you dig for us?"

Without question, Grumbuk began to dig with his hands.

"He looks like a dog digging for a bone," laughed Merik.

A few minutes later, Grumbuk stopped digging and pulled a bracelet from the ground. "This it?"

Edna frowned and walked forward. She took it from him and peered at the artefact. She shook her head. "For a moment I thought it was the right thing. This is too small. I'm looking for a torc, not a bracelet. This is just a trinket."

She paused and smiled at the Goblin. "Would you like it Mr. Grumbuk?"

"Me like."

"What's that noise?" asked Sheean.

"Your ears are better than ours, Prince Sheean. What do you hear?"

Sheean turned his head this way and that, trying to get a better impression. "It sounds like wood creaking, like a ship moving on the sea, it sounds like..."

Edna looked around in alarm. "The trees over there are moving! We must leave! Follow me, and don't step on anything. Don't eat the mushrooms. Oh, and if we meet any Demons, follow my lead. They don't really mean any harm, it's just the way they are."

Chapter 5

"Is this a river or a sea?" asked Merik, as he looked out across the dark, glass-smooth water. "How are we going to get to the other side?"

Edna brushed some of the dust off her skirts and looked up. "It's a river, one of the seven rivers of this realm. Someone will come." She peered more closely at the horizon. "Look, here she comes, the ferry-woman. Don't be afraid."

A shape appeared on the horizon, a shifting blackness on the water. As it drew closer, the form solidified into the shape of a boat. Sheean, Merik and Edna waited patiently for it to arrive, while Grumbuk sat in the dust, playing with his new bracelet.

After a while, the boat drew up against the beach. The ferry-woman was dressed in a tattered grey toga, her auburn hair trailing down her back into the bottom of the boat. Standing tall, she focused her piercing grey eyes on Edna. "You have the horde?"

"Not yet, but I will continue to look," said Edna. "These people wish to return. What price do you ask?"

"I have been rowing this boat for thousands upon thousands of years. It is time for someone else to take a turn. I will take you home if someone will take my place."

Edna shook her head. "That is not possible. We are on a quest."

The ferry-woman stepped down from her boat and approached them. She was tall and imposing, thin and pale. "On a quest. Everyone I meet is on a quest, so they say. If you cannot give me one of your people, then I wish for the Wyvernhope treasure. I have everything else. I have been paid riches beyond measure, but that is not what I seek. I seek an end to my torment."

Edna smiled and drew a deep breath. She was reminded of bargaining in the market for apples. "An end to your torment you say. Everyone here is looking for an end to their torment." Edna drew closer to the woman. She kept her face soft to show she meant no threat. "We seek a prize beyond the selfish needs of one. We seek a prize to liberate all. Will you co-operate with us?"

"My boat is the only way back for you. Bring me one simple necklace from the Wyvernhope horde and I will help you escape. I do not ask for much."

"Why not leave your boat and join us?"

"I am trapped here just as you are. I cannot leave this boat until someone volunteers to take my place."

Merik stepped forward. "Where is this treasure?"

"It is beyond the six rivers."

"Then how by the gods do you expect us to find it?"

"It will only be found when the time is right," said the ferry woman, returning to her boat. "The signs say the time is near. You will have to be quick, there are many who look for the horde."

"What signs?" asked Sheean.

The woman looked at Sheean closely, a small smile playing at the corners of her mouth. She raised one eyebrow a little as she spoke. "I have been told by other travellers that a Faerie prince has come to rescue a wizard. Also it has rained for the first time in the forests. These things have come to pass."

"Can you tell us the other signs?" asked Edna.

The ferry woman sat down in the boat, arranging her hair all around her like an auburn blanket. "A child will point the way. I am told there is a place for lost children where the fire runs into the sea."

"And that would be in which direction?" Merik asked.

"Follow the coast towards the mountains." She pointed along the coast.

Edna looked off into the distance, searching for signs of mountains. When she turned back, the boat and the woman had disappeared.

"She's got powerful magic," said Sheean.

Edna began to march off along the coast. "She is not to be trifled with. She's not getting that necklace though. That's for us. We can pay her with the rest of the treasure."

With the sea on their left and the forest on their right, they made their way along the soft, ash coloured beach. It wasn't long before they were all desperate for a drink. Sheean increased his pace to catch up with Edna.

"We're going to need water soon," he said. "The trees told us no one can die here, but if we don't find water, we won't have the strength to keep walking."

"We'll find something soon, I'm sure," said Edna.

"Have you noticed how the sea doesn't smell like the one back home?" said Merik.

Sheean paused to crouch down at the water's edge and scoop some water into the palm of his hand. "How do we know it's not poison?" he asked.

"I've already tried it and I know it's not poison," Edna replied. "It won't kill you, nothing will, but it won't refresh you."

Sheean ignored her and took a mouthful of the water. "Tastes like very strong Goblin ale."

Grumbuk's eyes lit up. "Sea of ale? Best thing ever!"

"If you drink that," said Edna, "you will end up drunk, and even more thirsty, which will make you drink even more. Eventually you will collapse and not be able to move from the edge of the sea. You will suffer horribly."

"S'pose," said Sheean. "But we do need water."

"Fayri make rain?" asked Grumbuk.

"I could try, but what would we catch the water in?"

"I have been here before. There are herbs further up that we can chew," said Edna.

They walked onwards. There was nothing to break the monotony. The forest lined the coast and the thick dust under their feet sapped their strength.

"You know..." said Merik through parched lips, "if every tree is a criminal of some description, there must be lots of bad people in the worlds."

"Aha. Here they are," said Edna, trotting to the trees. She bent down and pulled up some herbs. She gave everyone a piece and told them to chew. Putting a piece in her mouth, she felt precious saliva flow as the bitter taste filled her senses. Grumbuk spat his out on the floor.

"Tastes bad."

"You fool of a Goblin! Get some more."

Grumbuk hesitated, playing with his bracelet. To Edna's eyes he looked like a spoilt child in need of firm guidance. She drew herself up to her full height, calling on a mild magic of obedience. "Do as I say. NOW!"

To her amusement, Merik and Grumbuk both trotted off to the trees, pulling up the herbs and filling their mouths. They came back, smiling. "Tastes great," said Grumbuk, smiling up at Edna in adoration. "You is clever witch."

She leaned down to him. "I am no witch, little one, I am a Wizard, and don't you forget it."

They walked on, refreshed by the herbs, until they saw plumes of steam at the sea's edge. As they neared the foothills, sulfurous fumes filled the air. Mountains rose up ahead, their tops tinged red with fire. In front of them flowed a vast expanse of magma.

The ground was soaking wet. Every indentation was full of water. Sheean scooped up a handful and swallowed. The others watched for a few seconds, waiting to see if anything happened to him. When it didn't, they joined in.

"OK," chuckled Edna, "this tastes a lot better than the herbs."

When they had slaked their thirst, they sat for a while on the dusty beach. Merik took off his boots and rubbed his feet.

Edna knew Sheean could walk all day, and Goblins were renowned for their strength. She had her magic. But the soldier, he had to rely on his muscles and willpower alone.

"Do we follow the river of fire up into the hills?" asked Merik. "And what about the lost children?"

"The lava flow is too wide for us to cross," said Edna. "Sheean, you could fly across, but the rest of us would have to stay here, and I think we should stay together for now. As for the lost children, I just don't know. I would be surprised if they are real children."

"Like Seven Sisters, they is rocks," Grumbuk said, with a tinge of authority.

"You are very wise, Mr. Grumbuk," said Edna.

Grumbuk burped and patted his belly. "Yep. Me wise."

They made their way along the edge of the river of fire and into the foothills of the mountains. Sheean

140

paused, looking back over the twisted tree tops to the horizon. Merik continued to march up the hill ahead of them.

"Is everything alright?" asked Edna.

Sheean shrugged. "Nothing's moving. Not a bird, no clouds, nothing."

"This is the Demon realm," replied Edna. "Be thankful that nothing is moving."

Merik returned from scouting up ahead. "There's a cave up there. I've not been inside, only there's something strange about it."

"What do you mean?" Edna asked.

"I think it's the home of the lost children."

"Did you see any of them?" Sheean asked.

"No, but I could hear childish laughter coming from inside the cave."

* * *

Merik led the way up a steep, winding path, leading to a man-sized fissure in the rock-face.

"How you know was here?" Grumbuk asked.

"Listen."

"Am listen, you not say nothing."

Merik scowled at Grumbuk.

"Mr. Grumbuk," said Edna, "I think Merik wants us all to be silent and listen."

"Only need say."

"Grumbuk, shut up and listen!" hissed Sheean. He paused, tipping his head on one side. Then he heard it. "I can hear children's laughter."

"That's what I heard when I scouted up ahead," said Merik. "It's coming from inside the cave."

"It's good you didn't go in," said Edna as she examined the entrance. "Like everything here, this is

141

likely to be a trap. Mr. Grumbuk, pass me the bracelet I gave you."

"Not got."

"What have you done with it?"

"Bottom hill, is junk."

"Junk it may be, Mr. Grumbuk, but we need it to grant us access to this tomb. Kindly go and find it."

"Tomb?" Grumbuk repeated quietly. He wiped beads of sweat from his forehead. "Thought no-one die here."

"Intriguing, isn't it. Now go, or do I have to put another obedience spell on you?"

"Don't like tomb."

"If you wish, you can stay out here and wait for me to return."

"Grumbuk hero, not scared."

"Good, however we still need the bracelet. Please go and fetch it."

Grumbuk spun around and stormed back down the track, grumbling loudly to himself.

"Hang on, I'll help you find it," said Sheean, running after him. He caught up with the Goblin. "What's up Grumbuk?"

"Don't know if like woman boss."

"Edna's a good person."

"Grumbuk know, but remind of wife."

"You never mentioned you were married."

"Long time go, bad temper, think Grumbuk stupid."

"What happened to her?"

"Sold to best friend."

"Did it work out for your friend?"

"D'no, not friend no more."

Sheean went quiet for a time until they reached the bottom of the hill. "You don't recommend marriage then?" he asked quietly. Grumbuk didn't have time to answer. As they approached the spot where he had thrown the bracelet away, a small Goblin stepped out from behind a rock. It was the Goblin from the forest and it was wearing Grumbuk's bracelet.

"You again," said Sheean. "Why did you run off?"

"Wasn't scared!" it shouted in a high pitched squeak of terror.

"I didn't say you were."

"Give bracelet," demanded Grumbuk.

The Goblin covered the bracelet with his warty hand. "Sharnt. Is Krodbell's now."

"Is my bracelet!"

"Not. Found over there."

"Is mine, me throw away. Um, dropped it. Mine!"

"Not yours no-more."

"Give back or set Fayri on you."

By now the two Goblins were face to face, spitting saliva in their fury. Sheean stepped forward and grinned, showing his pointed teeth. Reluctantly, Krodbell took the bracelet off and gave it to Grumbuk. "Not fair," he mumbled.

Grumbuk strode off up the hill. "Come, whatever name you has, Krodbell was it?"

They set off. Sheean looked back and smiled as he saw relief showing on Krodbell's little green face. They hadn't gone far when a strong smell of lemons stopped Sheean in his tracks. So out of place in this world of sulphur was the smell, that Sheean drew Alex. He looked around.

"What stop for Fayri?" Grumbuk asked.

"Do you smell lemons?"

Grumbuk drew a deep, snotty breath through his nose.

"No smell nothing."

Krodbell shook his head.

"It's fading now. I was certain I could smell lemons."

"Fayri imagine things."

"S'pose," Sheean said as he slipped Alex back in his scabbard.

When they reached the rock face, they found Merik busy trying to carve a face into a lump of lava with a small dagger. "About time you two came back," he said. "I was just beginning to toy with the idea of coming to look for you. I see you've brought our little friend with you."

Grumbuk stood as tall as he could. "I rescue him. He called Krodbell."

"Did not," said Krodbell. The two Goblins glared at each other. Merik looked at Sheean for confirmation.

"We found him with the bracelet. It seemed wrong to leave him on his own."

"OK Grumbuk, but he's your responsibility."

"Course, I hero."

Edna joined the group. "Give me the bracelet please. I want to try and open the door."

As Grumbuk removed it from his wrist and handed it over, Krodbell whispered something in Grumbuk's ear.

"Yes, she powerful," replied Grumbuk. "Do as told or make you toad."

Sheean followed Edna to the entrance. They stood together in front of the harmless looking rock.

"Why do you need the bracelet?" asked Sheean.

"The doorway is locked by magic. If you were to try and enter without unlocking it, something nasty could happen to you."

Sheean peered into the darkness. "How did the children get in?"

"We'll find out in a minute," said Edna, as she pushed the bracelet into a depression cut into the rock. For a moment nothing happened.

"Knew bracelet junk," muttered Grumbuk.

Edna dusted down her skirts. "It's safe to go in now. There was an invisible, magical seal across the entrance."

"How you know it gone?" asked Grumbuk.

"I don't for sure. We'll find out when one of us goes in," chuckled Edna.

"Send Krodbell first," said Grumbuk.

Krodbell looked frantically from Sheean to Merik. "I not good at brave."

"It's OK," said Sheean, as he headed for the entrance. "Me and Alex will go first."

"Excuse me," said Alex, as he was drawn from his scabbard. "I don't remember volunteering."

"Someone with magic should go first. As Edna is the only other person here with magic, it wouldn't be very gallant to let a lady go first."

Alex's blade glinted in the murky light. "Spoken like a true future king."

Sheean changed his glamour to give off a bright light and entered the tomb. Merik followed closely behind.

* * *

Edna's round face beamed with joy as she gazed at the wonders in the tomb. Above their heads, two stone beams supported a black, concave ceiling, decorated with thousands of sparkling stars as bright as jewels. On the walls were colourful, painted scenes depicting everyday life in the Human realm, long ago. The paint was peeling, but by Sheean's Faerie light, the colours showed their original brilliance. The room was long and narrow, leading away into darkness.

Edna peered at hieroglyphs between each picture. Each line of text hinted at a deeper meaning to the murals. Edna saw an arch of green stone, framing an open doorway. The eerie laughter of children floated towards her. Sheean shivered.

"This is wonderful," said Edna. "I've only ever seen this sort of thing once before, and never expected to find something like this in the Demon realm."

Grumbuk touched the wall paintings. "What is?"

"It is the tomb of an ancient king. Certainly someone very important."

"I can still hear laughter," said Merik. "Where are the lost children?"

"I think you'll find them here," said Edna, pointing to a painting of a small group of children huddled together at the edge of a cornfield.

The children appeared to be cowering away from a large, dark shadow. One of them, a small boy, pointed towards the darkness that loomed over them. In the distance, a number of adults could clearly be seen searching for the children, their faces distressed and anxious. The laughter grew in intensity, filling the room with echoes.

"Where's the laughing coming from?" asked Merik.

Edna moved closer to the painting and examined the children carefully. "Look."

She pointed. On each child's face, where the mouth should have been, was a small hole in the wall. Edna bent her ear to the face of a little boy. She could hear wind and water rushing past the tiny opening. She stood back. "Don't be afraid. It seems innocent enough. There are holes in the walls and something behind the wall is making the sound. It isn't the sound of children."

"But it sounds just like the children at May Dance," said Merik, peering at the carvings.

Sheean examined the painting. "Clever isn't it? From this angle the boy appears to be pointing at the doorway at the end of this room."

"Yes, but like everything else in this world, it could be a trap," warned Edna.

"Can you read the picture-writing?" Sheean asked.

"I think so. It's very old and hasn't been used for centuries. Sheean, come with me to look round."

"I can't help with reading the pictures."

"I know. I just need you to be my light."

"I can do that."

Slowly, Edna and Sheean worked their way around the room. Most of the writing referred to everyday life in an ancient village. There was even a recipe for making cheese. The writing over the far doorway was different. It appeared to tell a story about a man and a serpent.

"This may be important," said Edna.

"What say?" asked Grumbuk.

"I will read it to you as best I can. It's an old language and I may get some of it wrong."

She craned her neck back to get a good view of the letters. Her voice echoed around the room.

"Suddenly I heard a noise like thunder. I thought it to be that of the waves of the sea. The withered trees shook. The earth moved and I was frightened. As I uncovered my face, I saw a serpent draw near. His scales were edged with gold, and his colour was that of lapis lazuli. He coiled himself before me,

addressing me by my true name of Wyvernhope. He told me a
story of future events, both evil and good, and how a magic torc
will save the realms from demonic rule. My magic torc.

If you have read my tale so far, then our destinies may be
entwined. However, I have hidden my treasure well and the way
to the torc will not be easy. Seven rivers must you navigate
before you can possess its magic. One, you have already crossed.

As you pass through this doorway, you will be judged.
Only the brave and true will pass safely. Those that do will find
a boat to speed them on their quest. I am old now, and must
soon die here in this realm, alone. Do not feel sorry for me, I
am happy. My part in this story is complete. It is I who should
feel sorry for you."

She turned to the others. "It's by Wyvernhope,
the Great Mage. Now we can find the torc and stop
Grizelda."

No-one said anything. Edna tipped her head on
one side and smiled. "Well?"

Everyone started to talk once, each suggesting
different courses of action. After a few seconds, Edna
shouted over them. "Stop! We need the torc to free
my husband, defeat Grizelda and put everything right
in the Human realm. Therefore, I must go on. I
would be happy for you all to accompany me, but I
understand if you would rather stay here. Once I have
the torc, I will make certain you get home."

"What if not find?" Krodbell asked.

"I will not go back without it."

Everyone started talking at once again. Eventually
Sheean managed to quiet them down. "I think we're
all coming with you," he said. "Although Grumbuk's
not certain about the brave and true bit in the story."

Edna came closer to the Goblin. He shrank away
from her. She touched his arm gently and he calmed.
"The words sound a little like the Knight's Code from

148

the time of the Wizard Wars," she said. "We are all brave, otherwise we wouldn't have got this far. The true part usually means being true to yourself. To be true to yourself, you must have integrity."

"Wazzat?" asked Krodbell.

Edna smiled at her party of treasure seekers. "Are we ready?"

"Are you ready Alex?" asked Sheean. "Am I brave enough and true?"

"Don't ask silly questions boy."

Everyone laughed.

"Very well," said Edna as she gathered her skirts and strode through the arch.

* * *

Sheean followed Edna through the doorway. Beyond was a rocky, ash covered island in a sea of lava. The island was tiny. At some point there had been a single tree growing, but that had died long ago. Its hollow trunk lay rotting in the sulfurous fumes. The heat was suffocating.

Sheean looked over his shoulder. The doorway back to the cave had disappeared. There was no way back. He glanced at Edna. She was gazing out over the red hot sea, seemingly unconcerned.

Sheean watched as Merik walked along a small outcrop and looked down at the edge of the river of lava. "Have you seen this?" he said.

Sheean and the others joined him. A short way out from the shore, a narrow boat bobbed up and down, hovering just above the lava flow. It was slim and made from some kind of woven plant material. There were oars and seats inside. The prow curved upwards like the neck of a swan.

"I guess that's our transport," said Edna.

"How are we going to get to it?" Sheean asked. "It's too far away for Humans to jump. I could fly across, and maybe carry the Goblins."

Grumbuk frowned and shook his head. "Not think so, nearly drown last time."

"My wings are full size now."

"Was two Fayris last time and still got wet."

"S'pose your feet could get a bit hot," Sheean said, giving Grumbuk a big grin.

Grumbuk scowled back.

Edna looked around. "Well gentlemen, we are going to have to be inventive."

No-one spoke. Grumbuk scratched his backside and sat down. Krodbell sat next to him. Edna laughed, her apple cheeks shining in the heat. "It's simple," she said, "there's an old hollow tree trunk over there. We can use it as a bridge to cross to the boat."

"That rotten tree will never support our weight," said Merik, "and getting it across the gap is not going to be easy."

"Can you think of a better idea?" asked Edna.

Sheean flew out over the lava to the boat and back, keeping his wings well out of danger. "How heavy is the tree trunk? Could I fly across holding one end?"

Merik shrugged. "Mmm, that might work. Let's have a go. We can practise before you fly out over the lava with it."

Merik and Sheean got hold of an end each and heaved it off the ground.

"It's heavy," Sheean groaned.

"It is a bit," said Merik. "Have a go at flying, see if you can manage."

Sheean spread his wings and flapped them slowly, gradually building speed until the air was choked with dust. Twice Sheean thought his feet were clearing the ground, but the tree was too heavy. He gave up.

Merik peered through dust filled eyes. "It's no good lad."

"Now what?" Sheean asked.

"Well, if we were back at the castle, we would make an A frame and use rope to lower one end onto the boat. But as we don't have any wood to make a frame, or for that matter any rope, we're going to have to lift one end and let the tree drop across the gap and hope it lands OK. What do you think Edna?"

"That sounds a wonderful plan."

"Right lads," Merik ordered. "We need to carry it to the edge and stand it on end."

Everyone heaved and pulled at the tree trunk and eventually they had it balanced on its end at the river's edge.

"Right we need a couple of large rocks to put at its base to stop it slipping backwards when it falls."

Edna laughed again. "Oh Merik, you're in your element aren't you?"

Merik looked puzzled.

"I mean," said Edna, "you were born to do this sort of thing."

"With respect, Ma'am, I'm highly trained."

"Of course," Edna chuckled. "Of course."

Grumbuk and Krodbell rushed off, returning with two large rocks. Merik placed them against the tree trunk and stamped them into the dust a little way. Then he turned to Edna. "At your command."

"Very well. 3, 2, 1, Go."

Merik and Sheean gave it a push towards the boat. The tree trunk hesitated in midair for a second, then fell to one side, away from the boat. Just before the trunk was about to touch the burning surface of the river, it bounced back up, moved forward and settled in place across the gap.

"Did you see that?" Sheean asked.

No one said a word.

"And did you smell lemons? Like before."

Edna frowned.

Merik crawled across the trunk on his hands and knees, followed by Edna, while Sheean flew across. Grumbuk was about to walk across next, when Edna stopped him. "Wait a second Grumbuk." Turning to Merik she said, "Is it my imagination, or is the boat sinking a little every time someone comes aboard?"

"I come now?" Grumbuk shouted from the bank.

"Yes, but one at a time. Krodbell, wait until Grumbuk is safely across."

Sheean leaned over the side, keeping an eye on the boat's height above the lava. On Edna's signal, Grumbuk stuck his arms out and walked across, jumping onto the deck of the boat.

The boat lurched. For a second the hull touched the lava, making smoke billow up the sides. The boat lifted again, settling just above the lava flow.

"It won't take any more weight," said Edna.

"I could fly," said Sheean, "that would take my weight out of the boat."

"This quest could take days," said Edna. "No matter how strong a flyer you are, you couldn't stay air born that long."

Everyone looked across the gap at a very lost looking Krodbell.

"You not go!" Grumbuk shouted.

Edna grabbed his arm. "Grumbuk!"

"What? Is true."

"Yes, but you shouldn't be so blunt."

Edna looked over at Krodbell. He was stomping up and down the bank, his lower lip stuck out in silent protest. "I promise when I have the torc," she called, "I'll rescue you."

Krodbell said nothing, he just kicked dust in the direction of the boat and wandered off to the other side of the island.

"I think we should get a move on," said Edna.

Merik pushed the trunk from the edge of the boat into the lava, while Edna settled herself down on a seat, gathering her dusty skirts round her. "There was a picture in the tomb showing a boat just like this." She touched the woven material at her feet. "The papyrus is quite cool to the touch. It must have powerful magic. Good. On we go."

"How do you suppose we make it move?" asked Sheean.

Merik picked up an oar and gave the other to Sheean. "Row."

* * *

Sheean sat opposite Merik on the rowing deck. "So how do these things work?"

"If we were floating on water," Merik answered. "You would put the oar in this holder on the side of the boat. It's called a rowlock. Then you hold the pole shaped end in your hands and push it down and forward, which lifts the oar out of the water, then lift it up so the oar dips into the water, then pull it towards you. Then you just repeat." Merik mimed the gesture in the air. The boat slewed sideways in the lava flow.

"Won't the oars burn if we dip them in the lava?" asked Sheean.

"Mmm... I'd not thought of that."

Grumbuk sat next to Edna, gripping the sides of the boat and peering at the orange river in terror. Edna put her hands on the side of the boat, closed her eyes, then nodded. It was well designed. Opening her eyes again she said, "Try doing it without dipping the oars in. Just wave them about in the air and see what happens."

Merik looked at Sheean and shrugged. "OK, we have to do this together, at the same time, or we'll go around in circles. One, two, three, Go."

As if reluctant to move, the boat lurched one oar's length, coming to a shuddering stop as the oars were lifted and pushed back. They were still only a few yards from the island of ash.

"This is going to be hard work," Sheean mumbled.

Krodbell came back to the island's edge and stood shouting obscenities and making rude gestures at anyone who looked in his direction.

"No need rescue," Grumbuk said. "Wasted space."

Edna patted Grumbuk's arm gently. "He's annoyed with us for leaving him there."

"Would think he be nice, so we come back and get."

"I suspect he thinks we won't be coming back for him."

Merik and Sheean put the oars in the rowlocks and practised synchronising their movements. They soon got the hang of how to wave the oars in the air, and the island faded away into the distance. The boat moved into the centre of the river and picked up speed. The lava flowed strongly now, still only inches below the bottom of the boat. It seemed to pull the boat along, making rowing easy.

After a time, Merik and Sheean were able to relax, only needing to use the oars now and again to make corrections.

"Does anyone know where we're going?" Merik asked.

"If my memory serves me right," Edna replied, "all the rivers converge in the centre of the Demon realm in a great marsh."

Merik shivered, despite the heat. "Didn't the writing in the cave say we had to cross seven rivers?"

"To be precise, it said we had to navigate seven rivers. The only way to get to the other six is to follow this one to where they all meet up."

"Does this one run into the sea of beer?" Sheean asked.

Edna smiled. "I'm not sure. This river is called the Phlegethon, the River of Fire."

Grumbuk snorted. "Fleggy thon? Stupid name!"

Edna ignored him. "Then there is the Styx, that's the one that tastes like Goblin beer. It separates the Human realm from here. There is Lethe, the river of unmindfulness, which flows round a cave. There is Cocytus, the river of wailing and Acheron, Eridanos and finally Alpheus."

Grumbuk peered up at her. "How you know this? You bin school?"

"Yes, it was part of my schooling. Before the wars, children learned about the other realms and their people. It was quite common to see the Faerie folk in the Human realm at that time."

"Did Humans ever go to the Faerie realm?" Sheean asked.

"There were no laws against it in those days, but few did."

"No-one said anything about Faeries and Humans visiting each other when I was at school in Taranor."

"Yes, it's a shame. The Faerie folk became very insular after the Wizard Wars. It became taboo for the two races to mix. I remember strict rules being made that are kept to this day."

"How long ago was this?" asked Merik.

"Many thousands of Human years. Watch out for that boulder!"

Merik grabbed an oar and waved it. The narrow boat shifted sideways. Merik looked at Edna. "But you said you learnt about it in school?"

Edna smiled, her eyes crinkling up at the corners. "I come from a long line of Wizards. I am, shall we say, quite old."

No one liked to ask Edna her age, all of them finding interesting things to look at over the side of the boat. There was no land to be seen, nothing to break the monotony, nothing to gauge the distance travelled. The heat rising from the river was almost unbearable, affecting everyone's mood apart from Edna's, who remained stubbornly positive. Fanning herself with her shawl she said, "Don't despair everyone, we'll soon be there." She kept watch as the others slept in the boat, lulled by the rocking motion as it sped over the lava.

Grumbuk woke first. He crawled out from the bottom of the boat to sit in the seat at the front next to Edna. Islands appeared up ahead, misty in the heat haze. Grumbuk pointed at the river.

"Look, river go slower."

"Yes," said Edna. "It seems to be splitting into different channels."

"Which way we go now?"

"We're getting near the end of the river. Let's wake the others."

The islands drew closer, covered in dense jungle and dripping vines. Between the islands the river ran in boiling red rivulets, just wide enough for the boat to pass through. Every time they came to a fork in the river, the boat seemed to hesitate for a second before continuing down one of the branches, sometimes even against the river's current. Impenetrable jungle guarded the riverbanks, looming over the boat as it made its way through the overhanging vines.

"It's like someone's guiding us," said Sheean.

"Yes, and I think I keep getting a faint whiff of lemons," Merik added.

Edna frowned and rubbed at the whiskers on her chin. "The smell of lemons in the Demon realm. That's not good."

"Me like lemons."

"That's not what I mean, Mr. Grumbuk."

Edna lost track of how many times the boat changed course, taking one river branch or another. Suddenly they rounded a bend to find themselves in a vast area of marshland. The boat slowed to a stop.

Edna peered ahead. "The old stories tell of this place being the centre of the underworld."

"Is the underworld part of the Demon realm?" Sheean asked.

"The underworld and the Demon realm are one and the same place. Most of the stories of Hades and the underworld are just references to manifestations of the Demon realm."

"What we do next?" Grumbuk asked.

157

Merik picked up his oar again. "I guess we start rowing."

Sheean and Merik waved the oars as hard as they could, but the long grass of the marshlands made it impossible to make any headway.

"We need to lose weight," said Edna. "We need the boat to float higher, high enough to travel above the grass."

"I guess it's my turn to stay behind," said Merik. "I'll be fine. I can defend myself."

"I'm sorry Merik, it can't be you. We need you to help row the boat," said Edna.

Grumbuk swallowed loudly as everyone turned to look at him.

"Grumbuk can row."

"I'm sorry, Mr. Grumbuk. You will be safe here in the marshlands until we can rescue you."

Grumbuk's face fell. "How I know you keep word?"

Sheean patted his friend on the back. "Whatever happens I promise I'll come back for you."

* * *

With Grumbuk placed safely on a grassy mound at the edge of the marshland and the boat now floating just above the reeds, Edna, Sheean and Merik prepared to set off in search of the Wyvernhope hoard. Edna waved at Grumbuk, who turned his back, sulking.

"Where do we go from here?" said Sheean, picking up his oar.

"We continue," said Edna. "We have another five rivers to navigate. The torc could be anywhere."

"On three then?" said Sheean.

"Let's get out of here," said Merik, picking up his oar. "I can't bear to look at Grumbuk anymore. He's making me feel guilty." Merik positioned himself on the rowing bench. "THREE!"

Sheean and Merik pulled at their oars. The boat shuddered forward.

"Like you said before, this is going to be hard work," grumbled Merik.

"You sound just like Grumbuk," joked Sheean.

Merik gave him a sour look and carried on rowing.

"Keep going slaves," laughed Edna. "No time for arguments."

Hours went by. It was much cooler now that they had left the lava behind. Edna dipped her finger in the water of the marsh and sniffed at it. "This water is neutral and free from magic." Merik and Sheean continued to row, while she filled their water bottles and gave each of them a drink. As they neared the next river inlet, the boat started to rock increasingly violently from side to side. A whining noise filled the air.

"Good job I haven't eaten anything," said Merik.

"What is that noise?" asked Sheean, trying to row and cover his ears at the same time.

"I can't hear anything," Merik said, sticking a finger in his ear and wiggling it about.

"The river Cocytus," said Edna. "Sometimes called the Wailing river."

"I still can't hear anything."

"The wailing is very high pitched Merik," said Edna as she shielded her ears. "It's probably above your hearing range. You should consider yourself

159

lucky. Maybe you two could row a little faster and get us out of here."

Merik and Sheean pulled hard on the oars, and gradually the boat picked up speed as it made its way across the Wailing River's estuary. The sounds of wailing seemed to be coming from the water itself. Sheean was convinced he would go mad as every ripple screamed in his mind.

Eventually the boat passed through the estuary and back into the tranquil marshes.

"Thank the gods," said Sheean as silence once again washed over them.

Merik grinned at Sheean. "Don't know what all the fuss was about."

Sheean poked his tongue out at his friend.

"When you two have quite finished," said Edna, "we have a quest to complete."

"Yes, sorry. Right lad, stop messing with those pointed ears and put your back into some rowing," said Merik with a grin.

Before long, they found themselves at the mouth of another river. No matter how hard Sheean and Merik pulled on the oars they couldn't control the boat. It turned to face upriver and began to make headway against the river's flow.

"I think you can stop rowing now," said Edna. "The boat seems to be working on its own again."

Merik and Sheean joined Edna on the main deck. "Is this a good thing?" Merik asked Edna.

"I don't know. I'm hoping that we're being taken to the treasure."

Merik yawned.

"Good, I could do with some sleep," said Sheean.

"Try and fight it, Sheean," Edna warned. "I think this is the river Lethe. It's said the river will induce drowsiness, and anyone drinking the water will forget everything. If you come here after your death and drink from the water, you completely forget the life you just left."

"I could do with forgetting a few things," mumbled Merik.

"Be careful what you wish for. Anyone drinking the water will forget everything."

They continued onwards. The river spoke to them gently, lapping soothing lullabies against the boat. The waves hushed the world. Sheean felt all his cares and anxieties falling away.

Eventually he fell asleep, leaving the boat to weave its way along the narrows and into the main river. Occasionally he woke and looked around at the passing land, but noticing the others were asleep, he soon shut his eyes and succumbed to the voice of the river once more.

The boat jolted on a sand bar, jarring Sheean awake. He was lying on the bottom of the boat next to Merik. Edna lifted herself to a seated position, gathering her skirts around her. Sheean felt like he had been asleep for days. Merik grabbed him by the arm in a panic.

"I can't see anything," he hissed. "I think I've gone blind."

"Don't panic Merik," said Edna. "It's dark."

Merik rubbed his eyes. "I thought there was no day or night here."

"While you lot slept, the boat took us into a cave. Sheean do you think you could make a little light?"

"Yep," Sheean said as he altered his glamour. "What is this place?"

"I think we have arrived at the cave of the god Hypnos."

"Is this where the treasure is?"

"I don't know, but it would make a good hiding place. I think maybe we should explore a little."

Sheean noticed the boat was quite a long way from dry land. He unfolded his wings and lifted Edna in his arms, carrying her gently to the cave floor, then he went back for Merik.

"This place is creepy," said Sheean. "It reminds me of a dream I often used to have. There was always something evil hiding in the shadows."

The floor of the cave was slippery. Pointed lumps of rock hung down from the ceiling, dripping.

"I sense something here," said Edna.

"Ever since we found the boat I've had a feeling someone is watching us," said Merik.

"At least I can't smell lemons," said Edna. "I think we should try and find the back of the cave, away from the river. The further away we get from the water, the more alert we should feel."

Sheean stepped in front to lead the way, but Edna pushed him gently to one side.

"I'll go in front, young Fay. I'm a lot tougher than you think. You watch our backs."

Gradually, the noise of the river faded into the distance and they began to feel much more alert. Sheean drew Alex from his scabbard. "I'm convinced there is someone else in this cave."

"How close?" Merik asked, drawing his own sword.

"You're right," said Edna. "Not a good energy."

"I feel eyes watching us. Not a threat at the moment, just watching."

"Be alert lad," Alex warned. "People who hide in the shadows are usually up to no good."

With the aid of Sheean's Faerie light they made their way to the back of the cavern.

"Look," said Edna, "there is a patch of picture writing, just like before, and a doorway. Now be quiet both of you, let me read."

* * *

Jerremoy fluttered at the entrance to the Meeting Room in Taranor Castle, his wings flashing mulitple shades of blue in anxiety. Fable stood behind him, tossing his head and pawing the marble floor with his hooves. Guards held them back, looking questioningly at the Queen. She gestured for them to enter.

"Let them through."

They rushed to the table and bowed low.

"I humbly beg your pardon, Your Majesty," said Jerremoy. "I have terrible news."

The queen nodded her permission for him to speak.

"The future king and queen are missing."

Queen Rhyannon shot out of her seat. She hovered over the table, her wings pale.

"I believe they have returned to the Human realm," continued Jerremoy. "Fable says they have gone to rescue a friend!"

"Agaric," she said, lowering herself back down to her chair, "This is not foretold in the prophecy! You have my permission to open a portal and bring them back. Immediately!"

Chapter 6

As Bryony went to bed one cold night, she paused near the family tent and smiled at the guards. Their tiny eyes twinkled in the torchlight. A couple of them smiled back.

"When is Gobfest?" she asked.

A short, fat Goblin grinned. "Next moon. Is good time."

Bryony moved a little closer, ready to bolt at any second, but keen to appear to make friends with them. She warmed her hands at the perimeter torch.

"Do you drink ale and tell stories?"

"Yes."

"Lots," said another.

"That's great. Is there a story about Gobfest?"

The fat one pushed his friend forward. This one was wearing a yellow hat to keep his ears warm.

"This is Storyteller of our village. He tell you."

Bryony settled down on the sand. Although her heart was hammering in fear, she kept her face composed and her posture relaxed. She noticed a Goblin, the one that had let her out of the jail, walking closer to listen. The Goblin in the yellow hat stepped forward and cleared his throat.

"I use proper storytelling speak."

Bryony and the Goblins nodded. The story was long, involving Goblin heroes, dragons and monsters. The single moon was high in the sky by the time it was finished. Bryony stood up, gave a small curtsy and thanked them. They laughed and punched each other on the arm.

"Not like other Humans," said the Storyteller, "this one clever. She like Goblin stories. Got cultcha."

The following night, she talked with her guards again. They seemed happy with the diversion from their boring job. She asked about the pale Goblins who seemed to be in charge of the camp.

The fat Goblin lowered his voice to a whisper. "They is special. They is soldiers. They think they cleverer than us but they is not."

There was a rumble of assent from the gathered Goblins. Bryony glanced along the fence, careful not to make a show of her thoughts. She noticed the guards were no longer in a neat line. Many were coming closer, hopeful of another story and warmth from the torch.

"We is frighted of them," said the one in the yellow hat.

"Yes." An old Goblin with grey whiskers protruding from his nose stepped forward. "They beat us. For fun."

"How awful," said Bryony.

"Look." The old Goblin rolled up one trouser leg. There were scars, healed, but still ugly.

"What happened?"

"Big one bit me. 'Cos didn't want to work here. Have wife, have ten Grandgobs at home."

That night, Bryony wept. She wept for the Humans and Goblins caught up in this charade. She wept for the loss of her bright home and her glorious future. As her tears ebbed away, she felt a wave of rage flood through her being. In the dark, her green eyes flashed gold.

* * *

Edna examined the picture-writing. "Only two people can pass through. A third would most certainly die."

"I'll stay behind," said Merik. "I'm convinced someone's following us. I think it's best I guard your backs."

Edna nodded. "The writing says the horde is through this doorway. It talks of a fiery crevasse too wide to jump, but I think that shouldn't cause you any problems, Sheean."

Sheean grinned. "Shall we go then?" he asked as he took a step towards the door.

"Stop. We have to go through together. The doorway will only allow someone to pass once in both directions, and will not open twice in a row in the same direction."

"I hope you understood that, Sheean," laughed Merik.

Sheean chuckled. "I think so. How are we going to go through together? The doorway isn't big enough."

Edna beckoned Sheean over to a section of the wall. "Look, this picture shows two people standing back-to-back in the doorway. I think that means we go through sideways."

Sheean brushed the dust away from the picture and stared intently at it. "Has one of those people got wings?"

"It does look like they have wings doesn't it, but it could equally be just the texture of the rock."

Edna placed Sheean in the doorway, folded his wings out of the way and got herself into position. "On three."

Sheean wriggled against her back. "Three."

Trees appeared all around Sheean, closing in. He trembled and looked down at his feet. They were bare. His leather clothing was gone. Instead he wore petals and leaves. There was something wrong with his back. He reached round. His wings were tiny and weak. He drew Alex. Instead of a long, silver blade he found himself clutching a toy sword. He called out, "Is anyone there?"

His child-high voice echoed in the darkness. He ran through the forest. Soon he was sweating from every pore, his chest heaving. He paused to catch his breath. All around came the sound of breaking branches, as if something huge was crashing through the forest towards him.

"Who's there?" he whimpered. No one replied, but the sound of breaking branches got louder. Sheean started running again. The chase continued. He stopped and hid now and then, but each time the sounds of pursuit moved that little bit closer. Finally, he burst out of the darkness into a bright clearing. He stood in the centre, turning round and round, looking for his enemy, ready to run at any second. "What do you want? Stop chasing me, leave me alone!"

The sound of breaking branches ceased at the edge of the clearing. Sheean listened. There was nothing, not even the wind, just silence all around him. Faceless eyes began to appear around the tree line, as though afraid to enter the circle of light. Sheean crouched down, hugging his knees, trembling with shock and fear. The circle of trees closed in on him.

Resigned to his fate, he stared blankly ahead. The trees moved closer, almost near enough to reach out and touch him. He closed his eyes and tried to tell himself that he would wake up any minute. The trees continue to edge forward. A root touched his knee. Sheean stood up to get away from it. Three more trees moved closer, trapping him. Bit by bit they moved together, crushing his young body and wings. Spindly arms reached down from the branches, scratching at his head and shoulders. He struggled for breath.

Somewhere in the distance a baby cried. Sheean opened his eyes. The pressure eased a little, allowing him to take a ragged breath. A distant but familiar voice said, "Don't worry you're perfectly safe. Everything will be fine. We're going to be such good friends."

"Kanthy?... KANTHY! It is you, isn't it?"

"Such good friends!" The sound of evil laughter came to him through the trees.

Suddenly, a ray of blinding white light came down from above, making the trees shuffle back into the darkness of the surrounding forest, their branches withered as though touched by fire.

An old woman's voice called his name. "Sheean?"

"Who are you?"

"It's me Edna. Where are you?"

"Trapped in a forest."

"Use your magic, Sheean. It's not real."

"I can't, I'm only little."

"You're not a child, Sheean. Something is messing with your thoughts."

Sheean looked at his hands. The sword in his hand was real. He was tall and strong and bathed in turquoise light. He sheathed the sword and looked around. Something made him think of fire, and a ball of flame appeared in the palm of his hand. He panicked, trying to throw it away before it burned him. The ball of fire hit one of the trees, turning it to dust. He looked at his hands again. Two more balls of fire appeared. He threw them again. Another tree turned to dust. Sheean destroyed more and more of the evil forest. With each throw, his memory of where he was returned.

Without warning, Sheean's world tilted. He found himself standing next to Edna, returned to his normal adult form.

"Sorry," he said.

"What for?" asked Edna.

"For leaving you on your own for so long."

"You haven't. We came through the door together, only a second ago."

"I was in a forest. The trees were closing in on me."

"An old nightmare?"

"Yes. How did you know?"

"The door's magic is designed to use our insecurities to debilitate us. You were saved from being stuck in the forest forever when you realised it wasn't real."

"Did you know about all this dream stuff before we came through?"

"Yes, but I didn't want to frighten you."

"Did you have a nightmare?"

"I'd rather not talk about it."

Edna and Sheean stood at the edge of the crevasse, staring at the far side through the steam rising from deep underground. Sheean peered at an object on the edge of the crevasse.

"Is that a small chest over there?"

Edna smiled. "I think that's what we are after."

"Could it be that simple?"

169

"It has been rather easy getting here hasn't it?"

Sheean sat down for a moment. His legs were still a little shaky from the bad dream. "When I think about it. Finding the boat so quickly, then finding it could steer itself. Even the visions as I came through the door. It was almost as though someone reached into my head and picked a few memories to put together. And what about the smell of lemons?"

"The lemon smell is bad news I'm sure."

Sheean spread his wings and flew across the crevasse. It wasn't far, half a dozen beats of his wings and he was standing next to the chest.

Edna called out to him. "Don't try to open it, Sheean. I need to make certain it's safe before we look inside."

Sheean bent down and heaved the chest off the ground with its two side handles. "It's heavier than it looks," he shouted. As he flew over the edge, the weight of the chest seemed to increase suddenly, pulling him down into the gaping, jagged slit in the ground. He heard Edna scream his name.

It took all his strength to fly across, but he managed to get the chest onto the edge. Edna dashed forward to help. As soon as it was safe, Sheean joined Edna and together they pulled it away from the edge.

"It seemed to get heavier the further away from that side I went."

"Yes, I didn't expect that. We can't take it out of the cave, but that doesn't matter. All we need is the torc and a trinket for the ferry woman."

Edna knelt down next to the chest and examined its markings and locking mechanism.

* * *

"Can you open it?" Sheean asked.

"I think so. The box has picture symbols on it. If I can work out what they say, we should be able to open the chest."

Sheean watched Edna study the symbols closely. "The wavy line is a letter N and the picture of the reed next to it is a letter E."

"What about the bird?"

"That's a letter M, then another E, then a T, an R, another E and a B."

"NEMETREB," they both said together.

Nothing happened. Edna looked at the picture writing.

"Silly me," she said. "The reed has a double meaning. It can be a letter I."

"So," said Sheean, "it could be NIMETREB or NEMITREB or... err... NEMETRIB."

The lock clicked open.

"Wow, did I do that?"

"Yes, well done."

Edna lifted the lid, exposing hundreds of gold coins. "I hope the Torc is inside somewhere."

"Maybe it's buried under the coins."

"Don't touch them. This is Fay gold. Anyone touching it will be cursed."

"Why would any of my people curse gold? It could harm someone."

Edna smiled. "Not everyone is as nice as you, Sheean."

"Will it hurt me?"

"I don't know for certain."

Sheean dug his hand into the coins.

"That was very brave Sheean... or reckless."

"I can't see any other way of finding out what's under all the coins," he said as he rummaged about

171

inside the box. A second later he drew his hand out, gripping two identical torcs. "Is this what you're looking for?"

Edna squinted at the jewellery in Sheean's hand. "One of them will be the right one, but I don't know which. For now it would be safer if you carry both of them."

Sheean adjusted his glamour to provide him with a leather pouch. "Would this be Ok?"

"I think that would be perfect. Now, get a trinket for the ferry-woman and we can go and find Merik."

"OK. I'll get a few coins as well, they may come in handy."

Edna and Sheean stood back to back in the doorway. "On three again?" Sheean asked.

"Three."

Merik knelt on the floor, facing them, his face as pale as death. His sword lay on the floor and the air reeked with the scent of lemons. "I'm sorry, I didn't see him. He just appeared behind me."

"Who?" Sheean asked, looking around the cave.

A shadowy figure materialised behind Merik, holding a serrated knife to the soldier's neck.

"Give me the torc."

Edna stepped forward. "Grantra?"

"The very same. I am the rightful owner of the torc."

"If you are the rightful owner, how come it was in the cave," asked Sheean.

"The Wizard Wyvernhope stole the torc from me and hid it in the cave, protecting it with an ancient Faerie curse. He set up the obstacles of your journey here to dissuade treasure hunters from finding it."

"You helped us find it then?" Sheean asked.

"Yes. You would have wandered around for an eternity if I had not helped you. As you have already seen, I wish you no harm. All I want is the torc."

Edna glared at him. "If we don't give it to you...?"

"That would be foolish. I will kill to get it back."

"And if we do give it to you."

"I will allow you to leave here unharmed."

Edna looked at Sheean then back at Grantra. "That's not good enough."

Grantra moved the knife a little way away from Merik's throat, but not enough to give the soldier room to move. "You can keep the rest of the gold."

"I know you, Grantra," said Edna. "I know of the power you wield in this realm. If we willingly give you the torc, you must promise to take us all back to the Human realm. Including the creatures we have left behind."

"You ask too much, Witch. I will just kill you all and take it from you."

Sheean took one of the torcs out of his bag and turned to the doorway. "If you harm anyone I will throw it through the doorway, where you cannot get it."

"Sheean!" screamed Edna. "No!"

"STOP!" cried Grantra. "Very well. Give me the torc and I will take you all back to the Human realm."

Sheean stepped forward, his hand ready on Alex's hilt. "Release Merik."

Grantra released Merik, holding out his wispy hands for the torc. Once it was in his grasp he mumbled an incantation. The world span and everyone found themselves standing on the beach next to the river Styx.

173

"The ferry woman will take you across the river to the Human realm," said Grantra. "I will see you there in a while. I have great plans."

"You promised you would take us," said Edna. "Great Demons keep promises made."

"Do they? Oh, very well."

The ferry boat appeared on the horizon and made its way steadily towards them. When it arrived, the ferry woman moved to the front of the boat and smiled at Edna. "You have brought me the treasure?"

"I'm afraid I have failed you."

"No treasure, no journey back."

Grantra approached the ferry-woman. "Do you know who I am?"

"No."

Grantra closed his eyes and took a deep breath. His voice when it came was tight with control. "What will it take for us to use your boat?"

The woman paused, staring without fear at the vapourous figure before her. "Someone else must pilot the boat."

"That's easy. I can control boats," Grantra bragged. "Get off and let me take your place."

"That's very kind of you," said the ferry-woman, moving to get off the boat. Grantra climbed on board. As the ferry-woman eased her way past him, Grantra lost his balance. While flailing his arms to right himself, he dropped the torc in the water. The ferry-woman jumped clear of the boat, concealing a smile. Sheean rushed forward and grovelled in the river to find the artefact.

"Give it to me!" snapped Grantra.

"No," shouted Edna. "Give it to me, Sheean. This is it! This is our chance of escape!"

Sheean shook his head. "Great Faeries keep their promises. We said we'd give it to Grantra."

Sheean handed the torc to the Demon.

"SHEEAN! NO!"

"Well done, Faerie Prince. I never forget a good deed done. You will be rewarded."

As Grantra stood at the front of the boat examining the torc, trying to work out how to get it around his thick-set neck, Grumbuk and Krodbell appeared on the dusty sand. They gawped around them in surprise. Edna scowled at Sheean and took both Goblins by the arm, bustling them onto the boat.

Sheean took a gold ring from his pouch and handed it to the ferry-woman. She gave it back saying, "I don't need this. Thanks to you, I have my freedom. I will come with you over the river and go to my own realm."

Edna put a finger to her lips to silence the Goblins who had begun to squabble. Everyone sat at the back of the boat, as far away from Grantra as possible.

A blanket of fog enveloped the boat as it moved away from the shore. "Does Grantra know that he's freed the ferry-woman and doomed himself?"

"No. But we are in deep trouble. The torc will allow him to get free of the boat, enter the Human realm and kill us. You just made a huge mistake."

"No I haven't. The torc he's holding now is useless to him."

"What do you mean?"

"When he dropped it, I swapped it for the other one. He's going to be very annoyed when he finds out he can't get off the boat... ever!"

175

Everyone laughed. Edna gave Sheean's knee a little squeeze. Her eyes twinkled in the gloom. Grantra turned and scowled at them. "You had better not be laughing at me. I could turn you to dust with a look."

A few moments later the boat pulled alongside a pier. The fog here was so thick that the wooden structure seemed to be floating in space. Grantra turned to them. "Walk along the pier and you will find yourself in the Human realm."

Everyone climbed out of the boat and stood on the pier, hugging themselves against the cold, while Grantra turned the boat back towards his home.

"I'm popping back for a quick spot of vengeance," he shouted, "and then I'll come and terrorise the Human realm. What fun! You fools have no idea what you've done! There's no limit to my power now!"

As the boat disappeared back into the fog they heard him call out, "And say hello to Kanthy for me."

"How does he know Kanthy?" Sheean asked.

"It's best you don't know, Sheean," said Edna. They all waited while the ferry-woman walked away, gazing around her in joy, then Edna said, "Pass me the torc. I need to make certain we arrive back in the right place."

* * *

The day of Gobfest dawned. All day long, barrels of the finest Goblin ale had been rolling into the prison camp. In the dining tent, decorations made from green paper festooned a makeshift stage. A group of Goblins hammered pieces of wood together, making a scaffold to hang David.

176

Bryony looked away from the ghastly structure, standing tall and dark against the early evening sky. She entered the exercise yard, catching up with Malichai and Elliott, and falling in step beside them.

"Don't act like I'm saying anything extraordinary. Just look bored and tired."

The boys kept their heads down, walking round and round in the warm sand.

"We're breaking out of here tonight," whispered Bryony. "I'm picking those I trust and I'll come back for the rest when I've dealt with Grizelda."

Malichai looked at her in wonder, then back down at the ground.

"I've arranged with the others what to do," she said. "I'm going to get the guards drunk and allow some of the Humans - I mean people - to escape. Once you're clear of the camp, I'll signal to you with an orange scarf. When you see me do that, I want you to throw a stone at the corner torch by the family tent."

"When?" asked Elliott.

"During tonight's celebrations, before the... before we rescue David."

Again Malichai glanced up. Elliott touched his hand. They continued their march.

"How?" asked Malichai.

"Don't worry about that," said Bryony.

In truth, she had no idea herself how she was going to get David from jail. She had almost no magic and everyone here was weakened by hunger and forced labour. "When the torch falls, I'll make my escape and meet you in the bushes. Do you understand?"

The boys nodded.

"Supper time!" shouted a guard. "Then Gobfest entertainment! All must attend!"

* * *

Edna spread the open ends of the Wyvernhope Torc and placed it around her neck, thinking of her cottage on the outskirts of Gavelkind. The air shimmered. Her stomach lurched as her cottage materialised around her. To her relief, her team was still with her, looking shaken and a little nauseous, but unharmed.

She gasped when she saw her front door lying smashed across the kitchen. The window was open and there was no sign of Azabyandee. She looked at the setting sun through the window. Maltbrook Lane had been decorated with green bunting. Goblins lay around in various stages of drunkenness shouting, "Gobfest Cheer," to passers-by.

"It looks as though these revellers have tried to see what's in my kitchen. Merik, would you mind helping me to clear up?"

"Of course," said Merik. He lifted the door and propped it against the frame, while Sheean swept the splinters into a dust-pan.

"That's better," said Edna. "Make yourself at home gentlemen. I'd like to celebrate our success with a pot of herbal tea and some cake. You two Goblins won't have time to celebrate Gobfest as you'd like, but I guarantee this will be the best Gobfest you've ever had. Come on, don't just stand around like a bunch of fools, sit down at the table." She looked around the kitchen. "Has anyone seen my husband?"

The others seated themselves.

"What he look like?" asked Krodbell. He was sitting on a chair and swinging his warty little legs. His pointed boots were inches from the flagstone floor.

"He's in the form of nine cream cats right now." She peered into the living room. "Dee? Azabyandee, where are you?"

Edna came back into the kitchen. "He must be out mousing. I expect he's gone rather hungry while I've been away." She clicked her fingers at the fireplace. Grumbuk and Krodbell gasped as the neatly piled wood in the hearth burst into flames. She hung the kettle on a hook to boil and gathered a spotty teapot and cups from the cupboard, placing them on the table. Next, she opened a cupboard and brought out a cloth-covered bundle. She unwrapped this to reveal a fruitcake.

"Help yourselves."

Grumbuk leaned forward. "Is all mine?"

"No, Mr. Grumbuk, it's to share. Would you be kind enough to cut the cake, Merik, while I pour the tea?"

Grumbuk sat back, disappointed. "Should be mine. Was left with nasty snakes on ownio."

Sheean looked around. "How come we arrived back in your kitchen Edna? Surely there isn't a portal to the Demon realm here."

"I'm sorry we left you alone, Mr. Grumbuk. As to how we got home, I used the Torc to bring us here. If I hadn't used it we would have ended up somewhere in the mountains, and we simply don't have time for that sort of journey."

"Coulda died," Grumbuk whimpered, looking longingly at the cake.

"Mr. Grumbuk, I'm sorry you had to deal with snakes. I was unaware there were any. Have an extra piece of cake."

Krodbell wriggled, stuffing his cake deep into his mouth. "Me left on ownio too."

"Have an extra slice too, dear Goblin friend."

As they sat around the table stuffing cake into their mouths and sipping herbal tea, Edna smiled at Grumbuk. "Tell me, Mr. Grumbuk, how did you become a hero of legend?"

Grumbuk wiped his mouth on his sleeve and puffed up his chest. "Many reasons: rescue Fayri, kill Ogman, kill beast. Was in prophecy."

Edna sat forward. "You killed Ogman?"

"Grumbuk accidentally fell down an air-shaft," said Sheean, "and landed on Ogman's crown, smashing the crystal that had kept him alive over the centuries."

"Ah," said Edna, hiding a small smile.

"Still killed him," muttered Grumbuk.

"And what were you doing at that moment, Sheean?"

"I was fighting Ogman hand-to-hand. In the struggle, his crown fell off. Grumbuk saved my life."

"I see. So, Mr. Grumbuk, you truly are a hero of legend."

"Me have extra slice again?"

Edna smiled. "I think you've had enough, my friend." She looked around at her companions. These people had helped her in ways they could not imagine. She felt choked with emotion. Now she was going to have to ask them to face a battle with an uncertain outcome. Lives could be lost. The future King of Taranor was at risk. "I want to thank you all for helping me find the Wyvernhope Torc."

"What is the Torc?" asked Sheean.

Edna took a deep breath. "Wyvernhope was the most powerful Wizard of his time. Before he died, he managed to transfer his power to this gold and silver necklace." She touched the torc around her throat, feeling its power thrum through her fingers. "The torc is very valuable, and in the wrong hands very dangerous. Anyone wearing it can draw on its power."

"What are your plans for it?" asked Merik.

"To rescue Azabyandee, my husband, to free the Human realm from Grizelda's tyranny and to put a final end to the damage done by that loathsome crone during the Wizard Wars."

Merik nodded. "Sounds like a worthy cause."

Krodbell scratched his head. "Who Grizelda?"

"Evil Witch," said Grumbuk. "Make Humans slaves."

"That bad thing?"

"Goblins next," growled Grumbuk.

Krodbell nodded. "Sound good cause then."

Edna rose from the table and looked out of the window. "Sheean, have you seen Bryony? Is she safely in Taranor. It's just we could do with her assistance."

Sheean played with some crumbs of cake on the table. "She's in trouble. That's why I came here. She's in the prison camp. I have to get her out."

"Oh dear. We must rescue her. There's so much to do. First I have to find Azabyandee. Sheean, I'd like you to go with Merik to the castle and find out what you can. Then, when we have suitable collective power, we can kill Grizelda, close the portals to the Demon realm forever and rescue Bryony."

"That won't be easy," said Merik. "The castle's very well guarded."

"I know. I want you to go and find out its weak spots. No matter who... or what... guards that dreadful queen, she will have left a weakness in her protection somewhere."

"As you wish, Edna," said Merik. "Sheean and I will go on ahead and make certain the Human guards understand the situation. They will support us."

They heard the sound of marching. A few minutes later, a platoon of Goblin soldiers made their way past the window, heading towards Cucapha Castle.

"I got idea," whispered Grumbuk. "Me an Krodbell join army."

Sheean looked irritated. "How would that help?"

"Cause confusion. Get info. Get help."

"Why you include me?" muttered Krodbell.

"You want be hero of legend?"

"No."

"You will. You come with Grumbuk."

Sheean reached into his bag and fished out a few coins. "Here, Grumbuk, put these in your money pouch. Don't touch the money, it's cursed."

"Thank you, Mr. Grumbuk," said Edna. "Gather what information you can. We will meet at the Maltbrook Arms, the inn just outside the castle, at midnight."

* * *

Bryony queued for her supper in the dining tent, listening to people discussing David's impending execution. As she got closer to the front of the line, she saw that they were being given rice and greens as usual, but tonight they were also given a small lump of meat. She arrived at the head of the queue and held out her bowl.

"No meat thank you," she said in her politest tones.

"Gobfest. Must have fried Bugrat. Eat!"

The Cook slapped a lump of dead flesh onto her rice. Swallowing hard, Bryony turned and made her way towards Ruth. She whispered her escape plans.

Ruth nodded. "We'll be ready."

Bryony then moved to the back of the dining tent, where she could see Kerry, Malichai and Elliott, already eating. She sat down and spooned her meat into their bowls, leaving a little rice at the bottom for herself. She noticed Kerry looked pale. She was rubbing her head where the Goblins had hit her.

"Kerry, are you alright?"

Kerry looked at her brightly. "Yes, she's a lovely mouse."

Elliott rolled his eyes and tossed his fringe out of his eyes. "She's been talking nonsense all day. I think it must be the bump on her head. It's still quite swollen."

"Oh dear, I thought I'd made her better. Kerry?"

Kerry smiled vacantly at Bryony.

"Kerry, we're escaping tonight. Keep close to the boys. Ruth will look after you."

Kerry nodded. "OK. I think it's in the cupboard."

Elliott took his mother's hand and squeezed it. He looked at Bryony. "Can we take Little Eric with us?"

"He isn't feeling well," added Malichai. "He's not eating his food. Can we have it?"

Bryony looked at the skinny boy sitting nearby on the sand. His food was untouched. He looked up at Bryony with his pale green eyes and gave a brave

183

smile. "I don't feel..." His attempt at speech failed as a paroxysm of coughing doubled him up. She touched his arm gently, sending as much healing to him as she could risk, without showing her Fay light.

"Be ready," she whispered to Malichai and Elliott. "Don't go to the main tent tonight, stay under your blankets in the sleeping area. The guards will think you're just another pair of sick children."

As people filed into the tent for the first part of the Gobfest entertainment, Bryony slipped out and approached the guards. The light of the guttering perimeter torch touched their green faces with a sickly orange tinge. They greeted her warmly.

"Gobfest Cheer!" they shouted.

"Um, yes, Gobfest cheer to you," she replied. Her mouth felt dry.

The Goblins laughed and slapped each other on the back.

"She almost Gob-kin," the fat one chuckled.

Bryony smiled her most disarming smile. "It's not fair is it?"

"Wot?" said the old one with grey whiskers.

"All the other Goblins are drinking ale, but you can't because you're on duty."

Two or three guards muttered agreement.

"Did anyone say you couldn't drink?" asked Bryony.

There was a muttering of voices and a general nodding of heads.

"Are you sure?" she asked sweetly.

The Goblin guards looked confused.

"Would you like me to get you some?"

A chorus of, "Not fair," and, "Gobfest ale!" came from the guards. Bryony smiled.

Holding a large, earthenware jug she found outside the tent, she approached the bar. The stink of Goblin ale made her feel sick. She held out her jug. "The guards need more ale."

"Gobfest Cheer!" said the little Goblin bartender. His skinny green arms trembled with the weight of the jug as he filled it to the brim.

After three more visits to the bar, the Goblins guarding the corner near the tents were hopelessly drunk. Many lay sprawled on the ground, while others clustered round the Goblin with the yellow hat as he launched into another epic tale.

Bryony laughed loudly as she filled their cups. She gave the signal to Malichai and Elliott; a celebratory high pitched whoop. "OK!" she shouted out, laughing, "OK! Steady on, there's plenty for everyone!"

From the corner of her eye she saw Ruth and Kerry, followed by a string of children, crawling out of the family tent, under the ropes and off into the bushes away from the prison camp.

"More ale!" shouted Bryony.

"More ale!" came the reply as another Goblin sank down unconscious onto the sand. For a split second Bryony felt a flash of guilt at the thought of the beating these poor guards would get when the children were found missing.

With a deep breath, she made as if to go to the bar, but doubled back instead to hide at the edge of the family tent. She waved an orange scarf at the bushes on the far side of the fence.

At her signal, a stone flew through the air, striking the torch from its holder. Sparks scattered in the sand. Giggling, the Goblins patted out the flames with their leather boots.

"Why that torch fell?"

"Dunno."

While they were busy putting out the flames, Bryony crawled from the tent, keeping flat to the ground. She glanced to her left where the guards, jealous of their colleagues, were squabbling over a jug of ale. She felt the magic dampening spell that surrounded the camp fall away as she moved further into the desert.

When she reached the safety of the bushes she crouched down. There, well hidden, were twelve children in all, including Little Eric.

"Well done," she whispered. "Now, I'm going to rescue David. Elliott and Malichai, can you help me? I'll meet the rest of you under that big tree."

Ruth nodded and set off with the others towards a tall solitary pine tree in the foothills.

Bryony, Malichai and Elliott made their way, keeping hidden among the bushes and cacti, to the fence nearest the jail. Bryony felt Faerie power flowing almost freely through her veins once more. The remaining pain in her right arm reminded her she was not yet at full strength.

"I need to test my power," she whispered.

The boys looked at her strangely. Malichai kept glancing back to where he had last seen his mother. Bryony drew energy from the moon and stars, the sand and earth and the distant ocean. "Sorry, I've no time to explain." She looked at Elliott. "Freeze."

Elliott stood as still as a statue. Malichai almost squeaked in fright, covering his mouth with his hand to stop any sound.

"He's fine. I just needed to test my magic. Just touch him gently, he'll wake up."

Malichai reached out, brushing Elliott's hand. Elliot blinked and smiled. "Well, what are you sorry about?"

Malichai giggled. "She froze you."

"No she didn't."

"Keep your voices down and stop arguing. I'm going to freeze those two guards down there. I want you to run down, open the door and bring David up here. Then we can join the others. I can't go down there myself because my magic won't work near the fence."

The boys stared at her.

"Go on."

"But... that was magic."

"I know."

"What else can you do?"

"Lots, now get down there before I turn you both into toads."

She watched the two boys scuttle towards the fence. Despite the pain in her right shoulder, she used both arms, pointing her fingers at the guards, giving the command silently, yet shouting it in her mind. "*Freeze!*"

The Goblins sat on their chairs as still as stone. The boys looked back. She gave them a signal to carry on. It was only when they were at the door of the jail that she realised her mistake. The sound of the rusty bolt being moved aside disturbed the guards. She could see them looking around in a daze. Desperate to save her friends, she screamed the command in her mind, "*FREEZE!*" and flung both arms forwards. Never before had she used such force.

Icicles hurtled from the fingers of her left hand towards the guards. Like birds of ice, they flew, stabbing deep into the backs of the waking Goblins. Malichai and Elliott hesitated for a second, transfixed in shock and horror.

A banging sound from inside the jail jolted them into action. Elliott threw the door open and David rushed out. Together, they made their way under the ropes and up the hill to Bryony.

She placed her finger to her lips and led them to the big tree where the others were waiting. Although Bryony felt sick at the thought of killing two innocent guards, she was quietly thrilled at her new discovery.

* * *

It took Merik and Sheean two hours to walk fast to the Castle at Cucapha. They huddled in the shadows of the castle walls, watching Kendro single-handedly push a blackened, smouldering wagon through the courtyard and out through the gates. Panting, Kendro closed the fortified doors and staggered to the gatehouse. Leaning against the wall for support, he slid down a little to pick up an earthenware jug placed there in readiness. He began to take great gulps of ale from its frothy depths.

Merik strode forward.

"Stand to attention, soldier!" he barked. "You know better than to slouch around when an officer is present. You're drunk!"

Kendro dropped his jug of ale, spilling its contents. He jumped to attention, saluted, and then broke into a grin as he saw Merik.

"About bleeding time you came back, Sir."

Sheean had been using his glamour to blend in with his surroundings. He adjusted it back to his usual Human form and stepped out of the shadows.

"By the gods, Sean, isn't it?" said Kendro. "Does the old witch know you're back? 'Course she doesn't. Quick lad, get inside the gatehouse before anyone sees you."

Looking around nervously, Kendro ushered Sheean and Merik into the gatehouse.

"If Grizelda finds out you're back," he continued, "she'll have your guts for dinner, for real."

"It's good to be home," said Merik, slumping into his old chair by the table. "How are things?"

Kendro pulled out a chair for Sheean. "Where have you been? Things are going from bad to worse around here. Most of the Human guards have left or been arrested. There's Goblins everywhere you look, and Grizelda's moved out of the royal apartments and into the North West tower."

Merik laughed. "How does she get to the top of the tower? It must take her weeks to climb the steps."

"There aren't no steps, she had them all removed."

"How does she get up the tower then?" Sheean asked.

"She's got this pet blacksmith fellow, calls himself an engineer. He made her a winch system or something, says it's called a lift. She stands in this giant bucket and pulls a lever and it takes her up and down the tower, without no walking. The engineer fellow says there's no magic, says it uses science. Whatever that is."

"Is she on her own when she's in the tower?" Sheean asked.

"Yes. Although she has guards on the battlements. Now it's Gobfest she's let the Gobs off for the night and got Demons up there."

Merik looked at Sheean. "This is going to be easier than Edna thinks. We could have this all sorted before she even gets here."

"I don't know what you're planning," said Kendro, "but easy isn't a word I'd use to describe a Dragon and a couple of large hell creatures."

Sheean opened his mouth in amazement. Merik didn't seem to be listening. "Edna is coming here at midnight," he said, "to kill Grizelda."

"Edna? You mean Edna the old woman who delivers the cakes and makes herbal remedies?"

Sheean smiled. "The same."

Kendro stared in amazement at his superior officer. "With all due respect Sir, is this a good plan?"

"Edna is very much more powerful than you know," said Merik. "She and her husband are Wizards or something."

"I never knew she was married, and a Wizard you say?"

"Yes, very powerful."

"If they're so powerful, why haven't they sorted Grizelda out before now?"

"It's a long story, so just take my word for it. I need you to make certain no Humans are around when she arrives. It would also be good if you could empty the dungeons. I want to avoid Human casualties."

"Yes Sir. All of the Human guards will have to go by midnight anyway, as I'm expecting a platoon of Goblins to arrive any minute."

"We passed some of those earlier on. What are they coming here for?" asked Merik.

"The old witch doesn't trust Humans no more. She's arranged to have all Human guards replaced by Goblins by tomorrow morning. That's why it won't be a problem making certain there are no people left here after midnight. Most of them were going anyway."

* * *

Grumbuk and Krodbell just managed to tag onto the stragglers at the end of the column. They followed at a shambling pace to Cucapha castle. The soldiers marched out of step, kicking and tripping over each other's feet as they made their way along Maltbrook Lane. Someone shouted something unintelligible at the front, causing a wave of mumbling to ripple down the column. As word reached the back, the pace picked up to a trot.

A few minutes later, the conscripts marched off the road and into the yard of an inn.

"See?" said Grumbuk. "We at Pig and Thistle."

"So. How this delay army?"

"Pig and Thistle roudy place. Watch, learn." Grumbuk strode through the middle of the milling soldiers in the inn courtyard. "Gobfest Cheer! Drinks on me," he shouted. "I Grumbuk, hero of legend."

All the Goblins cheered, hats were thrown and calls of "Gobfest Cheer!" echoed down the lane. The yard was teeming with other conscripts from the southern territories, many of whom joined in the cheering. Grumbuk pushed his way through the crowded door and into the bar, fighting his way to the front.

"We hear of you," said one of their commanders as he moved out of Grumbuk's way. "You kill monster. Yes?"

"That me, Grumbuk, hero of legend, your men want drinks? I buy."

The commander looked thoughtful for a second. "Have orders from Queen Grizelda. Only stop for one."

Grumbuk got the bartender's attention. "Ale all round, as much as wanting."

The bartender scowled at Grumbuk. "You got lots money?"

Grumbuk unfastened a leather pouch from his belt and placed it on the bar. "See for self."

The bartender untied the pouch and tipped its contents onto the bar. Six shiny gold coins glistened in the candlelight.

"That enough?" Grumbuk asked.

"It'll do." Greedily the bartender scooped up the Faerie gold and put it in his pocket.

Before long, the two groups of Goblins were singing songs and praising Grumbuk for his bravery and his generosity. One stout Goblin with brown leathery skin leapt to the table and began to sing "Hero of legend, Grumbuk is. Monster killer, Grumbuk is. He saved the realms from Ogman's wrath. And stopped a Goblin bloodybath. He buys us ale, we sing his song. Grumbuk's stories can't be wrong."

"You famous," said Krodbell, with a tinge of hero worship in his voice.

"Told you was."

Round followed round. They drank their ale and listened to the soldiers sing Grumbuk's praises for the twentieth time. Grumbuk's smile refused to fade.

"Getting bit boring now," muttered Krodbell as he watched a happy group of Goblins drown one of their comrades in the horse trough. "I still not see how this help."

"Watch."

Krodbell watched as Grumbuk walked over to one of the commanders and engaged him in conversation. A minute later, Grumbuk returned.

"What you say to him?" asked Krodbell.

"You see. Come, best get out way." Grumbuk picked up a full jug of ale and headed for the gate. The two friends sat on a low wall, swinging their legs as they drank their ale and watched.

"Watch commander."

The commander looked around with a grim face. Spotting his sergeants, he called them over. After a brief conversation the sergeants became agitated. They stamped their feet in frustration and grumbled to each other. The soldiers started pointing and scowling at the other group, who continued to drink and dance.

Eventually, one of the sergeants walked over to one of his counterparts in the other group, picked up his jug of ale and tipped it over his head. For a second, all anyone could hear was the wind in the trees. The tension broke, and with the ferocity of a herd of Demons let loose, the Goblins flew at each other's throats. Windows were smashed, ale was spilled, and tables were turned over.

The bartender rushed out of the inn, trying to get them to stop, promising them another round of ale if they didn't break anything else. No one listened. The fighting soon spread to the inn itself.

Grumbuk and Krodbell watched the confusion of flying fists and kicking feet with glee.

"What you say to make fight?"

"Say the others say they useless sod diggers."

The yard and doorway became littered with Goblins, many hopelessly drunk, others knocked out, some dead. A flicker of orange rose from the roof of the inn, spreading in hungry flames across the thatch. Three Goblins jumped, screaming from an upstairs window and landed on the bartender, squashing him flat.

A few moments later, the inn was a smouldering ruin, surrounded by groaning Goblins.

"Job done. Better go."

Calmly, Grumbuk and Krodbell finished their drinks and set off towards the Maltbrook Arms.

"Fayri gold, bad luck," chuckled Krodbell.

* * *

Finally alone, Edna went out into her garden to look for Azabyandee. In the distance, a few Gobfest fireworks were lighting up the darkening sky.

"Azabyandee! I'm home! Come in now, the fireworks are starting."

An eagle called in the sky high above. She looked up. It flew over the cottage, dipping its wings.

"Hello, Aram old friend," shouted Edna. "Have you seen my husband?"

Before the eagle could reply, nine cream cats streamed through the garden hedge and ran to her. The eagle landed in a nearby tree, bobbing up and down with excitement. Edna scooped one cat in each arm while the others climbed her skirts and rubbed round her legs. She found herself laughing and crying with relief at the same time.

"Oh, my love!" purred the cats' minds in unison. *"I'm so glad to see you."*

"Me too, my sweetheart, me too."

Covered in cats and still laughing, she bustled into the cottage and sat on the floor by the hearth, allowing all the cats to climb over her equally.

After a while her hips ached, so she sat on the chair and cuddled as many as she could at once. It was then that she noticed the kitten. It was sitting, with its feet tucked neatly together, by the door.

"Come in, come in. Timothy isn't it? I'm glad you're alright."

Timothy bounced in, landing in the middle of the pile of cream cats. *"Me happy too."*

"I'm glad. Well done Dee, she looks very healthy."

"She is naughty and undisciplined. I doubt she will be able to manage even the most basic of the Wizard Arts."

Edna let her head relax onto the back of the chair, her hands stroking each cat as it came past. She felt tired. "I don't expect anything of Timmy other than to be a wonderful companion. Mind you she could surprise us. Anyway, what am I thinking? I've got a present for you."

All nine cream cats lined up in a perfect diamond formation on the floor. Timothy fell off the chair, chased her own shadow for a second and then ran up Edna's skirts and onto her shoulder.

"Back in a second," said Edna, "close your eyes."

Edna walked back into the room with Timothy still perched on her shoulder like a ginger parrot.

"I have the Wyvernhope Torc."

"Well done, my beautiful beloved," purred all the minds of Azabyandee.

Edna placed it round the neck of the cat at the front of the diamond. "Now you can be free."

The gold and silver necklace shrank just enough to create a perfect fit. The room filled with light and a vibrant purring.

A few seconds later, the purring ceased and where there had been nine cats there stood a man. He was tall and slim, wearing a full-length cream robe with matching cloak fastened at his neck by an ornate golden brooch. Around his neck was the gold and silver torc.

His hair hung long and cream across his shoulders and down his back. In his handsome dark face his brilliant blue eyes shone with love and new-found freedom. He stepped forward to embrace his wife.

"It is time you revealed yourself too," he said, taking off the torc and placing it gently round Edna's neck. Timothy patted at the necklace as it changed size to fit Edna. There was a flash of light and Edna stood, taller and younger, dressed in the same cream robes. Her grey hair hung loose and long down her back. All the stress of her time in the Demon realm fell away. She smiled. Timothy seemed to glow, and her fur stood on end.

All around them, Wizard Magic crackled; an ancient, powerful magic, held in check, waiting to be released. Silently, they held each other, heart pressed to heart.

After a timeless moment of love, they separated.

"We have a job to do," said Edna. "I said I'd meet the others at the Maltbrook Arms at midnight."

"Let's go," said Azabyandee. "Once we're done here we can go home. At last."

Chapter 7

Once they were safely back under the big tree, Bryony relaxed.

David and Luci hugged each other silently, shedding tears of joy, while Kerry embraced her two boys.

"I don't know how you did that Bryony," said Ruth, "but well done."

"She did it by magic!" shouted Malichai. "You should have seen it!"

"Ssssshhhh!" hissed Bryony, her eyes darting back to the camp. "If they hear us, they'll have fourteen executions to celebrate at Gobfest tonight."

"Ice arrows! Peeow! Peeow!" laughed Malichai, mimicking Bryony's arrows of ice.

"We need to get out of danger," said Bryony as she moved away from the tree. "I'll explain once we're safe."

Luci stepped forward. "Thank you for rescuing Uncle David. I don't mind if you are a witch, you saved his life."

Bryony shot her a quick smile and began marching up the hill.

"I know the paths around here," said David. "There is a track running parallel to the main road. It leads to a cave just before the pass. We can shelter there."

The mouth of the cave was much smaller than Bryony expected; it was barely tall enough for an adult to walk through, and the smell of Bear was almost overpowering. David went to go in first, but Bryony put her hand on his arm.

"I think there's a bear inside," she said.

David hesitated. "Well, maybe we should go on up to the pass. We can't stop here."

Bryony looked at the children. "But we might get stopped at the pass and taken back to camp!"

They were all exhausted by the late hour and the climb from the prison camp. Kerry had carried Little Eric on her back the whole way and looked ready to collapse. David scratched his head. The older children shivered in the cold as they waited for a decision from the adults.

"Let me see what I can do," said Bryony. "Please keep an eye on the track. Whistle like a kingfisher if you see anyone."

"A kingfisher?" said David.

Bryony sighed. "A bird. Any bird. Just make a bird noise if you see anyone."

She walked into the cave, her mind projecting love and peace into the darkness. Using her Faerie sight, she saw a bear right at the back of the cave. It watched her intently.

"Hello Mr. Bear. I'm so sorry to intrude, but I have a problem."

"You do," said the bear in a low rumbling growl. "Yes. You have a big, brown, hairy problem."

"I'm Princess Bryony of Taranor and I need to shelter some Humans here until dawn."

"Your problem, little morsel, is that I'm going to eat you and then the rest of your friends."

"No, really, I'm Fay. You can't eat me, it's against the rules."

The Bear growled and shifted towards her. It placed a massive clawed paw on the dust between them. "Just watch me."

Bryony released her glamour a fraction, just enough to reveal her wings and her pointed teeth. "I forbid you to eat anyone!"

The bear stopped. Bryony's sharp ears caught a murmur of Human voices outside the cave.

"I just hope no Goblins saw my light just then," she said, shifting back to dull, Human form.

The Bear bowed low. "I apologise, Princess Bryony of Taranor. I am Brunhilde. Please bring the food - sorry - I mean the people inside. I will shelter them."

"Thank you, noble Brunhilde. I will see to it that you are rewarded."

It was dark and warm in the cave and the scent of bear was soporific. All Bryony wanted was to close her eyes and sleep for a year, but she fought the temptation. She was the leader. For a fleeting heartbeat she thought of her future as Faerie Queen. Maybe now she could find Edna, rescue her, and get home. She did a quick calculation. She hadn't been in the Human realm long. There was still plenty of time to get home before the banquet at Taranor Castle.

Ruth's voice jolted her back to reality.

"Who's on watch?"

"Luci and David," said Bryony.

Ruth patted the warm, packed earth floor near her. "Good. Come on little ones, snuggle up."

"The bear is called Brunhilde," said Bryony. "She's perfectly safe." *"Aren't you,"* she added into Brunhilda's mind.

"Perfectly safe. Sorry I called them food earlier, I was joking. Mind you that little one looks tasty, just a snack." Bryony heard mind-laughter, as thick and warm as treacle on nut porridge.

The children lay down at the back of the cave, hidden from view by the bear.

"Where's the tablecloth?" asked Kerry.

Soon, many of the younger children were asleep. The adults huddled together, listening to the hoots of owls in distant trees and watching bats flit across the entrance to the cave.

Bryony had no idea how much the Humans could see in the darkness. Ruth and Kerry looked exhausted. Like everyone else, they had lost weight and their faces were pale. Some of the children whimpered in their sleep. Little Eric coughed.

"Will Luci and David be all right out there?" asked Ruth.

Bryony nodded. "I've asked them to keep watch and tell me if they see or hear anything. As soon as I know that the bear has accepted the children, I'll go out and take a turn at keeping watch."

Ruth tipped her head on one side. "Who are you?"

"I'm Bryony."

"That's not what I mean. How did you manage to rescue David? There's something really odd about you."

"No. I'm just Bryony."

"Malichai said you fired arrows at the guards, yet you don't have a bow."

Bryony felt another wave of exhaustion, deeper than the last. Her very bones ached with the continual tension of the past few hours. "I want to tell you everything Ruth, but..."

"Don't you trust me?"

"No, it's not that."

They heard a stone rattle down the slope near the entrance to the cave. Luci ran inside, looking terrified. "Goblins!" she hissed. "Three! Coming up the hill, they're... they're crawling! Like rats!"

Bryony pushed Luci into the cave, slipped outside and hid behind a bush. She saw David further up, watching the track. He pointed. A little way downhill, Bryony saw three small Goblins crawling on their hands and knees, sniffing along the ground. One was in the centre, following the track, while the others flanked either side, shoving their noses into the bushes. They moved slowly, purposefully, following the Human scent towards the cave. Bryony could hear them sniffing. She stepped out onto the track.

"Freeze!"

The Goblins stopped moving. She glanced back at David, who made a cut-throat gesture with his finger. Bryony moved closer to the Goblins. They were barely more than children; their skin was smooth and light green and their noses were still rounded. She went to each in turn, taking their weapons from them with the skill of a backstreet pickpocket. She was careful not to touch the iron on them. Next, she whispered, "Goblins be Rabbits."

Immediately, three faintly green rabbits hopped along the track, nibbling the grass under the trees. David joined her at the entrance to the cave, his mouth hanging open. Ruth joined them, followed by the older children.

"Bryony, it's time to explain," said Ruth.

Bryony handed out the Goblin blades, one to David and one to Ruth. She looked across at Kerry and hesitated. Kerry seemed blissfully unaware of any danger as she smiled down at Little Eric, soothing his hair and singing quietly.

Malichai jumped up and down, his voice as unrestrained as steam from a boiling kettle. "Me me me! I need the dagger!"

Elliott turned on him. "You do not. You'd only hurt yourself with it."

Luci laughed as the boys argued. There was a steady glint in her eye that Bryony liked. She had taken first watch without complaint. Bryony handed the blade to her.

"That's not fair!" shouted Malichai, stomping back towards the rear of the cave.

"Every weapon," said Bryony, "whether it is a blade, axe or spell, can be used against the wielder. To carry a weapon you must have the mind and soul of a warrior."

Bryony hoped she didn't sound too pompous. She was simply repeating what her mother told her when she got her first dagger. "I was about eight mortal years old when I got my first blade. I had to learn to use it safely. Luci got the dagger because she remained calm."

Ruth looked horrified. "Who gave you a dagger at eight years old?"

Bryony's fingers touched her belt where her silver dagger should have been. She regretted not picking it up when she left Taranor in such a hurry. "My mother."

"Your mother gave you a dagger?" hissed Ruth. "What kind of a mother was she? That's outrageous!"

Bryony's eyes flashed gold. "My mother was the most beautiful, the most powerful..."

David stepped forward and touched her arm. "Ruth doesn't mean to offend you, Bryony. It's just that things are a little weird right now. We're all here in a cave with a bear that hasn't eaten us. I saw you

202

turn three Goblins into rabbits with a word. Your eyes flash gold when you're angry. If you could just explain..."

Bryony took a deep breath, calming her eyes back to green. "I'll explain in a moment. First we need someone to keep watch. Those little Goblins were probably scouts."

David sat on a rock at the entrance, looking down the track towards the prison camp far below. Bryony took the others deeper into the cave.

"I'm Bryony, Princess to the throne of Taranor. I'm due to be crowned Faerie Queen tomorrow night. I came here to rescue my friend Edna, but I got captured by the Goblins."

There was a silence for a moment, disturbed only by forest sounds and the gentle snoring of Brunhilde. Little Eric coughed.

David darted back inside the cave. "They're coming! The big ones, with armbands. They've got weapons and they look determined."

"Quick everyone," said Bryony, "get to the back of the cave. Give Brunhilde a nudge to wake her and get behind her"

David hesitated.

"Go!" hissed Bryony. "I can fight them. I don't need your help."

By the time the marching of feet could be heard, all the Humans were hidden. Bryony shrank to the size of a bird and sat on the rock at the entrance to the cave. There were ten soldiers in all, each bristling with savage looking axes and swords. They marched in a manner unlike any Goblins Bryony had ever seen. These were disciplined warriors.

They marched past the cave, moving away, up the hill, with just the steady tread of feet and creaking of leather armour giving them away. Bryony breathed a silent sigh of relief.

Little Eric coughed.

The army stopped.

"What was that?" said a huge Goblin at the back of the group. He held a throwing axe loosely in his hands as he approached the cave entrance. Another drew a mace and twirled it round and round. Bryony flew into the cave, grew to the size of a Human child and walked out into the night, rubbing her eyes as if sleepy. She gave a little cough.

"There! It's a kid!" shouted the one with the axe.

"Come here little kid," said the mace wielder. It held the chain in one hand, letting the heavy iron ball swing. It stretched out its other hand. "We won't hurt you... much."

When they were close enough, Bryony erupted, bursting into full Faerie form, her wings blazing red.

"FREEZE!"

Nine of the Goblins stood still. One remaining Goblin, a female, was unaffected by the spell. Without hesitation, she moved forward, tapping each soldier as she passed, waking them.

"You will have to do better than that, Faerie girl," she cackled. Her thin black lips drew back into a snarl as she sent a bolt of lightning from her palm towards Bryony. The light slammed into the rock, filling the air with the smell of sulphur. All the Goblins were now awake.

"Dead or alive," sneered the magic user, "we don't mind."

Bryony grinned, showing her pointed teeth, and flung herself into the air. She made wide gestures with her arms as if sowing corn to both sides of a field. Icicles flew from the fingers of her left hand, impaling two of the Goblins. They fell by the entrance to the cave writhing and squealing.

Bryony shook her right hand to try to wake up the magic in it and flew high over the Goblin troops to land further up the hill. The soldiers turned towards the cave, sniffing the air like tracker dogs.

"It's me you want!" shouted Bryony, flying dangerously close. "Come on! Come and get me!"

As they turned back towards Bryony, she saw David emerging from the cave, followed by the older children.

A tall, pale Goblin, wearing an armband, crouched low, tossing a knife with a serrated edge from hand to hand. It looked just like the sort of knife Mrs Hogarth had used when cutting the fresh, warm, early morning loaves at the bakery in Gavelkind.

Suddenly, the Goblins rushed at her. She shouted, "STOP!" at the top of her lungs. The Goblins stopped.

"GA!" shouted the magic user, "NA FAYRI SHPEEE!"

Woken from Bryony's magic, the Goblins moved again and were on her in an instant. Surprised, she tried to fly away, but the tall Goblin caught her leg. She was hauled down, unable to fight back, unable to change form. It was as if her magic had never been. She couldn't utter a word. The Goblin held her.

From the corner of her eye, she saw Malichai and Elliott stealing the weapons from the fallen Goblins by the door.

"EERON FIRE!" shouted the magic user.

The Goblin placed the flat edge of the serrated blade against Bryony's cheek. The world went white. Green fire exploded in her head, screaming fury and death through every fibre of her being. She twisted in the soldier's grip, unable to breathe. Her face burned as through a hundred sewing needles raked across it; her eye burst in a shower of sparks.

The Goblin let go and dropped her to the floor. The pain lessened enough for her to understand it was her, and not the ironfire, that screamed. She clutched her face and curled into a ball. All around her were shouts of battle.

Despite the pain, she made herself look up. Luci was on the back of the Goblin who had burned her, stabbing it again and again in the neck. Luci's trousers were soaked in blood from gripping round the Goblin's chest. Before the magic user could draw breath, Malichai drew back his hand and threw a knife at her. She lifted a palm. The knife fell harmlessly to the floor.

Brunhilde and the adult Humans were fighting near the cave entrance. As Brunhilde ripped each Goblin in half, the Humans picked up weapons and used them.

"Over here, smelly breath!" shouted Elliott. The magic user turned to him. Malichai threw again. His knife hit. The female Goblin fell. Elliott rushed forward and hacked her head from her shoulders.

Bryony tried to cheer, but the movement of her jaw brought another wave of agonizing burning. Tears came to her eyes as she curled round the pain. She heard the sound of feet running away.

She looked up again to see the bear catch the fleeing Goblins. Each was ripped asunder by her powerful claws until all were still. Elliott and Malichai leapt up and down among the Goblin debris, whooping their victory. As her cheeks curled into a smile, Bryony fainted.

* * *

After a while, Kendro reported back to the gatehouse at Cucapha castle. "The kitchen staff have been dismissed, and the dungeon emptied. There's no people anywhere in the castle. Are you certain you don't need any help, Sir?"

"No! We're fine," said Merik. "We're going to meet Edna soon, at the Maltbrook Arms. Until then I want to watch the castle."

"It's been an honour serving with you, Sir. I'm heading for the docks. There's a merchant ship due to leave in three hours, and I intend to be on it."

Merik and Kendro hugged and slapped each other on the back. "Take care," said Merik. "I'm sure we'll meet again one day."

Merik and Sheean settled down to watch the courtyard. A few Goblins scuttled to and fro in the darkness. As the clock struck eleven thirty, a fearsome yell echoed around the castle.

Sheean jumped. "What was that?"

"Grizelda sounds hungry," laughed Merik.

"Won't she come looking for someone?"

"I hope not."

A grinding mechanical noise started up, quickly rising to a high-pitched whine. They peered out of the gatehouse window and watched as Grizelda descended the outside wall of the North West tower in her new machine.

"Pox! I was hoping she would stay in the tower until later," said Merik.

"What are we going to do?"

"I'll go and make nice noises at her and try and persuade her to go back up the tower. I'll promise her supper."

"Is it safe?"

"I've been a guard at this castle for years. She won't do anything to me."

Merik strolled across the courtyard. Grizelda sat in her machine, hanging, just above head height. Her bulk was wedged into the device like uncooked dough in a loaf tin.

"Your Majesty," said Merik. "There has been a small delay with your evening meal. No need to come all the way down here. I will bring it up in person as soon as it arrives."

Merik went to walk away.

"Stop right there! There's something going on here. Don't think you can fool me."

"There's nothing to worry about. Just a small hiccup with the catering staff. It's all in hand."

Grizelda's machine grumbled down to ground level. "So you think I should go back up to my room, do you, Merik?"

Merik's face paled. "I think it would be in your interest, Your Majesty." His hand rested on the knife at his belt. He heard a low wheeze, like the wind in a forest at night. He looked up. Perched on the battlements next to Sheean's old tower stood a Dragon.

Grizelda looked up at the golden beast as it paced to and fro; smoke leaking from its nostrils. "I'm not the only one who thinks there is something wrong here," she said.

* * *

Sheean watched Merik talking with Grizelda. Why was it taking so long? He saw Merik looking up at the battlements, his face transfixed with horror, his hand straying to his knife.

"Nooooo!" screamed Sheean, giving up his Human form and flying across the courtyard like a turquoise arrow.

Merik turned to him. "Stay back Sheean! You're in the way!"

Spittle flew from Grizelda's lips as she screamed her orders, her sharp-nailed, pudgy hands pointing at Sheean.

"FAERIE! FAERIE! KILL IT! KILL IT!"

The Dragon let loose a blast of sulphurous flame. Sheean tried to raise a Faerie shield, but he was too slow. As the fireball lit up the courtyard, Merik threw himself in front of Sheean, taking the first few seconds of the flame onto his own skin.

Sheean's shield held back the flaming Dragon breath, but it was too late. Merik collapsed. Sheean glanced up. He saw Grizelda struggling to make her contraption rise to safety. The Dragon peered down at him, its golden claws gripping the edge of the battlements. Just behind the Dragon, Sheean recognised the tower in which had been held prisoner for so long as a child.

"Merik, why did you do that?"

Merik took a shuddering breath. His face was blackened, his armour still hot to the touch. "I owe you my life, for stealing your childhood, for not rescuing you when I should." He coughed weakly.

Their eyes met. Sheean held his friend and mentor, vaguely aware of the tears that flowed down his cheeks. Merik closed his eyes and sighed, slumping heavily in Sheean's arms.

Anger rose from Sheean's chest like bubbling lava as he lowered Merik's body gently to the ground. The grinding of gears came to Sheean's ears. Grizelda was half way up the tower.

"KILL THE FAERIE!" she cried.

Sheean paid no attention to her. His first clear thought was of revenge. The Dragon paused for a second. It tipped its splendid head on one side then drew in a deep breath, releasing another barrage of fire. Calmly, Sheean raised a hand, drawing the flames into his outstretched palm. The Dragon stopped. It moved from foot to foot uneasily, backing up against the wall of the tower.

Grizelda screamed more orders, but this time the Dragon didn't respond. Sheean breathed in deep, concentrating the energy of the Dragon into his palm and drawing more from the trees around him. With a shout, he released all his pent up emotion in a ball of fire directed straight at the golden beast.

He knew it was forbidden for the Fay to kill another magical creature, but right now, he didn't care. With a deafening boom of thunder, the wave of angry magic hit the Dragon squarely on the chest. With a snort of smoke, it fell backwards, knocking against the castle stonework. Sheean's old tower collapsed in a pile of rubble and dust. With tears in his eyes, Sheean turned his attention to Grizelda.

"You're next!" he shouted.

Before he could raise his hand, the air around him sparkled in turquoise light, the courtyard disappeared and he began to fall through space.

* * *

"More ale, barman," Grumbuk bellowed across the noisy taproom of the Maltbrook Arms.

"Should look for Edna?" asked Krodbell.

"Plenty time."

They sat down at a window seat with a view of the lane and the castle. A massive explosion outside made everyone dive to the floor. A second later, the Goblins were back on their feet and as noisy as before, standing ten deep around the bar and shouting for more ale. The Human bartender struggled through the crowded room and slammed a jug down on Grumbuk's table, mumbling something.

"What say?" asked Grumbuk, cupping his grubby hand around his ear.

The barman scowled. "Bloody fireworks," he grumbled as he peered out of the front window into the smoke filled lane. "Bloody Gobfest."

"Is good business," said Krodbell.

"Only if you lot don't do more damage than the small profit I make on your Goblin ale."

"Is cheap in Goblin realm."

"Not by the time it gets here, it's not."

Grumbuk and Krodbell nodded knowingly. "Middle Goblin take big slice of profit," said Grumbuk. The barman just shook his head in response. The sound of smashing glass drew the barman's attention. "Bloody Goblins," he mumbled under his breath and forced his way back to the bar.

Another explosion rocked the inn.

"Is very loud fireworks," said Krodbell as he poured himself a tankard of ale.

Grumbuk pushed his tankard forward for more. "Is best Gobfest I seen."

* * *

A flash of light blinded everyone in the Meeting Room of Taranor Castle. When it cleared, they saw Sheean trembling in the middle of the meeting room, covered in dirt and soot. Agaric lowered his arms.

"Prince Sheean," said Agaric, "I hope you can explain why you left Taranor without permission! Where is Princess Bryony?"

Sheean's anger at the death of Merik, and at being dragged back to Taranor before he could avenge him, was too much to bear. Without warning, he attacked Agaric, wrapping his hands tightly around the officer's throat. The guards rushed towards them, trying to pull them apart without injury.

Queen Rhyannon raised her wand.

* * *

By the time Bryony and her charges arrived at the village of Dringle, the Gobfest fireworks were in full blaze. Explosions shattered the air. Goblins of all ages lay around in the streets, most of them hopelessly drunk, many dead from bar brawls.

Bryony lay low over the back of Brunhilde. Just conscious, she held her injured cheek away from the coarse fur, her arms and legs wrapped around the bear's chunky body. To avoid detection, her Faerie light had been covered with a blanket. Sharing Brunhilde's back was Little Eric, whose cough had got worse since the fight.

David and Luci walked quietly by Brunhilde's head, leading the way to the safety of a derelict farmhouse on the outskirts of the village.

Once there, Ruth checked that all the children were gathered together and opened the door to the house. It was cold inside, but there was a fire grate and a kettle to hang above it, a table they could sit at, and a separate room big enough for all the children to snuggle down.

Bryony and Little Eric were lifted from the bear's back. Brunhilde sat on the floor in a corner of the kitchen and waved a paw at her tummy, encouraging the Humans to put Bryony against her soft fur.

"There'll be water outside in the well," said Luci. "I'll get it."

She left the house with Malichai and Elliott carrying the kettle and jugs, while Ruth lit the lamps and settled the children. Kerry found some mugs on a shelf above the sink. David stood guard by the door.

Bryony lay against Brunhilde's belly, watching her friends organise themselves. Although her face tingled as if brushed by nettles, it had been a while since she'd had a wave of that terrible pain. It was bearable if she didn't move her face, or speak.

The children came back with the water and offered Bryony a cup. She gulped half of it, then looked into the bottom of the mug. She thought of Edna. Nothing happened. She tried to rise, but the burning stabbed right through her again. She cried out.

"Don't try to get up. You need rest," said Ruth.

Shaking her head stubbornly, Bryony struggled to her feet, using her wings to support her. "I need to get to Cucapha. I need to kill Grizelda."

"We all do dear, but not right now. Lie down again."

Bryony heard Brunhilde speak in her mind. *"The Faerie Princess is badly hurt. You will need strong magic to recover. Rest against me for a while. We will get help."*

"Thank you Brunhilde."

As she sank back against the bear's warm coat, Bryony noticed Ruth shooting David a questioning look. He nodded wisely.

"She's like Kerry," he said. "They're both not quite right in the head. Pain can do that to you. My old Aunt Agatha had something like it, she used to be alright for a while, then she'd wander off, muttering all sorts of nonsense."

Kerry smiled vacantly and moved to the doorway, gazing out at the darkness.

"I am NOTHING like your Aunt Agatha!" shouted Bryony. "Kerry had a bump on the head, but I've... Ow!" She clutched at her face. Ruth came over to her and tried to stroke her hair, to soothe her, but it just felt irritating.

"Get OFF ME!" shouted Bryony. Then tears filled her eyes. "Oh I'm so sorry, Ruth. I know you're trying to help. If only I could reach Edna."

"Who is Edna?"

"The herbalist at Gavelkind. She could help me but she can't because she's in the Demon realm. I have to go and get her out of there."

"You're in no fit state to go anywhere young lady," said David.

Kerry looked over from the door. "You're Fay. They used iron on you. That will stop your magic for quite a long time."

Everyone looked at her in astonishment.

"How do you know about that sort of thing?" asked Ruth.

Kerry smiled again. "I'm not sure. I guess I've never really wanted to live here." She looked at Bryony, a gentle smile playing round the corners of her mouth.

"Right," said David, "we need a plan."

214

Ruth gave a shriek and pointed. There at the door, behind Kerry, stood a Goblin. It was peering into the farmhouse.

"Oh, hello," said Kerry pleasantly, "do you want to join our party?"

"No!" said Elliott.

Kerry smiled and led the Goblin inside. It pointed at Bryony.

"Fayri!"

"Yes," said Kerry. "Isn't she pretty?"

"Reward for Fayri. Plenty money." The goblin looked around. "All got green eyes. Plenty, plenty money."

Ruth stuttered, "Kerry, I think..."

Kerry reached into her pocket, her voice remaining charming and pleasant. "It would be such a shame if you got stabbed, wouldn't it?"

The Goblin looked at her, its eyes narrowing in confusion. Kerry made a sudden movement, thrusting forward with her hand. The Goblin gave a gasp. As Kerry pulled her hand back, the Goblin sank to the floor.

"There," she said, wiping the dagger on her skirt, "that's better."

Bryony lay against Brunhilde's warm fur, feeling the burning pain calm down to a tingle. Ruth sat at the table, lying with her head on her arms, exhausted.

"The children are asleep now, Ruth," said Luci.

Ruth's reply was muffled by her arms. "Thank you, Luci."

"Would you like tea?" asked David. Ruth nodded without lifting her head. Kerry hunted in her pockets for some money. "I'll pop to the shops shall I? Get some oatmeal?"

Bryony tried to smile, but it still hurt her to move her face much.

"No thank you, Kerry."

Ruth looked up. Her eyes were puffy and red. She sighed.

"Kerry, we can't get to the shops. We'll be recaptured. We'll have to steal our food."

Kerry went to the door again. "What shall we get?" she asked brightly.

"Nothing for now, Kerry," said David. "There is a box of tea here. When we've rested, we'll go for a forage. Just before dawn would be good, when all the Goblins are asleep."

At that moment, Little Eric poked his head round the corner to the kitchen, rubbing his little fists against his tired eyes. His hair was tousled. "Can't sleep," he said.

"Come here, Little Eric," said Kerry. She knelt down and opened her arms to him. He padded barefoot across the floor to her and relaxed in her embrace. She cradled him, crooning a soft lullaby that took everyone, adults included, back to a safe time, back to a time before the Goblins, and before Grizelda became Queen.

"Bryony, are you planning on going to the castle at Cucapha when you're a little better?" asked Ruth once the song was over. "If so, I'd like to come with you."

Bryony nodded, holding onto Brunhilde's fur to steady the dizziness that threatened to overwhelm her.

"She can't," said David. "She can hardly talk, never mind fight Grizelda."

"It's just a little bit of dizziness," said Bryony through gritted teeth. "I'll be better very soon."

216

Ruth rose from the table and knelt down by Bryony. "I want you to have this," she said, placing a delicate gold chain into Bryony's hand. Attached to the chain was a golden oak leaf, perfect in every detail.

"Oh," breathed Bryony, "I can't possibly, why...?"

"I want to thank you," said Ruth, as she fastened it around Bryony's neck, "for rescuing all the children from the camp, and for giving me a chance to see my beloved Merik again."

Bryony felt the quality of the chain in her fingers. For a piece of Human jewellery, it wasn't bad. Of course, if it had been made in Taranor it would have been thrown back into the fire as crude, but it was quite a fine chain and the leaf was beautiful.

"Merik gave it to me many years ago at Dragonfest. It's not valuable, but I want you to have it."

"Thank you. It reminds me of the oak trees at home."

"Where is home?" asked Luci.

Bryony smiled. "Taranor. The Island of Taranor."

"You see, she's not well," said David. "Taranor is just an island in the sea; a place for sea birds and trees."

"No," said Bryony. "It's another realm. The Island of Taranor you know is in the Human realm. My home is..."

The pain in her face made further speech impossible. She shrugged her shoulders and drooped her wings in a gesture of defeat. Her hand strayed to the pouch at her waist where she kept the Portal Stone. Its magic would work now they were out of the camp. It was time to move on: time to leave these wonderful Humans, time to say goodbye.

"Sorry," she said, "I must get to Edna. She can heal me and then I can rescue her and then I can kill..." Again the pain stopped her.

"But Bryony, you can't go," said David. "You're still ill and besides you'd be spotted the minute you left the house. It's alright for the children, they're good at sneaking. We've been lucky so far. But if the Goblins notice us, we'll be in trouble, even with Brunhilde's help."

Bryony looked at each precious Human in turn, ready to thank them for their help, but before she could utter a word, her world shimmered. The farmhouse kitchen became misty. She heard her friends calling out, but she was powerless. She fell through white mist.

* * *

Queen Rhyannon lowered her wand. Bryony appeared in the meeting room in a swirling misty light. She staggered and collapsed onto the floor. Fable rushed up to her and nuzzled her, looking around to the Queen for help. Guards, attendants and healers flew in from all directions to tend to the wounded princess.

Sheean let go of Agaric and stood back, shaking, tears streaming down his face. The Security Chief flew back a few wing beats and felt his throat.

"Merik's dead," sobbed Sheean, "I have to go back!"

Agaric dragged in a ragged breath and looked at the queen. "You see, Your Majesty," he wheezed. "He is not suitable to be king. He has been tainted by his time with the Humans."

Queen Rhyannon turned on him. "As we discussed, there is no one else. Sheean will have to learn how to behave. Maybe you could see to his rehabilitation personally." She called out to the healers. "Use your finest skill to restore Bryony. The crowning and the marriage will go ahead as planned. Please see to it. And the valets must be called. The future king needs to be cleaned up... again. As soon as he is presentable, physically and emotionally, and Bryony is strong, we will have the banquet. Then they can explain what they have been doing."

* * *

"Edna here soon?" asked Krodbell.

"Not long," said Grumbuk. "Be here soon, nearly midnight." The two Goblins sat back and drank their ale.

A knock on the window startled them out of their stupor. Peering through the window was a younger version of Edna, dressed in a long cream coat, with a golden broach at her neck. Mesmerised, they sat staring until Edna knocked on the glass again. The bartender shouted obscenities as the two Goblins tumbled over each other, knocking tables over in their rush towards the door.

Azabyandee smiled and held his hand out for Grumbuk to shake. "It is good to meet you as one entity," he told them.

Grumbuk stepped forward, taking hold of Azabyandee's hand, shaking it vigorously. Krodbell looked up at the tall black human standing in front of him and almost curtsied in his confusion.

"Where are Sheean and Merik?" Edna asked.

"Not know," Grumbuk answered. "Been here long time, not see."

"We must start without them," said Azabyandee.

"Yes dear. However I'm concerned something has happened to them. If Merik makes a promise, he keeps it."

Grumbuk nodded. "Is true. Fayri not let down. Something wrong."

"Let us go to the castle. They may be there already," said Azabyandee. "We must strike soon or we will lose the advantage of surprise. Soon the celebrations will be over and Grizelda's army will be back to full strength."

A group of drunken Goblins stepped out of the inn and almost collided with Azabyandee. He scowled at them, waved his hand, and they all fell to the floor.

"You kill?" Grumbuk asked.

"No, they are just asleep. They will wake up in a few hours with a headache and remember nothing. "Listen, Goblin friends," said Azabyandee, "and listen well. Edna and I need you to make a reconnoitre of the castle gatehouse."

Grumbuk and Krodbell saluted, shouting, "Yes, Boss," in unison. Grumbuk had no idea what the Wizard was saying.

"There's no need to salute."

"Yes, Boss," repeated Grumbuk, fighting the desire to salute again. He looked at Krodbell briefly. His friend was standing like a soldier, his chest puffed out and his warty chin in the air.

"Right, Sir," said Grumbuk, "we know what to do, Sir. Don't we, Krodbell?"

Grumbuk hoped his friend understood the big words, but Krodbell merely shot him an anxious glance, utter incomprehension showing in his little eyes.

"What is it we have to do, Kroddy?"

"Erm..."

Edna stepped forward, smiling. "Go to the castle gatehouse and find out who is guarding it. Then come back here and report what you see."

"That's right," said Krodbell. "I knew that."

Azabyandee waved his hand in the direction of the castle. Grumbuk and Krodbell, assuming they were dismissed, scurried off along the lane, eventually slowing to a stroll as they neared the gates.

"Act casual," hissed Grumbuk.

"Am casual," replied Krodbell.

"Why you keep looking behind then?"

"Feel cat-man watching."

Grumbuk grunted. "Naw. If he see this far, he not need us go look."

"Still feel someone watch."

"Shush, nearly there."

They were rounding a ruined tower, walking in single file, when Krodbell stopped suddenly. Grumbuk walked smack into his friend's back

"What you stop for?"

Krodbell gasped for breath. "Merik," he squeaked.

"Where?"

"There," he said, a little clearer, pointing at the top of the gates.

Merik's bloodied head hung impaled on a pike staff. His sightless eyes, almost closed by scorched skin, stared out at Maltbrook Lane with a faintly shocked expression. Grumbuk swallowed nervously. "Is war now."

"Why they put head above gate?"

"Warning to us."

"Why?" asked Krodbell, panic beginning to show in his eyes.

"She know Merik not on ownio."

"Where Fayri?"

"Not know. Go back now, report what find."

As they turned to go back, a tall fat Ogre pushed his way sideways through the gatehouse door.

"Ay you. Thtop there!"

* * *

Edna pulled her cloak tight round her shoulders and huddled under the trees by the Maltbrook Arms, while Azabyandee crouched down in the dark, his long legs bent at the knee, his hands clasped together in front.

"We must get home as soon as we have finished with Grizelda," she said. "You need to find your staff and resume your title."

Azabyandee looked up at her. "And you, my dear, will be able to continue your training and prepare for your exams."

"Yes dear. Although I think I might rather retire to the coast."

Azabyandee shot her a withering look. Edna pulled a face and stuck out her tongue. She couldn't help it. She knew Azabyandee hated her being childish, but she felt like a teenager now that he was once more by her side in Wizard form.

"Our life together has been restored," said Azabyandee. "Injustice and wrong-doing will tremble before us. There is no time to retire to the coast."

Edna watched a Goblin commander kicking at his men, trying to get them to line up.

"Yes dear. Do you think we really should kill Grizelda? Is there no other way?"

"We could throw her down Ogman's crater," said Azabyandee. "I have to admit though, that killing in cold blood is not my style."

"I think we should keep her alive. She might learn her lesson and turn out alright in the end."

Azabyandee gave out a short, sharp, humourless laugh. "That witch is a sheep tick. She is evil."

"Sheep ticks are not evil, my dear."

"Wait until you've had one stuck to your ear for a few days, and then tell me they're not evil. That woman sucks the blood of her people, takes their energy and their food. She's become bloated and blood filled. She should be squashed."

Edna looked at her husband squatting on the ground. There was still a lot of cat in the symmetrical way he sat and the hint of cruelty in his bright blue eyes.

As if reacting to her scrutiny, he stood up. "We'll find a container and bottle the old bat."

"Hit her with a bottle? That's a bit beneath us isn't it, darling?"

"I don't mean hit her with it."

Azabyandee came closer to Edna and peered into her eyes. She felt the hair on her head rise with static electricity.

"I think," he said quietly, "it will be better to take her with us to the Wizard realm and to deal with her there. We can place her in a jar of some kind."

Edna laughed. "How on earth are we going to get that obese obscenity of a Human being into a jar? We would have to squeeze and squeeze and squeeze."

Azabyandee smiled. "With the torc, I can control her and shrink her."

223

"Please don't be cruel, dear."

"All the time I was in cat form, I refrained from playing with my prey. I excelled in a swift bite through the neck. No creature suffered by my paw." Azabyandee grabbed in the air at an imaginary target. "However, here we have a mouse that needs to learn a lesson."

"Didn't you always say that negative actions will come back to harm you?"

"Yes, but this action is positive. Grizelda will understand all her wrong-doing before she dies. Her soul will be clean."

Edna could see there was no point in arguing.

"Now," said Azabyandee. "While those two green creatures are on their errand, let's see how you handle the torc."

Edna fingered the necklace round her neck. It felt heavy on her collar bones. "What do you mean, dearest?"

"I want to see how you react to it. Close your eyes and see what you need to see."

He reached out to hold her hand, closing his eyes and waiting. Feeling a little silly, Edna closed her eyes.

In her mind's eye she saw a lake surrounded by seven trees. Some were in bloom, some were withered. The surface of the lake was ruffled as if by a powerful wind, yet the air was still. Beyond the lake stood range upon range of snow-capped mountains. She felt her shoulders relax a little as she saw Azabyandee standing next to her, still squeezing her hand.

"Talk to the water," he said. "But beware. If I say 'pull away', then you must drag yourself away from this place and back to your physical form."

"Isn't this all rather long winded? Your blue crystal works much faster for simple scrying, and my crystals..."

"Edna! Just get on with it. This torc has a power that we both need to understand and control."

Edna sighed and turned to face the lake. "Please show me the castle at Cucapha."

The surface shimmered. Bubbles rose. Two Dragons emerged, one of gold, one of silver, both rising out of the water into the evening sky. They swam into the air, flowing round and round, heads chasing tails to form two rings. The rings merged and intertwined, flowing gold into silver, silver into gold. One of the Dragons looked at Edna. "Wizard Edna?"

"Yes. It is I."

"You wish to see the castle at Cucapha, in the Human realm, at the time of the Goblin alliance?"

"Yes, please."

Through the centre of the ring, she saw the castle. Goblins staggered drunkenly along the battlements. In one corner, she noticed a hazy outline of a portal from which stepped Demons of all shapes and sizes. It looked as though there had already been some kind of battle. One of the towers lay in a heap of rubble. Edna recognized it as the tower where Sheean had been held prisoner during his youth. She could see no sign of Sheean or Merik.

Edna looked closer. There seemed to be a body lying on the floor of the courtyard. It had no head. She shivered. "Show me Grizelda," she asked.

The image shifted to the inside of Grizelda's Tower. The fat queen lay on her back in her bed, eating some kind of sweetmeat. On one side of the room lay a large egg on a finely sequinned cushion.

Edna looked away from the image to check with Azabyandee.

"What do you think that is?"

"It looks like the egg of a Wyvern. We must put a stop to whatever evil this witch has in mind. Let us leave. We have seen enough."

"Thank you, Dragons," said Edna in her politest tones. "I have seen enough."

The Dragons broke their ring formation and hovered in the air, their bodies still intertwined, gold around silver, silver around gold, their two heads facing her. "But are you sure you've seen enough? Would you not like to see yourself in the future?"

"We have seen enough," said Azabyandee firmly.

The Dragons separated with a hiss that sent chills down Edna's spine, and sank once more beneath the water.

Azabyandee gave her hand another squeeze. "Open your eyes, darling," he said.

She opened her eyes and found herself back outside the Maltbrook Arms. She shivered. "I'm not sure I like those Dragons, dearest. They exerted a strong mental power. Would you like to wear the torc for a while?"

"I have the strength my dear. I need to see whether or not you do."

Edna touched the necklace with her fingers. The metal was warm. Almost alive. She had a very bad feeling about it. Before she could argue further, she saw Grumbuk and Krodbell running towards them down the road.

"Why did you send those two Goblins off into danger, my dear," she asked, "when we find that we can see more clearly for ourselves?"

"I want them to feel important. I want them on our side."

Krodbell wrapped his arms around Edna and buried his head in her robes. Azabyandee shook his head and addressed Grumbuk. "Report."

Grumbuk pulled himself up tall and saluted.

"Castle guarded by huge thing, and Merik is deadid."

"Oh, how awful!" said Edna. "Did you see Sheean?"

Grumbuk shook his head. Edna wiped a tear from her eye and smiled warmly at the two little creatures. Fortunately, they had no idea how much power they held in the balance of the worlds. If they knew, they would surely stumble. Azabyandee leaned down a little towards the Goblins. "Listen closely. This is the plan..."

Chapter 8

The Ogre at the castle gate smiled. It was a ghastly sight. Thick lips parted like giant slugs to reveal a stinking cavern of a mouth. The tongue, thick as a slab of dead meat, lolled out, almost to the creature's knees.

"Thay again?" it said. Its tongue flapped with each syllable, spraying saliva.

"We have been summoned," said Azabyandee, "by her Royal Majesty on a matter of the most urgency."

The Ogre frowned, shifting its enormous bulk to a more upright position. "Av yer come about the toileth?"

Azabyandee looked the vile creature in the eye, sprinkling his speech with the faintest hint of persuasion.

"Yes. That is correct. We will go through the gates, mend the toilets and leave again."

"Well, why didn't ya thay! They ith over in corner. Come back here when done. I'm goin' for my lunch. Got thotheegees."

The Ogre hauled its tongue back into its mouth, squeezed through the gatehouse door and slammed it behind him.

Edna, Azabyandee and the two Goblins walked into the courtyard. Merik's body still lay on the charred flagstones. Above him, on the western battlement, sat a golden Wyvern, licking its singed hide. A few Demons wandered around looking dazed. To Azabyandee's experienced eye, none seemed to pose a threat. As yet.

"Goblins," he said, "I've already told you what to do with regards to the Wyvern egg. Off you go. Edna,

I will talk to the Wyvern while you close the Demon portal. When you have finished, meet me back here. Can you manage that alright? Make sure you stay out of sight of Grizelda."

Grumbuk and Krodbell started towards Grizelda's tower.

"Of course I can manage, my love," said Edna. "The portal is in the outer courtyard, she shouldn't see anything. Don't worry. I can handle a few Demons. It's only like sweeping the floor of some rubbish and closing the door."

"True, however, it's not the Demons that I'm worried about."

"Oh you always did worry so. At least when you were nine cats you just glared at the world. Now..."

Azabyandee's eyes flashed. "Have you any idea what it was like being split like that? I will ask you, Wife, never, ever joke about my trauma again!"

With a whirl of his cloak he walked smartly towards the Wyvern, his hands outstretched in greeting.

* * *

"You know what do, yes?" asked Grumbuk, as the two Goblins reached the base of Grizelda's tower.

"Erm, yes," answered Krodbell.

"What do then?"

"You forgot?"

"No, just testin."

Krodbell looked confused. He stood scratching his head. "I go fix toilets?"

"No dumbnut! We get egg, but don't know way in. Ask Edna."

"Yes, ask Edna, she nice lady."

Edna was gazing into space as Grumbuk and Krodbell returned to her side and pulled at her skirts.

"Big Dragon," said Grumbuk. He could feel his knees knocking with fear.

Edna looked down and patted him on the arm. He felt a wave of peace and confidence pass through him, as if he'd had a draught of the best Goblin Wine.

"She is protecting Grizelda," said Edna.

"Big Dragon eat us?" asked Krodbell.

"Grizelda has the Wyvern's egg in her room," said Edna. "As long as she holds the egg, the Wyvern will protect her at all costs. If we rescue the egg, the Wyvern will be our ally. As my husband already explained, rescuing the egg is your job, Mr Grumbuk."

Grumbuk put on his bravest face and nodded.

"How we get egg from witch?" Krodbell asked.

Edna sighed. "Did you not hear a word of Azabyandee's plan?"

Grumbuk cleared his throat. "Can't understand him. He speak long words."

"Fair enough," said Edna. "One of you must keep Grizelda busy, while the other gets the egg from the room."

"How we keep her busy?"

"I don't know. Sing to her or something."

"Easy then," said Krodbell. "I good singer."

"Yes easy," said Grumbuk. "I do difficult bit. Brave bit."

"You only have to keep her occupied for a few minutes, Krodbell," said Edna. "When you have the egg, Grumbuk, bring it to its mother."

"Why not use magic?" asked Krodbell.

Edna sighed. Grumbuk elbowed his friend in the ribs.

"Ow. Was just askin."

"It's OK, Mr. Grumbuk. I know when Azabyandee explains things it can be hard to understand. I'll tell you what he said in plain language."

Grumbuk blushed.

"If we attack Grizelda before the egg is safe," continued Edna, "the Wyvern will try to stop us. They are magical creatures and there are very few left in any of the realms. We cannot afford any harm to come to either the egg or its mother."

"Understand?" Grumbuk asked Krodbell, elbowing him in the ribs again.

"Yes. Stop hurting me, or you do on ownio."

Edna concentrated for a moment, using the torc to see into the tower. "There is a maintenance door to Grizelda's room. It looks as though it has been blocked off. You can get through that way. Be careful, the stairs are steep and broken. If you get into trouble, just yell."

* * *

Krodbell ran round to the base of Grizelda's tower while Grumbuk began to climb up to the battlements. He ignored the guards who lay, slumped against doorways, with stupid, drunken grins on their faces. One of the unconcsious ones had an arm band.

Carefully, Grumbuk pulled off the band and placed it on his own arm. Then he ran along the battlement and up to the entrance of Grizelda's tower, where the ground was littered with blocks of stone. In front of him stood a small door, blackened by fire and barricaded with wood. He pulled the planks clear and began to climb the stairs. Krodbell's voice echoed round the courtyard. He was singing a Goblin love song. Grumbuk shook his head and carried on up the narrow stairs as quietly as he could.

* * *

Edna walked through the archway into the outer courtyard and climbed the staircase to the lower battlements. There, using the power of the torc, she herded all the Demons to the portal. They fled in terror from her. She chuckled. They stood just the other side of the portal, cowering together on the hot grey sand of the Demon realm.

The sight of the river Styx reminded her of the twisted trees and her promise to free them all.

* * *

Grumbuk reached the door to Grizelda's room and pulled down on the handle. There was a slight click and the door swung open. Grumbuk saw Grizelda standing on the balcony, her back to him, listening to Krodbell's awful voice. In the washbowl near the bed was the egg. It was huge, smooth and pale blue. Grumbuk took a step forward. A floorboard creaked. Grizelda whirled around.

"How did you get in here?" she screamed, raising her hands in attack.

"Your Majesty," Grumbuk replied, bowing gracefully and showing her his arm band. "Am new Security Chief."

Grizelda lowered her hands. "Where the old one?"

"Is dead, Your Majesty."

Grizelda looked at him suspiciously. "Where are the castle guards? I've not seen any for some time."

"Is Gobfest, Your Majesty, guards drunk. Is OK. Keep eye on you."

"You still haven't answered my question. How did you get in here?"

"Is problem with maintenance door."

"Maintenance door?"

"Is broken, anyone get in."

Just at that moment Krodbell got to a part of the song with a rousing chorus. Grizelda looked back down over the balcony.

"Who is the singer?"

"Is simple minstrel, Your Majesty. He in love with you."

"Really? When he is finished send him up here, I may play with him for a time."

"Yes, Your Majesty."

The chorus finished and the song changed into a yearning verse in which Krodbell expressed undying longing for a lock of his lover's hair. Grumbuk took a few steps towards the egg. Grizelda turned to him again.

"Security Chief?"

"Yes, Your Majesty."

"Take my breakfast plates away."

"Yes, Your Majesty."

Grizelda leaned over the balcony again. Grumbuk looked around for the plates and was pleased to find them next to the washbowl.

* * *

Edna glanced back towards the inner courtyard. She couldn't see the two Goblins, but she could hear the awful singing. Azabyandee was no doubt deep in conversation with the Wyvern. She hesitated. It would take her a long time to free each tree. She would need a lot of water.

She fingered the torc at her throat, wondering if the souls trapped in the twisted forest were in fact all that innocent. She wondered whether she might be making a mistake, whether by interfering they would be made to suffer in another way. There was of course the possibility that some were truly evil. It was probably better if they stayed there. For the first time in her long life she saw that the realms needed Dark to balance Light, and that there was something rather beautiful about Shadow.

* * *

Watching Grizelda all the time, Grumbuk picked up the Wyvern's egg and placed it in the extra large breakfast bowl on the tray. Covering both the bowl and tray with a towel, he headed for the door. Grizelda turned round again.

"Don't think you can get away with it," she growled.

Grumbuk's heart missed a beat. "Y, Y... Your majesty."

"The cup! You've missed the cup."

"Sorry, Your Majesty." He spotted the cup on the floor next to Grizelda's bed. As he bent to pick it up, the egg shifted violently, almost making him drop the tray. With difficulty, he straightened up and walked to the door.

"One more thing!" Grizelda screeched at him.

"Yes, Your Majesty."

"Get that door fixed."

234

"Yes, Your Majesty."

* * *

Leaving the twisted trees to their own fate, Edna shut the portal to the Demon realm and returned to the gatehouse. She paused, watching Azabyandee talking to the Wyvern. She'd always been in awe of her husband, but actually, she now saw he was really rather puny. Did she really want to spend the rest of her long, Wizardly life with him? She looked at him talking Latin with the Dragon. What a pompous fool.

Edna turned to stare at the unguarded gate. The ogre was still inside the gatehouse, snoring like a thunderstorm. It occurred to her that she could just go to Taranor and meet up with Bryony. With the Faerie Queen as her ally...

She felt a tug at her neck as if an invisible hand were grabbing at the torc. She heard Azabyandee shouting. "Pull away, Edna! Pull away!" She whirled round to see him running towards her, his cream cloak billowing behind him.

She wanted to fly away. Surely she could fly? She felt another tug at her neck. Her throat burned with a terrible pain. Her vision grew dark.

When she opened her eyes again, she felt the arms of her husband holding her close and safe on the cool stones of the castle courtyard. In his hand he held the gold and silver torc. He looked at her sternly.

"We will talk of this later."

* * *

235

Grumbuk scurried along the western battlement towards the Wyvern, trying not to worry about the noises coming from the egg under the towel.

"I got egg," said Grumbuk. The mother Wyvern glared at him, her eyes filled with suspicion. He removed the towel. A baby Wyvern sat in the broken shell, its long snout smiling. Its wings were still crumpled and folded, covered in slime from the egg.

"Nice Dragon," Grumbuk crooned.

The baby Wyvern belched smoke into Grumbuk's face and licked him. The mother growled. Carefully, Grumbuk placed the newborn down on the battlement next to its mother. "Is safe."

The Wyvern sniffed its baby and picked it up by the scruff of its neck. She spread her wings, and as she took to the air, she grabbed Grumbuk in her talons, lifting him from the battlements.

Within seconds, the ground and castle were tiny dots far below. Grumbuk saw Krodbell running towards Azabyandee and Edna near the gatehouse. Azabyandee looked up and waved.

* * *

As Edna watched the Wyvern take to the sky, she felt Krodbell grabbing at her skirts. Azabyandee waved until the Wyvern could no longer be seen, then he turned briskly and began to march towards Grizelda's tower.

"Grumbuk come back?" Krodbell asked.

Edna smiled. "I'm sure he will. Let's hurry, we have a queen to overthrow."

They soon reached the maintenance door and made their way to Grizelda's room. Azabyandee spoke a word of power, throwing Grizelda onto her back. Edna watched Grizelda wriggle on her back like a bloated beetle, while Azabyandee held her down with a stream of blue light. The room crackled with counter magic.

"Krodbell, get that broomhandle!" shouted Azabyandee.

"Remember, don't be cruel," said Edna.

Azabyandee glared at her for a second, his eyes glinting like sapphires, then he turned his attention back to Grizelda.

"I have witnessed your crimes," he snarled. "You used a stick to open the mouth of a helpless Faerie child and you gave him mind-death to drink!"

Grizelda's eyes widened. She struggled.

"Edna," said Azabyandee, "get me a bottle of mind-death potion."

Edna looked along Grizelda's potion bottles. She soon found a bottle of black, viscous liquid. "Why don't you just use the torc to shrink her, dear?"

"Because I want her to experience the torment she made Sheean endure, everyday, for his entire childhood."

Krodbell held the witch's nose. When Grizelda opened her mouth, the Goblin shoved the broomhandle sideways between her teeth.

"I saw everything you did to him," continued Azabyandee. "You are now going to know how it felt. Edna, pour the liquid in."

With a shaking hand, Edna poured a gulp of the liquid past Grizelda's white lips. The witch's back arched and her eyes rolled up in her head.

"She is safe now," said Azabyandee, "let her go."

Krodbell took the broomstick away.

"Is she all right?" asked Edna.

Azabyandee patted at Grizelda's cheeks like a kitten patting a ball of wool. "She's fine."

Grizelda's eyes opened. Her pupils were black. She tried to sit up, but the vast bulk of her belly held her down.

"Excuse me?" asked Edna. "Do you know your name?"

Grizelda looked around the room frantically. "I'm not sure."

"How old are you?"

"I don't know. Am I sick?"

"She can go in the potion bottle," said Azabyandee. "Plenty of room in there, and I can keep an eye on her as we travel."

Back in the castle courtyard, Edna lifted her face to the heavens, enjoying the soft rain and the first streaks of dawn in the eastern sky. She gave silent thanks to all who had helped rid the Human realm of Grizelda's tyranny. She looked back at the headless corpse in the courtyard.

"Krodbell," she said, "go and get Merik's head from the gate. I'll hold Grizelda's bottle. Husband dearest, would you mind bringing our fallen friend out onto the lane? I'll find a nice spot for his resting place."

Within minutes, Edna found a suitable place for the grave under some trees at the edge of the road. She looked up to see Azabyandee dragging Merik's body towards her, leaving a trail of blood behind him.

"Oh do be careful!" she shouted. "That's not very respectful."

Azabyandee growled low in his throat. "He's pretty heavy in this chain mail, dearest."

Krodbell joined them, holding Merik's head by the hair. Edna tried not to look. Azabyandee laid Merik's body down and pointed at the ground, muttering words of magic. A shallow grave appeared. Edna helped pull Merik's body into position, while Krodbell placed the soldier's head where it should have been.

Edna felt her eyes fill with tears now that her old friend looked whole. Together, the three friends carried stones and rubble from the collapsed castle wall and covered the body. Azabyandee said a few words and waved his hand in the air. A flat stone, streaked with white quatrz, floated into place as a head stone. Then, satisfied all was in order, he took his wife's hand and bowed his head.

"He was a good man and brave. May his spirit find the light and fly to peace."

"He was a good man," whispered Edna. "Fly to peace."

Krodbell hopped from foot to foot, looking nervously up and down the lane.

"Why we have to carry stones, Boss? Could have used magic."

Azabyandee sighed. "One must use some effort when honouring the transition from one form to another. To do otherwise would show disrespect."

Krodbell scratched his head and looked down the lane again. Azabyandee spoke a few more words of magic as he wrote on the stone with a stick. Ornate letters appeared carved into the headstone.

Edna smiled through her tears. "Come now," she said, "we must be on our way. It's still dangerous here. We can't afford to dally, especially with what we have in this little bottle."

She held up the potion jar. Inside, Grizelda's face was squashed against the glass, glaring at the world, red with fury.

* * *

Once safely back in her cottage, Edna put the bottle containing Grizelda on the table. Azabyandee marched into the living room. He had a deep frown on his face and the torc in his fist. Krodbell collapsed onto a chair and put his head on the kitchen table. Timothy the kitten, sensing the Goblin's despair, climbed up his leg and purred into his ear.

"You've been a very brave, little Goblin," said Edna.

"Gone," he moaned. "Gone!"

Edna put her hand on Krodbell's back.

"Do you mean Grumbuk?"

"Gone!"

Krodbell began to cry.

"I'm sure he'll be back soon. And think of the wonderful adventures he's going to have."

"Adventures!" wailed the Goblin. "Adventures is horrid!"

Edna moved around the kitchen, packing things into a big bag. "Soon you'll feel alright. Soon you'll want another adventure."

Krodbell shook his head, sobbing silently, wetting his little green arms with tears.

Edna went through to the living room to find her husband sitting cross-legged on the hearthrug deep in meditation. "While you meditate, dear," she said, "I'll pop down to Gavelkind and get Bracken. We can ask him to pull the cart for us."

Azabyandee's bright blue eyes popped open. "Why do we need the cart?"

"I'm not leaving my things here. I spent all this time making a lovely home. There's my rugs and cushions, my kettle. And the cat baskets - we could take one for Timmy. We'll look like a normal family moving house, rather than a pair of Wizards, carrying a Witch in a bottle to another realm."

"I had hoped to travel light, my love."

"Hope again, sweetest. Enjoy your meditation."

"I'm not meditating for pleasure. I'm doing this to save the realms."

"Yes dear. I'll see you in a bit. Oh, I think Timmy has brought up a furball on the sofa. Would you mind?"

"Furballs! I'm sick of furballs."

Edna chuckled as she went back into the kitchen, calling back over her shoulder, "You only made them dear, I had to clean them all up."

After a few minutes brisk walking, Edna arrived at the Blacksmith's forge in the centre of Gavelkind, where she found Sandy and Roger in the forge, arguing.

Roger was talking and hammering at the same time, making so much noise that Edna couldn't hear herself think.

"Roger Gladwyn! What are you doing?"

Roger turned, his hammer held high, sweat glistening on his face. "Edna! You made me jump. I was just trying to get this funnel into the right shape. Only it's got to look right, as it will stick up above the cart."

Sandy sighed and wiped her hands on her apron. She and Edna came closer to look.

"What's it for?" asked Edna.

"It's to take the smoke away from the passengers. I'm trying to design a heater for the driver and passenger on a cart, only you know how cold it gets, sat up high behind the horse on a winter's day."

"How's that going to work?" said Sandy. "I keep telling him it's a waste of time. The heat will all escape because you're outside."

Roger made big gestures with his work roughened hands as he spoke. "I thought of that. I'm going to make a box with a window in it and a slot for the reins. Then mount it where the seat is and put some chairs in it. That would keep the heat in."

He brushed his hands through his curly brown hair and looked at the women.

"And how are you going to make the heat?" asked Edna.

"Fire."

Sandy sighed. "So you want to carry a fire around on a wooden carriage. Don't you think that's a bit dangerous?"

"Well, the fire would be in a metal box."

"And what would you burn?"

"Wood."

Sandy laughed. "You see Edna? I mean it's been great having Roger around since Albert's dad..." her voice trailed away for a second, then came back strong and artificially jolly, "But look what I have to put up with. Roger you silly man, anyone wanting to have one of these would need to carry a load of wood around with them, and stop every mile or so to stoke the fire."

"Yes, good isn't it"

"I can see what side of the family Albert gets his ideas from," said Edna.

She immediately wished she hadn't mentioned the lad's name. It broke her heart to think of him in trouble; he was just too nice a lad to get hurt. A tear ran down Sandy's cheek.

"Have you heard from him?" asked Edna.

"No, we thought he had eloped with Bryony, but she's been back recently and she says she hasn't seen him."

"Bryony's been back? When?"

Sandy pulled herself upright and attempted a smile. "A while back. No need to worry, he'll turn up somewhere."

Edna mentioned that she wanted to buy Bracken from them and the old cart. Sandy went with her to the stables, apparently happy with the deal.

Bracken was grazing peacefully on a nosebag of hay in his stall. Sandy leaned over the gate and stroked his nose. "You've got a new owner now, Bracken. You always liked Edna didn't you?" Sandy turned to Edna. "The animals are lucky not knowing about the Goblins and the camps."

Bracken stopped eating and gazed at her.

Edna smiled. "I think things are going to get better now."

Sandy sighed and turned away, unaware of Bracken's deep look of love and understanding.

Soon Bracken was trotting down Maltbrook Lane towards Edna's cottage. The road was littered with the unconscious forms of Goblin revellers too drunk to get home. Bracken clopped along as if it was just an ordinary day, taking care not to run anyone over. Shortly, Edna brought Bracken to a gentle halt outside her cottage.

"Wait here, my sweet horse. I'll get Azabyandee to carry my belongings and we'll be off as soon as possible. Things might be difficult round here for a while, and you've been such a good horse to me over the years that I want to reward you by taking you to my realm, where you can live in peace and comfort, with all the carrots a horse could possibly wish for."

Bracken gave her a puzzled look. She got down from the driver's seat and patted his neck.

"It's true, my glorious husband is better now."

To Edna's delight, all her favourite things had been piled on the kitchen table. Her rugs had been bundled with rope. Her pots and pans and potions were stacked in crates, neatly labelled. There were boxes of books and numerous bags of spices and precious stones.

She looked around her house. There were so many happy memories deep within the thick stone walls. She remembered looking out of the pretty curtains as Bryony arrived to take the delivery every morning to the castle. She touched the chairs and thought of Albert; young, confused and deeply in love.

In the living room she found Azabyandee in deep meditation. In this room too were so many memories; of Dragonfest and Bryony's delight in all things that shone. Of presents under the tree and of long summer evenings with the back door wide open.

Timothy jumped onto the sofa and up onto Edna's shoulder, where she sat, like a parrot, clinging on with needle-sharp claws.

Azabyandee opened his eyes, stood up, stepped back into the centre of the room and lifted his right palm. "I'm sorry my love. I'll explain in a moment."

A bolt of power came from him, hitting the wall between the kitchen and the living room like a cannonball. Stone and mortar fell onto the floor. Dust filled the air. All Edna could manage was a tiny squeak of dismay at the destruction of her precious cottage.

Azabyandee removed the torc from round his neck and placed it in the hole he had created. He turned to her. "Pen and paper?"

Edna still couldn't speak. She gestured weakly to a desk in the corner. Azabyandee scribbled a note and held it out for her. Edna opened her mouth to read aloud, but Azabyandee silenced her with a finger to his lips and a stern look towards where the torc lay. She read quietly to herself.

This message is destined for one who is to come in centuries hence. One skilled in the furnace, in metal making and new ideas. This one will understand how to make all well with this treasure, in whose structure truth and non-truth intertwine, and through which power beyond measure is found.

Edna met Azabyandee's eyes.

"This information came to me in a vision of the future," said Azabyandee. "I couldn't make out the face of the person who will claim it."

Edna nodded. Azabyandee sealed up the wall with a strong binding magic, hiding the torc and the message until the right time.

As Edna turned to leave her cottage she thought of Bryony. She sent a stream of loving kindness to her, wherever she was.

"Come along, Krodbell," said Edna, "come along, Timothy. We have a long journey. Bracken awaits. Don't forget the little bottle, darling."

* * *

245

The day after Gobfest, David and the other green-eyed escapees made their way from Dringle to Cucapha. Rain lashed down continually. Decayed and tattered pieces of bunting, left over from the celebrations, lay in the road like old green handkerchiefs, muddied by the puddles.

The rain had soaked through David's thin cotton shirt and now the chill was setting in, despite the smart pace of their march. He could feel Little Eric's legs quivering in the cold as he rode high on David's shoulders.

"David?" whispered Little Eric.

"Yup," answered David, trying to put energy and jolliness in his voice.

A paroxysm of coughing wracked Little Eric's body. After a while his small voice came again. "Is Queen Grizelda really gone?"

"So the messenger said. No-one can find her. Without their leader, the Goblins don't know what to do."

"Are we safe now? Are we free?"

"It's looking good so far. We won't know until we get to Cucapha and find out what's happening."

"So, who is queen now?"

Darkness brooded under the trees. David watched out for attack. He still feared random violence from the Goblins.

"I have no idea, but anyone is going to be better than Grizzly."

Little Eric's laughter turned to coughing. David turned back for a moment to admire the fortitude of the group of women and children trudging through the dark behind him.

246

"Keep going," he called, "we're nearly there. Just up here is a pub where we can rest and get some hot food."

He led them as briskly as he could past the castle battlements and on towards the welcoming lights of the Maltbrook Arms. To one side of the road, near the gatehouse, lay a pile of stones and rubble. A grave. It looked Human by the size and had been hastily but lovingly constructed. He paused to read the headstone, giving the others a chance to catch up.

Here lies Merik.

A brave and loyal soldier.

A Mentor.

A Friend.

A Hero.

Killed in action at the Battle of Cucapha.

Ruth was the first to join him.

"It's the grave of a soldier," said David. "Look, he must have been a hero. There aren't many who have a headstone these days."

"MERIK!" shrieked Ruth, collapsing onto her knees in the mud by the grave. "Oh Merik! NO!" She threw herself over the rubble as if to protect and comfort the dead soldier.

"Merik?" asked David. "Is this your Merik?"

Ruth lifted her head from the stones to look at him. Her eyes were huge. "Merik is a soldier," she shook her head, "was a soldier at the castle. This is his..." She lay over the stones again sobbing.

David turned as the rest of the group caught up. The children ran up to Ruth, patting her back and trying to pull her free.

"Kerry," said David, "we've just found the grave of Ruth's husband. Take the children to the

Maltbrook Arms, just up there. Get hot drinks down them. We'll join you soon."

With a nod, Kerry took Little Eric into her arms and led the children away.

David knelt down beside Ruth. She lifted her head. David watched quietly as she read the inscription.

"A hero," she said. Her voice caught in her throat. "I wonder what happened."

"We'll never know, Ruth, but we can rest assured that he died a noble death, probably saving life, and was loved and respected enough to be given the honour of this headstone. Someone must have been with him at the end."

David stood and offered Ruth his arm to help her stand.

"He must have helped to overthrow Grizelda," she said. Her voice was a whisper. She offered David a quavering smile. "Which means he helped to free us all." She paused, her face beginning to crumple. "I hope he didn't suffer."

"We can't know what he went through," said David, steering her gently away from the grave. "What we do know is that his death has helped to give these children their freedom and the safety to rebuild our world. Let's get to the Maltbrook Arms and get warm and dry. Little Eric needs us."

* * *

Bryony woke from her faint to find she was floating in mid-air on a small, fluffy cloud. Panic flooded her. She gripped the edges as hard as she could. Above her was a blue dome, lit by crystals of every hue. She shut her eyes and swallowed hard.

She hadn't been on a cloud since that awful day: that terrible day when she was tiny, when her world ended. She tried to fly away, but the cloud held her firmly in place. Her face burned where the knife had touched her cheek and her right arm ached with a gnawing pain.

"Bryony?"

The voice was gentle. Through her terror, Bryony felt the presence of someone calm nearby. She opened her eyes. A Faerie with the pale wings of a healer hovered over her, light and love flowing from her clear, green eyes.

"Get me down from here!" shouted Bryony.

"Why don't you like the cloud, Bryony?" said the healer. "Isn't it comfortable?"

"GET ME DOWN NOW!"

The healer waved her hand and the cloud transformed into a soft, supple oak leaf. Bryony relaxed.

"Your Royal Highness, My name is Miriam. I need you to lie on the leaf for a little while. The crystals in the dome will heal your burns."

"Alright, but not on the cloud."

"Certainly. You are quite safe and it won't take long. I will be as quick as I can."

"OK."

Bryony felt embarrassed at the tremble still showing in her voice. The memory of the cloud of her childhood hovered at the edge of her mind like a nightmare, as the leaf flew slowly around the chamber, pausing at different coloured crystals. Each resonated with a gentle music, and soon she felt the pain of the mortal iron melt away.

At last the leaf descended. Miriam steadied the oak leaf with her hands. "You may leave the leaf now and fly free. How do you feel?"

Bryony flexed her wings and rubbed her arms. She felt her face with her fingers. There was no pain anywhere. Her arm, which had ached all the time she was at the camp, felt normal.

"I feel good, thank you. I'm sorry about... earlier."

"That's perfectly alright. I'd like you to fly with me now to the Fountain of Healing. We can talk on the way if you like."

"But I'm all better now. Can't we go to the banquet? I want to wear my dress and tiara."

"We need to seal the magic. I want to be sure that the pain does not return. Sometimes ironburn, especially if wielded within a negative energy field, can return, and then your magic will be useless."

They flew out of the castle and into the Royal Forest. There, in the middle of a clearing of smooth green grass, stood a turquoise fountain. All around its edge hung tiny cups made from the petals of harebells. The water was as clear as crystal and as deep as a pond.

"Please, Your Highness, drink this elixir," said Miriam, handing Bryony a cup of water. She took one for herself. As they drank together, Bryony felt happiness and health flow through her. All her fatigue and despair vanished.

"Thank you."

"Would you like to talk about what happened on the cloud?"

Bryony hesitated. She couldn't see the point. Her parents had died that day and talking wouldn't bring them back. Despite her thoughts, she found herself telling her story. "I was a little girl, with baby wings. I went cloud hopping... you know..."

Miriam nodded. "I did the same as a small child."

"I fell." Awful memories flooded her mind. "No, I don't want to talk about it."

Miriam laid a gentle hand on her arm. "That's fine, you don't have to."

The image of Bryony's parents drowning as they tried to reach her filled her mind. "A gust of wind took my cloud over the cliff and out over the sea and I panicked. I fell off." She drew a deep shuddering breath. "Fable saved me. He was only a foal. He lay beside me on the beach, keeping me warm until help arrived."

Miriam gazed at her tenderly. "Your parents?"

"They died trying to get me out of the water."

Bryony stared at Miriam as if the Faerie healer could somehow erase those terrible moments; make them unhappen. She could hardly breathe. Miriam scooped two more tiny cups of water and gave one to Bryony. They both drank together as before. Bryony saw the rest of the story. She saw herself being rescued, loved, and adopted by the Royal Family. She saw the love that surrounded her now. She felt the presence of her parents. She felt their love.

"That is a terrible experience for one so young," said Miriam. "I will help you bear the burden as best I can. I have been assigned as your healer for the first five thousand years of your reign. I hope that once the coronation is over, we can meet to see if we can heal some more of the unresolved pain surrounding... clouds."

Bryony smiled. Miriam continued. "Please call me any time, day or night, if you need me, or if you are disturbed by bad dreams. Now, by your leave, we must prepare for the banquet."

* * *

Sheean sat impatiently in his bath, enduring the attention of the Royal Bathers who fussed around him with sweetly scented cleansing lotions and offers of wing moisturiser. One particularly annoying one called Marvil kept on trying to touch his hair.

'I wonder,' thought Sheean, 'if anyone would complain if I got Alex and sliced their heads off.'

"I'm sorry Your Royal Highness," said Marvil.

"What?"

Marvil gulped. "I... I'm sorry to interrupt your thoughts. I need you to look up so that I can sort out your hair for the banquet."

"What's wrong with my hair? It's how all the young men at the castle had it."

"Yes, Your Royal Highness. I'm certain it was perfect for blending in with the Humans."

Sheean scowled. "You say that like there's something wrong. What's wrong with Humans?"

"Well..."

"Yes?"

Sheean's voice held a hint of menace. The other attendants paused, their sponges dripping, and looked at Marvil. The one washing Sheean's feet gave the slightest shake of his head in warning. Marvil gulped again.

"Er nothing. I was just trying to say your hair needs a few small changes, maybe a griffin feather above each ear. I have some gold spider thread, it would look very..."

"Naff."

"But, Your Royal Highness, the banquet."

"My hair is clean, isn't it?"

"Yes of course, but..."

"Then it will be fine as it is."

Sheean clambered out of the bath, almost slipping back into the scented water as his foot found a bar of soap. He stood, his skin glistening in the torchlight, refusing to raise a glamour to hide his nakedness. He looked around the room to make sure he had everyone's attention.

"From now on" he said, smiling at their embarrassment, "I bathe myself, I dress myself, I decide how my hair is. And you can tell the toilet assistant, I can clean my own backside."

The attendants flew out, low to the ground, holding their heads down like scolded children.

"And tell my valet to knock before entering," he shouted after them.

* * *

Bryony looked at herself in the mirror, twirling round and round to see the golden petals of her dress billowing outwards like a flower.

"Please, Your Royal Highness," squeaked one of the glow-worms, "please can you stop twirling. We're feeling sick."

"Sorry."

Bryony stopped. She felt the tiny, gripping feet of the insects in her hair relax.

"We felt, Your Royal Highness," said Lorella, "that, due to the uncertainty of Sheean's coronation, the royal blue of victory should be reduced. And, with the deepest respect, I notice you are wearing a necklace. I'm concerned about that."

"What's wrong with my necklace?"

Bryony whirled to face her maidservant, dislodging two butterflies, one of which fell to the floor. Bryony knelt down.

"Oh, you poor thing. Are you the butterfly I asked to fly round the meadow?"

"Yes," squeaked Butterfly. "I'm fine, just a bit tired, but I'll be fine. It is an honour to decorate your hair, and I will try not to fall again. Please put me back."

Bryony helped the creature back to her hair, where it perched, leaning against her tiara. Bryony glared at Lorella through the mirror's reflection.

Lorella lowered her gaze and spoke softly. "The royal blue, Your Royal Highness, not only represents victory over adversity, but the inevitability of the coronation and a continuation of Taranor as a happy and carefree kingdom. Also the gold chain is a piece of Human jewellery and does not befit the occasion."

"Ah," said Bryony, sitting down on the rose-petal bed. It sank beneath her, releasing the pure scent of summer. "Is Sheean not going to be king then?"

Lorella curtseyed. "I am not at liberty to discuss such matters, Your Royal Highness. It was remiss of me to talk so freely."

"I don't care if this necklace doesn't befit the occasion. I'm not taking it off. It's important to me."

Lorella paled a little, simply curtseying again in reply. "If that is all, I should be helping with the seating at the banquet."

"Alright. I'll have a fly about and look around."

"As you wish."

Lorella curtsied once more and left the room. As the curtain billowed behind her, tiny bells tinkled.

Bryony went closer to the mirror and peered at her face. Despite the healing, she could still make out the long, pale scar that lay along her cheek. Its serrated edge was still clear. She shuddered at the memory of its touch, then straightened up and tucked her silver dagger into her belt. At least her burns didn't hurt anymore.

She flew out into the garden and over to the meadow to find Fable surrounded by Pixies. They were arguing about how to plait his tail with flowers.

"Hello, little one," said Fable. He was chewing on sweet grasses.

Bryony gave him a hug, wrapping her arms around his neck and upsetting the daisies in his newly brushed mane.

"Sorry, Pixies," she said, trying to put the flowers back into place, "I didn't mean to upset your work."

"Excuse me, Noble Horse," said a Pixie in green, curly toed boots, "but which is best? Daisies all the way down your tail, or daisies and ivy leaves as well, only Sarah here says-,"

Fable smiled and interrupted. "I'll leave it to you."

The Pixies continued to argue, some even slapping each other.

"Stop it," said Bryony.

They all stopped at once and hovered in the air in a neat line.

"Just use daisies. They remind me of my sixteenth birthday. Do you remember, Fable, when I had them in my hair, the night I turned sixteen and got my first-level powers?"

Fable nuzzled her cheek. "I remember it well, little one."

"Oh! I just thought. It must still be Sheean's birthday."

Fable chewed thoughtfully for a bit. "Well, yes and no. When he was kidnapped it wasn't his birthday. However when we flew back here, he had just got his second-level wings and had reached the mortal age of eighteen. It isn't twelve petals yet so I suppose it is technically still his birthday. It's all rather confusing."

"What shall I get him?"

At that moment Dog came running up to join them. He was grinning all over his face. Around his neck was a turquoise ribbon. "Am so happy!"

"Hello, Dog," said Bryony, giving him a hug. "That's a very pretty ribbon. I'm not surprised you're happy."

Dog tipped his head on one side. His ears flopped. "No. Me hates ribbon. Me happy they is going to cook me honey and nut sausages and magic any flavour I like. Whatever I think of, I get. So excited!"

Dog ran round and round Fable, scattering the Pixies away from their task. "Me having sausages! Me having sausages!"

Fable thought for a moment. "I think Sheean would like the freedom to decide his own future."

"That's not a very jolly present," said Bryony. "I'll have to think of something."

* * *

Sheean flew out into his private garden and sat on a bench of finely wrought silver, letting the warm breeze dry his wings. Looking up at the stars, he spoke aloud. "I know I was tough on the servants, Merik, but it's not what I'm used to. I so wish you were still alive, sharing adventures with me, and

256

telling me what the right thing to do is. I don't want to hurt Bryony, but I don't love her. Should I go through with the coronation? Maybe I could change things here, maybe I could make them help Humans."

He looked at the garden. All around were deep, velvet hued flowers, some hiding their light and resting, others wide open, feeding on the light from the two moons. Glow-worms hovered nearby, quivering, feeling his distress. As he glared at them, one of them squeaked and flew off as fast as it could into the castle. He looked up at the night sky. "Maybe I should just run away."

Dog galloped up to Sheean, his tail wagging, and sat lazily at the foot of the bench. He looked up at Sheean with big brown eyes. "Just had loadsa sausages."

Sheean scratched Dog's head. "What would you do, Dog, if you were me?"

"Dog do what Dog like."

Sheean sighed. "It's easy for you. You don't have to be king." He thought for a moment. "Do you remember Kanthy? I wonder where she is?"

"Remember her, good fun. Make good bitch."

Sheean smiled as a clouded memory came back to him. "Yes Dog, she did make a good bitch."

"Not be good like Dog though."

"No, I'm certain you're right."

There was a noise from inside Sheean's bedroom. Sheean and Dog both looked to see what had caused it.

Jerremoy stood at the garden doors and coughed. "I'm sorry, Your Majesty, I did knock but you didn't hear me. I will have the tinkle bells on your curtains mended. We have only a short time to get you ready for the banquet and get you there. You cannot be late."

Sheean stood and raised a glamour of a loose fitting white shirt and trousers. "What do you think Jerry?"

"A little plain, Your Royal Highness, but if that's what you want to wear."

"Yes, this is what I want to wear."

* * *

Lorella felt sick at the thought of what Queen Rhyannon would think when she found out Bryony was wearing a Human necklace. She flew out into the scented gardens where she found Jerremoy counting glow-worm lanterns.

"Jerremoy, have you got a minute?" she asked.

"Certainly. How can I help?"

"Princess Bryony is wearing a Human necklace."

"My dear, simply tell her to adjust her glamour accordingly." He turned to her, his eyes wide with alarm. "Did you say Human?"

"Yes. She said a Human gave it to her, and that she wants to wear it."

Jerremoy fluttered around a jasmine bush in agitation. "That's disgusting!"

"I know. What should I do?"

"She can't possibly wear that to the banquet." He gave Lorella a conspiratorial wink. "Tell her that it's the necklace or the tiara. Her choice. That should sort it. If not, we will have to take the matter to the queen. And that won't do because she's terribly busy at the moment."

"That's a good idea."

"And can you inform Princess Bryony that there is a delay. The banquet will not start until the eleventh petal."

"Why so late?"

"Because Queen Rhyannon wishes longer for all the guests to arrive. Some are still on their way?"

"How many people are we expecting?"

"Queen Rhyannon has invited the entire population of Taranor. After all, Princess Bryony and Prince Sheean will be ruling not just the city of Taranor itself, but the entire Faerie realm. This banquet allows the subjects a chance to meet their new king and queen."

"Are the Grey Elves invited?"

"Oh my wings no! Whatever gave you that idea?"

Lorella decided that bringing up the Grey Elf issue now was not a good idea. She gave Jerremoy a dazzling smile and flew back to find Bryony and tell her the news.

Chapter 9

Bryony took off the gold necklace Ruth had given her, and placed it with Sheean's Portal Stone in a pouch at her waist. Then she checked her tiara in the mirror and set off towards the forest, followed at the correct distance by Lorella.

As arranged, they met Sheean and Jerremoy at the Scented Rose Garden at the edge of the forest. Fable was there too, his mane and tail covered in daisies. Dog sat on Fable's back, wagging his tail proudly. His ribbon looked wonderful in the moonslight.

They made their way to the start of the Avenue of Wisteria, where they met Agaric. Bryony was alarmed to see how many security staff were gathered. Many hid among the trees, while others stood guard on either side of the Avenue in full view.

As if in answer to her look, Agaric said, "We are not expecting trouble, Your Royal Highness. However it is wise to take precautions. We have heard rumours that some of the dwellers of this realm are preparing to make protests. They are using this wonderful occasion to make their voices heard. Of course Queen Rhyannon has always been one to listen to the lower beings, so they will be allowed to gather. However they will not disturb you."

All around them hung clusters of glow-worms, illuminating the path into the depths of the forest.

"We will fly though every clearing," said Agaric, "each will be populated by our brothers and sisters of the Faerie Realm." He handed Bryony and Sheean a purse each, containing a fine pink, glittery dust. "Here are bags of love mist. Smile at all you see, no matter what they say to you, and sprinkle them to show your good intentions for the future."

Bryony checked her tiara self-consciously, her wings tinged with a happy sky-blue. The first sound of trumpets came to her from far ahead. She glanced across at Sheean, hovering on her right. He looked solemn, like a proper king, carrying Alex in his belt. All he needed was a crown and he would be perfect.

They flew for half a petal, travelling high up, through every clearing in the forest. They flew over Pixies, Nymphs, Dryads and Centaurs, sprinkling them all with love mist. The pink glitter looked so pretty in the moonslight as it twinkled over everyone's upturned faces. The security guards flew alongside, keeping to the trees, their glamour rendering them invisible to anyone unaware of their presence.

Agaric paused. By now they had reached the outer margin of the forest, far away from the castle. "This is where we might have trouble," he said. "This is where the people who have alleged grievances are gathered."

Bryony felt suffocated by the proximity of the guards as they closed in around her.

"Fly higher here. We can't risk them grabbing at you," one of them said.

"Come up here," called Fable as he flew up near the tops of the trees. Dog whimpered and crouched down on Fable's broad back.

"What's to stop them flying up and grabbing us?" asked Sheean.

"These people are forbidden to fly while in our city."

Forbidden to fly. The words echoed around Bryony's mind as they flew into the clearing. It looked strange to see so many Fay sitting or standing on the ground. She hesitated, sprinkling some love mist on their upturned faces. Many brushed the dust from their wings and shook their hair. They were quiet and their faces were grim. Agaric reached for Bryony's arm, but she pulled away. "No, I want to hear what they have to say."

A small cheer rose up from some Dryads on the far side of the clearing. A Centaur walked forwards to speak. He had long white hair and a tail just like Fable's. His coat was the colour of ripe chestnuts. He lifted his head high. "I have a message from the Grey Elves and from us all."

Muscles rippled across his chest as he gestured towards the crowd. "Every 46,000 years or so, the ordinary Fay get to feast on Royal Food during the coronation. The rest of the time we have to hunt for dried flowers, damaged nuts and fallen leaves in the Northern lands. Pixies work in your castle all night, afraid for their lives should they make a single mistake. The mist you shower down is not filled with love, it is just mist. It has been this way for thousands of years."

An ugly murmur came from the crowd. Bryony felt puzzled. She was sure she had sprinkled the powder with love. Agaric dragged her away. "This is not your concern, Your Royal Highness."

She looked back. The Centaur's deep brown eyes met hers. She gave the Centaur a look of genuine goodwill and peace. Just before she turned away, she winked. The Centaur bowed.

They flew on, returning to the glittering spires of the castle, where glow-worms flew dangerously close together to provide decoration. Soon they entered a clearing, filled with a throng of her own kin. The forest was scintillating with multi-coloured, winged creatures. All were silent, their eyes on the new royal couple; the holders of the Light Prophecy.

The sound of trumpets ceased as Bryony and Sheean took their seats on a giant red and white toadstool. In the very centre of the clearing grew a clock flower. Eleven of the petals were lowered down, leaving one remaining upright against the gem in the centre.

Queen Rhyannon sat cross legged on a tall, slender mushroom. Her golden wings spread light all around. Fable and Dog made themselves comfortable nearby, while Miriam the healer, Lorella and Jerremoy sat at a discrete distance. Bryony noticed castle guards in armour hovering all around, alert and steely eyed.

With a flourish of pipe and drum music, tables of food materialised in front of the guests, laden with delicacies from across the whole of Taranor. The queen's food taster stepped forward. Queen Rhyannon pointed to the dish of her choice and the taster had a sample. He nodded and the queen began to eat, smiling at Sheean and Bryony to encourage them.

Bryony chose a bright green leaf rolled around cherries. Her taster nodded. She took a bite. The juices from the cherries burst sweetly on her tongue, mixing with the tang of the leaf so beautifully. All those months of rice and greens at the prison camp faded away as she reached for another leaf. The music grew faster and louder as the people relaxed and the banquet began.

* * *

Course followed course, each being brought to the table by the castle servants. Everyone was smiling. The music was continuous. High pitched pipes and flutes combined with Pixie songs, and Faerie ballads

263

flowed from musicians perched high in the trees above the revellers. Sheean's head was beginning to hurt. He looked sideways at Bryony who seemed deep in thought. She hadn't touched her cake.

"What's wrong?" he asked. "Are you not enjoying the banquet? I would have thought the finery and flowers would be perfect for you."

Bryony sighed. "Sorry. I'm happy, really I am. It's just that I keep thinking about that Centaur and all the unhappy faces we saw earlier. Non Faeries are forbidden to fly. Is that right? Then I keep thinking about Edna. I feel so bad that I couldn't rescue her. She's trapped in the Demon realm. I went back to Gavelkind to find her. I failed. Now they'll never let me go back."

Sheean interrupted when Bryony paused for breath. He'd forgotten how busy her mind was. "Don't worry," he said. "Edna's fine."

Bryony whirled to face him, dislodging some of the butterflies in her hair. One of them fell onto the top of the mushroom with a squeak of terror. Bryony picked it up and held it in her palm. "Oh, little Butterfly. You should have rested when I gave you the chance. You're too tired to decorate my hair."

Sheean cleared his throat and continued. "I helped Merik and Grumbuk rescue her. Last time I saw her, she was at home safe and sound."

Bryony's face lit up with relief. She looked as though she was going to fly up out of her seat in happiness. Wisely, she stayed put. "Thank the gods!" She looked back at the butterfly. It was struggling to its feet, pumping its wings back and forth. "Butterfly, why don't you rest?"

Sheean heard the tiny voice of the insect. "No," it said, "I must do my job. I'll be thrown away if I fail."

Bryony laughed. "Don't be silly. No-one's going to throw you away. You're a living being, not an object. Now sit up inside my tiara if you really want to. But I'm quite happy for you to sit on the mushroom instead."

"Please put me back. I can manage."

She placed the butterfly back on her hair where it sank down among the deep brown strands, clinging on for dear life. Trumpets sounded and players, dressed in bright clothes paraded into the clearing.

"Your Majesty, Your Royal Highnesses," bellowed a young male in yellow and pink glamour. "By your leave, the Taranor Players will perform for your delight, a new play called 'The death of Ogman.'"

The crowd went wild. The actor bowed low before Queen Rhyannon and then Sheean and Bryony. The actors flew into the air, pirouetting and dancing in the moonlight. Soon they settled on the grass and the play began.

Sheean forced a smile. Bryony looked at him, puzzled. "Are you alright?"

"No," he said. He was beginning to feel sick. He just wanted to get away to talk things through with Bryony privately. "Edna is OK, but Merik isn't."

Her face fell. "What happened?"

"He died, saving my life. He died so I could do this..."

Sheean waved his hand to indicate the glittering finery of the forest, the lights and the players. Some of the courtiers noticed his gesture and bowed in response.

Bryony and Sheean sat silently for a time, pretending to enjoy the play. A young female with her wings held tight back, pretending to be Human, danced with a male wearing a crown. Some of the larger actors, dressed as guards, captured the king and mimed throwing the two lovers into a hole in the ground. The strident voices of the players filled the clearing. "And so King Ogmantiguthra, as punishment for loving a mortal, was imprisoned in the Goblin realm in a deep, deep cave." The audience was rapt. No-one made a sound.

The players acted out the kidnap of Sheean and mimed Bryony's brave trip into the Human realm to rescue him. The audience applauded. The players mimed the journey through the Goblin realm and the fight in the cave. Sheean noticed a single tear trickle down Bryony's cheek.

"Albert will really old now," she said. "He'll be in his fifties, which for a Human is really old. And Edna. She could be dead by now!"

Bryony began to cry quietly. Many of the nearby kin gazed at her in compassion, clearly assuming she was moved by the story.

"Bryony?" said Sheean, quietly.

She sniffed and rubbed her nose on her sleeve. "Yes?"

"We have to talk about our future."

"Now? Wouldn't it be better if we talked later?"

"After tonight, they won't give us much private time together. Not until after the coronation and the marriage."

Sheean studied her face. She was beautiful in a way, but not like Kanthy. Kanthy was homely and rounded.

Bryony sighed. "I'm sorry Sheean, I can't think of our future right now. All this seems so shallow."

She looked up at the players who were now fighting Ogman with swords. He saw her take a deep

266

breath. "I suppose," she said quietly, "we have to keep going don't we?"

"Did you fall in love with Albert?"

Bryony blushed. "No... well, yes I was getting very fond of him. Not like a husband sort of thing, but I did like him." She paused. The actor playing Ogman fell to the ground, his crown smashed. "Well, maybe I did love him a bit."

She looked quickly at Sheean. "But I wouldn't have married him. I'm supposed to marry you. I've thought about it. I know we don't love each other, but we are good friends. We could be happy. We have a lot of experience of the world outside Taranor. We could make a difference. We could truly fulfil the Light Prophecy."

"Yes, but shouldn't we be marrying for love?"

"The people need us. We can work something out, and anyway we may fall in love, given time."

"S'pose," said Sheean thoughtfully.

The play came to an end. Everyone applauded by rising into the air and flapping their wings. Sheean and Bryony played along, thanking the actors for their performance.

There was a pause. Everyone watched the clock flower in the centre of the clearing.

"As it was your birthday in the Human realm, just before we jumped," muttered Bryony, "I brought you some Cowslip wine."

She gave a gesture and a servant poured a buttercup full of golden wine and placed it on the mushroom near Sheean. He smiled. "Thanks. That's kind of you, but what I'd really like is Merik back."

Bryony gave a small squeak of inspiration and reached into her pouch.

"Here," she said, "your Portal Stone. I took it. And..." she hesitated, shooting him a strange look. "I think you might like this." She handed him a gold chain with a leaf on it. "Merik's wife gave it to me. It was a present from him to her. Would you like it?"

Sheean reached out his hand and took the delicate chain, closing his fist around it. He clenched his jaw to stop the sadness that threatened to overwhelm him. Now was not the time for grief.

Before he could thank her, a cry sprang from the mouths of the gathered Fay. All the glow-worms dimmed their lights. The twelfth petal in the clock flower lowered slowly, to reveal the full brilliance of the gem in the centre. Twelve bells sounded throughout the land. Cries of delight could be heard all round the forest as clock flowers in every clearing did the same.

Queen Rhyannon raised her wings and flew high in the air; so high that all the guests throughout the forest could see her glow in the sky. She revealed her wand of power and lowered it towards Sheean.

"Happy Birthday, Sheean, and welcome home," she cried. Everyone cheered and flew up into the air again. The pipers and singers resumed their places in the tree tops and soon a lively tune filled the air. The food tables disappeared, revealing the soft grassy clearing speckled with wild flowers.

"It's the dancing now," said Bryony. "We're expected to be the first."

Sheean panicked. "Who told you that?"

"My personal assistant, Lorella. Are you nervous?"

"Of course I am! I have no idea how to dance!"

Queen Rhyannon looked across at them, smiling.

"What do I do?" asked Sheean.

"Stand up, bow, and ask me to dance."

He did as he was told.

"I like you in plain white," said Bryony as she took his hands and led him to the dance area.

"Thanks, they wanted to dress me like a..."

"Faerie?"

"Yes."

Bryony grinned. "And we can't have that, can we."

"You look like a proper Princess."

"Don't lie Sheean. I know you don't like all this pompous stuff."

They were both giggling by the time they were in position.

"You know, I'd rather fight Ogman than be standing here in front of all these people," said Sheean.

"Relax. You'll be fine. Hold my right hand, put your left hand on my waist, and hover just clear of the ground. I will make it look as though you're leading, and don't fight me when I move us around the clockflower."

On the first step they collided as Sheean moved in the opposite direction. "Move with me, Sheean," laughed Bryony.

Most of the time it worked, but every now and again they ended up standing on each other's feet. Sheean kept his wings relaxed, which was a problem whenever they did a quick turn, as they slapped round him like wet laundry. Bryony grinned from ear to ear, letting her wings relax as well. Soon they were flapping and flopping, tripping up and stumbling, all in time to the music.

Sheean heard a small group talking and pointing. He looked across at them, noticing they were trying to copy the new dance steps. Before long, the clearing was full of people following the new trend.

"See?" said Bryony. "They think we're great!"

"I'd still rather fight Ogman."

Sheean twirled Bryony round and round, smiling as her wings flapped against his face. "Thanks for my present Bryony. It means a lot to me."

* * *

Bryony lay on her bed later that night, enjoying the light from the two moons as it shone through the curtains at her window. She felt gentle hands smoothing out her wings.

"There's no need to do that," she said kindly.

"But your wings, Your Majesty," said a little Pixie. "Your wings must look their best for the coronation tomorrow night. We have to keep them smooth."

Bryony sighed and rolled onto her back, nearly crushing her attendant. "Oh I'm sorry, did I hurt you?"

"No I'm quite alright," said the Pixie as she straightened her hat.

Bryony looked around. The room was full of tiny Fay creatures, most of whom were picking up rose petals and putting them back on the bed.

"Do you stay here all night, every night?"

One of the Pixies stopped what she was doing and curtseyed. "Yes, Your Royal Highness. It is our job to make sure your bed is at least one Pixie deep in rose petals."

"So," said Bryony, "every time I turn over in my sleep, you rearrange the rose petals so that I'm comfortable? Is that right?"

"Yes, Your Royal Highness."

"Do other people have this?"

"Yes, Your Royal Highness. Sheean, Queen Rhyannon and yourself all have this service."

"What about the ordinary Faeries?"

"Oh they sleep very well. They have a leaf each or a flower. You mustn't worry. Everyone is happy in Taranor."

Bryony sat up, scattering rose petals as her wings opened. "Oh sorry. Look, please don't worry. Have the night off."

"No we couldn't. It just wouldn't do."

"I won't tell. It isn't fair that you work hard all day and all night."

"We don't mind. We can't possibly bother you with our trifling troubles."

Bryony got out of bed. "Please my little friends, go out into the garden and sleep together in the leaves. I'll be fine."

Bryony was still awake when she heard the clockflowers chiming three. She was worried she might look dreadful in the morning. She turned over again, this time feeling the floor through the thin layer of remaining petals.

She gave up and flew through the window into her garden, where she saw the Pixies curled up asleep. They looked so cute. She yawned and stretched, searching out a suitable place for herself. Shrinking down to the size of a butterfly, she wrapped herself in a leaf. There, rocking gently in the breeze and listening to the lullaby of the fountain, she finally fell asleep.

* * *

Albert slept fitfully until the first rays of dawn woke him. The pale pink sky was flecked with tiny golden clouds and the air was already deliciously warm. His heart sank as he realised he was not dreaming. His stomach growled with hunger. He heard gulls calling again, although now the sound seemed more like tiny babies calling. Their cries echoed off the cliffs. He listened harder. It was babies! Crying babies!

He walked along the beach at the base of the cliff face, looking behind rocks and boulders, searching for the source of the sound. After a while, he discovered the opening to a cave, the entrance of which was flanked by two tall pointed rocks, both covered in unfamiliar symbols. Despite his fear and his desperate wish to return home, he was beginning to enjoy himself a little. "Something to tell the grandchildren," he said aloud.

As he crossed the threshold, his eyes blinded by the darkness, the crying noise stopped. Straining to see inside, he thought he saw a woman lying asleep on a bed. In her arms she cradled two very small babies. As his eyes adjusted to the gloom, he realised the woman was lying asleep on a huge four poster bed. She was covered by a rotten quilt, embroidered with intricate designs of flowers and animals. It looked ancient. Flowers were growing under the bed. Right underneath where she lay.

The babies watched him silently. He came closer and recognized the woman. She was from the castle. He searched for her name for a moment, looking intently at her sleeping features.

"Kanthy?"

Kanthy opened her eyes. She mouthed something, but no sound came through her cracked lips.

He approached the bed and leaned closer, putting his ear near to her mouth. "Sorry, I didn't catch what you said."

"Get me some water, dunderhead."

"Oh, right, of course," he said. "Water."

He could hear a dripping sound at the back of the cave. "There's a spring back here. I'll collect some for you."

He walked to the rear of the cave. "This is amazing. There's a pipe with water coming out of it. A golden pipe! I wonder if it's real gold. And there's a basin. It looks like marble. Have you got anything to drink from?"

There was no reply, so he searched around on the floor. There, by his foot, lay a dusty, dirty goblet, brown with age and dented. He picked it up and filled it with water. Albert wondered quietly whether there was any treasure in the cave. That would make his adventure worthwhile.

One of the babies giggled, snapping Albert out of his daydream. Kanthy struggled to sit up as he approached. She placed the babies on the pillow and sat on the edge of her bed. Albert put his arm around her shoulders to support her and put the goblet to her lips.

"Thank you," she whispered.

"Are these your babies?"

Kanthy looked deliberately slowly round the cave. "I can't see any other women here can you?"

"When did you... um, give birth?"

"Yesterday."

"What are you doing here?"

"Will your questions never stop? I had to keep the children safe. Keep them away from King Yuppick and my mother."

She seemed terribly weak and there was blood on the floor and on the bed covers. She was as pale as death.

"What's happened to you? Have you had these babies on your own?"

Kanthy nodded. "Needed to get away." She coughed and reached for the water again.

"Where are we?" asked Albert.

"We're on Taranor, not the Human one, the proper Faerie Kingdom of Taranor."

"Wow. I jumped through a hole in the sky after Bryony and her friend. The one with the funny name. Sheean, that was it. How did you get here?"

"Sean's alive?"

"Yes. My best friend Bryony helped him escape. A wolf jumped out off the castle balcony and Bryony and Sheean fell." His words rushed from him in a torrent. The news seemed to interest Kanthy. She lay back down, cuddling her babies, listening quietly to his tale of flying horses and windows through worlds. When he had run out of steam she lifted a finger. "Food. Get me some food."

"Oh, food. Of course. Gosh, yes. Sorry."

Albert waded out to his waist and looked down through the clear turquoise water at the sand below. He stood totally still, holding a straight piece of driftwood carved to a point at one end. He remembered doing this on his holiday with Bryony. He also remembered her reaction when he brought her his first kill. She had reacted really weirdly.

The sea was teeming with fish. They were large and brightly coloured, seemingly unafraid of him. They came close to his legs, tickling him with their fins. It was easy to stab one. He ran to the beach to kill it quickly. "Bryony would hate to see you suffer," he said to the fish, "but Kanthy and I need to eat." He gutted it carefully as his mother had shown him, and placed it on a flat rock. "Now, a fire to cook it."

There was quite a bit of driftwood around, but he had no flint or tinder. He ran to the entrance of the cave. "Do you mind the fish raw? Only I could light a fire, but it would take a long time, and I expect you're hungry."

Kanthy shook her head. "Give me the fish now."

Albert felt pleased with himself as he brought Kanthy the food. He was behaving like a proper man in front of a damsel in distress.

"What are you smiling at?" she snapped. "How long does it take to catch a fish?"

Albert's smile faded. He watched her devour the food. Every now and then she stopped eating, and fed chunks of fish to the babies.

"Should they eat that?" he asked. "I thought babies drank mother's milk."

"They told me they wanted it."

Albert had expected to share the food. There had been enough for two, but now that the babies were eating as well, he had nothing. He left the cave and spent the rest of the morning catching fish for himself. Not wanting to eat the fish raw, he lit a fire at the entrance to the cave and cooked his lunch.

While eating, Albert thought about Bryony. Now that the initial shock had worn off, he was beginning to feel annoyed at her. She should have told him she

275

had real magic; powerful magic like Wizards and Faeries have. He remembered seeing Bryony's magic for the first time. She'd been able to change his appearance with a click of her fingers. He'd seen Fable leap into the air. He'd seen Bryony's wings.

He chewed his fish and stared at the sea. She'd always said she was promised to that man. Sheean. The food in his mouth tasted like sawdust. He swallowed. Here he was, trapped in an alien world because he'd been stupid enough to think she might love him one day. Maybe she'd never loved him. Maybe she never would.

He went back into the cave to talk with Kanthy. She was feeding the twins; one baby crooked in each arm, one baby for each breast.

"Who is the father? Couldn't you have stayed with him?"

"I couldn't exactly stay with Sean at the top of the castle tower, now could I? The babies would not have been safe there."

"Sheean's the father? Were you and Sheean lovers? It's just that Bryony kept saying she was going to be his wife. That he was a prince and that they were going to be married."

"Nonsense. Do you know where Sean is?"

"His name's pronounced Sheean not Sean. He's here. I followed them both through a magic window like I said."

Kanthy thought for a minute. "You have to help me. I have to find him and tell him I have his children."

"You can't. I told you, him and Bryony are going to be married. I feel so stupid. I was daft to follow them. Bryony's not interested in me. She never was, she never will be. And now my parents will be worried sick about me."

Albert paused, looking out of the cave at the sea. The sun was very hot and he was glad of the cave's shelter. "Is it true what they say? If this is truly the Faerie Kingdom, will I be very old when I get back?"

There was no reply. Kanthy had fallen asleep. The two babies sat up on the bed staring at each other, without blinking, as though they were having an intense, silent conversation.

"I don't know much about babies," said Albert. "But I do know that at one day old you two shouldn't be sitting up like that."

* * *

Dog left Bryony having her hair brushed and trotted down a long corridor towards the kitchens, hoping for sausages. He could smell something delicious. He jumped in surprise when a tall thin Faerie dressed in deep blue glamour stepped out in front of him. His wings were small. His dark green eyes sparkled. He leaned down towards Dog, bending in the middle like a blue lamp post.

"Ah, there you are. Please allow me to introduce myself. My name is Yewed Ukak. I am the Royal, Senior Liaison Officer for Animal Welfare. I understand you are the new royal animal companion."

"Go way," said Dog. "Am busy, getting' sausages."

"Oh dear, oh dear. Is there something wrong with your mouth? All I can hear is a garbled noise. Pray tell me your name."

"Dog."

"I am terribly sorry, I did not catch that."

"Didn't throw nothing. You stupid?"

"You seem unable to pronounce words in a coherent fashion. Am I making a correct assumption?"

"What you think I doing?" said Dog. "Just told you. You stupid."

"This will never do, the royal couple cannot possibly have an animal companion with such poor enunciation."

"I talk clear. Maybe you deaf."

"And you're so... common. Look at your fur, it's so rough and tangled. Who picked you for this position?" Yewed pushed his fingers into Dog's fur. "Oh my goodness, you're so... so filthy."

Dog growled deep in his throat and bared his teeth. "Why you nasty to Dog? I think I bite you. Teach you manners."

"What are you d-doing? S-stop that, go away. Stop... Ouch!"

* * *

A commanding voice ricocheted around the servants' quarters of Taranor Castle. "JERREMOY-DROFORD-ROSETHORN! REPORT TO SECURITY CENTRAL IMMEDIATELY. BRING A HEALER!"

Jerremoy dropped his cleaning wand into its holder, taking a careful mental note of how much more cleaning the royal banqueting table cloth needed, and flew towards the Healing Fields. His entire being buzzed with a vibrant energy: the energy of action. His mind leapt about like a rabbit, trying to imagine what terrible calamity was going to meet him.

Jerremoy and the healer materialised in the sparse, grey room of Security Central. Yewed was flying around in the middle of the room, holding onto one leg. His tiny wings were almost black with fury.

"What on Taranor is the matter?" asked Jerremoy.

"He bit me!" shouted the officer.

"Who bit you?" asked Jerremoy.

The healer, a soft round woman with pale hair, pale eyes and white wings, flew near to Yewed, her hands outstretched, already sending healing.

"That dog!"

"What dog?"

"The one brought in by Princess Bryony. Look!"

Yewed rolled his trouser leg up to show teeth marks. The healer suppressed a small smile as she completed the healing. Only a few small marks remained.

"I don't think you'll need any more healing, Sir," she said. "You will feel no more pain."

"Thank you. You may go."

At the door the healer gave a mock curtsey, the nature of which was not lost on Jerremoy. He had to suppress a smile. Yewed landed on the floor and hovered near his desk, fury palpably beating in his wings.

Jerremoy made his wings paler to try to calm his colleague. "Of course, it doesn't surprise me at all. You are aware the dog is from the Human realm, aren't you?"

"Yes, and I totally disapprove. We cannot have a dog from the Human realm living with the Royal Family. Such a thing has never happened before and will never happen again. You and I agree don't we, Jerremoy, that change is a bad thing?"

He ignored Jerremoy's polite nod of agreement and began looking at his schedule for the evening. "We must dispose of the animal at once."

"It will not be easy to dispose of. The dog apparently helped save their lives, and it is also a friend of Fable."

"Well, what would you expect? That horse has always been a bad judge of character."

"What do you mean?"

Yewed looked up and met Jerremoy's eyes. "Well, the princess is a commoner you know. Why she was picked to be the future queen, I don't know."

Jerremoy felt his colour darkening. He tried to keep the pale blue of agreement and lower status, but it was a struggle. "As you are aware," he said, "she did pass all of the tests and there is a shortage of suitable children from the upper classes. I am more concerned about the future king."

"Why?"

Now that he had managed to change the subject, Jerremoy had no trouble in staying subservient. "How shall I put this? He seems to have been tainted by his time in the Human realm. Either that or he is the result of poor breeding."

"Poor breeding? Have you met his father?"

"Only once. He was running an errand for his wife. Do I need to say more?"

* * *

After a late breakfast, Sheean sat in his garden on the low wall surrounding the pond, watching Bryony fly from flower to flower. She was sniffing them and making delighted squeaks of pleasure, while Dog ran around and around, chasing his tail.

"Bryony, stop flitting around like a demented bee and talk to me."

"Is it about us again?" she asked, giving Sheean an exasperated look.

"Yes, it's important. We, or at least I, need to understand why we're doing this."

"Very well then, I'll stop being a demented bee. But I don't know what to say to reassure you. I mean, what do you want me to say?"

"I just want you to tell me what you really think about the future that other people have mapped out for us."

"You think I haven't given it any thought, don't you?" said Bryony.

"Well it does seem that way, sometimes."

"As I said before, I think we can make a difference."

"The coronation is bad enough, but what about the marriage?" said Sheen. "We're just friends, we're not in love."

"People don't always marry for love."

"I always thought I would."

"You're a prince, you don't have that luxury."

"S'pose... It just doesn't seem fair."

"What's not fair?" asked Bryony as she joined him on the wall. "We were chosen for each other. It was predestined."

"It still doesn't seem fair." Sheean poked petulantly at the water lilies with a little stick.

Bryony took the stick from him. "We've been best friends since we were children. It's better to marry each other than strangers. We're perfect for the position. We know what needs to be done to save the Faerie realm. We've had lots of experience in other realms."

Sheean took the stick back and threw it. Dog ran after it, barking with delight. "It's such a huge responsibility. I'm not sure you're taking it seriously. How would we keep order?"

"We would be kind and benevolent."

"And what about our heirs?"

Bryony put her nose deep into a rose. "What do you mean?"

"They would expect us to produce children, lots of them."

"Oh," she said, pulling her face from the flower. "I hadn't thought of that."

Dog came back and dropped the stick by Sheean's feet. "That is one of the reasons you were picked to be the queen. The whole point of our union is that we will have children of our own, and those children will eventually have children of their own, helping to strengthen the ruling class."

Bryony thought for a minute. "We will just have to deal with that when the time comes."

Dog picked the stick up and dropped it again, tipping his head on one side.

"I'm still not convinced we're doing the right thing," said Sheean, absent-mindedly picking up the stick again. "I think we should step down now, before it's too late."

"Look, Sheean," said Bryony, "I want to make sure the other races are looked after. There's something going on here that needs attention." She came close, her wings touching his, gently. Dog bit at the stick beginning to tug at it.

"It would really help if you ruled with me," said Bryony. "You understand other races, and you like Humans like I do. There's trouble brewing. I know it. Please help?"

"S'pose. I guess there's no alternative." Sheean pulled the stick away from Dog and threw it again.

"Good," said Bryony, "are you going to relax now and enjoy the celebrations?"

"I'll try."

A discrete cough from beside the rose arch drew their attention. "Your Majesties," said Jerremoy, bowing low. "I'm sorry to interrupt. It is time for the coronation rehearsal. I would like to introduce the Master of Ceremonies.

The official bowed low. His hair had a vaguely bluish tinge and his wings were large and strong. "Your Royal Highnesses, my name is Ashley Pelagon. I am the Master of Ceremonies for tonight's coronation. I wish to walk you through the events that will unfold this evening." He indicated for them to follow him. "If you will both do me the honour of accompanying me to the Standing Stones."

Jerremoy fluttered his wings politely. "Will you be needing me anymore, Your Highness?"

"No, thank you, Jerry," said Sheean. "Why don't you have the rest of the day off?"

Just outside the castle they were met by a group of guards. It was the first time Sheean had seen their armour properly. It looked like the chainmail he knew, but seemed a lot lighter. It didn't seem to encumber their movements in any way. He could see no weapons, yet the look in their grey eyes was stern enough to make his knees shake.

Fable and Dog met them as they entered the forest. Dog jumped up and down, leaping at everyone in excitement. Ashley flew up high to avoid Dog's enthusiastic muddy paws. His action only made Dog leap higher.

"Oh Dog! You'll be flying soon," giggled Bryony as she ruffled his fur. "Why don't you come too? It'll be fun."

Fable nodded. "I think we are meant to join you."

"That is right, noble Horse," said Ashley. "You, too, are part of the ceremony. You are too young to have witnessed a coronation before, so you all have a lot to learn. It is important that you pay attention."

Ashley continued to talk as they made their way through the forest.

"This will be my third coronation. It is a complex ceremony and everything must be done in the right way at the right time, or the crowning will be ineffective."

"What do you mean ineffective?" asked Sheean.

"And why do we always have to have guards?" asked Bryony.

"There are some," said Ashley, "that would wish the coronation to fail."

"Why?" asked Bryony.

"You haven't answered my question yet," said Sheean.

They reached the edge of the forest and flew out into open grassland. The sun shone down strongly from a deep pink sky. Dog collapsed panting in the cool grass. "Me need wings."

Fable smiled. "You can always sit on my back. You do not need to run."

"Bit scary that. Me like ground."

Ashley pointed to a distant track winding up the hill in front of them. "Ahead of us is the coronation pathway. On either side you can see the Standing Stones of the Golden Arch, which lead the eye most delightfully to the far mountains. It was designed in the wonderful days before the splitting of the realms."

Sheean noticed Ashley's eyes had gone all misty and he stood with his hands clasped together in a weird way, his right hand held by his left as if begging.

"We will go now to the Stones," Ashley continued, "and I will explain everything. I will answer all your questions."

The path sloped upwards to the horizon, flanked by three pairs of standing stones. On the brow of the hill, Sheean could see two thrones. "Are they made of glass?" he asked.

"No, they are crystal. Can you see the mountains ahead of us? Can you see the shape of a bird?" Ashley Pelagon asked, pointing to the horizon.

Sheean looked up. He could just make out three distant, white-capped peaks. He couldn't see a bird. Bryony nudged him.

"Look, oh look," she squeaked, "those three peaks, the middle one is the body and the other two are the wings. That's amazing, they look just like a bird."

Sheean peered, still unable to make out anything but rocks jutting up into the air. He shrugged his shoulders. "S'pose."

"As you can see," said Ashley, "the Standing Stones line the ceremonial walkway. There are six, representing six of the seven realms. Each is carved with the figure of a powerful Fay king and queen."

"Where's the seventh?" asked Bryony.

Dog ran up and down the stones, sniffing each one. For a ghastly moment it looked as though he was going to cock his leg and wee, but he ran off into the trees after a squirrel instead. Fable followed him, a concerned frown in his deep brown eyes.

"Ah yes," said Ashley, "I thought you might ask that. The Faerie realm, the seventh and the most important realm, is represented by the Crystal Thrones."

"Sort of symbolic then," said Sheean.

Bryony looked puzzled.

"Like, how all the other realms should defer to us."

Ashley bobbed up and down in agreement, his wings turning pale blue in subservient delight. "Yes, yes," he enthused, "you've got it! Well done, Your Royal Highness!"

Sheean grinned. Bryony blobbed her tongue out at him. He gave her a stony glare, broken almost instantly by a wide grin.

"First, the way will be prepared by two children, representing you as you were when first taken from this world. You will walk down the path together. As you get to the first pair of stones, you will pause and you will each place a hand on the face that is carved into the stone.

"Then what happens?" asked Sheean.

"An archway of light will form between the two stones."

Sheean smiled. "Cool!"

"Yes, there is no need to worry; the light is perfectly cold and safe. The same action and speech is performed at the next two stones and the two after. When you touch the last two, all the arches will join into a sparkling canopy. You will then go and stand by the thrones and face the walkway."

"That sounds simple enough," said Bryony.

As they walked down the track to the thrones, Fable came cantering back with Dog clinging to his back.

"I've told him to pay attention and not run off," said Fable.

Dog jumped down and sniffed the thrones. Ashley Pelagon ignored Dog and continued with his explanation. "At this point there will be a fanfare of trumpets, and Fable and Dog will give speeches of acceptance of their roles in the Royal Household, followed by your own declarations which will take the form of poetry. After this the queen will start her procession down the walkway, under the canopy. Oh yes, I forgot to mention. On the thrones there will be two gold crowns."

"One each?" joked Sheean.

The official's face stayed serious. "Yes, one each."

Bryony frowned at Sheean.

"Then Fable and Dog, who played their part in your prophecy, will come behind Queen Rhyannon and will stand in front of the third stones with their right legs fractionally in front of their left as is appropriate to the occasion."

Fable nodded, shooting Dog a quick sideways look. Dog carried on sniffing round the thrones, paying no attention to the official's droning voice.

"As the queen gets to you, you will both kneel on the cushions provided."

Sheean and Bryony looked at the floor.

"Yes. They are not there at the moment, but rest assured they will be when it is time. At this stage, you will have to try not to fidget, as you will be kneeling for some time. The queen will give a speech and abdicate her position in favour of you both. This could take between half and a full petal, depending on what instructions the queen chooses to give you. Effectively it will be her last decree."

"Then we will be King and Queen of Taranor?" asked Bryony.

"Almost. The queen will ask if there are any objections. If there are no objections then you will be tested for your wands of power. If you succeed, then the crowns will be placed on your heads, and you will be declared King and Queen. Then of course, the celebrations will begin, and exactly twenty-four petals later, you will be married. Over the next few days there will be further training, followed by the test in the Big tree. Have you any questions?"

Sheean watched as Bryony span round and round in delight.

"I can't wait! I'm so excited!" she squealed. He felt his heart sink. He looked around, almost as if he might see an escape route somewhere.

"Will there be fireworks and dancing?" asked Bryony as she settled down next to the throne. Her delicate hands traced the carvings of leaves and petals in the pure, clear crystal. "And will we have new thrones to sit on?"

"Of course, Your Royal Highness. The throne room will be refitted to accommodate two matching thrones, and there most certainly will be fireworks and dancing."

Bryony got hold of Sheean's hand and smiled at him. "It will be OK, Sheean, we will be happy together. I promise."

Sheean felt his guts tighten. He tried to relax his jaw and smile, but his face simply wouldn't obey.

* * *

Agaric placed some light silver bells on the curtain to his room and turned to face Yewed.

"That way," he said, smiling a thin smile, "if anyone comes near, they'll make a noise and I can close the connection."

Yewed scowled, flapping a hand in a dismissive gesture at the security chief. "Why the secrecy? Everyone wishes for the rightful king to take the throne do they not?"

"Yes they do, but very few favour Prince Liedinroad."

Yewed snorted. "Prince Liedinroad of Goldendale? Are you mad?"

Agaric poured water into a bowl. Before he made the connection, he turned and fixed Yewed with a glare. "Surely you, who understand the purity of the Faerie Law and the Conservation of the Way Things are Done, can understand the power of having Prince Liedinroad as king!"

Yewed fluttered to the window, his dark blue wings holding him in mid-air. He rubbed his leg where the dog had bitten him and watched Agaric prepare the water. "You are correct. Prince Liedinroad would not accept mangy, stinking mortal dogs into Taranor. That is for certain."

Agaric looked up. "Exactly. Now let me concentrate. Scrying is not my strong point."

"Why do you not use a portal?"

Agaric sighed. "Because the queen will notice."

"Surely not. There are portals opening and closing all the time in this city. Even you cannot keep track of them all, can you?"

"Quiet. Let me concentrate."

Agaric relaxed his mind and pictured the hills of Goldendale. Soon he saw a castle. It was far smaller than Taranor Castle and only had a few turrets and towers. He noticed with a smile that there were no flags flying. No frippery. No fancy decorations. Just as a castle should be.

Soon the image of a room appeared in the water. The walls were of light golden marble, inlaid with lapis lazuli. Very tasteful. A young male Faerie walked into view. He peered at Agaric without recognition.

"Can I help you?" he asked.

"Fancy not recognising me! Mind you, you look no more than a child."

"I'm sorry. I'm the valet to Prince Liedinroad and I've just celebrated my eight thousandth year. I put my good looks down to a daily glass of nettle juice."

"Agaric, Chief of Security of Taranor Castle here. I wish to speak to the prince."

"I'm sorry, he never talks in water. He considers it vulgar. I can take a message."

Agaric sighed. "He will no doubt have received his invitation to the impending coronation. Tell him to make haste. If Prince Liedinroad wants a chance at true power and orthodox rule, then he needs to be here to contest the king's throne."

"Thank you. Is the queen's throne taken?"

"Yes. But if you have another, send her. We need all the help we can get to keep order in Taranor."

Agaric cut the connection and smiled.

* * *

Albert spent the day gathering wood and catching fish. By evening he was feeling a little panicky. "I really should be getting back," he said.

Kanthy watched the babies crawling about on the sand outside the cave. "You could stay here and be useful."

Albert shook his head. "My parents are relying on me to run the business. I can't stay here. Can you help me?"

"I suppose so," said Kanthy. "You've helped me get my strength back. First you can bathe me, and then I'll open a window into the Human realm for you."

Without embarrassment, Kanthy took off her dress and waited for him to help her. "Come on, dunderhead. Get some water. And wash my dress."

Albert kept his eyes averted from her as he helped her to wash, then he took the dress outside and washed it in the sea, hanging it over a rock to dry.

Kanthy walked gingerly out of the cave, wrapped in the rotting quilt. The children were near the edge of the sea, squealing with delight as the surf touched their toes.

"I'll send you back to the Human realm now."

The babies looked back at Albert. He could see now that their eyes were bright green, just like Bryony's.

"Stand on that rock."

Albert did as he was told.

"When I open the window, be quick," she said. "I can't hold it open for long."

"OK."

Kanthy closed her eyes and drew a symbol in the air. There was a shimmering above the sand, and then, with a crackling sound, a portal appeared in front of them.

"Jump, quickly!"

"I can't see anything on the other side."

"Just do as I say! Jump!"

Chapter 10

The day of the coronation dawned without a cloud in the sky. Birds stretched their wings and sang of the joy of the celebrations to come.

Bryony lay low over Fable's neck as he flew over the trees of Taranor forest. She laughed gaily every time he dipped down and touched the leaves, only to bounce up again like a white ship on a golden sea.

Minutes later they landed near the edge of the crystal pool, where the early morning sunlight slanted through silver birches, dappling the ground and rocks near the waterfall in pink light.

"Oh Fable," said Bryony, leaning forward along Fable's mane and wrapping her arms around his warm neck. "Life is so wonderful. I can't believe that tonight I'm going to be Faerie Queen! After all this time!"

At her words a group of ladybirds flew into the air, squealing with excitement. A bee droned heavily among the flowers. Fable dropped his head suddenly, chuckling as Bryony slipped off his neck and onto the ground.

Bryony lay on her back in the grass, laughing. "Faerie Queen!"

Fable nuzzled her. "You will have a lot of responsibility, Little One."

Bryony rolled over and looked out at the crystal pool. "This is where it all began." Her voice became smaller. "It seems so long ago."

She shivered.

"It is a long time for us," said Fable. "However for the people here, only a few petals have passed."

Bryony flew up into the air and twirled in a circle. "I'm so pleased we made it. Fable you are wonderful.

Thank you for looking after me. I was so scared in the mortal realm at first."

"You showed great courage, my sweet."

"Do you think I should wear golden boots with toes that curl upwards, or maybe go barefoot with anklets of daisies?"

Fable sighed.

"I know I have to wear gorgeous robes," continued Bryony, "and follow the council's colour code, but no one has made rules about my shoes. Have you seen the dress? Oh, and the crown... have you seen it yet?"

She flew round and round her white horse in a blur of turquoise light.

"Bryony," said Fable, "being queen is not just about dresses and shoes. You will have to govern the entire kingdom and deal with conflict. Real conflict."

"I know."

Bryony landed near him. She placed one hand in his mane near his ears, enjoying the feel of his silky hair. "I'm not shallow. I can be queen. I thought hard about it all night. I'm going to be fair and reduce the workload of the Pixies. Everyone will have good food to eat, not just the rich people."

Fable snorted in approval.

"And," continued Bryony, "I'm going to allow Humans and Goblins and everyone to be friends." As she jumped up onto a branch of a nearby tree to caress a robin, she noticed Fable glancing around nervously. She laughed. "Nobody's listening. And anyway, I'm nearly queen and I can say what I like."

Fable looked up at her. "No sweet one, you cannot say what you like. Not anymore."

Bryony kissed the robin and flew down to Fable. "What do you mean?"

"I advise you to be cautious, Little One. Although I agree with you wholeheartedly, there are many here who would oppose such views. At first I think you should maintain tradition, hide your true feelings, then, when you have the confidence of the council, you can introduce changes, little by little."

"Oh Fable," she said, hugging him again. "You're so wise. Shall I write my poem now?"

Fable nodded. "That is why we have come."

"Poetry's not my strong point. In fact I've never written anything before."

With a click of her fingers, a scroll appeared in the air, covered with a fine silver frost of diamonds. As she spoke, words appeared on the parchment written in a fine turquoise ink. Each sentence began with an embellished capital letter.

"Frosted diadems of Paradise,
Entwine the City Walls.
Each happy smile, like a rose of cream
Shall pour from our hearts
Into the stream of love."

She turned to Fable. "That's not bad is it, for a start?"

Fable chuckled as her last sentence wrote itself across the paper with a flourish.

"Oh no!" said Bryony, laughing, "No. Stop writing everything I say."

The parchment emptied itself of all words. Bryony clapped her wings together in frustration.

"Patience, Sweet One," said Fable. "Patience. Imagine all the long, boring meetings you're going to attend. If you get irritated with a dictation parchment, you'll never deal with the council."

"OK."

Bryony took a deep breath and repeated the lines she wanted. "Do you think Sheean's done his?"

Fable shook his head in amusement. "That lad writing poetry? Probably not."

"Then I'll write one for him as well. It's quite fun. I think I'm quite good at it!"

By lunch time, they were flying back towards the city. The spires and turrets glittered in the sunshine and flags fluttered in the warm breeze. Bryony clutched the scrolls tightly.

"Do I have to learn all the words?" she asked.

"No," said Fable, "you'll be far too nervous. You can read the scrolls when it is time."

Bryony held onto his mane as they came to land in her private garden. Attendants were gathering. She could smell the rose scented bath water. Already a group of Butterflies and Bees were jostling to be chosen as her hair ornaments.

"Isn't it rather early to be getting dressed?" she asked.

Lorella curtseyed. "This is the first bathing of three, Your Royal Highness, and your hair decorations need to be chosen."

* * *

An Elf walked over to the window of his mountain retreat. A streak of grey hair shone in his long brown hair. His grey eyes were calm. He looked out over the distant rooftops of Londale, where crystal towers jutted into the cloudy sky. In the distance, he saw the river Thalmes as a thin silver snake. Far below, on the outskirts of the ruined Delphi temple, disaffected people huddled in their

295

tents, trying to keep warm. Here and there he saw camp fires. He smiled gently, knowing the time was right.

He went over to an ancient scroll lying open on his polished desk and ran his finger down the right margin, pausing now and then to peer at the tiny handwriting. His finger came to rest on a name. "The Human female," he mumbled. "She would be the one to approach."

Concentrating on the female's name, he peered into the depths of the seer's bowl. Slowly a young woman's face filled its waters.

"Kanthy? Am I talking to Kanthy, the witch's daughter?"

* * *

Kanthy noticed the water in a rock pool, right by her feet, become cloudy. The smiling face of a man with pointed ears appeared, suspended in the water.

"Who are you?"

"My name is Kelpor."

"I don't know you."

"That is true, but soon you and I will become friends."

Kanthy looked up at the twins. "Put the crab down this minute," she shouted. They dropped the crab and stared silently at her. Kanthy looked back into the pool. "I don't think so."

"Don't be too hasty. How are the children?"

"How do you know about the children?"

The twins began to crawl towards the rock pool.

"I know all about them, and you and Sheean. I know Sheean killed King Ogmantiguthra."

"How? Who are you?" She paused, letting his comment sink in. "Sean killed Ogman?"

"Of course, you wouldn't know about that. You missed Sheean's heroics when you left him for dead."

"Don't blame me! I had to protect the children."

The children crawled closer, their round faces focused on the pool.

"So Ogman is dead?"

"Yes, very much so."

"Where are you?"

The picture in the pool broke up for a few seconds.

"Some distance from you."

"Are you in the Fay realm?"

"Yes, but as I said, many petals... sorry, days from your location."

"Have you taken Ogman's place?" she asked.

Kelpor laughed. "No. I represent a number of enlightened individuals, and we ask for your help."

"What do you want with me?"

"You are part of the prophecy. You and Sheean. The realms have been waiting for this moment in time, for an enlightened leader to come of age and bring about the joining of the realms; someone with magic at their disposal and a strong interest in the people of the other realms."

"And you want Sean to be this person."

"He is destined to bring the realms together, and possibly rule them. We thought at first that Bryony would rule with him, but the children have changed all that. It is now clear that you, a Human, are destined to be at the king's side."

"Didn't Ogman have a Human companion, and didn't he try to rule the realms?"

The children sat silently at her side, staring into the rock pool.

"Ogman wasn't always evil you know. He was a good and caring ruler and he would have worked tirelessly towards the unity of the realms. It was the prejudice of the Fay ruling classes that destroyed him."

"Won't the same thing happen to Sheean?"

"Possibly, but you and the children will be at his side, and I will be there to guide you."

"You said Sean would rule?"

"It is not clear. Our best visionaries seem to be in disagreement about his future. Some say his children will be his downfall."

* * *

A knock on Kelpor's door brought the conversation to an end.

"Kanthy. I have to go. I will contact you again soon. I advise you to find Sheean." He closed the connection.

"Enter!" he called, as he poured two fingers of golden liquid into a crystal glass. A middle-aged Human woman entered the room, carrying a steaming plate of root vegetable stew. As she placed it on the desk, she scowled at Kelpor.

"That whisky will be the death of you."

"Yes mother, you say that every time," Kelpor answered with a grin.

* * *

Kanthy used a piece of sailcloth she'd found on the beach to wrap the children up in a sling. She'd

298

thought of using the embroidered quilt, but it was too rotten to hold their weight. She tied the cloth so that her babies were against her chest, secure enough for her journey up the cliff path. "You two are going to have to be good if this is going to work. No poking and definitely no biting," she said sternly.

The children grinned toothily at their mother. Kanthy didn't know much about babies, but she was fairly certain they didn't normally have teeth until they were a few months old.

It was going to be a hard, painful journey, travelling on foot with two small children, but she could see no other way. She sighed. She picked up a pretty shell from the beach and tucked it in her waistband, gathered her water bottle and began to walk to the cliff path.

"Right children, let's go and find daddy."

Kanthy stood by the side of a track, trying to get her breath back after the long climb from the beach. The sling with the two children was heavy. She was panting, feeling light headed and dizzy. She looked around. The sea was behind her. Ahead were golden hills and woods. The track was paved in tiny blue stones and seemed more to mark the way than to walk on. In the distance she saw a valley filled with golden trees, glimmering against the pink sky. In the distance was a castle.

The air was warm enough to cause the shifting, golden trees to shimmer in the distance. As she watched, the mirage seemed to come closer, gradually resolving into a group of Faeries flying in formation.

"Snuggle deep, and try not to draw attention to yourselves," she muttered.

The cloud of golden light approached. Soon she could make out five distinct Faeries. Three were armed with swords, while one, a lot smaller than the others, carried a banner. She saw white stars on a golden background. The fifth wore a crown. He flew up to her and looked down his thin, pointed nose at her.

"What are you doing here?" he said. His voice was pompous and regal, as if coming through his nose. Kanthy instantly disliked him.

"Catching my breath from the climb."

His guards hovered nearby. They looked bored. The one with the crown coughed quietly, holding his hand to his mouth with his little finger crooked up. "Catching my breath from the climb, what?"

"What?" said Kanthy.

"Your Majesty," prompted the one with the banner.

Kanthy suppressed a grin. "I'm not of royal birth."

The royal Faerie's glamour flushed orange. "No, you stupid girl. I am. You should address me as Your Majesty!"

The soldiers laughed. The one with the banner looked uncomfortable. Kanthy lowered her gaze and looked at the ground.

"Sorry, Your Majesty. I was not aware of your status."

"What? Why not? Everyone knows who I am. I am Prince Liedinroad."

Kanthy kept her head down, trying unsuccessfully to hide a smirk.

"I saw that. How dare you laugh at my name?"

"Sorry."

"You will be! You do realize, I could have you imprisoned for... for something or other! Shame. You could be quite pretty if you weren't deformed. What happened to your wings?"

The scroll holder leaned across and whispered something in the prince's ear. The prince scowled at a Kanthy. "My valet says he thinks you're a Human. Is this true? You certainly smell like one."

Kanthy decided there was no point in lying. "Yes, Your Majesty."

"How did you get to Taranor? There are laws against mortal scum like you polluting our land."

The prince rose higher in the air and kicked one of his pointed, felt boots hard against Kanthy's ear. She staggered backwards, raising her arms to protect herself. The prince flew close and pushed her. She crumpled to the ground.

"Who have you robbed? What is in your sling?" shouted Prince Liedinroad.

A soldier grabbed at the sailcloth.

"Please," Kanthy begged, staggering to her feet and turning away from the soldier. She was afraid to reveal her magic.

"Shut up," said the prince. "I do not want to hear excuses from the likes of you. All Humans are thieves and liars."

As Kanthy faced the prince, both babies wriggled round to look at the Faeries. There was a blast of light and a shower of green dust. The children giggled as a miniature whirlwind picked up the ashes of the prince and mixed them with those of the other members of his party.

The air nearby vibrated with a high pitched alarm for a few seconds, then went quiet. "I hope that's not because of us," said Kanthy, brushing the Faerie dust from her clothes. Both babies squirmed round in the sling so that they were facing her once more. They looked up at their mother and grinned. Kanthy smiled back with some pride.

"No one had better mess with us," she joked. The children giggled in response.

Kanthy looked around, uncertain which way to go. She gave the babies some water and took a long drink herself. Then, when she felt refreshed, she poured a little into her shell. Although tiny, the scrying pool worked.

She concentrated on Sean and soon she saw an image. It was hard to make out much detail, but the room looked sumptuous. Huge tapestries hung on the walls and in the centre was a curved table with tall wooden seats all round. She saw Sean relaxing. She smiled to herself. It had been some time since she had seen him. She'd forgotten how handsome he was. Spending the rest of her life with him did not seem like a bad thing after all. "Behind every strong man is an even stronger woman," she muttered.

She drank the water in the shell and looked the way the stupid Prince had come. She smiled at her babies. "The idiot who assaulted us must have come from over there. I think that would be a good place to start searching for Sean."

The babies gurgled.

* * *

"I can't believe it!" shouted Agaric, flying around his room in a rage. Two guards bowed their heads to the appropriate level. Their hands were clasped just right. Their feet made no sound and their wings were the perfect shade of blue.

"It's ridiculous!" continued Agaric. "We suspect there may even be death threats, yet Queen Rhyannon insists on people being invited."

"What do you recommend, Sir?" said the taller of the two guards.

"Put anyone who objects to the coronation in the far regions. As far away from the royal couple as possible. Tell the queen that they have all been invited and are free to express their objections in a polite and dignified manner. No bad behaviour will be tolerated. And treble the protection round the royals."

"Yes, Sir," said the guard.

"All this protest nonsense makes me so angry. Do you have any news about the recent Sentinel Tree alarm?"

"The Sentinel Trees reported malignant magic, Sir, in the coastal region. However there appears to be no source. It is quite possibly a false alarm. We are investigating."

* * *

Sheean sat on the edge of the pond in Bryony's private garden, watching her flit around the flowers, pausing at every shiny surface to check her appearance.

"I'm really pleased everything is working out for you," he said.

"It is wonderful, isn't it?" Bryony answered as she buzzed up to a full-length mirror deeply hidden in an ivy clad wall. She span around, trying to get a good view of her wings. "Do you think I look fat in this dress?"

"What?"

"It's important, Sheean. I've got to make a good impression."

"How can you get fat? You only eat those stupid petals. You could eat a ship full and not put any weight on."

Bryony stopped spinning around, put her hands on her hips and frowned at Sheean. "What is a ship full? Is it a lot? You know you could do with losing weight."

"What?"

"Well, you are a bit flabby in places."

Sheean jumped up and flew across to the mirror. "Where am I fat?"

"You're not going to sulk, are you?"

"No. Where am I fat?" Sheean asked as he turned around.

"Well, your stomach is beginning to bulge over your belt a bit and your bum's looking a bit too round."

"What? How can you say things like that? It's not fat, it's muscle."

"Albert didn't have any fat."

"Albert! What's Albert got to do with anything?"

"Oh, nothing. I keep thinking about him. He was so nice; he used to follow me around like a puppy."

Sheean smirked at her. "You had a thing for Albert, didn't you?"

"No!"

"Well how come you looked close enough to know he wasn't fat."

"Well I... It wouldn't have worked anyway."

"If things had been different, would you have married him?"

Bryony looked thoughtfully at her reflection. "No, he's... he was Human, and anyway he was even more immature than you."

"And you're not, of course."

"Of course I'm not." Her light laughter faded. "It's going to be good between you and me, isn't it?"

"I will do my best to make certain you are happy."

"What do you mean, do your best?"

"Well, it will be difficult," said Sheean. "I mean, you're so immature... and fat."

Sheean scowled at Bryony until he couldn't hold the laughter in any longer.

* * *

Agaric wandered over to the office of the City Gate Supervisor.

"Have you seen Prince Liedinroad?" he said.

The supervisor shook his head. "No Sir, I'm informed he left Goldendale with his entourage some time ago, but no one has arrived as of this time."

"I wonder what's delaying them? Please send word to me immediately on his arrival."

"Certainly Sir."

* * *

After about a mile, Kanthy came to a line of oaks stretching across the landscape like a living boundary between the coast and the rest of the island. She hadn't seen them from the cliff, which surprised her, as each tree was huge; as wide around the girth as a man's outstretched arms. They stood close together, their leaves intertwined with each other, forming a line as far as she could see from left to right. Their leaves and branches moved gently in the sea breeze. Beyond them stood a castle. She was surprised at how plain it looked. There were only a few turrets and no flags flew.

She felt the children fidgeting. "Alright," she said, "let's have a rest under these trees. I'm feeling a bit tired and you two need feeding."

To her surprise both children had their hands over their ears as if they could hear a loud noise. "What can you hear?" she asked. The trees nearest the road began to sway more wildly as if tossed by a winter wind. "I can only hear the wind in the trees."

Her children both shook their heads and clamped their hands harder over their ears. Kanthy looked up. She felt a shiver down her spine as she realised the breeze she felt on her skin couldn't possibly produce that much movement in the branches.

Then she heard it. A high-pitched whine, just on the edge of her hearing.

"Hang on kids. We'll run through and get to the other side of them. We'll be OK."

She put her arms around the sling and began to run. As she drew level with the trees, the sky darkened from pink to violet and all the birds stopped singing. A branch slapped down in front of her, another one behind. She felt something hard and strong wrap around her waist. "Babies! Do something!"

She was plucked from the ground and held high up in the canopy. The bough round her middle held her tightly, but not painfully. Slender branches draped their leaves over her head and body, brushing her arms and the babies in the sling. The leaves brushing

306

her head twined into her hair, pressing down on her scalp.

She heard music, a soft gentle song, and saw a young girl and boy smiling. They had tiny turquoise wings and vivid green eyes. She saw herself there with them, seated on a throne. She looked a few years older. The boy and girl were her children; beautiful, noble and regal.

The leaves receded. She was lowered to the ground with a soft ringing sound like a bell. Kanthy moved away from the trees, without looking back. When she was a few yards away, she stopped and checked on the children. They smiled up at her sweetly.

"Well done," she said. "Let's take a look at that castle."

* * *

The children were growing at a phenomenal rate. Every time they ate the fruit from the hedgerows along the road, they seemed to mature by another month or two.

The daytime sun was cooled by a gentle breeze blowing from the sea. She walked for about a mile and stopped for the children to play.

They made their way up a small hill and found themselves looking down on the walled town of Goldendale, nestling in a wooded valley. At the far side of the town stood the castle.

By the time they arrived at the outskirts of the town, the children had matured to the point where they were able to toddle happily along at Kanthy's side. Both had tiny wings.

Kanthy watched with great delight as the children tried to fly, their wings humming like honey bees.

As they walked down the road, they passed a sign painted in gold letters, stating that they were about to enter the principality of Goldendale. "Be good children," said kanthy, "and don't do any magic unless there is real danger."

Both children smiled and nodded, displaying mouths full of pointed, gleaming white teeth.

As they neared the outer walls of the town they came across a workman hovering in the air, fastening a banner above the main gates. Kanthy and the children paused to look up at its message. The workman looked back down at them. "Have you come for the celebrations?" he asked.

"Err... Yes, although I'm a little confused."

"Why might that be?"

"The sign says, congratulations King Liedinroad and Queen Bryony."

"Yes that is correct."

"Wasn't Bryony supposed to marry someone called Sean?"

"Prince Sheean, yes. It turned out he had been tainted while he was in the Human realm and may no longer be suitable for a royal position. Our Prince is a contender for the throne."

"Oh I see."

The workman frowned at Kanthy. "Where have you come from?"

"A tiny hamlet on the coast. It's so small it doesn't have a name."

"And you walked?"

"Yes. Is there a problem with walking?"

"Most people fly. Are you injured?"

Kanthy realised she needed to be cautious. She knew nothing of day-to-day life in the Faerie realm. "As you can no doubt see, the children's wings are too small for them to fly, and it seemed like a good opportunity to introduce them to the beautiful countryside."

"I see," the workman said suspiciously. "It's still unusual though."

"Where is the coronation taking place?"

"At Taranor city. Prince Liedinroad has gone there this morning. Why have you not had an invitation?"

"It's probably waiting for me at home. So, Taranor city is where Prince Sheean will be?"

"Yes." The workman flew down to ground level. "There's something wrong here. You should know these things. Why are you not showing your wings. Show me."

"What if I refuse?"

"I'll summon the guard and have you taken before the magistrate."

"And where would this magistrate be?"

"In the city, of course."

"The city where Prince Sheean is?"

"Yes. Now stop playing around and show me your wings."

"No."

"GUARDS!"

* * *

Drofox, the local law enforcement officer, scratched his head as he looked Kanthy and the children up and down. He could tell there was something different about Kanthy. He could sense

309

her magic, but it tasted different to anything he had experienced before. The children on the other hand, were definitely Fay, although there was something not quite right there as well.

He sat back in his chair, unsure of what to do. Eventually he decided he would take no chances and arrested Kanthy on suspicion of not being Fay and for kidnapping two Fay children. "Do you understand the charges?" he asked.

"Yes."

"Have you nothing else to say?"

"No."

"Then you and the children will have to spend a few days in the tower, until the coronation is over and things are back to normal in the city. I will arrange for your transport to Taranor city at that time. Is that acceptable?"

"Yes."

"I'm certain this is a misunderstanding, and it could so easily be sorted out if you were to show your wings. Are you certain you want to take this course of action?"

"Yes."

"Very well then, I respect your wishes. I will escort you to the east tower of Goldendale castle."

* * *

Kanthy stood on the balcony, her arms wrapped around the children as they looked out over the Taranor countryside.

"You were very good children. Mummy is very proud of you for not killing anybody."

One of the children turnd to look at her. "When do get names?" he asked. His sister joined in. "Yes, when do get names?"

Kanthy smiled. "This is so exciting. Daddy will be so disappointed that he's missed your first words."

"When will we be getting our names?" the children asked in unison.

"When we find your daddy."

The boy tugged at Kanthy's earings. "Mummy?"

Kanthy removed his tiny fingers from her jewellery. "You are both very special and he will love you dearly. It is only fair that he's involved in such an important decision."

The children nodded in agreement as Kanthy moved them from the balustrade and carried them into their room in the tower.

"Not big enough," said the girl.

"It's not too bad, and it will only be for a few days. Your daddy lived in a tower like this when he was a child."

Both children's eyes lit up with excitement. "Tell us about Daddy," they pleaded.

"Your daddy is a very brave, handsome man," she started. "He is a Faerie Prince."

"Am I a Faerie Prince?" the boy asked.

"Yes, and before you ask," she said, turning to the girl, "you are a Faerie Princess."

* * *

Grumbuk gripped the edge of the massive Wyvern nest and looked down towards the river as it made its way through the valley thousands of feet below. He decided that looking down wasn't a good idea. He still wasn't used to being so high up. The

311

baby Wyvern showed a voracious appetite and was already as big as a horse. To Grumbuk's dismay, it had started to talk in his head.

"Mother coming back with food," it said.

"Good, Grumbuk starving."

Grumbuk saw the mother Wyvern gliding over the nearby mountains, coming closer and closer. She had something in her mouth. The baby Wyvern began to screetch with hunger.

A few minutes later, the mother landed with a flurry of leathery wings, her talons gripping the branches of the nest. As it took her weight, the nest shuddered and dipped down alarmingly. To Grumbuk's relief, the creaking branches sprang back, levelling his new home once more.

The mother dropped a dead goat at her feet and proceeded to rip it apart, giving Grumbuk and her baby equal shares. Grumbuk grabbed a leg and held it in front of the baby's face.

"Could roast food a little?" he asked.

The baby obligingly spat out a stream of fire. It only took a few minutes for them to finish the goat. With his stomach full, Grumbuk lay back and belched. "Goat delicious," he said. The mother gazed at her baby.

"Mother says you welcome," said the baby, "and asks have you thought of name for me?"

"Yes, very important. Grumbuk hero of legend. Had adventures, been strange lands. Killed Ogman. Rescued good witch. Hope old friends be safe. Call you Hope."

* * *

Sheean noticed the royal guards settle into position on both sides of the avenue of stones, each one a wing's length from the next in line. Guests crowded together, chatting excitedly and getting in the way of the guards. Some of the ladybirds were asking questions, trying to find out which flowers to perch on. Sheean's mind was spinning with all of the fuss and commotion. He looked across at Bryony and gave her a weak smile. She smiled back and mouthed, "Are you ready?"

"S'pose," he mouthed back.

Fable and Dog arrived. Dog looked uncomfortable, like he'd just been washed. Both animals were covered in ribbons and flowers. Alondil and Fionna pushed their way through the crowd to stand before Sheean. Fionna gave him a hug and then held Bryony close.

"Protocol dictates that we musn't make a fuss," said Alondil, shaking Sheean by the hand, "but we had to come and tell you that we are very proud of you both."

They were far too stiff and formal. 'Are they really proud?' Sheean wondered.

"Thank you Father. I will try not to let anyone down."

"I'm certain you will do just fine," said Alondil. "It is nearly time for the ceremony to start, so we will make our way to the thrones. We will see you at the feast."

Sheean was just about to turn to Bryony to tell her that he didn't want to go through with the ceremony, when the music started. It was too late. He looked at Bryony's smiling face, her perfect hair, her perfect gown. Bryony's eyes met his, their sparkle reflecting her joy. He tried to smile. She leaned forward and kissed him on the cheek.

Sheean watched as two children with turquoise wings flew between the standing stones, pausing occasionally to spread flower petals on the grass. Fable nuzzled Bryony's cheek and began the journey between the stones. Dog sat on Fable's back, grinning at the crowd.

Ashley Pelagon arrived with tremendous pomp. "It is time. I will stop at each pair of stones and hit the ground twice with my staff. You will place your hands on the stones. You will say the words of the incantation, wait until the arch of light forms, and then move onto the next. Do you understand?"

Sheean and Bryony nodded.

Agaric stepped forward, looking in disgust at Sheean's leather armour. "Your dress is not appropriate. No-one has ever broken protocol before."

Sheean opened his mouth to tell him what he thought of his protocol, but before he could say anything, Bryony interrupted.

"He is dressed as a warrior and carries his sword with pride. Do you want a king that is content only to count the petals in the garden? Or do you want a brave, courageous king? Do you want a warrior king who will protect Taranor and its people?"

Agaric gaped. He started to stutter a reply, but was drowned out by the cheering of the crowd as the music changed key. It was time. Sheean and Bryony went to their starting positions.

Ashley Pelagon struck the grass twice with his staff. Sheean and Bryony placed a hand on their respective standing stones and said the incantation in unison.

"Taranor lux itermatay."

No one had told them how bright the light would be, so when the arches of light exploded from the top of the stone pillars, Sheean ducked. Agaric's wings went dark with fury.

As they flew down the avenue, the shimmering light-filled arches formed, each one accompanied by a change in the intensity of the music.

* * *

Bryony almost couldn't breathe with excitement as she walked towards the thrones. She waved her hand and smiled to acknowledge her people. In the deep night sky floated the two moons. They were low on the horizon, almost level with each other, their light shining into her eyes. She could see that within the next few heartbeats their light would shine through the thrones of crystal. Just how gorgeous was she going to look, sitting up there with all that light streaming through her?!

She saw Fable and Dog standing to one side. A tear of joy ran down Fable's white cheek. She could see his brown eyes smiling with fulfillment and pride.

There, on her very own throne, lay her crown. It sparkled in the moonlight. It was finely wrought with golden leaves and sparkling diamonds.

"Turn and face the guests," said Ashley Pelagon.

As they turned, Bryony touched Sheean's hand. He looked pale and distant. "Are you alright?" she asked. Sheean nodded.

Ashley Pelagon turned to the crowd and bowed. At this signal, a fanfare of trumpets echoed across the land. Fable, with Dog balanced on his back, walked to a place where he could be seen. He tossed his mane and lifted his magnificent head.

"I imagine many of you will have been a little surprised by the events of the last few petals," he said. "This morning, Bryony and Sheean were juveniles, bathing at the Crystal Pool. Now they stand before you, about to be crowned. They have endured eight, long years in the mortal realm. They have aged accordingly. As have I. They have grown in maturity and wisdom. I have watched them struggle. I have watched them overcome difficulties. Sheean was brave. Bryony never gave up. Even in her darkest hours, Bryony never gave up."

Dog jumped down from Fable's back and sniffed the stones. Fable glanced at him nervously, then continued his speech. "I remember, on that awful day that bryony's parents died, I lay by Bryony's side, keeping her alive while help came. It is a day I will never forget. I will continue to stand by her. I will give my life if necessary to save her. I, Fable, hereby pledge to honour and support Bryony for as long as she may live."

The crowd went wild. Pointed hats were thrown, wings thrummed against wings. Some of the smaller insects fell off their leaves in their enthusiasm.

Ashley Pelagon stepped forward and the crowd became still. His voice rang out loud and clear. "Do you, Dog of the mortal realm, accepted ward of Queen Rhyannon, pledge your loyalty?"

Dog ran up to Fable and jumped up. He had managed to scratch most of the ribbons off. "Yus," he said. "Me be good Dog."

Some of the crowd applauded, while others simply stared in surprise. Ashley turned back and smiled at Bryony. "You will now recite your poems of acceptance of the Crowns of Taranor. You have both prepared? Yes?"

Bryony nodded.

"Prince Sheean?"

"Er, I didn't have time."

"That's OK," said Bryony. "I wrote one for you."

She clicked her fingers. Two scrolls appeared in the air and four hummingbirds, waiting near the thrones, flew forward to hold the parchments open.

* * *

After Bryony had read out her poem, Sheean scanned the parchment in front of him. "Do I have to read this out loud?" he whispered.

"Yes," hissed Bryony. "It's good."

Sheean looked at Bryony. She nodded reassuringly. He took a deep breath.

"Speckled petals I will bring,
Ornamental magnificence in perpetual spring."

He looked at Bryony again.

"Keep going," she whispered.

"Monumental suns will light our land.
Gentle waves on coastal sand."

The crowd gasped. Sheean wondered if they'd been ordered to respond like that. 'No one could possibly like this stuff,' he thought. He took another deep breath.

"I promise you my subjects, dear,
I will protect you with my spear."

Sheean scowled at Bryony. "I don't have a spear," he hissed.

"It rhymes," Bryony hissed back. "Keep going."

Sheean took another deep breath and continued.

"No one dare to take our lives,

Pink bees will swarm from golden hives."

Sheean chuckled. "Bryony," he whispered. "Pink bees? Are there such things?"

Ashley looked at Sheean and frowned. "You can stop now. The poems are complete."

* * *

Thousands of pairs of wings flapping in applause filled the warm, night air. Bryony flushed pink with pride as a fanfare sounded, high above their heads, announcing the arrival of Queen Rhyannon.

"I am going to meet the queen," said the Master of Ceremonies. "You must kneel down and wait."

Bryony watched him fly back to the start of the avenue of stones as the fanfare sounded again. Everyone looked up. Bryony gasped. Queen Rhyannon, in the most gorgeous robes of gold, descended from silver clouds high above the crowd. All around her flew soldiers in violet glamour, almost invisible against the night. In her hand the queen held her wand of power. As she flew slowly under each arch of light, the guests bowed low.

"Have you seen the people?" chuckled Sheean, nudging Bryony. He was smirking. Bryony sighed.

"You're not taking this seriously, are you?"

"Everybody looks so funny."

She looked around. "What do you mean?"

"Look at the guests when the queen gets level with them. They're trying to bow, but there's no room. They look like they're sniffing each other's bottoms!"

Bryony stifled a smile.

Queen Rhyannon arrived at the crystal thrones and turned with a flourish of turquoise sparks to face her subjects. A hush fell on the land as the soldiers fanned out, their faces grim and beautiful.

Everyone waited patiently while Fable moved into position behind the queen, his right leg just in front of his left. He turned his graceful neck to look at Dog.

"Oh," said Dog, grinning sloppily. "Me do trick now."

Fable nodded. Dog jumped down from Fable's back and sat bolt upright in between Fable's hooves. Fable nudged him with his nose, trying to get him into the right place.

Queen Rhyannon smiled. "Dog is fine where he is," she whispered. She gestured to Ashley Pelagon that she would continue. "This is a glorious night!" she sang, her voice ringing through the realm, as high and clear as a golden flute. "It is a rare and blessed night in which we see the end of an era and the beginning of another. I have had a long and happy reign. With the Coronation of Sheean and Bryony comes the fulfillment of the Light Prophecy. Soon peace shall reign in all the realms."

Bryony's heart wanted to burst with happiness. At last, everything was going to be fine. Soon, the crown on the throne behind her would be resting on her head. Soon, as long as she passed the final tests, the wand would be in her hand, and with it, the power to rule. Queen Rhyannon rose in the air a little and addressed the crowd.

"Protocol dictates that I ask whether any creature objects to the Coronation of Bryony Winkleweed as Queen of Taranor?"

There was a hush.

319

"As I thought." She turned to face Bryony, smiling. "Bryony Winkleweed. Are you ready to ascend and claim your wand?"

Bryony glanced upwards then shouted out, "Yes!"

Queen Rhyannon leaned forward, took Bryony's hand and glanced briefly at Sheean. "I'll be back for you in a moment," she whispered.

Bryony felt herself lifted up into the air, high above the crowd. Soldiers flew alongside, keeping a discrete distance, their bows strung. Below, the crowd stayed quiet, all looking upwards. The queen took a deep breath and called out, "Let all the clockflowers and lights of the land be extinguished. Let the dark hold you safe until Bryony's light appears."

Taranor was plunged into total darkness as all the petals of every clockflower closed, hiding the light of the gems. Bryony was carried higher. Soon the dark of night changed to silver as they entered the cloud. The queen hovered in front of Bryony, still holding her hand, her wings a halo of gold around her slender frame. The crown on her head radiated shafts of light in all directions. She dimmed the light of her wand.

Chapter 11

It was a lovely spring evening in Gavelkind. Albert normally enjoyed this time of day, when his work was over. The sun was setting and the blackbirds sang beautifully. However, this evening, he felt nervous. His heart thumped as he knocked on the door of Doctor Klein's consulting room.

After a few moments, the door opened and the portly doctor invited Albert inside. The room was rather musty, with enormous pot plants here and there and bell jars containing stuffed birds from foreign lands. The room was lined with bookcases. Albert was led past a folded screen of oriental design to a couch.

"Please lie down, Mr. Gladwyn," said the doctor.

"But I'm not sleepy."

Albert heard the doctor sigh. "I require you to lie on the couch. I will sit here at your head," he said, indicating a leather armchair. "You will not look at me, you will relax and elucidate, allowing your mind to go where so ever it wishes."

Albert lay down. On his left was another enormous plant, standing over three feet tall. He heard the creak of leather as Doctor Klein sat down. Albert lay rigid. He could see the sky through a window at the far end of the room. He could hear the traffic going past the window: horse's hooves, the rolling of wheels, people talking.

"Please relax," said the doctor. "Let your eyes close if you wish, or use your surroundings for inspiration. Tell me about your childhood. Say whatever comes into your mind, without censorship."

To his utter dismay, Albert began to cry.

"Good," said the doctor, "this is good. Please tell me what is on your mind."

"My parents are dead."

"Aha."

Albert could hear the scratching of the doctor's pen on a notepad.

Albert took a deep breath. "I made a terrible mistake."

"Go on."

"I loved a girl you see, but she jumped through a portal to another world. I followed her, but I couldn't find her." His tears flowed freely. "When I got back here, two hundred years had gone by. My parents and my sister... I never saw them again. I never got to say goodbye."

Albert sobbed. The pen scratched.

"How long have you been having these dreams?"

"This is real."

"Aha."

There was a slight pause. The gas lamps hissed softly. A carriage rolled past the window.

"Do you read a lot, Mr. Gladwyn?"

"No. I'm too tired after work."

"What is your work?"

"Engineer. I like to invent things, design new things. I have an idea about making a machine, a horseless carriage."

"You have a vivid imagination, Mr. Gladwyn."

Albert sat up, suddenly furious.

"I am NOT imagining things!" His outburst reminded him of Bryony's temper. He sank back onto the couch with a whimper.

The doctor's voice stayed calm. "Please remember the rules we discussed. If you become unruly, we will have to terminate the therapy."

Albert stared at the plaster carvings round the edge of the ceiling. "How is this going to make me better?" he asked.

The doctor cleared his throat. "By unlocking your unconscious mind, you will bring blocked memories and emotions to the surface, and then you will be able to sleep. You will stop your obsession with drawing the girl."

"But..." Albert's voice was feeble. He felt hopeless. What was the point in talking to this quack? A few of Edna's herbs would have made him better in no time.

"But?" prompted the doctor.

"I like drawing Bryony."

"I'm sure you do. However, you told me when we first met, that you cannot sleep unless you have a new likeness of your lost love gazing at you from the wall. This is not normal. I am using the latest techniques in psychiatric medicine to cure you. You clearly have a wish to bring back your mother, in the form of this unattainable love, and I suspect the story you tell of travel of between the worlds and the ensuing time paradox is designed to wipe out the presence of your father, so that you can have your mother all to yourself. I have heard enough for this session. Please get up."

Albert wiped his eyes on his sleeve and followed the doctor past the screen to a leather-topped desk. The doctor took out a paper envelope and gave it to Albert.

"Please take these powders. They will help you sleep, and calm your mind. Come and see me next week and we will continue."

323

As Albert walked into the kitchen at Edna's old cottage, he looked up at the picture of Bryony above the range. "I'm back, my sweet," he said, addressing her image. He sighed. It was comforting to be living somewhere familiar. Edna's cottage was the only recognisable building in town. He lit the gas lamp. The mantle flickered red for a few seconds, slowly building to brilliant white.

He looked around. Bryony's face looked back at him from hundreds of drawings, pinned to every available space on the cottage walls. "I hope you've had a good day, Bryony. I went to the doctors and got some medicine to help me feel better. The good news is I may be getting a promotion. I finally plucked up the courage to show my boss my drawings for that horseless carriage I've been working on. He wants to see me in his office tomorrow. Yes, I know it will mean spending more time at work, and I did promise you more light in the living room. Don't worry, I'll do a bit every evening; it won't take long to knock that wall through. I'll just have a drink and some of the powders from the doctor before I start."

Albert poured some water into a cup and mixed in a spoon of white powder. He grimaced as the bitter taste coated his mouth. Carefully, he removed some of Bryony's pictures from the wall between the kitchen and the living room and put them into his keepsake chest.

"I'll get that old sledgehammer. I don't know what Edna used it for, but it's been in the garden for ages."

His arms, grown weak from years of work in the drawings office, trembled at its weight. He went into the house and smiled at the portrait of Bryony flying with Fable. Next to it was a sketch of Dog.

"Are you ready?" he said. "It's going to be a bit dusty."

Albert gripped the sledgehammer firmly in both hands and swung it as hard as he could at the wall. It bounced off, jarring his shoulders. He swung it again. This time one of the stones split in half.

"This is going to be harder than I thought. I wish you could use magic on it, Bryony. Still, it'll be worth it - a nice bright house for you."

As Albert removed the broken stone from the wall he saw something glinting in the gap. He reached in and pulled out a metal hoop and a piece of paper with ancient, spidery calligraphy on it. He read the message.

"Is this meant for me?"

He looked closely at the jewellery. It looked like some kind of ancient necklace, with two threads, one of gold and one of silver. At each open end was the head of a dragon.

"This must be worth a bit."

Without thinking, he placed the torc around his neck. The object seemed to adjust its shape to fit comfortably. Mystified, he went to the mirror.

"Oh Bryony, I wish you could see this, you'd love..."

The ground fell away beneath Albert like a mudslide. He grabbed with both hands at air that swirled in a kaleidoscope of colours, unsure whether the long, wailing shriek he heard was his own.

Firm hands held him, steadying him. As his vision cleared, the colours resolved into people in elegant capes and fine robes. They had wings of bright blue and green. He found himself crowded in amongst them. It was night, yet he could see fairly well.

A gentleman, with the kindest eyes he'd ever seen, held his shoulders until he could stand unaided. "Almost missed the show," the man said, smiling. "Still, better a petal unfurled than one curled as they say."

Albert managed a nervous smile. There were thousands of people all around. No, they weren't people: their ears were pointed, their eyes were slanted. They were Fay! The beings turned to look towards the centre of the silent crowd. Albert stared with them.

Centaurs paced gracefully under the trees, and to one side a group of Dwarves held beer flagons in meaty hands, toasting each other in hushed whispers. Tiny creatures in pointed hats jostled round his knees with trays of sweet cakes.

The air was filled with insects; butterflies, ladybirds, bees and dragonflies. High in the air Faeries with purple wings soared in the warm night air, as if keeping watch. In the centre of the throng was an avenue of stones lit by a soft golden light. The stones led to the brow of a hill where, in full view of the crowd, stood two transparent thrones. Above the thrones hovered a silver cloud. Two moons hung on the horizon. They were both full.

"Taranor," whispered Albert. "I'm dreaming of Taranor."

"As are we all," said the male who had helped him earlier. "The new king and queen bring in a new dawn."

"Ssshhh," hissed a butterfly. "Quiet."

Albert looked closer. There was no sign of Bryony. A young male in leather armour knelt by one of the thrones. Everyone kept glancing up with wide, bright eyes at the cloud in the sky.

Albert began to understand. He must have fallen asleep after all that hard work. It had been a long day. He smiled as a bee came close to his face. What a dream. If only he could see Bryony once more.

The bee flew close, hovering just in front of his eyes. It was the size of a bumble-bee but a lot fluffier, and it was pink. He shifted his head to maintain a view of the thrones. Soldier Faeries surrounded the young male. They scanned the crowd with stern eyes, their bows strung taut.

"Are you an Elf? Where are your wingz?" the bee buzzed.

Albert looked directly into the multifaceted eyes of the pink bee. Talking bees. Whatever next? Part of his mind skittered around like an alarmed colt, while the rest of him committed the bee to memory. He was sure it would please the doctor if he could draw something other than Bryony's beautiful face.

"My wings?"

The bee's eyes grew wider as it flew back a little. Albert had never expected to see astonishment on the face of a bee.

"I'm zo sorry, Zire," it said, in a tiny buzzing voice, "I didn't recognizze you."

Albert, going purely by instinct, bowed a little. "It is of no consequence. I shall pardon you." He almost laughed as soon as the ridiculous words were out of his mouth.

The bee flew back a little more. "If you would follow me, Zire."

Albert walked slowly through the throng, noticing that people made way for him easily, like the waters of a lake parting for a boat.

Soon, Albert was clear of the thickest part of the crowd and had reached the area near the thrones. The

327

soldiers took in his presence with a glance and made way, ushering him under a rope made of intertwined pink roses, into an zone set aside for rich members of the audience.

It was at this point that Albert noticed something wonderful. He was dressed in his normal trousers, waistcoat and shirt, but now had a stunning set of wings sprouting from around his shoulder blades. A soft brown light emanated from them. He smiled.

"This is the best dream I've ever had," he said. "All I need now is to see Bryony."

A woman, in a dress made entirely of lilies held together by humming birds, turned to him. "It is like a dream, isn't it?" she whispered. "It won't be long now."

She looked up at the cloud hovering above their heads. Albert felt his skin prickle. The lady smiled again, turning to gaze at him. "I am Prince Sheean's mother. My name is Fionna." She indicated the young male kneeling at the foot of the thrones. "Soon Sheean will be bonded to Bryony for eternity and they will rule Taranor as king and queen. It's a mother's dream come true. I'm so proud."

A tall Faerie with turquoise wings and robes of silver smiled at her. "A father's dream too," he said. "My name is Alondil."

Albert nodded, his mouth having gone dry. He looked back up at the cloud.

* * *

Bryony looked down at her people. She saw Sheean kneeling by the thrones and, near him, Fable and Dog waiting patiently in the moonlight. She saw Sheean's parents talking to a Faerie with brown wings.

328

Queen Rhyannon let go of Bryony's hand and spoke in a quiet voice, her face deadly serious.

"Bryony Winkleweed, in order to earn your wand of power, you must answer my questions. Please answer honestly. Question one: It is the purpose of the rulers of Taranor to ensure the well-being of all creatures. If those rulers fall into corruption and deceit, do the creatures have the right to challenge the law?"

Bryony swallowed hard. "Yes."

"Question two: There is a situation in which only a loved one can save Taranor. Someone like Fable. He asks permission to fight in war. Do you grant this?"

Bryony hesitated. The thought of her beloved white horse going to war filled her with horror. "Yes I would grant him permission, but I would advise caution."

Queen Rhyannon leaned closer. "Is that your real answer or is that what you want me to hear? Remember, no one else is listening. This is the last time you will experience personal privacy."

"I feel if my response is going to be swayed by emotion or sentiment," said Bryony, "then I may need to say what I think others want to hear, until my heart is settled on the right way forward."

The queen kept her face impassive. Bryony had no idea if she was doing well or not.

"Question three: You have been promised since birth to Sheean. If, however your heart fell for another..."

Bryony blushed.

"... *if* your heart fell for another, would you give up your role to be with that person and risk throwing the realm into chaos? Or would you ignore your love and put the realm at the forefront of your mind?"

"Of course the realm is more important than my own whims and fancies."

"For the fourth question, I will have to look deep into your soul."

"OK."

Bryony felt fixed in place rather like a mouse in front of a cat. Queen Rhyannon's deep gold eyes became green, an intimate reflection of her own. She saw fear and excitement there; the past and the future. She saw herself as a pastry cook in the Human realm. She saw herself on the throne at Taranor, yawning during a boring meeting. She saw an old wooden box labeled, 'Do not open'.

"I want nothing hidden, Bryony," said the queen. "Not from me."

Bryony stared at the image of the box in her mind. She had never seen it before.

"What are you protecting?"

"I have no idea."

"A friendship?"

"I had friendships in the Human realm but no secrets."

"Let me see."

A lock appeared, sealing the box.

"Very well, we will leave that for now."

"Honestly, I don't know what's in there!"

Queen Rhyannon smiled. "You will know soon. Last question. A soldier is at war and his friend is in peril. In order to save his friend he must face his worst fear. Should he attempt to overcome his panic, and possibly court with failure, or should he admit defeat and leave his friend, in order to get assistance?"

"He should overcome his fears."

Bryony saw the ocean in her mind's eye. She saw the Seven Sisters, the rocks jutting out into the sea. She saw the green sky of the Goblin realm and heard Sheean crying out in distress. "No-one should leave their friend in danger," cried Bryony, her voice breaking. "I failed him." Her voice rose to a wail. "I left him there to die! I failed at my quest! I'm not fit to be queen!"

She dropped her head in her hands and sobbed. She saw the truth now. All this time, she had been dreaming. Being queen was just a juvenile, selfish fantasy. There was no way she could measure up to the awesome being in front of her.

Rhyannon placed a hand on her shoulder. "You have just passed the test."

Bryony looked up. The queen's eyes held a smile as warm as a summer's morning. "You have been truly honest. You know your own limitations. You are modest and you have courage. You will make a wonderful queen. We shall now return. You have earned your wand of power."

With a trembling hand Bryony took a stick of silver birch from one of the soldiers. As the queen touched the tip of her own wand to the wood, Bryony felt warmth and power flooding through her being. The wand glowed with a silver light, as if one of the moons had entered into its very fabric.

She heard the crowd below gasp as they saw the light.

"We will now descend. You will be crowned queen and then it will be Sheean's turn. I am delighted that we have both thrones filled. It is hard to rule alone."

331

Soon they were back on the ground amongst the people. The queen stepped forward and, using her wand, floated a crown in the air just above Bryony's head. With a fanfare of trumpets, flutes and horns, the crown was lowered.

"By the power vested in me, I crown you, Bryony, Queen of Taranor!"

The crowd went wild. Ashley Pelagon indicated for her to sit on her throne, as the first few rays of light from one of the moons touched the crystal. Bryony smiled down at Sheean, noticing how pale he was. He looked like he wanted to run away.

Queen Rhyannon turned to the crowd and sang out, "Protocol dictates that I ask whether any creature objects to the Coronation of Sheean Meranon as King of Taranor."

* * *

"STOP!" shouted Albert. "I object!"

He was dimly aware of the young man's mother glaring and of everyone turning towards him. Despite the proximity of the soldiers and the icy gaze of the queen, he felt confidence and strength running through his body. He felt as if his whole life had been building up to this moment. He stepped forward.

"This man," he said, "I mean Faerie, should not be with Bryony. I should."

The crowd gasped. The queen flew closer to Albert. Her eyes blazed and her wand flickered red and gold. Albert took one risky glance at Bryony. Her pretty face was a picture, lit from above by her crown and from behind by the light of the moons. She gaped at him without recognition.

"If we were not in a dream, Bryony Winkleweed," he said quietly, "you would know me."

"Who dares interrupt the coronation?" demanded a thin Faerie in dark blue robes. His wings were dark and his face was thunderous with fury. Albert noticed the queen give a subtle gesture with her hand. The guards moved in closer.

Albert felt a peculiar calm come over him. He shouted out so that the entire crowd could hear, "I am Albert Gladwyn. Rightful consort to Queen Bryony."

* * *

Jerremoy was late for the coronation. He had spent too long supervising the moving of Sheean and Bryony's belongings from their temporary apartments to the Royal Lodgings. He flew as fast as he could to the coronation area and settled somewhere near the back of the crowd.

There seemed a lot of excitement at the front near the thrones. The kin near him seemed less animated. They watched with puzzled expressions as a Faerie with brown wings gave a speech about being Bryony's consort.

"Who is this stranger," Jerremoy asked a Dryad, perched on a low branch of a nearby tree.

The Dryad turned to him. "Says he's Prince someone, consort to Bryony. First we've heard."

The crowd in front clapped and cheered at almost every word the new Prince said. Jerremoy scratched his head in disbelief. The Dryad simply shrugged her slender shoulders saying, "I don't know. I don't understand politics."

"I'm Valet to Prince Sheean," said Jerremoy to the people blocking his way. "Please let me through." He squeezed his way through the crowd towards the thrones. 'This doesn't seem right at all,' he thought. 'Why is the queen just agreeing with whatever the new prince says?'

* * *

Albert felt completely unafraid. This was such a great dream. The torc round his throat felt warm.

"Sheean Meranon," he continued, "is destined to be king, it is true. But not at this time. His time will come." The words poured from him effortlessly, almost as if scripted by someone else, someone more powerful and with greater knowledge. "It has been seen in the stars." He pointed upwards. All eyes followed his gesture. Albert marvelled at his own inventiveness, almost believing in his own words. "The brightest star at the helm of the hunter will show brighter yet. There will be a second sun in the sky ere Sheean comes to the throne." In other words, chuckled Albert to himself, never.

The queen took her eyes from the stars and looked at Albert. Her wand calmed back down to pure gold as she scrutinised his face. "From whence have you come?" she asked. "There is no mention of you in the prophecy." Her silky voice sent shivers down Albert's spine.

"The prophecy..." said Albert, stalling for time. The answer came as quickly and easily as had his earlier words. "The prophecy has been misinterpreted."

Was it his imagination, or was Bryony grinning at him? "Sheean is the king to kill the king. Bryony is the queen upon the road. All this is true. The great news is that when Sheean, the Warrior Prince, killed Ogmantiguthra..."

The crowd seemed to shudder at the name. A few beetles hissed.

"... I was released from the bondage into which the tyrant had placed me. The evil king knew I was his greatest threat, and his magic was strong. He made me look, behave and act like a pathetic Human boy. However, it was in the guise of this young mortal that I was able to keep a watchful eye on your new queen. Thanks to the bravery of these two young Fay, I can, at last, take my rightful place by Bryony's side and help to bring peace to all the realms."

Albert wanted to laugh, but he held his face still. He felt almost embarrassed at the story he was making up, but it was fun. He knew he would soon wake up and be back in Edna's cottage - alone.

The crowd began to cheer and flutter their wings. He warmed to his theme. "... to bring prosperity to all." There were cheers from the back and the wings of everyone within a few yards became a paler hue. "... and to bring in the seventh glorious age of Taranor, a time when..." He now had to raise his voice above the cheering crowd. The queen and her attendants were smiling openly. "... Taranor rules all realms and war is finally annihilated."

* * *

Jerremoy started to push his way to the front. After a few steps and many insults from the assembled crowd, he stood still and listened some more. A young Faerie, probably no more than three thousand years old pulled on his robes. "Isn't it great that Prince Albert's arrived?" she squealed.

He shook his head. "Why yes," he said. "It's brilliant. Of course, it makes perfect sense. Sheean never wanted to be king anyway. I don't know why I thought there was a problem."

* * *

The crowd went crazy. Albert found himself guided forward by the tall, thin Faerie. "Sire," he said in low tones, "I am Agaric, Head of Security. I bid you welcome to Taranor City." He held Albert's elbow and led him to the front by the thrones. By now Sheean was standing, grinning from ear to pointed ear.

"Sheean Meranon," said the queen in a loud voice. The crowd hushed. "We are half way through the coronation. The moons will not wait long for a decision. Already the light of the second moon approaches the king's throne."

Albert stole another quick look at Bryony. She winked. His heart skipped a beat.

"Sheean," said the queen, "Do you wish to continue as King of Taranor, or do you accept Prince Gladwyn in your place?"

Sheean walked forward and shook Albert by the hand, just like a Human would.

"I accept Prince Gladwyn to rule in my place," he said. "I am willing to step down."

Sheean smiled with what looked like genuine relief and ducked under the rope of roses, walking towards his mother.

"Come forward, Albert Gladwyn," intoned another Faerie male. "I am Ashley Pelagon, your

Master of Ceremonies. You do not, as consort, need to fulfil the test of the wand of power. Nor will you wear a crown day to day, but tonight, you will wear the Crown of Consort."

Albert knelt in front of the throne. As the queen waved her wand, a crown floated up above his head. Albert just had time to admire the fine workmanship: oak leaves intertwining with ivy, all wrought from the finest copper coloured metal.

"By the powers invested in me," said the queen, lowering her wand, "I crown you Prince Albert Gladwyn of Taranor, Consort to Queen Bryony."

The crowd cheered. Many lost control, and flew into the sky as the clock-flowers of Taranor opened, bathing the wooded valley with light. As Albert felt the crown settle on his hair, the torc around his neck grew warm. He was guided to sit by Bryony's side on the other transparent throne. Bryony's hand slipped into his.

Albert felt a gentle pressure, as if tiny hands were pressing against his wings. The moonslight behind him flooded through the crystal throne and joined with that flowing through Bryony's. The entire area lit up like a silver beacon. He glanced sideways. He'd never seen Bryony so happy or so beautiful.

The queen flew a little into the air and hovered above the thrones. Albert heard her voice ring out over the hubbub. "The marriage will be tomorrow night in the Glade of Everlasting Happiness! Let the celebrations commence!"

* * *

Showing the wing colours of valet to the king, Jerremoy flew up and over the crowd to join those in the roped off enclosure. He was just in time to see the crown land on the new Prince's head. He joined the throng in their celebrations, happy that Bryony was, at last, marrying the right prince.

* * *

'It all makes perfect sense,' thought Sheean as he joined his parents in the enclosure. 'I thought he was Human, but he's Fay. Amazing. He'll make a great consort, and he's got me out of a situation I didn't want to be in.'

"Good luck to you both," he said aloud.

Fionna placed a reassuring hand on Sheean's shoulder. Sheean turned to look at his mother and smiled. Fionna smiled back, pity showing in her eyes. "You know, Sheean, your father and I had great hopes for you, but you have been a disappointment. It's a shame everything you've done with your life so far has been wasted, but be assured; we still love you and are hopeful you will manage to do something useful eventually."

"Thanks mother," he said, quickly removing the hurt expression from his face. 'After all, she is probably right,' he thought.

* * *

Queen Rhyannon stepped close to Bryony and created a scintillating barrier around them both, deadening the sound of celebration. Bryony's lips trembled as she struggled to remain regal and dignified.

With deep compassion, Queen Rhyannon took Bryony in her arms and held her one last time, as a mother would hold a child. A healing wave of relief, joy and exhaustion rushed through Bryony's entire being. All the frustrations and fears of her time in the Human realm left her. She sobbed and laughed at the same time.

After a few moments, Bryony stepped back from the embrace and looked at the crowd. The sounds of revelry were still dampened. "I wish..." she said, "I wish my parents could have lived to see this."

Queen Rhyannon spoke gently. "Your mother and father are here; they are in the wind and the stars. They feel your joy: they watch you with love."

Bryony gave a small smile. Although she knew and understood the Faerie notion of inter-being, she still ached for her parents.

With a swirl of her wand, Queen Rhyannon removed the barrier, deluging them once more with the sound of trumpets, pipes and drums. Petals filled the air. Songs burst from all directions, competing with, and complementing one another. Bryony smiled at Albert, who stood dazed and happy by her side.

An attendant bowed low.

"Jerremoy-Droford-Rosethorn at your service, Sire. I am valet to the king. It is my joy to serve you and protect you with my life. You are requested to attend the Coronation Banquet at the hall of Bountiful Feasting."

Bryony touched Albert lightly on the arm. "Albert?" she whispered. "Is it really you?"

Albert simply stared at her as if dazed. He had a silly grin on his face that made her want to hug him.

She knew that would not be proper, so she simply took his arm and led him back down the avenue of light, towards the castle.

The banqueting hall echoed with the sound of feasting. Bryony sat in between Albert and Queen Rhyannon at a semicircular table, heavily laden with fruits and flowers. Further down the hall, the lower tables were crammed with dignitaries and nobles from across the lands. She saw Sheean smiling and laughing with his parents. The air shimmered with jewels and exquisite light. Pixies and other small folk moved swiftly between the tables, filling goblets and bringing more food.

Sitting on either side of the semicircular table were various members of the High Council. The only one she recognised was Agaric. They all looked a sour bunch to her. Although she smiled whenever she met their eyes, not all returned the courtesy.

"What a banquet," sighed Albert.

"I know," replied Bryony, "I can't eat another thing."

A pink bee buzzed up to their table. It looked closely at Albert and then landed near a plate of sugarplums.

"What's in that cake?" asked Albert.

A Pixie popped up on the far side of the table. "Apples, pears and meadow-sweet," it squeaked.

Albert smiled kindly at the little creature.

"Did you make it?"

The Pixie blushed bright green.

"Oh no, Your Majesty. The cooks made it."

Albert offered Bryony a slice. She shook her head and patted her belly.

"No thank you, Albert, the hazelnuts have filled me up."

"No wonder you're so slender," he said. "You hardly eat anything. You're not going to get fat on a few petals."

She noticed Albert looking down briefly to where her hand rested on her stomach. She felt herself go warm all over. She was sure her wings were going pink. She moved her hand and sat forward.

"It's so good to see you, Albert. It was such a surprise when you turned up."

"You can say that again."

"I'll never forget that moment when you said, 'I am Albert Gladwyn, rightful consort to Queen Bryony.' It was amazing."

"Did I really say that?"

"Yes, don't you remember?"

"No. It's all rather vague. Dreams are like that."

Bryony leaned closer, talking over the din of the hall, right into his slightly pointed ear. "I've missed you."

She watched as Albert tried to hide his embarrassment by fussing with a lettuce leaf. He put it absent-mindedly into his mouth, along with the piece of cake and chewed. He caught Bryony's eye and burst out laughing. His soft brown eyes gazed at her in adoration.

"I've missed you too, Bryony. I've missed you more than the beach misses the sea; more than a tree misses its leaves in autumn."

Bryony felt her wings shimmer and tremble. She could see from the corner of her eye that they were now pearlescent, but there was nothing she could do about it. Everyone in the room would know she was falling in love - including Albert.

"What happened to you Albert, after Sheean and I went through the portal? I'm so sorry we left you behind."

"I jumped through to follow you."

"Here?"

"Yes. It was so strange. I landed on a beach all alone. I was terrified. In the morning, I found a cave with..."

Trumpets drowned out Albert's voice. Agaric rose into the air. "Your Royal Majesty, Queen Rhyannon, Your Royal Majesty, Queen Bryony, Your Highness, Prince Sheean and Your Royal Highness, Prince Albert, Dignitaries and Council Members, the junior minstrels are about to perform the firework dance."

A group of young Faeries entered the hall. They each held a short wand of oak. Bryony was itching to ask Albert more questions, but knew she had to be quiet. The youngsters looked so cute, standing in a circle, their tiny wings fluttering like fragile petals. The silence in the banqueting hall was absolute. Even the ladybirds held their breath.

Bryony realised they were all waiting for her to say something. She waved her hand in a gesture that she hoped was right. As the Faeries began to produce sparks of brilliant light from their wands, Queen Rhyannon smiled at Bryony.

"I will be leaving soon," she said. "Over the next few days, I will help with your training. Then I will go to the Golden Isles."

Bryony nodded. The fireworks were beautiful. Tiny points of light flew around the hall as the Faeries danced. She glanced at Albert. He looked transfixed. Sheean, at another table, looked distracted, as if something was playing on his mind.

After a while, the fireworks ended and everyone flapped their wings in applause. More food was brought.

"Albert," said Bryony, "what were you saying?"

"Nothing. I was just saying I was only in Taranor for a night and a day. When I got back, two hundred years had gone past. It was awful, Bryony. Everybody we knew was dead. My parents were long gone. Finella, my sister. Edna and her cats. Merik. All gone. It was all so different. There were big houses and doctors and gas lights. Men wore tall hats and gloves. It was the fashion for the ladies to wear enormous skirts and corsets that made their waists really tiny."

The tremble in his voice betrayed the horror, the sheer screaming loneliness of no longer belonging anywhere. Bryony looked down at her plate. A few beetles were busy clearing away the crumbs.

"I'm sorry," she muttered.

"I worked as an engineer," continued Albert. "I lived in Edna's cottage, dreaming of you. I'm still dreaming. I took some medicine."

"I'm sorry I didn't realise that you were Fay when I knew you in the Human realm. I would have tried to help more."

Her comment seemed to snap him out of his reverie.

"Fay?"

"Yes. My gorgeous Prince Gladwyn, held in Human form by the evil King Ogmantiguthra."

"Bryony, my sweet, you don't understand. I'm dreaming all this." His voice seemed so far away. "I'm going to wake up soon."

Bryony laughed. The pink bee finished licking the plums and took off.

Agaric sighed. It had been a wonderful banquet. A pink bee landed on his plate and danced. "Information," it buzzed. Agaric licked the strawberry ice from his fingers and nodded his acknowledgment. "Report."

"Prinze Albert confuzed. Iz zick. Iz taking medizine."

"What's wrong with him?"

"Unzure of factz."

The edges of Agaric's wings turned red with anger. "How many times do you need to be told?! FACTS, FACTS, FACTS! Do not bother me until you have facts! Monitor his progress."

"Yezzir!"

* * *

"Here we are, dear," said Azabyandee as he shut the portal behind them.

Bracken stamped his hooves and tossed his head, rolling his eyes in fear at the sheer drop before him. He backed up, pushing the cart against the mountainside. Edna gasped at the view. The air was thin, yet sweetly fragranced. They were on a narrow track. Eagles soared in the clear blue sky below them.

"Home at last," said Azabyandee as he tossed aside a small blue crystal.

"Don't litter the place, dear," snapped Edna. She jumped down from the cart and picked up the crystal, putting it in her pocket.

"Why are you doing that?" said Azabyandee. "It's empty now. The whole of the Wizard realm is littered with empty, magical items."

"That's no excuse," said Edna as she gazed out at the view of the beautiful, fertile valley, far below.

"Is it how you remember?" asked Azabyandee.

Edna tucked Timothy under her cloak against the chill. "Yes, dear. But why are we up here? Why aren't we down in the valley?"

"Because, my gorgeous wife," said Azabyandee, "this is our new home."

He got down from the cart and turned her gently to face down the track, to where a grove of rhododendrons sparkled in the sunshine. Among the foliage stood a log cabin. Krodbell jumped down from the cart and ran away, beyond the cabin and into the bushes.

"Come back here!" shouted Edna.

"Leave him be, darling," said Azabyandee. He led Bracken down the track towards the cabin. "He'll come back when he finds there's nothing to eat."

Edna followed quietly.

There was room inside the cabin for them all. Two little windows looked out over the valley. The walls were bare and the floor was made from smooth earth. There were no curtains, no carpets, no home comforts at all, apart from a cold, empty fire pit in the centre.

"If we hurry up," said Azabyandee, "we can have the cart unpacked and all our things set up before nightfall."

"At least Bracken will like it," said Edna. "It's just like a stable." She watched the horse clomping around the room, exploring. Azabyandee went out to the cart and came back in, carrying Edna's dining table. "Why here?" asked Edna.

Azabyandee put the table against the wall under one of the windows. He reached into the pocket of his robe and took out the potion bottle containing Grizelda. He shook it gently. A faint whimper came from inside. Grizelda's fat face was pressed hard against the glass, her eyes pleading.

"The mountain air," said Azabyandee. "The view. Solitude. I need to meditate, dear. I need calm and quiet."

Edna looked around the hut as if to make a point. "I was hoping for like-minded friends, warm fires, teacakes and laughter. I've lived for a long time on the outskirts of the Human world. I've been dreaming of coming back here amongst my own kind, amongst my friends."

They stared at each other for a long moment. Azabyandee's bright blue eyes held surprise and disbelief. Edna looked away.

"If you need quiet, my dear," she said calmly, "we can stay here for a bit. But when you are ready, I'd much rather go down to our old place in the valley."

"And you, my dear, can have a warm fire," said Azabyandee, putting Grizelda's bottle on the table and clicking his fingers. The cold ashes of the fire pit became a comforting blaze. Shadows from the flames flickered around the wooden walls. "Right, I'll go and get the rest of the stuff."

Edna gazed out of the window at the valley. From this height, the trees of home looked like lichen; the river looked no wider than a piece of blue thread. Using her shawl, she wiped away a tear.

Chapter 12

The first morning of Bryony's reign dawned bright and clear. Sheean was picking at his breakfast of flower petals, when an attendant rushed into his room. "You have been summoned to see the queen," said the servant. "It is a matter of the utmost urgency, Your Royal Highness."

"You're new. Where's Jerry?"

The attendant bowed low. "He is valet to Prince Gladwyn now. Please follow me."

Sheean flew to Queen Rhyannon's garden to find her lying on a bed of orange flowers. Queen Rhyannon indicated, with the slightest of gestures, for Sheean to lie in a hammock of scented leaves near her. Attendants fluttered all around, offering a breakfast of sweet nectar in silver bowls. She waved them away.

"Thank you for coming so promptly, Sheean."

"Your Majesty." Sheean bowed low before her and settled himself into the hammock.

"I will get straight to the point," she said. "I realise you must be deeply disappointed with the turn of events. I imagine you were looking forward to the life of privilege that someone of your position would normally expect."

Sheean wriggled, trying to get comfortable. His wings kept folding up around his face. "I'm fine, Your Majesty. Bryony will do a great job as queen, especially with the help of her new consort."

Queen Rhyannon smiled. "It's very magnanimous of you to say so. I cannot imagine the pain you must feel."

Finally, Sheean got his wings under control. "Pain?"

347

"Yes. Giving up your childhood sweetheart, your love, for the good of the realm. Only someone with a deep love of his people could do such a thing."

Sheean cleared his throat. "As I said, Your Majesty, I'm fine."

"I am very proud of you. Your bravery and sacrifice have enabled the prophecy of light to have a chance of total fulfillment. When you killed King Ogmantiguthra, you saved our realm from destruction and its people from a life of slavery."

"Well, I didn't really, besides, most people would have done the same."

"I think not, Sheean."

"Most of my friends would have done so."

"Then you are very lucky to have friends like that."

"I agree."

Queen Rhyannon nodded knowingly. "Your realm owes you much, Sheean. I cannot give you the position you deserve, or Bryony's hand in marriage, but I can give you land and status as a small compensation."

"That's not necessary, Your Majesty."

Two Pixies approached the queen, placing hibiscus flowers in her hair. They flew back, admiring their work.

"Of course it is, Sheean. You will leave immediately."

"Immediately! Where to?"

The Pixies turned towards Sheean and muttered something he couldn't hear, then flew away as if having made a decision.

"We still have no knowledge of the whereabouts of Prince Liedinroad. So, I have given you his principality in Goldendale."

"That should make me popular," Sheean mumbled.

Queen Rhyannon continued. "It is a nice, quiet part of the realm. You should fit in very well there."

The Pixies returned with a sprig of ivy and began fluttering round Sheean's head, trying to stuff it into his hair. He waved them away. "But..."

"As I said, you will leave immediately."

"Can I say goodbye to Bryony?"

"Of course. But be quick, she is getting ready for her wedding."

Queen Rhyannon flew up from her bed of flowers, making it clear the meeting was over. Sheean got out clumsily, scattering leaves everywhere.

"One more thing, Sheean," said Queen Rhyannon. "Please take Dog with you."

* * *

Despite the glorious weather and a breakfast of honey-nut sausages, Dog felt sad. He slunk underneath Fable's belly, tucked his tail between his legs and laid his ears flat. Fable bent his strong white neck to look between his hooves at the unhappy creature.

"What's the matter, Dog?"

"Have been posted."

"Posted?"

"Queen says gotta go and live with Sheean."

"But I thought you were Albert's now."

Dog lay down, placing his muzzle on his front paws. The comforting warmth of Fable above him and the cool grass beneath his belly made him feel a lot better, but he still felt sad.

"Sending me away. Will miss you, Fable."

Fable bent his neck further and kissed Dog's nose. "I'll miss you too, but Goldendale isn't far away. We can meet halfway, on the cliffs. Then you can look out over the sea to the mortal lands if you want."

"Don't want. Nasty place."

"Faerie nuff."

Fable shook his mane and laughed out loud. Dog wriggled out from underneath Fable and tried to smile.

"It's a joke," said Fable. "I am a Faerie..."

"I know," Dog interrupted, "I am Faerie and my name is Nuff. But am still sad."

"Sorry, Dog."

"Albert was good to me. Always kind words and lots of treats."

Dog looked up. He saw Albert flying towards them. At a discreet distance flew three armed guards.

"You know funny thing?" said Dog.

"What's that?"

"Bestist food here is carrots."

"Carrots. That's good. They're my favourite too, apart from apples."

"Not tried them yet."

"Ask Sheean to get you some."

Albert landed nearby in a flurry of twinkling lights. He bent down and held his arms out to Dog, who responded instantly, running into his embrace, placing his paws on Albert's shoulders and licking his face.

Albert laughed at first and then began to cry. Dog hugged him tighter. Albert seemed unable to speak, he just sobbed, burying his head in Dog's ruff, while Dog snuffled at his hair.

Albert took a deep breath and sighed. Dog lifted his paws from his Master's shoulders and sat down. Their eyes met. Dog wanted to look away, but he held the gaze, knowing this was not a contest of power, but a look of love.

"I'm so sorry that you have to go," said Albert. "I'll come and see you whenever I can."

Dog felt too upset to reply. He couldn't imagine life without Albert. Their time together had been good, with lots of games. No scolding. No threats. Dog remembered all their walks together in the Human realm; the regular meals and the warm stable he shared with Fable. "Miss you. Miss Fable too."

"I know. Listen. As soon as Sheean seems happy, I, as Prince Consort of Taranor, request the presence of the Royal Dog at my side."

Dog tipped his head on one side, feeling his ears flop. "Um?"

"As soon as Sheean seems happy, come back to me. Queen Rhyannon only wanted you to go to keep him company."

"Was naughty too."

Albert laughed, wiping the tears from his face. "You're not naughty. You're just naturally bouncy and inquisitive."

"What's inkywhatsit?"

"Curious. Nosey."

"Ah, nosey. Yes. Am. Is good thing for Dog to be."

"It's the only way for Dog to be. I shall look forward to our reunion."

"Albert?"

"Yes?"

"Why you use long words now?"

Albert frowned. "I don't know. Maybe it's because I'm royalty now. The words just seem to come out of my mouth without me thinking about it."

"Promise me?"

"What?"

"Promise me, when get back here, you speak like old Albert. Like did before."

"I promise. Sorry, Dog."

A guard shifted a little to attract Albert's attention. Albert gave Dog one last hug. "We have to say goodbye now."

"Dog never say goodbye."

Albert's lips trembled as if he was going to cry again. "Alright. Not goodbye. I'll see you soon."

Dog wagged his tail. "See ya!"

* * *

Drofox was busy doing his rounds at Goldendale Castle. All seemed to be well. Then something caught his eye, high up near the balcony of the strange woman's tower. He gasped in horror as the children, far too young to fly, jumped off the edge of the balustrade and plummeted towards the ground.

He leapt into the air, trying to get to a place where he could catch them both. The girl fell more slowly. The boy twisted in the air at the very last moment, knocking Drofox on the head and flying off with the Hat of the Highest Rule in his fist, chased in fits of giggles by his sister.

The woman appeared at the balcony.

"Children," she called out, "give the nice man his hat back!"

The children flew around the castle battlements, forcing the guards to duck out of their way. Leaning over the balustrade, the woman made eye contact with Drofox. "I'm sorry about the hat, Mr. Drofox. I'll make certain you get it back as soon as they return."

Drofox found himself smiling back at her. "It's alright, children will play. It's only an old hat anyway."

"You're very kind, Mr. Drofox."

Drofox had been watching his guests closely for any sign of their identity. Not once had the children called each other by name. There was something strange going on. The children obviously were advanced, and yet, they and their mother refused to identify themselves. He remembered that when they first arrived, the mother said the children could not fly. But that was obviously untrue.

He wondered for a heart stopping moment whether the officials at Taranor City could have sent them as a test. What if these people were from the ruling class? You shouldn't lock the ruling classes in the tower. Oh my, Oh my.

The boy threw the hat to the floor. Drofox picked it up, brushed it down and flew away slowly, shaking his head.

* * *

"Now then, Hope," said his mother, the golden Wyvern. "It's high time you learned to fly. We've been resting in this nest for long enough." She gave a little nudge with her nose and Hope fell over the side. Grumbuk leaned over the side of the nest and watched his new best friend spiral head over heels towards the river far below.

"Spread wings," he shouted.

He could see Hope's mother hovering near the nest, watching her baby struggle to right himself. When it became clear he was not going to manage it in time, she dived towards the ground, her wings beating frantically to get there before him.

Grumbuk put his hands over his eyes and peeped between his fingers. 'This not going well,' he thought.

Just before Hope hit the river, he managed to right himself. It looked as though the young Wyvern might manage to glide onto the grassy bank, but a sudden gust of wind made him lose his balance again and he dived headfirst into the water.

Hope's mother was there in a second, grabbing the spluttering youngster in her talons. She lifted him clear of the water, and carried him back up to the nest. She plonked him down unceremoniously at Grumbuk's side.

Hope got to his feet and shook himself vigorously, drenching Grumbuk in the process.

"That was fun," said Hope through the clouds of steam coming from his mouth.

Grumbuk shook his head. "You be a worry to me, boy," he said.

* * *

Kelpor sat with his back resting against a tree, looking across the valley towards Taranor City. From the look of the forest, the wedding preparations were going well. Already a faint light emanated from many of the trees and the occasional flash of light showed him when new arrivals appeared into the area near the city. The line of Sentinel Oaks that ringed this part of the island glowed in the early morning light. Their music was quiet, yet content.

Suddenly, his keen eyes saw two Grey Elves running along the blue stone path from Taranor. As they approached him, they saluted.

"At ease," said Kelpor. "What news do you have? I want to know whether we can trust this new queen. I suspect she will unwaveringly follow the traditions set out by her predecessors."

"She seems different," said the first Elf.

"We feel she may be trusted," said the second. "The wedding preparations are going well. Are you not attending the celebration, Sir?"

Kelpor stood as still as stone, his long hair gleaming in the light of the sun. He scanned the horizon and the woods. "No," he said. "I am on my way to Goldendale. I am going to take the position of valet to Prince Sheean."

* * *

Azabyandee sat at Edna's dining table, glaring at a cloth-bound spell book. Grizelda, in her bottle, screamed. Edna wiped her hands on her apron and peered over his shoulder. "Could we let her out a bit more often? I wonder if she would scream less then."

"She's even louder when we let her out. Right now, I'm tempted to throw her out over the mountainside."

Edna shot him a disapproving look. "So am I, but she's too dangerous for that. I think we have to imprison her in a more compassionate environment, yet make sure she cannot escape."

Azabyandee passed his hands wearily over his face. "I can't seem to find a spell to counter the evil in her. I wanted to give her a chance of becoming good."

Edna tickled behind his ears absentmindedly. "I approve of your hope, darling, but I think she's beyond redemption."

Azabyandee butted her hand with his head. "That's lovely. A bit to the left."

Their laughter temporarily drowned out Grizelda's cries. Bracken rose from where he'd been lying and clopped over to them, accidentally knocking over a vase of flowers. Azabyandee felt a wave of irritation. "The noise from that wretched bottle is really beginning to irritate me. And does Bracken really have to clomp around indoors all the time, dear? He's distracting me."

"Come on, Bracken," said Edna. "Let's give him a bit of peace. You and I can get some herbs for soup and look out for Krodbell while we're at it."

Azabyandee watched as the brown rump of the horse squeezed out through the door. The silence, once they've gone, was wonderful. All he could hear was the wind in the trees and a few birds singing. Birds. He opened the door and looked out. There were a few chaffinches hopping around, pecking at the crumbs that Edna had put out that morning. He smiled. For the first time in a long, long time, the birds didn't fly away from him. His mouth watered. A muffled yelling behind him brought his attention back to his task.

He sat down at the table and began to leaf through the book again, turning the heavy pages with care.

"Let me out!" yelled Grizelda.

Azabyandee glanced out of the window to check Edna was nowhere in sight. He grabbed the bottle and rolled it along the table like a toy. The shouts of dismay and rage coming from inside pleased him enormously. He rolled the bottle back and forth, tapping it from side to side with his long fingers.

Then, bored with that, he pulled the stopper from the bottle and hauled Grizelda out with his fingernails. He dangled her in front of his face for a few moments then plopped her on the desk. She began to run. Just as she reached the edge of the table he caught her and brought her back to the middle, where she sat, refusing to move.

"I will NOT play your games, Azabyandee!" she yelled.

He flicked her with a fingernail. "Go on," he said, "run."

"No!"

Azabyandee sighed. "I've been trying to find a way to make you a good person, but I don't think it's possible." He licked his lips. "I have a much quicker and more effective way of dealing with you."

"What's that?"

With great care and tenderness, Azabyandee picked her up and held her between thumb and forefinger like a piece of cheese. With one fluid motion he popped her into his mouth and crunched.

* * *

Kanthy stood on the balustrade, looking down into the courtyard at Drofox, who was still standing around, talking to the guards. She smiled at the children.

"This should stop any rumours about me not being Fay," she said. "You will catch me if this all goes wrong, won't you?"

"Yes Mummy," they said in unison.

Kanthy leaned forward and pushed herself away from the balcony. The children had created a pair of very realistic looking wings for her and cast a spell that effectively made her weightless. She hesitated. "So, all I have to do is float down to ground level?" she asked, for the third time.

"Yes, Mummy!"

Kanthy floated around the courtyard, slowly spiralling down to ground level, landing gracefully in front of Drofox. As she straightened up, the children clicked their fingers, removing her wings, and making it look as though Kanthy had simply chosen to go wingless.

Drofox stood open-mouthed for a second, and then a look of relief spread across his face.

"I wonder if we can have a key for our rooms?" asked Kanthy.

"Yes, yes. My apologies. You should have been free to come and go from day one."

"Thank you," she said, turning to walk up the steps to the main doors.

"Are you not going to fly?" asked Drofox.

Kanthy turned, her eyes meeting his. "No, walking is good for me. You should try to do more of it yourself."

At that moment, a guard came flying towards them. "Drofox, Sir, there is an Elf at the main gate. He said that he is to be Prince Sheean's new valet."

Drofox frowned. "Prince Sheean? I wasn't informed about this! Prince Sheean is coming here? Oh dear. Send the Elf here."

"Yes, Sir."

"Wait," said Drofox. "Is he a Grey Elf?"

The guard hovered. "I don't think so, Sir. His hair is brown."

"Ok. Let him in. The Brown Elves are alright."

Drofox turned to Kanthy. "You needn't concern yourself with this, Madam."

"I'd like to see who it is," she said. "After all, if I don't like him, I don't want him in my household."

"Understood."

A tall Elf, dressed in a fine cloak, walked towards them, escorted by the guard.

"Kelpor!" shouted Kanthy. It was the Elf she had seen in the rock-pool; the one who seemed to know all about her. The Elf bowed. "Hello, Kanthy. We meet at last."

"By whose order?" said Drofox.

There was an awkward pause.

"Mine," blurted Kanthy. "Probably by Sheean's order as well."

"Very well," said Drofox. "Take him through to the servant's quarters. Give him his lists of jobs."

The Elf bowed once more and followed the guard into the castle. Kanthy followed, smiling.

* * *

Sheean sat in the back of a sedan chair, watching the countryside drift by. It was warm, and the rocking of the chair lulled him into a doze. Two Centaurs carried him: a white one in front and a chestnut one behind. He felt a bit embarrassed about being carried, but Agaric had insisted. He could have flown to Goldendale and saved the creatures the effort, but that would have meant leaving Dog to be sent on later.

He had tried to start a conversation with them a few times, but had given up when they talked about Humans and how dirty Sheean must feel for spending all that time with them. Sheean leaned forward and scratched Dog's head. He sent a message into Dog's mind. *These creatures seem a bit unfriendly. I guess it's just you and me now."*

"Be OK, I keep eye on you," said Dog.

"And me," said Alex.

"Alex, did you hear my mind-speech?"

"Not directly, but there's not much that goes off in your head that I don't know about."

"You never said you could read my mind."

"It's not as simple as that. It's more like I pick up feelings and emotions."

"That's still a bit frightening," said Sheean.

"Don't be stupid, Sheean, I have to have contact with your mind, otherwise how could I anticipate your next move in a fight."

"S'pose. I guess there won't be much work for a sentient sword now that I'm not going to be king."

"Now that you mention it, that's something we are going to have to talk about."

"Not now though. Later, yes?"

"Later," Alex confirmed.

As they rose over the brow of the final hill, Sheean got a view of his new home. Below them lay a wooded valley and a town. At the edge of the town, stood a simple castle, glowing in the sunshine.

They continued their journey, finally arriving in the late afternoon at the gates of Goldendale Castle. A pompous official stormed out of the main building, pointing at Dog.

"Where have you picked up that disgusting mortal animal?" he shouted. "He can't stay here. You will have to take him away again."

The Centaurs lowered the sedan. The chestnut one handed a scroll to the official. "Drofox, I think you will find the High Council at Taranor City has other plans. This is Prince Sheean. The animal belongs to him."

Drofox read the parchment, glancing at Dog every now and again. As he read further, his eyes fixed on Sheean. Sheean got out of the chair, followed by Dog, who bounced up and down around the Centaurs' hooves.

"When you have finished talking about me as though I'm not here," said Sheean, "I'm hungry and tired and want food."

Drofox looked at Sheean with obvious contempt. "I cannot lie to you. You're not welcome here." He hesitated and gave the faintest of bows, adding "Your Highness."

"OH YES HE IS!" a familiar voice shouted from a nearby window. "STAY RIGHT THERE!"

Sheean stood open-mouthed as Kanthy burst through the main doors and ran towards him, taking the steps down to the courtyard three at a time in her rush to reach him.

Through a tear-fogged mist he saw the girl he had known all his time in the Human realm, the girl he had once planned to spend the rest of his life with, the only girl he had ever loved, reaching out for him. They met in the middle of the courtyard. Sheean spread his wings and lifted her off the ground, spinning them both around in a spiral of happiness. The children buzzed around them, smiling and giggling as their parents laughed with joy.

* * *

A short while later, Kelpor walked along the corridor of Goldendale Castle towards Sheean's rooms. He could hear Kanthy laughing and the squealing of her children. He hesitated outside the curtain to the first reception room and jingled the string of silver bells.

Sheean opened the curtain. He was shorter than Kelpor expected. His hair was dishevelled and he wore a glamour of a leather tabard and long trousers. His royal wings were fully unfurled. Kelpor lowered his head. "Forgive the intrusion, Sire. I have been told to report to you. I am your new valet."

Beyond Sheean, Kelpor saw the children flying near the ceiling, drawing pictures on the immaculate marble with grubby hands. Kanthy nodded to him in quiet recognition.

"Come in," she said. "What is your name?"

"My name is Kelpor."

* * *

The late evening sunshine warmed the colours of the grasses in the meadow at Taranor Castle. Midges played happily above a stream. Most of the staff at the castle were busy getting ready for the great event; the Royal Wedding.

Albert had been sent to his chambers to be bathed for the second time, leaving Bryony alone for a while. Her bath would be next, once the design of her dress had been chosen. She lay on her belly across a spotted mushroom, near the stream, while Fable grazed nearby. Her wings quivered in annoyance. "But why can't I choose my own dress?"

Fable lifted his head and chewed thoughtfully on a mouthful of sweet grass. "You must follow protocol, little one."

"But if I was getting married in the Human realm, I'd choose my own flowers, my dress... everything! It's supposed to be the happiest day of my life!"

Fable smiled and sucked at a daisy caught on his lower lip.

"We are in Taranor now. Besides, it's the happiest day of your life because you are marrying the one you love, not because you're choosing a new frock."

Bryony frowned and tugged at the edges of the mushroom, throwing them in angry little gestures onto the grass.

"To be honest," said Fable, "I'm a little disappointed in you. You're being selfish and childish. That was alright in the Human realm, while you were suffering and you were much younger. Now you are Queen of Taranor and you can no longer put yourself first. It gives the people around you great joy to choose your dresses and your flowers."

Bryony sat up on the mushroom, crossed her legs and swept away her tears.

"You're right. I'm sorry. I keep acting like a petulant child. It's time I grew up. I'm a queen now. I should learn to act like one."

"Would you like to see the wedding preparations?"

"Oooh, yes please."

Fable nuzzled her cheek. She giggled as his long white whiskers tickled her skin.

"Come with me," he said. "We'll look in one of the forest clearings. The fountains there are often unused. Besides, everyone is busy. No-one will notice us taking a quick look."

They flew over to the fountain in the centre of a clearing and gazed into the clear water. After a few seconds the water revealed trees filled with sparkling lights. Bryony gave a gasp of delight as she saw, for the first time, the Glade of Everlasting Happiness. She'd heard about this place as a child, but never seen it.

The silver birches were being decorated with thousands of glow-worms, each obediently occupying an allotted twig. Pixies, Nymphs and Dryads were busy placing magical decorations in the air, while dark robed Royal Administrators walked in elegance through the trees.

"You see the oak in the centre of the glade?" asked Fable. "The one with the golden platform?"

"Yes."

"That is where you and Albert will stand when you take your vows."

"Why is there a platform? Surely we can hover in the air?"

Fable smiled patiently. "It takes energy to do that. The wedding requires a lot of concentration and magical focus."

Bryony turned from the image and hugged her horse. "Thank you, Fable. Thank you for everything you've done for me. I'm sure the ceremony will go well." She paused. "Just one more question."

Fable dismissed the image in the fountain.

"The glade isn't very big," said Bryony. "How will the rest of my subjects get to see the wedding?"

"Storytellers will be memorising the details. They will then travel the land, telling everyone what your dress was like, what Albert said and how the moon fell on your crown. By next moon, the whole of Taranor will feel as if they had been a guest of honour at your wedding."

Bryony lifted her ears. She could hear shouting in the distance. "What's going on?"

"They are allowing a group of your subjects from the north to voice their discontent."

"Discontent? Like at the banquet when we first arrived?"

Fable nodded his head. "I have been talking with many of the local creatures. There are a growing number who feel the balance is wrong."

"Fable, you're talking in riddles."

Fable smiled. "Queen Rhyannon believes that, for true happiness, all voices should be heard. She has allowed our kin, no matter what their status, to bring injustice to her attention. The High Council is against this. They want to keep things as they have been for aeons."

"Why are they unhappy about the wedding?"

"Many people outside the city fear that occasions like this use too much magic."

"I don't understand."

"Everything is in balance, Bryony. It takes a lot of magic to create a proper Royal Wedding. This means there is less for others."

"Where does magic come from?"

"From the stars, My Sweet, everything comes from the stars. Once it arrives here it needs to be shared. If we use a lot, there is less to go round for other creatures."

Bryony looked up at the points of light glimmering in the late lilac sky. To the west, the pink haze of the setting sun was as pale and soft as a rose. A rustle of leaves and a polite cough caught her attention.

"By your leave, Your Majesty," said Lorella, "it is time to dress your hair."

* * *

Albert knew he should have been happy, but the awful suspicion that he might never wake kept nagging at his mind. The doctor's medicine must have been really strong. Maybe he'd taken too much. He'd been dreaming for a whole night and a day, hour following hour, everything dream-bizarre yet making sense. Now it was the second night and he was about to marry Bryony, his childhood sweetheart.

He was standing high above the ground on a golden platform in a forest clearing. Two moons shone out over the trees and onto the upturned faces of the people below. The ceremonial build up to the exchanging of vows had been long, yet he felt no fatigue. Now they were ready to make their promises to each other. Not a sound could be heard from the crowd.

Bryony looked awesome. Her crown, held onto her head by tiny winged creatures, glittered in the lights of glow-worms. Her face was flushed and excited. She looked so happy. She kept stealing glances in his direction. Whenever their eyes met, she grinned and his heart skipped a beat.

This moment had been a fantasy of his for years, ever since he'd first seen her. At that time it had been the foolish wish of a young boy. As a teenager, he'd imagined asking for her hand almost every day. Now, as a grown man, it was still just a dream. Soon he would wake up and it would all be over.

The Master of Ceremonies approached, hovered in front of the platform, and called out, "Do you, Prince Consort Albert Gladwyn, take Queen Bryony Winkleweed as your wife? Do you promise to protect her, to honour her and to love her for all time?"

Albert looked out over the forest canopy and projected his voice for all to hear. "I do."

A short ripple of fluttering wings filled the air. A caterpillar, continuing to cheer far below, was shushed into silence by the guards. Albert's heart began to thump.

"Do you," said the Master of Ceremonies, "Queen Bryony Winkleweed, take Prince Consort Albert Gladwyn as your husband? Do you promise to protect him, to honour him and to love him for all time?"

As she opened her mouth to answer, a bolt of yellow light roared towards the platform. Like a puppet, manipulated by an unseen hand, Albert flung himself in the way. The blow knocked him sideways. Pain exploded down his spine. What felt like acid poured across his wing.

He opened his eyes. Bryony was on the floor of the platform with him, holding him, tears flowing down her pretty face. Her mouth moved but he couldn't hear. The pain lanced through him. All around the air was the deep dark blue of soldiers whirling, shouting orders, moving so fast he couldn't see one from the other. Maybe he was finally waking?

A Faerie with pale blue wings broke through the guards and touched his wing. The pain lessened. He heard Bryony asking if he was alright. The air around them cleared, revealing the trees and the people below. He stood, taking Bryony's arm for support. She gazed at him with open admiration. In a loud, clear voice she turned to the crowd and called out, "I do!"

The crowd cheered. Trumpets blazed a fanfare. Ashley Pelagon waved for silence. Once again, the forest was so quiet you could have heard an acorn drop.

"You may touch wings," said Ashley Pelagon.

Albert turned towards his wife. He felt weak with shock, yet elated that he had saved her life. That's what he'd done, he'd saved the life of his beloved! What a dream! Maybe it was better not to wake. Maybe it was better to stay dreaming forever, rather than wake up back at Edna's cottage, alone.

Bryony stepped closer and wrapped her gossamer wings around him. He lifted his wings to their fullest extent and enfolded her. For a timeless moment they remained encircled in love and light, their glamour mingling, their hearts and minds pressed close.

After a while he felt Bryony pull back a little. He released her and folded his wings. Where the pain had been, was now just a dull ache.

"Your Majesty Queen Bryony and Prince Consort Albert," said Ashley, "please face the crowd and show your wings."

As Albert opened his wings he noticed two things. One, he had a neat hole at the edge of his upper right, and two, he now had turquoise patches among the brown. He glanced across at Bryony. She was preening, showing the crowd the patches of autumn brown in her own.

Ashley Pelagon took to the air and flew over the forest, proclaiming, "Behold, Albert and Bryony Gladwyn Winkleweed, Prince Consort and Queen of Taranor!"

The crowd went wild. Fireworks filled the sky, butterflies and nymphs danced, and trumpets blared the news across the land.

* * *

That night, Bryony snuggled against the pillows of her bed. "Oh Albert, this is perfect! I never thought I could be so happy."

Albert smiled gently. He propped himself on one elbow and leaned over her. He looked lovely. There was a strange light in his eyes and a softness to his mouth.

"Any moment now," he said, "I'll wake up, but for now this glorious dream is all I could ever have wished for." He kissed her lightly on the lips.

Byrony giggled. He kissed her again, lingering a little longer. She pushed him away, laughing.

"Why are you kissing me?"

His face became serious, a tiny frown appeared between his brows. She noticed his hand shaking as he caressed her shoulder.

"I thought..."

He moved a lock of hair from her face to behind her ear.

"You don't need to do my hair. Lorella does that."

He smiled. His cool fingers traced the scar on her cheek.

"Don't do that," she said, squirming.

"How did you get that scar?"

"I don't want to tal about it. What did you think, Albert?"

"I thought perhaps we might make love, as it's our wedding night."

Bryony frowned. Albert removed his hand and gazed at her. "Only if you want to, of course."

"Make love? But love is everywhere. Why would we want to make more?"

Albert laughed. Bryony noticed how his pupils dilated when he looked at her, how they changed with his mood.

"Has no-one told you," asked Albert, "about the Birds and the Bees?"

"I know everything about them. There among my best friends."

Bryony sat up, scattering petals left and right. Instantly, a group of Pixies set to putting them back, and plumping up the pillows of thistledown. Albert lay back, sighing.

"Thank you, Pixies," he said.

"I like that about you, Albert," said Bryony.

"What's that?"

"You're polite."

He smiled. "Do you know what being married means, Bryony?"

"Yes I do. It means loving someone forever and ever. It means loving them more than you love yourself. It means being prepared to die for them. It means if they are remotely unhappy, you can't settle until they are happy again."

Albert gazed into her eyes, his hands behind his head, his brown wings spread outwards like velvet leaves. She loved the way that his long fringe still flopped into his eyes.

"I've always liked your hair like this," she continued, ruffling the strands of brown hair into chaos.

"Do you love me that much, Bryony?"

"Yes. Yes I do. It's just taken me a long time to realise it."

"When people are married," said Albert, "where I come from anyway, they make love on their wedding night and whenever they want to. They make love and celebrate being together by kissing and... making babies."

"Whenever they like?"

"Yes. If both want to, of course. It's supposed to be beautiful."

"Have you made babies before?"

Albert blushed. "No."

Bryony noticed a loose tendril of jasmine in the woven flower structure over the bed. "I am old enough, and I'm Queen of Taranor." As she began to weave the delicate yellow flowers back into place, she smiled. "Ooh, I like those words so much!" She ran her fingers through her hair, enjoying the scent of the flowers on her hands. "But in Taranor, both the male and female need to be in season. It's not my season for at least two or three months. I won't know exactly until the Healers tell me. They'll spot the signs."

Albert sat up. "Season? Like a mare?"

Pixies moved in to replace the petals lost by his movement.

"Yes. Why should I be different? I can't make babies all the time, I'd be exhausted. And besides, the place would be overrun."

"Are you serious?"

"Yes. Why, are you in season now?"

Albert stuttered, "I guess so. But I can wait. Don't worry. I am your husband now. Even if you never come into season, I'll stay loyal."

Bryony threw back her head and laughed. "Oh I will, don't you worry. It will be such fun. As soon as the right time comes, we'll go to the Glade of Everlasting Happiness and - make love, as you call it, and everyone will celebrate."

"In the Glade? In public?"

"Well how else? We need the energy of our subjects. In the centre of the Glade, surrounded by the love and warmth of selected subjects whose energy helps our union, we come together and then I can bring many children into the world, all with the potential to be queen or king after me. Of course only one will be chosen. Albert your mouth is open like a fish."

Albert shut his mouth. He breathed in deeply through his nose and then out in a long low breath through his lips, as though blowing out a candle. "We don't need lots, darling. A boy and a girl will do."

"True, but we won't know how many I am to provide until the time comes. The Council will know how many are needed for the realm to continue in happiness and peace." She looked out at the garden. Although trees now obscured the moons, the fountain and flowerbeds were flooded with a silver light. "I know. For tonight let's shrink down and share a curled-up leaf. It will be more private and cuddly."

Albert smiled. "OK."

Before she went out into the garden, Bryony took one of the Pixies to one side. "What is your name, little Pixie?"

The Pixie curtseyed. "Annabelle, Your Majesty."

"Well, Annabelle, my husband has spent so long in the Human realm that he has lost touch with our world. He will soon remember our ways. Please show him the courtesy of not talking among yourselves about his lapse of memory."

"As you wish, Your Majesty," said Annabelle. "We wouldn't presume to gossip."

The next morning, Bryony decided to take Albert to the Crystal Pool. They stood side by side, admiring the reflections of the soft pink sky in the water. "I think a beach of silver sand would be nice," she said.

Albert simply nodded, gaping at the beauty that surrounded him. Bryony waved her wand and gave a squeal of delight as the beach appeared, just wide enough for them to sit side by side. She ignored the polite appreciation of her attendants and, with due formality, invited Albert to join her on the silver sand.

Fable grazed on fresh grass nearby, occasionally looking up and smiling at her.

"I can hear the animals talk now," said Albert.

"Of course you can. Everyone can hear them."

Albert nodded. "I mean when I lived in the mortal realm, I couldn't hear any of them speak."

Bryony looked shocked. "Couldn't you? Why not? That's awful. How did you manage to look after Dog so well?"

Albert laughed. "So many questions my sweet bride. So many questions."

Bryony wasn't sure whether it was his honeyed words, his good looks, or the setting, but she felt weak with love.

"Albert..."

He toyed with her fingers, sending shivers across her wings.

"Albert, I was fond of you when we were both stuck in the Human realm, but now you're a bit older, and I'm far wiser..."

He gazed at her. His deep brown eyes had depths of golden-rod and nasturtium. Why had she never noticed before?

"I really, really love you. I meant every word I said at our wedding."

He leant forward to kiss her. It was like being caressed on the lips by a wild rose. She tilted her head for another kiss, breathing in to catch his sweet breath. To her surprise, he gave a troubled sigh and leaned back against a rock, watching the play of sunlight on the surface of the pool.

"The attendants," he asked, "are they always around?"

"Yes, for our assistance." Bryony kept her voice loud enough to be heard by all who surrounded them. "I'm really glad they're here to help. And the guards are here to keep us safe."

"Do they listen to everything we say, all the time?"

"Of course."

Bryony took a stick and began to doodle in the sand. "I can't rule without them," she said. The stick made nonsense patterns in the sand followed by the word *they* in Human script. "They help us choose the right clothes." *Don't.* "They advise on matters of state." *Watch.* "They make sure my food is safe."

Albert watched the words form in the sand without showing anything on his face.

They don't watch.

"Who would want to poison you?" he asked.

"Oh, no-one." *All.* "That hasn't happened for thousands of years." *The time.* "But they keep testing my food just in case."

They don't watch all the time.

"Doesn't everyone love the queen?"

"Of course they do." Her stick scribbled the words *but they listen.*

"I see."

She wiped the words away with an idle flourish.

"Shall we fly to the coast tomorrow? It's just that my work will start soon. Queen Rhyannon will be teaching me how to govern before she retires."

"May I kiss your cheek before we go?"

Bryony laughed and presented the side of her face. She felt his lips on her skin. His hair held the scent of autumnal leaves, his breath was a sweet as chestnuts. She felt a sudden urge to fly. Without warning, she shot up into the air. "Race you to the castle!"

Fable snorted, bunched up his hind-quarters and leapt into the air by her side. She flew to his back and gripped his flowing mane, beckoning Albert to follow.

With one fluid motion, Albert took to the air. As they flew side by side, escorted by their attendants,

Bryony was aware of a deeper shadow of purple; the ever present guards.

Chapter 13

Kanthy strolled into the kitchens and searched around for someone in charge. There were tiny beings running around everywhere, each wearing a pointed white hat. "Where is the head chef?" asked Kanthy.

A Pixie, wearing a taller hat than the others, came towards her, wiping her hands on a spotlessly clean apron. "Can I help you?"

"Do you know who I am?"

"You are one of the Noble Fay from Taranor City, m'lady."

"Good. I have a challenge for you."

"I can cook you anything you desire."

"You shouldn't make promises like that until you know what I want," chuckled Kanthy.

The Pixie looked puzzled.

Kanthy emptied a bag of potatoes onto the kitchen table "I want you to make mashed potato and tomato sauce sandwiches."

The Pixie stared wide-eyed at the vegetables.

"Do you know how to cook potatoes?"

"No, m'lady. They are of the deadly-nightshade family. We are not allowed to use them."

"The roots are not poisonous, nor are tomatoes. Scrape the skin off first, and then boil them in water. When they're soft, drain the water and crush them. I don't want any lumps. Do you understand? Boil the tomatoes until they are soft."

"Yes, m'lady."

Later that afternoon, Kanthy held onto Kelpor's arm as they made their way down the cliff path and onto the sand. The children flew off to look in the rock pools, with Dog chasing close behind. As

Sheean flew to Kanthy's side, Kelpor let go of her arm.

"This is great," said Sheean. "We have the whole beach to ourselves."

Kanthy smiled. "The folk at the castle don't seem to like outings."

Kelpor opened out a blanket for her to sit on, his eyes smiling at her all the while. "Kelpor, where do all the normal people live?" she asked. "We never see them unless they're doing things for us."

Kelpor was quiet for a few seconds. "The servants live in quarters in the castle."

"How do they get out of the castle to see their relatives?" asked Sheean.

"They are allowed a yearly holiday."

"We need to do something about the way the poor are treated," said Kanthy.

Kelpor bowed. "Shall I climb up the cliff and fetch the picnic hamper, Your Highness?"

Sheean nodded. "I'll come with you. I can carry the children's toys."

"No, Your Highness, it is my privilege to serve."

"Can we drop all that?" said Sheean. "Call me Sheean."

Kelpor bowed again and they walked off together up to the cliff-top.

Kanthy watched Caul and Libith playing with Dog at the water's edge. Dog leapt up and down, snapping at something in the air.

"Careful, Dog," Kanthy called. "Don't bite anything"

Dog threw himself this way and that to keep the creature in sight.

"Is buzzy thing."

"Don't bite it, Dog. It's a bee. It might sting you."

The bee flew away, zigzagging up the cliff path. Dog ran to Kanthy, shaking water from his fur in a wiggle that started at his nose and ended at his tail. Kanthy laughed, shielding her face from the spray. Kelpor and Sheean returned, carrying a hamper and a bag of toys.

"What have we got for lunch?" asked Sheean as he helped Kelpor open the basket. "The walk here has made me hungry."

Kelpor stood at a discrete distance from the royal couple.

Kanthy laughed. "It wasn't very far."

"In that case it's probably because I'm a growing boy."

Kanthy shook her head in mock despair. "You'll never grow up."

"Growing up is over-rated, don't you think? So what's for lunch?"

"Well, you know how difficult it is to get real food around here?" said Kanthy.

"Yes. Is it real food? What is it? My mouth's watering already."

"It's a bit strange. The children asked for it."

"Oh, come on, tell me."

"Mashed potato and tomato sauce sandwiches," said Kanthy.

"You're joking!"

"No."

"That's great. I love potatoes. Where did you get them from?"

"I found a field full of them, hidden away, on the far side of that wooded area we can see from our bedroom. I showed the cooking Pixies how to prepare them, and they had a good go at making tomato sauce. It isn't as good as cook used to make back in Cucapha, but it's not bad."

"The twins will love it," said Sheean. "Caul! Libith! Come on, it's lunch time, and your clever mummy's made us mashed potato and tomato sauce sandwiches."

* * *

After lunch, Sheean stared out at the shimmering patterns made by the sun on the sea. 'I wonder if I can fly out to sea far enough, so all I see is water?' he thought.

"It's probably easier to use a boat," said Kelpor.

Sheean turned and smiled. "Did I say that out loud?"

"No, but you've been standing there for a long time. I can guess what you're thinking." Kelpor handed Sheean a flask. "Would you like to try this drink? I'm rather partial to it."

Sheean uncorked the flask, sipped the golden liquid it contained, and gasped for breath. "By the gods, what's this? Is it poison?"

Kelpor laughed. "No, it's whisky, from the Human realm. I thought you might have tasted it before."

"No, I've drunk lots of ale as a youngster, but even Humans don't give children whisky to drink."

Kelpor smiled. "Try some more."

"No thanks." Sheean paused, looking out to sea once more. "Can you get things from the Human realm?"

"I have some contacts."

"Could your contacts get me something?"

"You do know it's against the Law to trade with Humans?"

Sheean frowned. "That's stupid. Humans are generally good people."

"I agree," said Kelpor. "I'll make enquires for you. What do you require?"

"A goat."

"A goat?"

"Kanthy and I are sick to death of Fay food. We manage to get fish occasionally, but we would really love some cheese."

Kelpor bowed. "I will do my best."

They gazed out to sea for a while, listening to the children playing. Kelpor cleared his throat. "Sheean?" he said, quietly.

"Mmmm?"

"I know Kanthy is Human."

"H... How?" Sheean stuttered.

"It is not a problem for me. I'm honoured to work for both of you."

"How many people know?"

"Only myself. I will not tell anyone. It so happens that my own mother is Human."

"Really?"

Kelpor nodded. "She is here on Taranor."

Sheean relaxed a little. "If the authorities find out, they will arrest them both."

"Don't worry. It is highly unlikely that they will find out. I will arrange to get the goat with great discretion. Do you intend to eat it?"

Sheean laughed. "No, milk it."

"You would drink the milk of the goat?"

"Of course, and make cheese."

Kelpor shook his head and pulled a face at the thought of it.

"You should try it, Kelpor, it's much nicer than whisky."

"I'll give it a miss if you don't mind," Kelpor said, as a big grin spread across his face. "Do you want another swig?" he added, holding the flask out for Sheean.

Sheean returned the smile. "I'll give it a miss if you don't mind."

* * *

Grumbuk and Hope stood on the edge of the nest. Grumbuk could see eagles flying far below.

"Sit in front of my wings and hold onto my neck," squeaked Hope, "it's easy."

"Easy you say."

"It's only difficult while we're in the nest. You'll feel much safer once we're flying."

"Goblins not fly. Goblins stay on ground."

Hope closed one eye and squinted at him. "Are you frightened?"

"What?! Course not. I hero of legend!"

Grumbuk grabbed one of Hope's neck spines and jumped astride, just like he'd seen Humans do with horses. Hope looked at his mother for reassurance. Grumbuk noticed a wink pass between the two creatures, then the baby Wyvern spread his wings and jumped over the edge of the nest.

They plummeted towards the ground at a nerve grinding speed. He closed his eyes and waited for the impact. The wind rushing past his ears changed direction and his stomach lurched. The expected crash seemed a long time coming. Grumbuk opened an eye slightly, peeping, ready to close it again at the slightest sign of danger.

382

The sight that met Grumbuk took his breath away. Hope was flying effortlessly a few feet above the ground, banking left and right as he followed the contours of the valley. Grumbuk found himself close to tears. "Well done boy," he shouted. "Grumbuk very proud!"

* * *

Agaric led his latest recruit through the Royal Woodlands and into the Gardens of Fragrant Joy. He flew slowly so that his officer could take in the illuminated quartz pillars lining the pathway. They radiated a green-pink light; very fitting for the season."Remember," said Agaric, keeping his voice low so as not to disturb the ambience, "I, as Head of Security, am allowed to go where I please, but you are allowed in the Royal Gardens only by invitation of Queen Bryony and Prince Albert, or by my direct orders."

The officer nodded, pausing to sniff at some roses. "Does this area have surveillance too?" he asked.

"Of course. However the insects posted here are not asked to cast doubt on the Queen, but to ensure her safety."

They both lifted their heads at the same moment, pricking their ears towards the sound of Queen Bryony's crystal clear laughter.

"She seems to be enjoying the cherry blossom orchard," said Agaric. "I shall introduce you."

The Royal couple were perched halfway up a cherry tree, legs astride a branch as if on a horse, facing each other. Queen Bryony seemed to be playing some kind of game. Agaric gave Thornfield a hand signal to approach quietly.

"Fay, Human, Fay, Human, Fay!" Each time Bryony spoke a word, she pulled a petal from a blossom and fed it to Albert. "Human, Fay, Human, Fay, Human!" Her laughter sprinkled the gardens with delight as she ate the petals herself. "It just depends on where you start. All these blossoms have five petals."

"Your point being?" said Albert.

"Well, you must be Fay. Your ears are pointed and you can fly. I'm starting from the obvious clues that I can see. Besides, whatever you are, I still love you."

Using his large brown wings for balance, Albert leaned forward to kiss her. Agaric gave a polite cough.

Bryony flew down. "Oh, hello. I didn't hear you coming."

Agaric bowed low. "Please excuse the intrusion. I would like to introduce a new recruit. Senior Security Officer Thornfield." He was pleased to see Thornfield was keeping his eyes averted and his head low. Bryony flew round them both.

"Hello, Mr. Thornfield. Do you have a first name? I can't call you Thornfield, it sounds frightfully stuffy."

With his head still bowed the officer said, "My name is Loosestrife Thornfield, Your Majesty."

"Pleased to meet you."

Agaric bowed again. As he lifted his head, he signalled for Thornfield to do the same.

"I am explaining the rules and showing him his territory." Agaric hesitated as Albert flew down to join them. "If I may be so bold," he continued, "I couldn't help overhearing your conversation, Your

Majesty. Can you please say what you meant by 'Whatever you are, I still love you'?"

Bryony flushed. Her wings shifted to orange as if fire swept along their veins.

"How DARE you!" she shouted. "WHAT are you IMPLYING?"

"I am implying nothing, Your Majesty. I was merely... interested."

Bryony's wings went back to turquoise. Albert stepped forward. His eyes were calm and steady, showing no sign of fear. "I can explain. I have been joking with Queen Bryony. She thought I was mortal when we first met, as I did her. Now we both know the truth, we like to jest."

Agaric bowed. "Please forgive me. I can only assure you that I have your best interests at heart. I did not mean to be rude."

Bryony flitted back up to the tree, where she began nibbling the blossoms again. Agaric glanced at the prince consort.

"Sire, is the queen more than usually hungry?"

"I've no idea," said Albert. "She's been eating a lot of petals today."

"She may be entering the first phase of season. This is great news. I shall inform the healers and the midwives."

Agaric noticed Prince Albert swallow nervously. "It is clear from your reaction that you know how this change will impact on you, Sire. Please rest assured we will protect you in the event of uncontrolled temper outbursts. The Royal Attendants will be alerted to potential changes in the queen's behaviour. All will be well. Your children will be plentiful."

Albert stared at him with his mouth open. Agaric stifled a smile and bowed. "I shall leave you in peace while there is still a chance of it."

The two officers left the gardens and returned to the palace.

"Here," said Agaric, gesturing towards a series of bee hives, "is the Pink Bee Zone. They work for us for three years and then are allowed their freedom. If any bee reports to you, please file the information in the Ledger of Detail in my office."

They paused to inspect the latest dances of the bees from the south.

"Any news of Prince Liedinroad?" asked Agaric.

"No zign," said a bee.

"Fan out further. We are looking for the prince and his entourage. I want to know where he is and why he reneged on our appointment."

The bees took to the air. Agaric turned to Thornfield. "He was supposed to arrive in time to challenge Prince Sheean, but he didn't turn up. Apparently he left Goldendale, but hasn't been seen since. I want to know what he's up to."

"Do you suspect foul play?"

"I am beginning to."

"Sir," said Thornfield, "did you get an odd feeling from Prince Albert? I hate to say this, but I feel he may be hiding something from us."

Agaric looked his officer in the eye. Their wings darkened.

"I agree," said Agaric. "I can't think what it is, but something doesn't smell right. When I was with him everything made sense, but now we're back here, my unease has returned. Post a senior bee nearby." He paused. "For the safety of our Royal Couple of course."

Thornfield nodded. "Understood, Sir."

* * *

The bells tinkled on the curtain that led to Kanthy's apartment. She opened the curtain a tiny amount and peeped out. She saw Kelpor standing there.

"Is it convenient?" he asked.

Kanthy opened the curtain wide. "How did you know it was me?"

"I would recognise those beautiful eyes anywhere." A mischievous grin spread across his face.

"Really?"

"Ah, caught again," he joked. "I cannot lie. It had to be you. Sheean's eyes are green."

"And there I was, thinking I had an admirer."

"Would that be objectionable?" asked Kelpor with a smile.

Kanthy shrugged her shoulders and beckoned him inside, placing a finger to her lips. "Hush, Caul and Libith are having a nap. Sheean and I are out in the garden."

"I hope you don't mind me asking, but has no one mentioned your eye colour?"

"No. They were funny with me at first, especially that Drofox fellow, but it's alright now that Sheean is here with me."

"I have always been able to see what you really are."

She smiled. "That's because you're special. What have you got in the bag?"

"I have something you will enjoy."

387

Kanthy led the way out to the gardens. Sheean was dozing on one of the many garden chairs, his feet balanced on the edge of the ornamental pond, the chair on its back two legs. Kanthy and Kelpor looked at his precarious position.

"The Pixies should make him a bed of petals incase he falls," said Kelpor.

"He gave them all a bag of gold and told them to go home to their families."

Kelpor nodded his approval.

Kanthy poked Sheean in the ribs, making him lose his balance and fall backwards into a flowerbed. Dog came running up and dropped a sticky, wet ball into Sheean's open mouth. Sheean's eyes bulged as he dragged a lung-full of air through his nose, expelling it through his mouth with some force. The ball shot across the garden with Dog in close pursuit.

"Sheean," said Kanthy, "Kelpor has something for us."

Sheean jumped to his feet, coughing. "Oh, hi, I was just playing with Dog."

"I see," said Kelpor, "an excellent game, no doubt."

"Yes, it's good fun," said Sheean, wiping his mouth. "What have you got in the bag?"

Kelpor pulled out a parcel wrapped in clean muslin.

"I bought this cheese in the Human realm," he said. "However it won't be long before your own goat will be producing milk and cheese for you. I thought you would not want to milk it yourselves, so I took the liberty of assigning it to a local family. Milk and cheese will be delivered to you daily."

"Have you got the goat?" asked Sheean.

"I have."

"So soon?"

"It only takes three heart-beats of time to go there and back for such an errand. It was no problem."

"You must pay that family," Sheean insisted.

"That's all in hand. As a reward for their silence, I have also taken the liberty of exempting them from all taxes and guaranteed their daughter a place in the sewing and mending school." He paused for a moment, watching Dog chase his tail. "I was wondering, since you both show an interest in the welfare of the people, would you like to accompany me on a tour?"

"Where to?" asked Kanthy.

"I thought you might like to see how people live and maybe visit my home in the north while we are at it. I know mother would love to talk to Kanthy. She spends so much time hidden away, and she is often lonely."

Kanthy looked at Sheean. "Can we? It would be great to get out of this stuffy castle and do something for a change."

"I think it's a great idea," Sheean said as he broke off a lump of cheese and stuffed it in his mouth. "When do we leave?"

"I will arrange porters and sedan chairs."

"I'd rather walk," said Sheean, with his mouth full.

"It is approximately five days walk to the Elf lands. Will the children manage that distance?"

Kanthy laughed. "The children will manage better than the rest of us. They love to be out in the countryside."

"Then it's settled," said Kelpor. "We will leave after the wedding."

"After the wedding is great," said Sheean.

Kelpor bowed and left them.

"I think he's a nice Elf," said Kanthy, once she was sure he was out of earshot.

"Nicer than me?" Sheean smirked.

"You are a Royal Faerie, not an Elf. Besides, no-one can match the father of my children," Kanthy said, laughing. "And while we are on that subject, I believe it's a full moon tonight."

* * *

Drofox addressed the nobles seated around the table. "I have arranged this meeting to discuss the wedding of Prince Sheean and his peculiar bride."

There was a rumble of voices.

"I fully understand your indignation at the commoner style wedding they have chosen, and the lack of celebrations," he said. "Prince Liedinroad would never have taken part in such a farce or tarnished the reputation of Goldendale's nobility. He would have declared a public holiday."

A few nobles nodded.

"Although, there is one good thing about the whole affair. It is clear Prince Sheean is a weak leader. The whole thing was his wife's idea. Of course a weak leader is a good thing for us, and we can use it to our advantage."

"Do we know what happened to Prince Liedinroad?" another of the nobles asked.

"No, I have to assume he has been moved to another principality, although I have not heard anything from Agaric at Taranor City. I expect our prince has been moved to make room for Simple Sheean... Prince Sheean I mean."

The nobles laughed.

* * *

Sheean and Kanthy stood at the far end of the old wooden barn, waiting for the people of the castle to join them for their wedding. They held hands nervously in front of the silversmith's anvil, the children buzzing quietly either side of them. Kelpor stood to one side. He was frowning.

The barndoor creaked open, and the people filed in quietly. Sheean turned to face the anvil. His palm felt sweaty in Kanthy's cool hand.

The silversmith coughed. "Does anyone know of any reason why these two cannot be married?" he said, looking round at the audience.

The gathered Fay looked down at their feet, and mumbling soon spread along their ranks. The children turn and scowled at them as if looking for the slightest hint that one of them might object to their parent's marriage.

"Very well as there are no objections, by the power vested in me and all silversmiths of Taranor, I declare you married."

The silversmith lifted his hammer and struck the anvil three times.

He bowed to Sheean and Kanthy. The people flapped their wings politely then filed out, followed by the silversmith.

"Well, wife," Sheean joked. "I guess you have to do as I tell you now."

Kanthy smiled. "Don't push your luck."

She looked around the empty room and shrugged. "I don't think the people of Goldendale like us very much."

"Do you care?" Sheean asked.

"Not in the slightest."

Sheean wrapped Kanthy in his arms and kissed her. "I love you so much," he whispered.

Kanthy smiled and kissed him back. "That makes two of us."

Later that evening, Kanthy looked out over her garden. She liked how the early evening sky bathed the flowers and pond in a lilac light. The two moons were just beginning to wane, but still looked almost full. A few stars were out, twinkling like gems.

She watched Sheean in his hammock, his chest rising and falling as he dozed after supper. He'd been enjoying the strong drink favoured by Kelpor. She tickled his nose. Sheean wafted his hand across his face as if at an imaginary fly.

* * *

Albert and Bryony were sitting high in the branches of a sweet chestnut tree in the Royal Forest, surrounded by attendants with lanterns, food and wine. Bryony looked across to where Lorella, perched on a nearby branch, held a plate of orange coloured sweets.

"Isn't this the best time of day?" said Bryony with a sigh. "I love the way the sky fades to lilac, and those early stars coming out are so pretty."

"Another sweet, Your Majesty?" said Lorella.

"Just one more nasturtium nibble," said Bryony, reaching for the plate. "They're so delicious."

Lorella held the plate closer to prevent Bryony losing her balance. Albert gazed up at the stars. He'd been quiet all evening. Bryony kicked him gently with her felted boot.

"A blossom for your thoughts, my love."

"I miss Dog," said Albert, continuing to look at the sky as if searching for his friend. "It's a shame he was sent away with Sheean. It would be so great if he was here. We could have such fun."

"Queen Rhyannon thought he was Sheean's dog."

"More drink, Sire?" asked Jerremoy.

"Yes please," replied Albert. "What's it made from?"

"It is our finest Canterbury Bell wine. The petals are harvested by hand and each barrel is aged for two hundred years. It is very strong, Sire. If I may be so bold, I would advise caution."

"Fill the cup."

* * *

Kanthy's attention was drawn to the centre of her garden where Caul and Libith were throwing sticks into the pond for Dog to retrieve. Their infectious giggling made her smile. "It'll be bedtime soon children," she called.

"Yes Mummy," they said with practiced patience.

* * *

Jerremoy poured a tiny drop of wine into a thimble-sized goblet and handed it to Albert, who drank it in one sip.

"Delicious," he said, gazing out again at the stars. "Dog was mine you know. Edna gave him to me." He sighed deeply. "I wish he could appear magically, right in front of me."

"You've had too much wine," laughed Bryony.

Albert turned on his branch as if to protest that he was sober, but lost his balance. He fell in a tangle of twigs, leaves and chestnuts to land on soft moss far below. He lay there, grinning up at Bryony.

* * *

As Caul threw his stick high into the air, Dog took a running jump. To Kanthy's amazement both the stick and Dog froze in mid-air.

"Children don't be cruel to Dog," she warned.

"It's not us, Mummy," said the children.

Kanthy nudged Sheean and got up to investigate. As she approached the pond, a circular window appeared just behind the frozen form of Dog, its edge taking on the form of two slim dragons, one of gold, the other silver, both intertwined to form a giant circle.

"Sheean! Come and look at this!"

"Mmm, coming," Sheean replied, without making any effort to move.

* * *

Bryony grinned back at Albert and launched herself towards his chest, feet first. By spreading her wings at the last moment, she landed fairly softly, merely knocking the breath out of him.

He grabbed her ankles and rolled over so that he was above her, looking down. She closed her eyes for a kiss.

* * *

Within the window created by the dragons, Kanthy saw two Faeries lying at the base of a sweet chestnut tree. Sheean joined her and pointed. "Bryony," he said.

It took Kanthy a second to recognise the other figure, because he had changed so much. "Albert," she said. "Older, but definitely Albert."

Dog's form started to faded.

* * *

Bryony recoiled from the rough, warm licks that slobbered over her face. Albert's breath stank!

* * *

The children shouted and pointed their pudgy arms at the window. Within seconds, Dog fully rematerialized within the ring - still held - frozen in its grip.

* * *

Bryony opened her eyes to see Albert roaring with laughter. Even the attendants in the trees were chuckling.

"Albert, that's disgusting! Don't you know how to kiss properly? And your breath! It stinks!"

"It was Dog," laughed Albert. "He appeared between us for a second, and licked your face. It was so funny!"

Bryony punched Albert on the chest. They rolled together in the moss, laughing as if they didn't have a care in the world. Bryony felt giddy with love. She threw herself on him, pretending to hold him down.

She knew he could lift her off him with one flick of his wings, but instead, he lay there, his eyes bright, gazing into her soul with adoration.

* * *

Dog hung in mid-air. He looked at the children with big brown eyes as if pleading to be let down. The gold and silver dragons writhed, hissing and spitting. Again, Dog faded.

* * *

Bryony brought her wings low over Albert for privacy and moved his fringe out of his eyes, but before she could plant a kiss on his lips, a damp muzzle appeared, pushing her and Albert apart.

Bryony sat back, amazed. Dog had appeared again, full of energy. His whole body wagged in delight and his barks filled the forest.

Albert hugged him. "Hello, old friend! Better keep the noise down. Not everyone here appreciates you."

Dog quietened, looking from Albert to Bryony with a huge sloppy grin on his face, wagging his tail in circles of joy.

* * *

"Let him go children," said Sheean. "We can't keep pulling him backwards and forwards. It's not fair."

They watched through the window as Albert and Bryony greeted Dog with hugs and smiles. "That's Queen Bryony," said Sheean, "and her consort,

Albert. Dog used to be his, back in the Human realm. It looks as though he wants him back, although I don't know why he couldn't just ask."

"Daddy!" whined the children. As the window slammed shut, the stick fell into the pond with a tiny splash.

"He's not our dog," said Sheean.

Caul stamped his foot. "But Daddy, he liked living with us."

Sheean looked at Kanthy and shrugged.

"Maybe someone in this realm has pets to give away," she said.

"What do you say to having a dog of your own?" said Sheean, grinning at his children. "Maybe a puppy."

Caul and Libith looked at each other, silent words passing between them.

"A puppy each would be good," said Libith.

Both children gave their parents a sweet tooth-filled smile. Kanthy smiled at Sheean and shrugged.

"A puppy each it is then, maybe." Sheean declared.

* * *

Early next morning, just as the sun was beginning to rise, Bryony gazed out at her husband as he sat on the edge of their private fountain. A light breeze ruffled his soft brown hair. Bryony laughed. "Look at him. I can't believe I knew him all those years in the Human realm and never realized his true potential. Isn't he gorgeous?"

Her maids giggled and lowered their heads in response.

"We cannot disagree, Your Majesty," said Lorella, as she smoothed a comb through Bryony's long brown hair. "But it wouldn't be right for us to say anything."

Bryony sighed. "As soon as he and I are in season, we'll bring a new generation of potential royals into the world. Won't that be lovely? A castle full of royal children."

"Yes, Your Majesty," said Lorella. "Do you want your hair free flowing again today?"

Bryony shook her hair, feeling it ripple down her back. "Yes please."

A pink bee flew in from the garden and landed on the dressing table with a thump. It rolled and then righted itself.

"Oh, Bee, are you hurt?"

The bee lifted off again, flying in slow circles between Bryony and the mirror. "Urgent," it buzzed.

Bryony noticed that one of her nails was unfinished. The others all sported miniature landscapes painted with great care by the Pixies.

"Zecret," said the bee.

"I didn't know there were secrets in Taranor," said Bryony.

The bee lowered its gaze.

"Very well. Lorella, please take the maids and prepare my bath. I'd like jasmine blossoms today."

Tiny bells tinkled as Lorella and the Pixies left her room.

"Now," said Bryony, "what is so important that it couldn't wait until all my nails were finished?"

The sound from the bee's wings changed. "Zorry. Realm zecurity."

Bryony laughed. "I was only joking. I'm not that vain. Would you be more comfortable on the table?"

The bee landed again, unsteadily.

"Are you hurt?"

"Hurt leg. Nothing."

"Oh you poor thing. I can heal you."

"Long time pazzed. Zpider web. No pain now."

"I shall have a word with the spiders. I'll ask them to make their webs more visible."

"Thank you. I report now?"

"By all means," said Bryony, picking up a spray of white flowers. She tested the colour against her skin.

"Prince Albert'z necklaze," buzzed the bee, "dangerouz."

"Dangerous? How?"

"Legend. Torc. Zeeks power. Mergez with mind."

"Is Albert in danger?"

"Great Wizard Wyvernhope last wearer. Now Prinze Albert wearing. Danger."

"What do you want me to do?"

"Azk him, take it off."

"How is that going to help?"

"He walk away. Get zpace between him and torc."

"Alright. But why can't you ask him?"

"Torc will fight. Prinze Albert love you. Truzt you."

Sighing deeply, Bryony stuffed the flowers in her hair and flew out to the garden.

* * *

Albert trailed his fingers in the fountain, displacing the lily pads and creating ripples of light on the water. Frogs jumped onto his hands and off again, while dragonflies darted here and there.

Bryony flew to him and kissed his cheek.

"Albert," she said.

His heart quickened. He could tell she was going to ask him a favour.

"Whatever you want, Bryony, I live to serve."

Bryony laughed. "No please don't. Live to love my lovely." Her smile faded. "But I do have a favour. It's a matter of Realm Security."

"Gosh."

Albert took both her hands and stood by her side. Bryony looked pale and serious.

"Please, Albert," she said, "will you do something for me that might be a bit difficult?"

"Of course. I would fight dragons for you."

Bryony's wings paled. "Oh no, we don't fight dragons! They are our best friends."

Albert made a gesture to dismiss his words. "I was using Human ideas. I'm sorry. It's a habit."

"That's all right, Albert. I understand. Please can you take off the torc and walk to the end of the garden?"

"Certainly. Is that all?"

As he took the torc from his neck, he felt the metal stiffen as if resisting. Leaving it on the fountain, he began to walk under the arches of laburnum and wisteria. Bryony's face was serious, even grim. What by the gods could be the matter? He stopped. "This is silly, Bryony. Why are you playing games with me?"

He went back to the fountain and picked up the torc.

"Please, Albert," said Bryony, touching his arm gently. "I just want to see if you can do it. I think the torc might be dangerous."

"Don't be daft." Albert turned the torc in his hands. "It's just a piece of jewellery."

Bryony tipped her head on one side. "For me?" she said in a small voice.

He put the torc down and flew under the arches again. Once on the other side, he felt terribly heavy, too heavy to fly. He landed and walked along the path, his felt boots making no sound on the turquoise stones. On either side, roses and marigolds beamed at him in the morning light. He looked up. The sky was sugar-almond pink. Stunning. He didn't want to walk to the shaded area at the far end, where the yew trees cast purple shadows. He turned.

Bryony gestured for him to go on. He took two more steps.

"Albert!" screamed Bryony.

He turned around. His body felt so heavy.

"Albert your wings!!" screamed Bryony. "They've gone!!"

* * *

The pink bee tucked his weak leg close to his body and flew as fast as he could out of Bryony's garden, towards the hive. His mind quivered at the thought of the reward he would get for this information. He rowed his wings as fast as he could to get some height. Ahead was the wild raspberry area - a tangle of fruit and vines. It was the quickest way, but it held dangers.

He paused on a leaf to catch his breath, feeling dizzy at the amount of information he held.

'Prinze Albert fake! Human. Zpecial zyrup reward. Wyvernhope Torc in Taranor!'

* * *

Kanthy watched Sheean stroll into the garden. He waved at her and opened his mouth to take a bite of an apple. Her eyes appraised his body as he walked. He was getting stronger. Her heart thrilled with the thought of her glorious future.

He bit into the fruit, put his hand to his throat and collapsed as if shot by an arrow. A gasp of horror escaped Kanthy as she ran over to him. His lips were tinged blue and his eyes had rolled up into his head, showing an illuminated whiteness through his partly open eyelids. His body stiffened in a violent fit. His back arched and his limbs jerked. A thin layer of foam lined his lips. Kanthy's heart hammered so hard she could hardly think.

Dropping to her knees at his side, she tried to hold him still. She smelled something familiar on his breath. Looking closer, she saw he still had some apple in his mouth. The fit subsided, leaving Sheean limp and still. Gently, she placed a finger in his mouth and pulled out the pulped fruit. She sniffed it. "Scourge Bane! Who has done this?"

She looked around wildly. The children noticed her distress. "Children! Come here, quickly, someone has hurt daddy."

The children were there instantly, buzzing loudly above her head.

"Who hurt Daddy?" they demanded in unison.

"I don't know. I need you to use your magic to make him better. Someone has poisoned the apple. There is no antidote! If we don't act quickly, he will die!!"

"Who did this?"

"How?"

"I don't know. This is beyond my magic. You have to try something, something that will make him well again."

The children looked at each other, silent words passing between them. Sheean gave a sigh. Bubbles of spittle fell from his handsome mouth.

"Quickly!" Kanthy shouted. "I can't lose him now!"

* * *

The pink bee took off and plunged into the fruit garden.

'Albert human. Wyvernhope Torc here. Web web web! Dodged it. Zpecial zyrup reward. Hive in zight. Tell Agaric.'

* * *

The air in the garden thickened, blurring the colours of the flowers and trees. The shadows shortened slightly.

Kanthy watched Sheean stroll into the garden. He waved at her and opened his mouth to take a bite of an apple. Her eyes appraised his body as he walked. He was getting stronger. Her heart thrilled with the thought of her glorious future.

One of the children flew at him like a turquoise dart, stealing the apple from his hand before he could touch his lips to the fruit. The other twin flew to an ornamental hedge, behind which one of the nobles was hiding and watching. The man felt no pain as the wind picked up his ashes and spread them over the roses.

The pink bee took off and plunged into the fruit garden.

'Albert human. Wyvernhope Torc here. Web web web! Wing! Caught in web! Zticky! Fight! Ztruggle! No! Keep still! - Too late. Zpider coming. Oh dear.'

5923140R00223

Printed in Great Britain
by Amazon.co.uk, Ltd.,
Marston Gate.